About the Editor

LIZ GRZYB was born in the middle of a thunderstorm in Perth, Western Australia. She is the editor of 10 titles, including acclaimed paranormal romance anthologies *Scary Kisses* and *More Scary Kisses*, paranormal-noir anthology *Damnation and Dames*, arabesque pantomime *Dreaming of Djinn* and steampunk romance *Kisses by Clockwork*. Liz is also the fantasy editor for *The Year's Best Australian Fantasy and Horror* anthologies from Ticonderoga Publications.

Hear Me Roar

Also edited by LIZ GRZYB

Scary Kisses
More Scary Kisses
Damnation and Dames (with Amanda Pillar)
Dreaming of Djinn
Kisses by Clockwork

The Year's Best Australian Fantasy & Horror 2010 (with Talie Helene)
The Year's Best Australian Fantasy & Horror 2011 (with Talie Helene)
The Year's Best Australian Fantasy & Horror 2012 (with Talie Helene)
The Year's Best Australian Fantasy & Horror 2013 (with Talie Helene)
The Year's Best Australian Fantasy & Horror 2014* (with Talie Helene)

*forthcoming from Ticonderoga Publications

Hear Me Roar

EDITED BY
LIZ GRZYB

Ticonderoga
publications

This book is dedicated to
ROBIN M^cKINLEY *and* TAMORA PIERCE
*the first authors I remember reading
and thinking, "so girls* can *do everything!"*

Hear Me Roar edited by Liz Grzyb

Published by Ticonderoga Publications

Typeset in Sabon and Chanticleer Roman

A Cataloging-in-Publications entry for this title is available from The National Library of Australia.

ISBN   978-1-921857-35-5 (trade paperback)
        978-1-921857-36-2 (ebook)

Ticonderoga Publications
PO Box 29 Greenwood
Western Australia 6924
AUSTRALIA

www.ticonderogapublications.com

10 9 8 7 6 5 4 3 2 1

Acknowledgements

Liz would like to thank Jenny Blackford, Faith Mudge, Susan Wardle, Janeen Webb, Stephanie Gunn, Kathleen Jennings, Kay Chronister, Alter S. Reiss, Cat Sparks, Kyla Ward, Eleanor R. Wood, Cherith Baldry, Kathryn Hore, T.R. Napper, Rivqa Raphael, Jane Routley, Marlee Jane Ward, Russell B Farr, Kate Dunbar-Smith, Deb Wilson, Jacinta Rosielle, Angela Challis, Shane Cummings, Amanda Pillar, Andrea Orlowsky, Jacintha Bell, Ruza Foster, Frankie Nathan, Kate Williams, Andrew Williams, Angie Rega, Carol Ryles, Nicole Murphy, Alan Baxter, Anthony Panegyres, Ambre Hillier, Michael Hillier, Tasmar Dixon, Mel Donald, Phil Ward, Lina Piscitelli, Nikki Irwin, Sammi Nimmett, Hilary Donraadt, Kim Astle, Giules Valuri, Helen Grzyb, and the Department of Fabulous.

Contents

Introduction

Liz Grzyb

Hear Me Roar is an anthology that is dear to my heart. It is a subject matter I feel passionate about, and one I feel should be much more common. It is about women, independent women, dealing with the world around them. It's celebrating the stories of women who, every day, need to be strong and brave in many different ways that aren't always recognised as such.

It seemed for a while there in the stories I was reading and viewing, that the only mighty women in popular fiction were either evil or two-dimensional. They were evil because they were powerful (even if it was limited to sexual power) and used their influence against the male protagonists. The other 'strong' women I saw frequently were physically dominant warrior women, who were only in the plot to either help the male protagonist reach success, to possibly became the prize for the protagonist, and/or because they looked/sounded hot in a chainmail bikini or skimpy leather armour.

Of course not all dominant female characters are reduced to being love interests, sex objects or villainesses, and many are masters of their own destiny, but these seem to be in the minority. They are the provenance of books squarely aimed at women, rather than being a common idea in books for any and all genders. It is generally accepted that although female readers will read stories about men and women pretty equally, that most males will rarely branch out from stories about men.

I decided I'd like to read, and show more stories about women who were fighting to control their own destiny, no matter what patriarchal structures were in their way. I hoped that these stories would be as engaging for male readers as for female readers, while demonstrating aspirational female figures.

When I first put out the call for stories, I mentioned a number of ways I thought women could be strong: "female superheroes, scientists, subversives and rulers". While I certainly read many wonderful stories about all of these possible characters (and you'll see some of these character types in the stories chosen for the anthology), hearteningly, I also received hundreds of stories about female characters showing toughness and resilience in so many other different fashions.

Narrowing down the submissions into the seventeen stories in front of you was a very difficult job, because once I'd whittled the stories down to a shortlist, they were all excellent works, and any of them I would have been proud to publish. The seventeen stories you are about to read stood together as a complementary, yet diverse group, from a powerhouse of Australian and international authors.

Just like the women we see around us every day, the characters in these stories show strength, make difficult decisions and sacrifices to do what they think is right, to choose their own destinies and fight against obstacles in the path of justice and freedom. The authors tell us of ordinary and extraordinary women, people who might make a spectacular impact on the world, or those who just keep making their small contributions every day. There are heroines who fight to save the whole of humanity, and those who struggle to keep one important person safe. These are all women who are navigating a dangerous world, and are drawn in a way that celebrates their different forms of resilience. As the tagline on the cover reads, these are *real* strong women, women we are all familiar with in our real world. Hear them roar!

Hear
Me
Roar

The Sorrow

Jenny Blackford

Lee lay strapped into the safety pod on the Mars Shuttle, staring at the screen. Already Penrith Spaceport was just a Lego set, with toy people driving tiny trucks across a concrete table. In no time, the ochre roofs and improbably-turquoise swimming pools of western Sydney had dwindled to Monopoly size, and the manmade structures were merging into the grey-greens and orange-reds of ancient vegetation and older land. Soon, Earth itself was a blue and green bauble, furry with clouds, hanging in the darkness of space.

With her eyes closed, though, all that Lee could see was red sand drifting over cratered highlands older than time. What strange life might that sand once have seen? The System fed the thin whisper of Martian winds into her auditory nerves. The billion-year-old lava flows of Mars were waiting, calling her—if the medical research team that she led could beat the Sorrow.

Was that a tiny flicker of too-professional interest in Grace's eyes, across the cabin? Slowly, carefully, Lee relaxed her fingers, clenched with longing close to lust for the feel of Martian dust trickling cool between them. Lee had hired Grace to psychoanalyse the rest of Mars Base, not to worry about Lee's own mental health. But dreaming of red dust was foolish. Unless a small miracle occurred, Lee had no chance of getting out of the Base to trek across the volcanoes of Mars, less even than before the near-useless trip to Earth. She'd wasted so many weeks on endless meetings with politicians and medical bureaucrats, and meanwhile the Sorrow had claimed another victim—yet another scientist who would never smile again, not properly, not right to the eyes, unless she left her life's work on Mars and flew back to Earth.

The memory of Sarah's sombre face haunted Lee. The Sorrow hit almost everyone who went to Mars, after two or three years. It started with an indefinable look in the eyes, a slight strain in the voice. Soon, it was unmistakable, and the only known treatment was to return to Earth—a tragedy for scientists who'd studied for Mars all their lives. There were too many scientists curled in foetal position in their bunks on Mars, faces puffy with dried-up tears, and even more dragging themselves in despair through the research they'd have killed for, a few years earlier. Lee's conscience burnt with the number who'd taken that one too-final step into despair. She couldn't let that happen again.

The Sorrow had taken too many of Lee's friends and colleagues.

This was surely her last trip to Mars, unless her team found a cure soon. The shielding was better every trip, and the longevity treatments mopped up most of the damage, but it accumulated with each journey in this infinitely-glorified tin can.

She looked back at the screen, trying against all probability to forget the Sorrow waiting on Mars, trying to find the blue-green bauble of Earth in the sea of stars. But it was a physical effort not to look back towards blonde Grace, at the dark-eyed redhead in the pod next to her. Whoever the girl was, she looked so like Zena: stubborn, lovely Zena. Oh, those stormy, exhilarating years that Zena and Lee had shared, and that week in Paris!

The girl was certainly pretty, though so very young, and not, of course, so gloriously pantherish as lovely Zena. Zena, who time and again refused point-blank to join Lee's team on Mars.

Sigh.

• • •

The sleeping pod was a marvel of engineering, a hundred times more comfortable than the earlier models. It almost made up for the permanently blocked nose and headache of microgravity. By bedtime, Lee had already stopped noticing the flat smell of recycled air, and the shuttle's quiet background hums and clinks were oddly soothing. All the same, after the few weeks back home, it wasn't easy to relax without the soft familiar weight of Mr Pudding curled in the empty space behind her knees.

Just as Lee's thoughts turned to hypnopompic mush, the three new medical researchers chattered their way inside the rest module.

A determined voice said, "I don't know why Doc Lee hasn't taken it seriously." It was Kiki from Singapore: peacock blue hair and a will of steel. "The problem should be blindingly obvious to anybody with the slightest grounding in biochemistry. The woman has two PhDs, but she just doesn't get it."

Damn! Lee was stuck. She had no intention of eavesdropping on her new team members—but it was too late already. She couldn't embarrass them all by emerging from the depths of her sleeping pod now.

Kiki went on: "Almost every bite of food on Mars is vat-grown, or synthesised. We haven't got a handle on all the micronutrients in common foods on Earth, let alone their interactions with one another. Look what happened with lycopene."

Mercifully invisible within her pod, Lee shook her head. She'd followed that possibility down its burrow, and the volunteers in the control groups on Earth were all healthy and cheerful. There was almost no chance that nutritional deficiencies triggered the Sorrow. *Almost.*

"It's the domes," a second voice said, lighter than the first. It was Claudine: small, pale, fiercely intelligent. "The radiation that gets through might look the same on the instruments, but I'm sure it doesn't look the same to our neurons." Her French accent was delicious.

A third voice, a little louder, chimed into the argument. "We evolved to seek out large bodies of water. *Anyone* would get sad in a place without lakes and seas and running rivers. I'm missing my runs on the beach already." That was blonde Grace, the psychiatrist. "But what do you think, Beth?"

The System pushed a list of Beth Venn's qualifications—geochemistry PhD, an excellent postdoc, and still ridiculously young—at Lee, with a photo. Oh—she was the girl who looked so like Zena!

Beth sounded baffled. "Why ask me? I'm not medical, like you three. What would a geochemist know about the mind?"

"Everyone's allowed an opinion," Grace said.

Lee snorted, silently. So, the new psychiatrist was starting a mental profile on Beth already. Lee was going to have to watch that sharp blonde!

Slowly, quietly, Beth replied, "Well—just one thing, about water. What about the desert peoples: the Bedouin, and some Aboriginal Australians? My grandmother's mob trapped eels around the Murray, but others might not have seen big rivers or decent-sized lakes for years, and they never got the Sorrow."

In her own pod, Lee nodded. When she finally slept, eels slithered through her dreams.

• • •

When Lee shouldered her way through the round entrance to the exercise module the next day, Beth was strapped into the microgravity lats machine.

"Hi," the girl said, her dark eyes curious. "You're the one everyone calls Doc? Is that right?"

Lee groaned. "The old Air Force types started it, on the first shuttle, and it stuck. Just call me Lee, please."

"And I'm Beth. So, Lee," she said with a smile, "can you tell me if I'm doing this movement right?"

Lee fixed her attention on the mechanics of the girl's arm and shoulder muscles, neck and spine. "Perfect."

"Oh, good! Thanks! I have to be able to lug bags of rock samples around once I get there. The exoskeletons don't do everything."

Lee tried to concentrate on her own exercise on the microgravity bike without staring at the girl who looked so like her lost, lovely Zena. After a few minutes, though, she found herself blurting out, "Look, I hope this isn't terribly rude, but you remind me of an old colleague . . . and friend. Are you by any chance related to Zena Sheldrake?"

Beth nodded. The movement almost sent her floating across the module, but she grabbed the machine in time. "Definitely! She's one of my grandmothers."

Lee had been suspecting some odd, random genetic similarity from a distant relative, a second cousin once removed, something like that, not a granddaughter. "Oh!"

"My father had two mothers, Mama Zena and Mama Elfie, but he mostly lived with Mama Elfie, because Mama Zena was always in the lab. His name is Charles Venn. He's up on Mars. Do you know him?"

Charlie Venn was Zena's child? With Elfie?

An icy arrow of ancient jealousy stabbed through Lee's chest. Deliberately, she pushed the pain away. Zena had never wanted to rub salt into Lee's wounds by talking about the baby that she'd made with the woman she'd left Lee for, and Lee had been too miserable to ask about the child. And then, of course, Zena and Elfie had broken up after a few years. Somewhere along the line, it seemed, Elfie had married again, and taken her new wife's name.

There was no need for any of that pain, not anymore.

"I do know Charlie," Lee said, "though less than I'd like to. Your father has a fine mind, and he's doing some fascinating exobiology. I had no idea that he was Zena's son, but I should have realised. He's got her look, like you, but it's not the same in a man."

"He doesn't look much like her, not like I do, especially with his hair so short, and hers, well—"

Lee interrupted: "A curling crimson mane, yes." Oh, Lee had so loved that roiling mass of hair! "She was about your age when I first met her. We did our postdocs in the same department—the early animal safety tests of the life extension technology."

"Ah. She's told me about them. Said it was totally exciting stuff."

"Oh, it was! She's a truly brilliant researcher, far better than I ever was, even before I went into management. I wish I could talk her into joining my team on Mars."

Beth grinned. "Oh! You're *that* Lee! The one who keeps nagging her to go to Mars! The one she flew to Paris with!"

Lee grinned back, feeling oddly pleased that Zena had mentioned that very special week to her granddaughter. "Yes. That's me."

"She'd *love* to work with you again. But she says she won't go until she can sleep through the trip."

Lee groaned. "That's right. Suspended animation: she's always been obsessed with it."

"But true suspension, *not* cryosleep."

"I'm not getting into a coffin until I'm dead," Lee said, a little lower than her normal tone, the accent a little closer to Zena's BBC Standard English.

Beth laughed at the imitation, and added Zena's next line. "I've read too much Poe. I will *not* be buried alive."

Lee ran her fingers through her short greying hair. No one younger than her and Zena would ever go grey again, unless they chose to. It was just one more incremental improvement to the quality of human life. Even she and Zena wouldn't be grey now, if they had tested the life extension tech on themselves back then, like Zena had wanted to.

"She's so stubborn, that Zena. There's no reasoning with her."

Lee found herself grinning as she spoke. Then she remembered something. "The last time we talked, she said she'd made a major breakthrough, but she wouldn't tell me what it was until she was absolutely sure."

"Yes!" Beth said. "She's tweaked the suspended animation process radically. It's not just insects, now—it's working well with small vertebrates. I helped her with some of the lab work."

"That's wonderful!"

"Lizards, frogs, that sort of thing," Beth said. Her face closed over a little.

Lee waited for a moment, in case the girl was going to add any more information. "I owe her a message. I'll ask her about it. Thanks for letting me know. It could be important."

"Yes, good idea, you do that. Sorry, I've got to go." The girl's expression was remote. She pushed off the wall with her legs. In a moment, she was through the circular hatch and away.

Lee looked after her, wondering.

• • •

Over the next months, Lee scarcely sighted Beth, though interfering Grace apparently felt compelled to report about her to Lee every few weeks. Beth was out of the sleeping module before Lee woke, and always seemed to be finishing her meal or workout just as the older woman was about to start. Lee didn't have much opportunity to notice, between endless administrative busywork—impossible to avoid even while crossing the solar system in a modified tin can—and working with her new researchers.

And every few weeks, there was another report of the Sorrow claiming a new victim. Every day, Lee woke dreading the worst. Halfway through the flight, it happened: a report on Charlie Venn, Beth's father.

The psychologists on site had sent a video that Lee watched obsessively, trying to deny the truth, the shadow growing behind

Charlie's eyes. They weren't certain. Lee tried to hang onto hope, however irrational it was.

. . .

It didn't occur to Lee that Charlie's daughter might be avoiding her until one day she reached the exercise module a few minutes after Beth, and the girl pushed out of the rows machine and headed for the iris of the door.

Before the girl could disappear, Lee said, "Grace told me about your Plushy."

Beth's face flushed pink.

Ah, so that *was* the problem!

After a moment, Lee said, "Anyway, what I wanted to ask was this: would you mind showing it to me? I've never seen any of those Plushy toy pets. I'd be very interested. It's for medical purposes, don't worry. I'm not doing a psychological checkup on you." *Not* like bloody Grace.

Beth said, "Yes, all right," in a small voice. "I'll fetch my pack."

Lee let her body pedal the exercise bike while the System filled her mind with all the product specs of the Plushy family of hyper-realistic animals, with their vat-grown fur and soft, heavy filling. There were so many of them, even just the cats—blue-eyed Ragdolls, sturdy Russian Blues, realistically neurotic-looking Siamese . . .

"I'm back," Beth said, and Lee looked around, startled, then untangled herself from the bike.

"Grace told me all about these Plushy toys," Lee said. "How she uses them in her work, to put her clients at ease. Not just the kids—adults as well. Even old people like me, or so Grace said."

Unsmiling, the girl opened her pack, and Lee peered in at a mound of shiny black fur like liquid silk. She could see delicate ears, and sweet jellybean toes. Her stomach felt fluttery, strangely joyful.

"Oh! I had no idea they were so realistic!"

"Yes, they're amazing." Beth didn't sound amazed.

"May I touch?"

The girl nodded, though all her body language was screaming *no.*

Lee carefully pulled the little cat out of the pack, its smooth weight so soothing in her hands. She stroked the soft black fur, then parted it to see the paler underfur and the faintly bluish skin. Her heart yearned.

"Oh, it's lovely," she said, and tickled the tender spot under the bony chin. "I've got my own theory about the Sorrow, but the higher authorities would prefer not to take it seriously. The UN won't even consider it officially. And I know it sounds simplistic, so please don't laugh at an old woman."

Beth made a vague sound of assent.

"We're animals," Lee said. "I think we *need* other animals around." She waited for the usual dismissive snort or yawn.

"Really?" Beth said. "That make sense to me, but what would a geochemist know?"

Lee was cradling the Plushy against her chest now, a soft silk sack of comfort. Emboldened, she went on: "Look at the way children react to animals, even just pictures in books, or tiny plastic toys that are hardly anything like the real things. Kids are hard-wired to love animals. Zoo animals, farm animals, whatever. We all are. How long would any of our ancestors have gone without interacting with animals? Half an hour, maybe."

"Maybe. Maybe even less. You're right."

Lee sighed. "The powers that be say it would be too great a risk to take pets of any kind to Mars, and far too expensive. Germs, viruses, parasites . . . They won't let me take even a single one for testing. I've applied so many times. That's one of the big reasons I went back to Earth, to plead with them in person. Still no luck." She shrugged. "But this toy kitty here is so very *interesting*. And *promising*."

She looked in the pink mouth and delicate ears, and pressed the soft furry paws until the sharp claws came out. She gently stroked the plush stomach, and weighed the cat gently in her pale hands.

"It's perfect," she said. "A beautiful specimen. I'm amazed."

Beth seemed to be holding her breath.

Lee nestled the cat gently back into the pack. "That's wonderful technology. Thank you so much for showing me. I really appreciate it."

She hoped the girl was too young and self-involved to spot the tears pricking at her eyes.

• • •

Beth seemed to grow less wary of Lee during the last interminable leg of the voyage, and Lee was careful not to mention the Plushy toy to her or anyone else on the ship. They often found themselves exercising together in companionable silence—Lee's only real retreat from the endless barrage of time-delayed but always-urgent work messages from Earth and Mars, and the constant demands of her frighteningly-intelligent new recruits. Occasionally, she allowed herself the luxury of personal messages to old friends on Earth, too many of them Mars scientists forced by unrelenting misery back to the unwelcome comfort of the green-blue planet. It stung her to have to tell them, again and again, how little progress she'd made on a cure.

• • •

Finally the shuttle neared the red planet, and set down next to Mars Base. Freed from the safety pod, Lee tested her ship legs against the unaccustomed pull of gravity. She tried not to jiggle too irritatingly with impatience while the crew performed endless post-landing checks in the pre-dawn darkness. Eventually a pressure-tube snaked out from the shuttle to the airlock in the side of the huge dome, and the shuttle door opened.

Lee felt the old joy bubble through her when at last she stepped from the shuttle's tube out onto that ancient red sand, even if it was blowing over the grey concrete floor of a bleak government shed, and the light of the harsh industrial lamps blocked any chance of her seeing out to the fourth planet.

All the passengers shuffled towards a workstation, where military-uniformed men were checking their IDs—as if they hadn't been scrutinised on Earth before they left. One of them took a bracelet of plaited leather from Grace.

"This needs irradiation," he said. "Organics. You'll get it back tomorrow."

Beth visibly stiffened, and Lee stepped forward a pace or two. It wasn't hard to guess what the girl was worried about.

"And what's in here?" the man asked, picking up Beth's pack.

Beth was silent, but her body language screamed misery. In a moment, Grace would turn around, and those piercing eyes would see everything.

Lee's long and honourable career flashed before her eyes. Which was more important—her reputation, if she was caught out, or Zena's granddaughter?

The choice was not so difficult. Before the man could open Beth's pack, Lee said, quickly, "Essential medical supplies. She's carrying them for me."

Beth's face, Lee was relieved to see, was a bland mask.

The man nodded. "No need to inspect it then, Doc. Go on, both of you."

Lee and Beth strode alongside without speaking until they were well away from the checkpoint, and Grace. Finally, Lee felt safe enough to say, "Your grandmother sends her love. I had a message from her before we landed."

The girl looked at Lee suspiciously, but she was *almost* smiling. "Thanks. I miss her."

Lee's mouth twisted. "Yes. Me too. Every day."

A big man in front of them moved aside, and Lee saw a handful of people at the end of the building, waiting to greet the new arrivals. Charlie Venn was there, waving at Beth, his reddish crewcut bristling. Once you knew, the resemblance to Zena was unmistakable. Lee could see the unmistakable lineaments of the Sorrow in the way he stood, but he wasn't too badly affected—yet—to be excited about seeing his baby girl again.

Lee edged closer to the girl and whispered, "When your cat wakes up from the suspended animation, will you let me know? Please? I've got a feeling that you just might have the cure to the Sorrow right there in your pack." A cautious stream of joy trickled through her bloodstream. If it worked—if animals were the key to the Sorrow—they were one important step closer to a permanent, self-sustaining colony here: new life on Mars. And renewed happiness for Zena's son.

Beth's mouth dropped open. "You knew about Felix all along?"

"I put two and two together."

"And you didn't tell me—or anyone else. You . . . you . . . And there I was, terrified that someone would find Felix and confiscate him, or that something would happen to my pack in an emergency, or . . . "

Then the girl smiled, and reached out a hand to Lee's arm. "Thank you. Thank you so much. And I *will* let you know. You can watch me wake him up, if you want."

"I'd like that very much."

The sun, further away than on Earth but still so familiar, slanted its first dawn rays through the dome and into the hangar. Lee pointed, and they both gazed at it. Mars was out there, waiting for them both.

Lee added, with a sly smile, "Oh, there's one more thing. That wicked grandmother of yours has gone and tested the new suspended animation procedure on herself, while you've been gone."

"Oh, no! It's far too soon!" Beth's smooth forehead wrinkled in urgent worry. "Is she all right?"

Lee patted her on the shoulder. "Don't worry, it worked. She's fine. Better than fine. The process is in full-scale testing now." She couldn't stop grinning.

Beth just stared at her. "There's something else, isn't there. What is it?"

The distant sun shone pink through the red-dust haze.

"They're going to test the new process on the shuttle, and she's in charge." Lee could barely speak for the joy filling her mouth, her chest, her whole body. "She says she'll meet us here next year."

Blueblood

Faith Mudge

It is an insult to die at midday.

In the mountain country where I was born, such things take place in the dark of night: the fall of an axe, the knotting of a noose. Here, it is a spectacle. From the narrow window of my tower room, I can see the road that leads away from the castle, down to the sea; it is already lined with people, jostling and squabbling amongst themselves for the best view of my execution.

In this place, a town will turn out to watch a man kill his wife, and call it justice.

My husband wants me to see this, to spend my last hours thinking about what will happen when the sun hits its zenith. Very soon he will step from the great oak doors, and a guard will come to bring me down. The crowd will get what they hunger for then. I hope it haunts them. It probably won't.

By this point it makes no difference. He can break every bone in my body and shed every drop of my blood and he will still be the fool.

Elyse will still be gone.

. . .

This is the story I stole. It began without me, in a city I will never see again.

Elyse was the queen's seventh child and the first to survive infancy. By then no one expected a son; it had begun to be doubted there would be an heir at all. The rumours that had plagued the queen from her first miscarriage grew louder, circumventions around a central point, delicately half-said by people who mattered. The outlandish death of the queen's mother. Her difficulty birthing a healthy child. In the early years of her marriage, the servants swore it had rained when she cried, and stormed when she raged.

Witch blood, was what they wouldn't say out loud.

So on her fifth birthday Elyse was paraded through the streets in a palanquin, a poppet princess waving solemnly to the curious populace, drowning out the gossip in a rush of loyalist sentiment. Daughters have their uses.

For the queen, however, it opened a new quandary. Elyse was now too old for a nurse, yet too young for lady's maid. She needed a companion—a handmaid close to her own age, quiet, quick and competent. There were plenty of servants to suit already at work in the castle, but while commoner girls were good enough to scrub floors and pluck chickens, even the daughter of a better sort of merchant was never going to be the confidante of a princess. To say the queen was a traditionalist would be to say that a tree is made of wood; her daughter had to have a companion of good noble blood, as generations of heirs had before her.

Unfortunately, while the practice was still favoured by the royal family, the sense of it being an honour had declined amongst the nobility. They would rather send their daughters abroad to the new academies, to forge friendships that might mature into advantageous political alliances and acquire a cultured polish that would appeal to wealthy husbands. Royal patronage could only take you so far; a future marchioness was much better off learning to talk about art in five languages.

That was never going to be my life.

My father's title was the only aristocracy my family could claim. Instead of keeping a house in the city or moving south to a villa for the winter the way our friends did, we lived in an ancient pile in the western valleys, held together more by ivy than mortar. Breeding racehorses was not a hobby for my father; it was the only way to pay the farmhands. I was the second eldest of thirteen and could turn my hand to any number of household tasks, including minding a horde of small brothers and sisters. When asked why she had not yet sent me away for a proper education, my mother looked hunted and made excuses about my 'weak heart'.

The royal summons was a reprieve for her, a way to save face. As for me, it was the adventure I'd never believed I would have. I could not wait to go.

The city of Celvre was two days travel to the north, close to the mountain pass for which it was named. I arrived at dusk inside the grandest carriage I had ever seen, bowling downhill towards the sweeping curve of the city that encircled moon-bright Lady's Lake. The way ahead was lit by glass lamps, blooming in the dark like captive stars. As the carriage rolled through wide winding streets, I knelt precariously on my seat, the better to stare. Women in jewel-coloured gowns alighted at a theatre, wearing lace masks of silver and gold; at one street corner a juggler spun knives between his fingers, while at the next a fire eater exhaled blue flame.

Above it all rose the shadowy weight of Mordan's Keep. It had been a fortress for centuries before it became a palace, and when I lifted my eyes to its night-shrouded walls, it stared back through narrowed arrow slits, a stone giant patiently awaiting the next war. Green banners snapped atop the turrets, bearing the white horsehead of the queen.

If her husband's banner was aloft beside hers, I did not see it. That was a fitting beginning. In all the years I spent at the side of his daughter, I never exchanged a word with the king. His ill health was notorious—if he left his sickbed for above a week it was considered a marvel and his physician of the hour might start dreaming of a knighthood. It never lasted, though. At length his gaunt, dull-eyed presence would fade away like a sad dream and the queen would sit alone once more in the throne room.

It was there I first saw Elyse.

Though I was not quite four years the elder, to her eyes I must have seemed almost grown up. Tall for my age, nerves pulling my mouth into a severe line, I towered awkwardly over her. She tried to hide her face in her mother's skirts but the queen pulled quickly away, as if embarrassed by her daughter's indecorum.

"You may approach, child," she said to me, her voice clear and brittle as glass.

I obeyed very carefully, afraid of using the wrong word, the wrong gesture, of being run through by that steely gaze. Not as afraid as Elyse, though. That woke a whisper of rebellion in me. As I curtseyed, my head was brought briefly level with the princess's, and I pulled a face where the queen couldn't see. The little girl frowned and tilted her head, like a dubious bird wondering whether to fly away.

She was the same age as my youngest sister Mardie, but for weeks I thought she was older. Mardie had never been silent in her life; she ran and laughed and screamed her lungs raw when she wanted attention. The princess was not allowed to run. She had been taught from an early age to cover every laugh with her hand, as if it were a dirty thing. The last thing she wanted was attention.

Is it terrible I liked that, at first? Yes. I think it is.

I was not at my boldest either, of course. Life in the castle could not have been more different from the mildly anarchic informality of my home. Elyse became my bellwether: by watching what she did, I learned when meals were meant to be eaten and where, what places I was permitted to go and which were forbidden. That way I knew what to pretend I was doing.

When we were not at lessons—it being rightly, if insultingly, assumed that I would be Elyse's educational equal—we were for the most part expected to keep to her rooms in the Maiden's Tower, on the east side of the keep. There were bell cords in each room to summon a servant should we need one, and an elderly attendant of indeterminate status stationed at the foot of the tower stairs, who was to catch any slack as I learned my duties. She was tiny and fiercely genteel, quick to crack down on any mistake. I discovered eventually that she had been lady's maid to the old queen, the one whose scandalous death still haunted this place like a ghost. As far as I was concerned, she had high standards and low expectations; Elyse was treated with distant, chilly courtesy. By unsaid agreement, we avoided her quarters whenever we could.

To be honest, accustomed as I was to a rabble of fractious siblings, having only the one charge threw me. What was I supposed to do with her? Any attempt at jokes or games was met with wide-eyed incomprehension. When in the same room as the queen, Elyse resembled nothing so much as a pretty clockwork doll.

It was only in the gardens she really came to life. Twice a day we were sent outdoors to walk the shrubbery paths that crisscrossed the royal estate. Elyse would politely ignore any attempt of mine to set our course, and go whatever way she wanted. The place was a maze, but she never got lost.

Often we'd go to the royal aviary and she'd poke crusts through the bars for the parrots. Another favourite haunt was the hothouse, where tropical fruit trees grew green all year round underneath steaming glass. Her mother would have forbidden it if she knew, but Elyse was a favourite with the gardeners and no one told. She only led me there once she'd known me a few weeks and seen my own minor misdemeanours. She had a soul of her own, the queen's daughter, but she held it close where no one could see.

As the months passed, it felt like the chill of the keep's stone walls was sinking through my skin. What child of five is never allowed to play in the dirt? What little girl is not even permitted to bend over and pick up a dropped toy, because it does not befit the dignity of her station?

"Watch," I whispered one day, when we were alone together in the gardens. Bay tree hedges rose high on either side, forming a corridor of dim green light. Hitching up my skirts, I crouched and dug my hands into the dirt beside the path. It was damp enough to be easily moulded. I made a messy man-shape and stuck twig arms to the sides.

"Go on," I urged. "Get your hands as dirty as you like."

Elyse stared. To a child schooled in obedience from the first moments of her birth, I must have seemed an utter radical. She looked from me to the hedge, where roots dug deep into the earth and little pillows of moss grew thick in the shadows. Stiffly, like the little old woman she was not, she bent over and poked her finger into the damp earth. She drew a frowning face and gave a gulping little giggle at her own daring—then flicked me a startled look as I started giggling too. It was all so *absurd*.

Footsteps on the pavement made us both jump up. The princess went white, hiding her grubby hands behind her back. A sudden gust of wind eddied around us, whipping up a cloud of dried leaves; when they cleared, we saw a garden boy carrying a basket of weeds, struggling to hold onto his hat. He froze at the sight of us, then bowed so low he almost overbalanced, and fled as fast as he could. I looked at Elyse. She looked at me. I was the first to start laughing and then she did too, only a little bit hysterically.

From that day onward, we were an alliance.

When the queen forbade sweets ("a princess's teeth must be as flawless as her reputation") I smuggled sugared violets and peppermint candies from the kitchen in my sewing box. We taught each other all the games we knew and made up new ones that could be played in secret, tracing shapes onto each other's hands during lessons or the dull afternoons when Elyse was trotted out to smile at strangers. When she wept into her pillow over a failed lesson, I wrote the answers in her place. A five-year-old's handwriting is not difficult to mimic, and I was old enough to actually understand what we had been told. Sitting in quiet corners with my head down and my ears open, I was learning fast.

The queen did not age with the passing years; rather, she petrified. She dressed as if in a perpetual state of half-mourning, and there was so much distance in her eyes that I sometimes wondered how she could see me at all. Though Elyse and I were taught how to dance, parties were unknown within the castle walls, supposedly on account of the king's ill health—as if he would even *notice*—and any excursion into the city was so carefully managed she might as well have had us on strings.

In response, we became mistresses of illusion. The princess would invent irreproachable employments of our time while I swept away the evidence: chalk scrawls, forbidden dice, powdered sugar. Once or twice, we were caught and punished, but our repentance was very visible and our next secrets better kept.

• • •

The guard is at my door.

There is a moment of surreal awkwardness as he grasps for the correct title. At length he settles for a curt bow. "They are waiting," he says.

I know him. I was here for his first day of duty, when he opened the wrong gate and was swarmed by geese—it was the first time I'd laughed in months. Poor boy. He does not know what to think. I leave my window, leave the room without any attempt at delay—there's no point now. The guard takes my arm very lightly, with a mumbled apology, then lets go again when he realises we must go single file down the stairs. He moves ahead of me. I lift my skirt daintily and follow.

"Will you stay and watch?" I ask, as if we're talking about a mildly amusing show.

He hunches his shoulders against my gaze. "I must. I—it's my duty."

"I see."

"I'm sorry," he whispers, almost whimpers, as if he's hurting. "I don't want—I don't know—*why?* Why did you do it?"

We have reached the last step. I pat his shoulder gently.

"That's for me to know," I tell him.

Let me make this plain: I do not want to die. More than anything, I don't want to die like *this*. But I paid a very high price for this pretence and a few kind words are not enough to earn the truth.

The doors swing open.

The crowd howls.

• • •

Elyse at sixteen: not a clockwork doll any more. Her hair had darkened to a deep buttery shade but retained its curl, with a tendency to spring out from whatever style I'd attempted to create. She was not thin or pale enough to suit the queen, who now gave uneasy attention to her daughter's looks, like an artist who suspects her masterwork is coming out wrong. There wasn't much of her in the princess, and not much of the king either. Sometimes people mistook the two of us for sisters. I really don't know why.

Me at twenty: still the taller, if only by half an inch, finally grown into my legs and nose, with hair a shade of brown that sometimes looked blonde in the right light. Quite an ordinary sort of pretty. My looks were a relief to the queen because they made Elyse look more fashionable by comparison.

By day we walked in careful steps, trussed into tight bodices, drinking bitter tea at soirees and tracing out frowning faces on each other's wrists instead of saying rude things. By night, we made it a mission to break every one of the queen's rules.

I patched together luridly colourful gowns with ruffled skirts and Elyse stole a rope ladder from the gardeners. We climbed out the window, swinging lightly down from the castle walls, and roamed the night markets, dancing with jugglers and thieves and learning to cheat at cards. When people asked our names, we laughed. By lantern-light we might be tumblers, storytellers, flower-sellers, minstrel's daughters—a pair of light-footed troublemakers always gone by daybreak.

If the queen had caught me, she would probably have killed me. She had fought all her life for the respectability we were so determined to throw away, had beaten it into armour, but that did not keep her safe. The whispers only ever grew louder.

In the night market, we heard them.

What woman never gets wet in the rain? Never gets dirty when she walks in the mud? My cousin said . . . my aunt saw . . . everyone knows . . .

"Remember her mother," the rumourmongers reminded each other. The old queen, they meant, who had ridden out in the last war with a bow on her back and never missed a shot—who had died throwing herself atop her lover's funeral pyre, screaming at the flames to give him back. "Never seen a storm like that before," we were told, warning looks exchanged above our heads. The lake had broken its banks that night, rushing through the streets.

Sorceress. Witch. Tainted blood.

It felt wrong to listen. I was, in my own way, a loyalist. But Elyse wouldn't leave, eating up secrets with her hands fisted under the table, and I couldn't go without her.

"You know it's not true," I said, walking back through the dark.

"How do *you* know?"

"They say she has a spell to watch her enemies. If she could do that, she'd know where we are right now." I stopped, melodramatically raising a hand to cup my ear. "Do you hear the guards on their way?"

Elyse smacked my arm. "Just because she can't scry—"

"She's not to blame for how her mother died."

"Are you sorry for her?" Elyse asked, incredulous. She spun to face me, bright skirts whirling around her ankles, long hair loose around her shoulders. She was pretending to be a travelling player and had painted flowers on her cheek. I rubbed them carefully away with my thumb.

"Do you really think your mother is a witch?" I asked.

Elyse looked away. I still had my hand against her cheek; I let it fall.

The queen never did catch us, and in the end the reward was worse than any punishment. A princess could not inherit the throne; only a son could. The queen needed a grandchild to be her heir, and had no time for sentiment.

The duke of Hamonsea was the chosen man, second son of a courted ally. He possessed a vast estate on the other side of the forest. A catch, the queen might have said if she didn't believe such terms to be disgustingly vulgar. "Fortunate," she called it instead, as Elyse stared at his portrait. The princess said nothing. Nor did I. We nodded and curtseyed ourselves out the door and into the gardens, where Elyse ripped branches off trees and smashed flower pots and spat out every curse she'd ever learned. Suddenly she collapsed in the grass and started to cry.

"I won't!" she sobbed, over and over again. "I won't, I won't!"

I had no words to comfort her. The duke of Hamonsea might be rich and titled with a throne just one brother away, but he was also twice the princess's age and had two wives already cold in the ground. From childbirth, we'd been told, but he had no children. He lived in a remote stronghold on the coast, as if even his father couldn't stand to have him close.

"He'll kill me," the princess wept, burying her face in her hands. Her hair pooled in heavy golden chains. "He'll cut me up and bury me with the other wives."

I knelt and put my arms around her. The day had seemed bright a few hours ago, but now clouds were bruising the horizon. There was a storm coming.

"He'll kill me," Elyse said again, very softly, against my shoulder.

"He won't," I promised. "He won't lay a hand on you."

She calmed after that; she believed me, you see. Night after night I lay awake, trying to find a way out. We could run away—sell some jewels to pay passage across the sea, or buy a small boat of our own. I could make a living for us as a seamstress. I allowed myself to fantasise about a house of our own, what it would be like to wear colour every day and laugh as loud as we wanted. Where neither of us would have to marry anyone. It was such a pretty, fragile thought.

But there were more guards outside every night, patrolling the castle walls, walking the gardens. When I tried to slip out, as I'd done so often before, I was caught and had to invent an excuse very quickly. This alliance meant a great deal to the queen. She was taking no chances.

Elyse was to marry in Hamonsea; all the preparations were made with the grim efficiency of a funeral. Several times I suggested errands that might take me from the castle, but none of my pretexts were enough to get away. Watching the queen dress her silent daughter in white wedding silks, my heart felt like a stone in my chest. It was like forgetting how to breathe.

Weeks passed. The day came for our departure.

The weather was foul. Thunder rattled the windows, and squalls of rain had turned the courtyard into a morass of mud. It seemed the queen must surely put off the journey, but she did not. Instead she stood at the top of the castle steps and pressed a kiss against Elyse's forehead, like a benediction, while I stood shivering beside our mounts. Mine was a placid brown gelding, the princess's a restless white mare I had never seen before. Elyse wasn't a good rider at the best of times—in this weather, on a horse she had not ridden before, I didn't know how on earth she'd keep her seat.

I reached over to pet the mare's neck, hoping to calm it down, and realised it was not after all entirely white. Three rusty red marks like smeared thumbprints spotted its forehead, between the eyes. My fingers stung when I brushed them and the queen looked up abruptly.

I dropped my hand, staring at the horse. It stared back at me.

The stone in my chest grew, expanding until it felt my ribs might crack.

"Go with my blessing," the queen said, and we rode into the rain.

Four guards travelled with us as protection from any danger on the road and, as I am sure the queen intended, insurance we would not bolt before we were safely delivered to our destination. It was spring, not long after the thaw, the trees overhead budding with newborn leaves. The princess, riding between her guards, stared at the ground without seeing a thing. She wouldn't talk. Now and again, her horse lifted its head to look at me.

They say the queen has a spell to watch her enemies. I should have listened.

Between the southern valleys and the coastline of the neighbouring kingdom lay the forest we called the Merewold. It was only four days ride from the castle, but here the chill of winter lingered among the evergreens; the air was cold, scented with pine and wet earth. We rode the path in single file, speaking little, for it seemed even to the least superstitious of us that something in this wood was listening. As Elyse rode, the trees swayed, bending as if to watch her pass. The leaves whirled in her wake.

Witch blood.

It never stopped raining.

For two more days we rode, until on the third morning we emerged from the trees and saw the road snaking downwards with the sea beyond.

The guards left us then. It would be an insult to the groom for them to stay, implying as that did that the queen didn't believe he could protect her daughter. The men were so glad to go, they did not even wait for the duke's appearance—he would be waiting at the road's end, they assured us, and with that they disappeared among the pines, leaving Elyse and I alone. I doubted they would go far today. They were more afraid of the queen than of the forest.

There was a stream somewhere to the left of the path, just visible through the trees. Without a word Elyse plunged towards it, forcing her way through pine needles and waist-high brambles, falling to her knees by the water and thrusting her hands into its icy current. They were bleeding from the thorns.

"Elyse." I bent, trying to pull her away. "Stop. I'll fetch a cup."

"You lied," she said, without looking at me. "We can't escape. You made me hope, and you *lied.*"

"No, I swear, we'll find a way—"

Something moved behind us, a crushing tread in the undergrowth. I turned sharply and found the white horse pushing its way through the trees. Elyse made a startled sound.

"*Queen's daughter, do your duty,*" the mare said. Its voice was a sibilant murmur, a courtier's tones from a horse's throat. I stifled a scream with my hands. "*Be your heart broken, be it whole, duty is all.*"

Elyse choked. She would have fallen into the stream but caught my skirts in time—she rose jerkily, still clinging to me.

"A witch horse," she whimpered. "I've been riding a witch's horse."

"Your mother's horse," I whispered. She was shaking in my arms. We stood together at the stream's edge, trapped under the mare's steady gaze. I grew up around horses; I learned to ride and walk at the same time. Horses did not stare like that.

"Away from the river, queen's daughter," it said, and we shuddered. *"The duke awaits. The day grows ever old."*

I decided then. It wasn't a conscious decision, a carefully laid plan—if it had been I think it would have failed. I let Elyse go and started running, breaking through the undergrowth towards the road. My gelding was patiently cropping grass; no one had thought to curse *my* mount. I scrabbled wildly in the saddlebags, pulling free a long blue gown that had buttons instead of laces. It was not quite long enough, but it would do. My hair and face I could do nothing about—I was no princess.

That didn't matter. Everyone knows portrait painters can't be trusted.

Elyse reached me as I was swinging into the saddle. The mare was trying to follow, but had become snared in the brambles and whispering trees; I could hear its struggles to get free.

"Where are you going?" What a sight my princess was, tear-streaked and muddy. She didn't understand.

"The duke is waiting," I said. I left her there on the road, calling out my name.

It wasn't my name any more.

The duke was waiting at road's end, as promised, with a group of his men. I slowed the gelding as I reached them, holding out my hand for him to kiss. His fingers were cold, his smile colder. I held my back regally straight, and smiled.

"My lord! Forgive my undignified arrival. It has been a most awkward journey. My horse threw me and so I am forced to ride my maid's. She is following on foot. Would one of your men go to collect her? Otherwise I fear we will be here all day, and I am wearied of these endless trees."

The duke had never met the princess before, and certainly not her handmaid. In these clothes, with my arrogant ease, the duke did not doubt my authenticity for a moment. At his swift gesture, a man detached from the party and rode back the way

I had come. The rest of us continued down the path, exchanging cool pleasantries.

"What would you have done with the guilty beast?" the duke asked.

"Oh, it is hopeless!" I exclaimed. "I declare it is more than half wild. Have its head cut off, for all I care, only do not allow it near myself or my maid again." A bubble of hysteria welled from my chest and escaped as laughter. "My, but I sound bloodthirsty! My mother would not recognise me."

The duke half-smiled. "We are not inclined to sentimentality, highness, here in Hamonsea. The beast will be slaughtered and a new mount found for you."

By the time Elyse arrived, riding with the duke's man, it was too late for her to stop me. She strained forward in the saddle, trying to meet my eye, but I turned away from her to laugh at the duke. He was saying something about hunting; I could not hear the individual words. He smiled again, and pressed my hand with his large heavy one.

There were ceremonies that night, fine lords and fine food and even dancing. I was so exhausted by then that I wanted to curl in a ball on the floor, but somehow I danced in the hard brawny arms of my fiancé, and smiled for his bleak-eyed father. My maid was, of course, excluded from the ceremonies. She had been sent to my chamber to prepare my things, but I was already thinking ahead to that.

"It is not that she's an ill-hearted girl," I said gaily to my groom-to-be at some point in the night, while I sat at his side and forced my aching face to smile, smile, smile. "But she has a sharp tongue and complains a good deal. I have a mind to dismiss her. Perhaps a purse to set her on her way could be arranged, and a new maid found for me tomorrow?"

"Of course," said the duke. "I am glad you, too, disapprove insubordinance."

"Well, naturally," I said. "I cannot stand people always expecting more."

Elyse was sent away that night. She knew I was watching and did not go quietly. She called for me, she kicked and wept and shouted, but the guards turned her roughly out the gates and threw her bag after her. My bag, it had been this morning. I'd slipped enough jewellery inside to buy her passage on the next ship out. I watched her disappear into the night, a defiant silhouette that kept turning back, as though she expected even now I might come down.

I did not. I went to bed and slept the sleep of the drugged and damned, until the sun of my wedding day came to wake me.

I married the duke of Hamonsea. The king blessed us without meeting my eyes, and we said our vows, and I wore a smile until it felt like a rictus. My hair looked almost golden in the sunlight, under my veils, and I knew the people who had come to watch our procession longed to be like me, to be the princess.

That night, in his bed, I bit down the tears until my lip bled.

We stayed a week after the wedding at the palace of the king, and afterwards rode in a beautiful white carriage up the steep and rutted roads to the duke's stronghold. My rooms overlooked the sea—the only kindness that stone tomb ever had for me. I spent a great many hours looking out over the water and dreaming of a day that never came, when I would step on a boat and sail off to find Elyse in whatever haven she had built for herself. I hoped she was happy. Surely I had paid enough for that.

Two years passed before the queen came to visit her wedded daughter.

We had exchanged no letters; that pretence was beyond what I could bear and besides, Elyse would not have done it. I can't say what kept the queen away for so long. I want to believe it was guilt; she did not want to face what she had done. Perhaps that is why she gave no warning of her impending visit—she thought Elyse would find a way to elude her. The first I knew of her arrival was when I saw horses coming up the road to the castle, led by the queen's pennant.

I froze at the window, one hand pressed against my mouth. As the queen rode through the gates, she looked up. Nailed to the arch was the head of the horse whose death I had ordered, hung there by my husband in mockery of my bloodthirsty ways. Wind and sun and rain had reduced it to an empty skull, but the queen guessed. Her eyes went wide and found me, at my window.

And I smiled.

. . .

I stand here in the sun, waiting to die.

The queen stands on my left, my judge; the duke on my right, my executioner. I wonder whose thought it was that I should die this way, thrust naked into a barrel studded with nails and rolled down to the sea, where my bloodied remnants will be washed away by the tide. I suppose it doesn't matter. They can do what they want. I have *won*.

With trembling fingers, I untie the ribbon at my throat and my white shift falls to the ground. The shouts of the crowd are deafening. The duke has trained them well.

He grips my shoulders and turns me to face him. I know him too well by now to hope for mercy—he should know me better than to hope for fear. The life I have is not worth begging for. His hands leave red prints on the bare skin of my arms. He thrusts me away and I stumble backwards, towards the barrel.

I fall on hard stone. All the breath in my body is knocked out of me.

The barrel is rolling away.

A wind has blown up from nowhere on this still, hot day. It fills my lungs, sweeps my hair across my face, blinds me for a moment—and in that moment, the crowd falls suddenly quiet. I comb the hair from my eyes and look down the road to the sea. A boat is bobbing in the water of the bay, and a girl is standing where the road meets the sand.

"Elyse," I whisper.

And—"Elyse," breathes the queen.

The wind whips at her, lashing the name from her lips. She staggers, holding up her hands as if to ward it off, but it is relentless. It whirls around the courtyard, leaving me untouched at the eye of the storm. The duke starts forward, drawing his sword; the wind beats him to his knees. At the end of the road, my death rolls to a halt at Elyse's feet, and she looks me in the eyes. She holds out her arms.

I push myself to my feet. The wind caresses my cheek like a kiss.

And I run as fast as I can, past the gaping guards and the silenced crowd, all the way down to the water, where a witch's daughter and her boat wait for me.

The wind fills our sails, and we are gone.

A Truck Called *Remembrance*

Susan Wardle

The buzzer sounded, reaching across the compound and through the depot. I looked at the screen. Short dark hair framed a distinctly feminine face, and large brown eyes met my gaze through the monitor. Behind her, a muddied but well made dirt bike leaned against the stump of the bloodwood we'd cut down last spring.

Archie would have called her a dame. That is, if Archie hadn't been locked up four days back, with my truck wheel clamped for unpaid tolls.

"Shall we let her in?" I looked across the room to my other business partner, Frank. His lanky frame was hunched over the scanner, bidding on jobs—trying to find us a load that would cover the tolls and let us retrieve Archie and the truck.

"Sorry Tal, you know we don't let strangers into the depot." He didn't look up from his work. That was the rule. Had been as long as I could remember. Competition in the long-haul freight business was too tight and the risk of sabotage too great. Not that we got many visitors here out the back of Yass. It might be a good location for getting onto the main routes that covered the east coast, but it was hardly suburbia.

She buzzed again. I ignored her, hoping she'd take the message and leave.

After about ten minutes, she realised we weren't going to let her in. Rather than heading off down the road, she dumped the bike up against the fence and sprawled in the shade of a lone scribbly bark.

"What's she doing?" Frank had left the office and was standing beside me at the garage door, staring across the baked dirt compound.

"Looks like she's settling in," I said and crawled back under the bonnet of Archie's rig, Remembrance. She was misfiring in the lower gears. Not a big problem—but enough to keep the truck off the road for a few days. I'd been off the road myself with a broken ankle when the word came in that the crops were ripe in the Riverina. That meant we had one functioning driver, Archie, and one functioning truck. So I'd handed the keys to my almost-new, top-of-the-line Argosy Prime Mover, Daisy, over to Archie and waved him out of the compound.

We tracked them to the privately owned Coonabarabran tollbooth where the radio was abruptly switched off. The payment notice for unpaid road tolls landed in my inbox shortly after. It was just one of the ways the large multi-nationals worked together to keep the small operators, like us, out of business—large tolls for little operators and a nod and a handshake for the large firms who all owned shares in each other anyway.

I didn't have the money. All I had in the world was tied up in Daisy: state-of-the-art road technology with yellow paint and alloy bumper bars.

Archie didn't have the money. He had Remembrance—a 1967 Mack Truck with a British racing green bonnet and an ANZAC montage painted down one side of his trailer depicting three generations of Archie's forebears.

All Frank had was tied up in this dusty block of land we used as headquarters, garage and depot for our small road freight operation.

We depended on Frank hunting down haulage jobs for Archie and me. Financially it was still touch and go—particularly at the end of the month when all the bills came due.

Late afternoon, I slammed the bonnet cover down and climbed up into the driver's seat. Remembrance roared to life at a turn of the key, engine timing sweetly.

"We're ready," I said to Frank as I swung out of the cab, my freshly knit ankle twinging.

"You'll go north," he said.

"When?"

"Tonight."

Sunny, our part-time mechanic-cum-chef and sometimes gardener, was creating a curry in the kitchen. The spicy smell permeated the workshop.

I wandered out of the workshop and across the hard-packed dirt drive to the gate. I looked through the mesh at the woman with the bike for a few moments. She rose and strolled over. She was just under six foot and better close up than she had been through the gate camera. "What do you want?"

"A soldering kit, a tank of fuel and a recommendation for where to go for a feed and a clean bed. I'll leave my weapons at the gate." She pulled out a thin sheaf of notes. "I can pay."

I nodded and walked back across the drive to the shed.

"What does she want?" Frank asked,

I repeated her request and Frank whistled. "Big risk."

"She's willing to pay and I reckon she weighs in at a little over sixty kilos. If she gets troublesome, Sunny could always sit on her."

"She's a professional gun. You don't know what she might have planted on her. Could be an agent for Vox." Frank's worry lines had multiplied since we heard about Archie.

"So I'll pat her down."

Sunny sniggered but Frank shook his head.

Over Sunny's home cooked curry, he weakened. "How much money was she offering?"

I shrugged.

"If she pays. Besides, it might be worth having a Gun around for the job. If her references check out."

I ambled back down the drive. "You can have the soldiering iron and fuel and, if you're quick, you might even get some curry."

She nodded and stood up. I saw the line under her coat. "Cash first. Then weapons in the safe box."

She handed them through the gate to me one by one. Two hand guns—a Glock and a Beretta, the wooden stock of an old style rifle, with a wooden stock and a stubby submachine gun. Four in all. "Anything else?" I asked, half joking.

She reached into her jacket pocket and pulled out two black ovals. Grenades. I took them gingerly and added them gently to the box. "Between jobs?" I asked.

"You looking at hiring?"

"Maybe." I waved to Frank back in the office and he hit the buzzer to let her in. She strode through the gate as if she owned the joint, and stood while I patted her down. Her body was firm, slightly built but strong. She smelled of dust and leather.

"Okay, you can bring the bike up to the shed." I waved her by. Archie would have offered to help her with the bike. But then Archie was the one locked up.

"Independent operation?" she asked.

"As if it's not obvious."

She shook her head. "You can't tell these days. Vox has started offering some of the smaller operators pizza run contracts with little margins—but regular earners."

Frank appeared in the doorway. "No-one owns us and no-one ever will. Those contracts are slavery."

She shrugged. "Suit yourself. It's none of my business."

"The name's Frank." He looked at her expectantly.

"Carol. Carol Stanton. Gun for hire."

I went into the garage and dug out the soldering iron and some metal. "You can work in that bay there." Not without a pang, I pointed to where I normally parked Daisy.

She pushed the bike over and bumped it up onto its stand before stripping off her jacket and getting down to work. Frank watched for a minute before turning back to the office. "Don't take your eyes off her," he muttered as he passed.

"My pleasure."

I settled back to enjoy the view and before long she'd roped me in to helping. Up close, a Honda label was visible under the mud coating the sculpted tank. "You do a lot off road?" I gestured to the knobbly tires.

"I've done my time working with the dirt farms. You need something that will do all terrains."

I nodded. "Have you got references?"

She shrugged. "Did a job or two for Bob Wilmot a year back. Runs a small independent operation like this down Melbourne way."

I knew Bob and trusted his judgement, but none of the other names she rattled off were familiar. "Give me some numbers."

She nodded. "What's the job?"

"There's still a few farms who prefer to deal direct rather than get screwed—the big freight companies don't like it."

She nodded and fired up the soldering iron, sending shadows dancing up the walls as she mended an almost invisible hairline crack in the tank.

My phone buzzed and I pulled it out of my pocket. Macy's face filled the small screen. "Hi Dad."

I turned away from Carol and plonked the phone on a shelf so Macy could see me on the screen. "What's on the homework agenda tonight?" We didn't get real time together anymore—but our daily online date was a non-negotiable in my diary.

Macy wrinkled her nose. "Lots of maths."

"Ok—get on with it. Give me a shout out if you need help."

She settled down to work, throwing me the odd question.

Eventually Carol strolled over, wiping her hands on a rag. "I'm done."

I introduced the two of them, and then wished Macy good night before pointing Carol in the direction of the bathrooms.

"Nice kid."

"The best."

"Where's Mum?"

"Still at work probably. Macy and I catch every afternoon without fail. I give her a hand with her homework—we hang out." My ex-wife wasn't aware of Macy's and my daily date—but that wasn't a story I felt like sharing. "Have you got family?"

"A sister."

I waited for more—but it didn't come. "Give me a shout once you're done in the bathroom and I'll take you down to the kitchen. Sunny said he'd keep you some dinner."

Sunny, inspired by the presence of a woman, had found a yellow tablecloth and covered the scarred laminate table we ate around.

I left her to his tender ministrations and hit the phone. Bob sounded pleased to hear from me.

"Carol Stanton. Good worker. I've used her a few times—and I'd use her again. I knew her father. He was a good man—lost his farm when the Farms Without Fences legislation came in. It destroyed him."

I grunted. The legislation had been supported by the large corporations. Another way to push out the small operators.

I checked out the other referees—none of them had anything bad to say about her.

"It's still a risk," I said to Frank.

"Everything's a goddamn risk. Why couldn't Archie have stuck to the free ways?"

I didn't answer. There was no point. In long-haul it was always a trade off between getting somewhere quickly and getting stuck with a large toll charge. How were any of us to know that a subsidiary of Vox had bought the tollway just that morning—yet another thing the government had sold from under us. Government tolls were cheaper and applied evenly; they weren't trying to push anyone out of business, and didn't have to be paid until the end of the month.

"I've put out the word on the networks that Archie's in lock-up. By tomorrow morning the media will be baying for his release."

I nodded. "It won't get us the truck."

"It won't get us the truck."

• • •

"You can sleep in the van," Frank said after Carol had finished dinner. "Just for a few hours."

The van is an old camper—older than me. No heating, no air-conditioning, no running water. Just a bed, a small camp stove and a bar fridge.

"So do I have a job?" she asked, standing on the step.

I nodded, still reluctant to share any details with a stranger.

She named a figure that was fair. "I've given you a discount on account of how you have helped me. Standard contract applies. If there's a valid threat to your life or business—I shoot. Anyone dies, you take full responsibility and lodge the paperwork. What sort of trouble are you expecting?"

I shrugged. "Not expecting any trouble."

She snorted. "If you don't tell me what to expect I can't do my job."

"Rest—we'll talk before we leave."

"Whatever." She stood in the doorway looking at me. In the

late afternoon sun she was all warm shades, her hair showing hints of russet.

"Do you want to come in?" She held the door slightly wider, an eyebrow raised, then laughed as I shook my head. I was still paying for the mistake I made with Macy's mother. "Your loss." The door shut on my face and I was left with an ache I hadn't felt in years.

Frank was still in the office, slumped back in his seat, gaze flicking between the scanner and his computer screen.

"You're heading north. Dalla Pozza's crops are ready. He promised the job to us—but now he's sounding nervous. God knows what Vox will have planted to try and get in your way. They'll be watching all the tollways—fifty-fifty chance they've got someone watching our front gate.

"I'll take the free ways as much as possible, I'll have to do some of the tolls around the city—just the government owned ones—maybe even the old road. They can't track Remembrance."

"They'll have watchers out. There's probably someone watching us now. Did the girl's references check out?"

"Solid. We're small fry, Frankie. Stop worrying. It's not worth them putting too much resource into us." I said it with more confidence than I had felt since Archie and Daisy's impoundment had rocked my world.

I was in bed by 8pm and up again around 2am. If we were being followed, I wanted to make it hard for them.

Carol knocked back a lukewarm coffee as we bumped through the gate, her bike in the back of the truck. "Where are we going and what am I looking out for?"

"Upper Hunter—it's possible Vox might try and stop us. "

She shot me a glance. "What have you done to upset Vox?"

"They want us to sign up with them. Sign up or go out of business."

"Why you? It's not like an operation your size is a threat."

"I used to work for them. They didn't want me to leave." That was the least of my offences.

"How you planning on getting there?" She was all business, her eyes reflected in the light of the console, flicking constantly over the surroundings.

"We'll take the old Hume, around the back of Goulburn then

Canyonleigh, through the back of Thirlmere and across onto the tollway to get us out the other side of Sydney . . . "

"No," she was shaking her head. "You'll end up stuck on the Pacific Highway."

"It's the main run. We're too big for anything else. We might take the Old Highway for some of it."

"Windsor, Northern Road, Putty Road."

"Putty Road? The Silence?" I shook my head. "It's off the grid. No radio reception, no road maintenance. We'd be lucky not to be ambushed and have the truck stripped out from under us for scrap."

"The road's alright. A bit rough—but nothing this old girl couldn't handle."

I snorted.

"True story. One of your big prime movers wouldn't make it—not through some of the tighter bends—but this truck is small—tighter turning circle I'll bet."

I grunted. "No power steering. Different to a joy run on a trail bike." The suggestion wasn't without appeal. It's not a route anyone would expect us to take—even if Remembrance could get through there was no guarantee we'd make it—there were enough stories about bike- and car-jackings from the area. Archie had done it a few times—but then Archie did things others only dreamed of.

"I can get us through," she said quietly. "I've spent some time in that area—if we run into trouble I can get us out of it."

"I don't know . . . "

She shrugged. "You're the boss. What are we picking up?"

I told her and she laughed. "It's a damn vegetable run. Why the hell do you need a gun?"

"We need to deliver." Dalla Pozza didn't just grow vegetables—he developed new strains. Our delivery service didn't try to hold him to ransom over the details of his research.

We cruised through a sleepy Goulburn, past empty shopfronts, broken windows reflecting jagged peaks back at us. Half a block further up, white light blasted from a 24 hour supermarket, its electric doors opening and closing like a hungry mouth.

Outside of Goulburn I picked out the flash of hazard lights up ahead. Carol pulled out her gun. "No stopping, maintain a steady speed."

She wound down the window and aimed.

"You don't know it's an ambush." Even as I spoke I was scanning the road ahead.

"Spike strip!" she called at the same time that my lights showed the dark line across the road.

I swerved left—aiming directly at the vehicle on the side of the road—figuring that they would have expected me to go right and away from the vehicle. "Hold on!"

There was a crash that bounced us around the cabin and then the ugly screech of metal as the car scraped along the side of the truck.

To the right a couple of flashes and a spiderweb crazed its way across the bottom of the windscreen. "Shit!"

Carol lunged forward, the front half of her body out the window. The report of her gun rang in my left ear. Once, twice, a third time, then we were pulling away from them.

"Are they following?" My voice sounded distant, distorted by the ringing in my ears and the thumping of my heart.

Carol slid back into her seat, her gun filling the cabin with the smell of burnt gunpowder. "I don't think so. Too risky."

I nodded. Sweat trickled down the back of my neck and greased my forehead.

"You alright?" she asked.

"Sure. A lot of fuss over a truckload of vegetables." I tried a smile.

"Yeah, but it's not about the vegetables—is it?"

"We'll reach Richmond around dawn. We'll take the Putty Road."

• • •

The next hundred kilometres rolled past in silence. As we bumped through the endless suburban sprawl around the arse end of Sydney she broke the quiet between us. "So what's so important about you that Vox give a damn?"

I started. "Nothing."

She snorted.

"Recently they've taken an interest in my career." There was more to it than that, but I was buggered if I was going to spill my life's story.

I felt her eyes on me. "It's a nice operation you boys have got—but as pretty as she is, I'd hardly call your truck serious competition."

"The truck's not mine." The words were out before I thought. "My truck's impounded at the Coonabarrabran tollway."

"Who's with your truck?"

"Archie—my business partner."

"As in Archie and *Remembrance* who got supplies through during the Queensland floods a few years back?"

I nodded. I could almost see the pieces falling into place in her head.

She patted the dash. "*Remembrance* is a hero."

Archie was the hero. He'd filled *Remembrance* with fresh water, blankets, food and empty sandbags and driven her up to Bundaberg. On the southern side of the Burnett River, just outside the heart of Bundaberg he'd come to the queue of Kenworths, Scanias and Argosies waiting to get through. All of them big trucks and none of them willing to risk the bridge—close to a metre deep in water.

The weather was wild enough to make airdrops out of the question.

"I saw the news footage. Saw him driving past all those rigs. Millions of dollars worth of high technology road machinery all stranded. He saved lives."

"He had water up to the foot pedals. He said the engine didn't miss a beat."

She laughed. "The day the underdog brought home the goods, hey? And then the big rigs tried to follow after him. Tried and failed. Truck after truck with engines flooded, computers fried by the water—lined up like rectangular islands. Best television I've seen in years."

"She's a workhorse," I agreed.

"So a national hero and a guy who used to work for Vox team up. And the big boys don't like it."

The radio squawked: Frank checking in. Relieved of the need to respond to Carol, I lifted the radio receiver and reported back in code. "Sheep Run One. Change of plans. Uncle's lost his hearing aid."

There was a pause at the other end and then the radio squawked again. "Good luck. Over and out."

"We should be safe through to Windsor. Wake me when we get there." She laid her head back and gave every appearance of sleeping.

I navigated our way around the city outskirts, yellow light falling in stripes from the street lamps.

The first tendrils of pink were lighting the night sky as we came into Windsor. I leant across and gave her a shake. "Toilet stop."

It was cold out of the cab. We took turns in using the facilities—one keeping watch over the rig. I bought a meat pie and two sausage rolls and inhaled them for breakfast while I waited for her to finish in the bathroom.

Even with sleep bruised eyes and ruffled hair she still looked good.

We rolled out of Windsor and through the surrounding farmlands, green and brown patchwork. Different to the other side of the Dividing Range with its temporary wind-blown topsoil farms.

"So why trucking?" Carol asked.

I shrugged. "Why a gun?"

"It's what I know. It gives me freedom."

I nodded.

"You don't look like a trucker."

"What does a trucker look like?" I liked her smile; it softened the hard line of her jaw.

"Fatter, hairier, more grease under the fingernails."

I laughed. "I'm working on it."

She shook her head. "You're what? Late thirties?"

She was being generous—I didn't deny it.

"Maybe I got sick of working for a multi-national—earning profit for someone else's bank balance. Maybe I didn't like what it made me." Maybe my wife hadn't liked the way my focus was changing. As my career became less important to me—hers had seemed to become more important to her.

"Multi-nationals, banks and politicians."

"What?" I shot a sideways glance at her.

"My pet hates."

I smiled. "Doesn't leave much to like." My father-in-law regularly spent time in each of the three camps. He had more pies than fingers.

"No," she said, her lips drawn into a tight line.

The road beneath us was growing steadily rougher, bitumen and pothole competing.

"Are you sure about this route?" I asked, trying not to let my growing tension show.

Orange light contrasted with the muted shades of dawn—an abandoned gas well in full flare. Crippled tree trunks lined the sides of the road, bare black silhouettes.

"Login." I tried my phone—no reception. The Silence.

"We'll be fine."

"It's amazing that the Government can't work out how to fix it." This had been one of the last great environmental battles—the war that the indigenous people won. Claiming land rights and using guerrilla tactics—they'd annexed this piece of bush from the rest of the country and worked out how to use high pitched frequency signals to block mobile and wireless reception.

She smiled. "They try. Let's go."

I brought the engine back to life and we bumped back onto the road. A kilometre further on we rounded a bend and left the burnt tree carcasses behind. In any other circumstance it would have been a pretty piece of road, full of sweeping bends, bush and hidden farm valleys. My hands tightened on the steering wheel.

We came to a narrow wooden bridge. I sucked in my breath. "Are you mad? Remembrance won't go over that."

"It's stronger than it looks," said Carol. "Slow down a bit."

I dropped a gear and we eased onto the bridge, the structure vibrating with the movement of the truck. Halfway across the truck lurched. My heart stalled as Remembrance tilted slowly and appallingly to the left. I hit the brakes.

"Tilt your mirror."

Carol reached through the open window and tilted the side rear vision mirror until I could see our rear wheels. One of them had broken through the rotten planks on the bridge.

I gradually eased on the accelerator, the truck lurched forward slightly. We cracked another plank and the truck tilted further.

"Fuck!"

"We need to get something solid under that wheel—give it some grip," said Carol.

"We needed to not go over this stupid bridge in the first place." I slammed my fist into the steering wheel.

She looked at me side-on. "Let's fix the problem—then you can kick the hired help."

She was right. I ran a mental checklist of what we had onboard. "There might be an old packing case in the back."

"I think that's just become the least of our worries," said Carol.

"What?"

She motioned with her head at the road in front of us. I turned. A row of ten-gallon drums now blocked the road ahead—guarded by two men holding shotguns. My heart doubled pace.

"Crap," said Carol.

"I thought you said you could get us through,"

"It's not over yet." Carol leaned out the window, hands empty and extended. "Stay here."

I remained in my seat and hated myself for it. I hadn't ever been one to let others fix my problems. Why had I listened to her? I left the engine running, hoping for a chance to rev it up and get out of there. A bearded man with more than a little of the old blood in him gestured at me with his shotgun. I turned the key to off.

The engine died and the silence that filled the cab was louder than the engine had been.

In front of me, Carol reached the roadblock.

I watched, a sick feeling in the pit of my gut. I wished I'd told Macy I loved her more often. I conjured up the clean smell of her wrapped in her pyjamas ready for bed.

Carol spoke with one of the men, her hands held out in front of her, palms up. I was too far away to hear anything. A flock of cockatoos flew over, their raucous shrieks grating on my nerves.

A minute passed, and then another. Sweat beaded on my forehead and trickled down the sides of my face. I tried to take hope from the fact that she was still talking.

Without moving, I shifted my gaze to the mirror: nothing. At that moment a Vox truck swaying into view would have been welcome—anything to break this awful silent tableau.

A movement caught my eye. Carol walked towards me.

She swung up the side of the truck and opened the cab door. "Let's go."

"What?" I stared at her dumbly for a moment.

"Let's go." She gestured at the road and I watched as three of the men dragged the ten-gallon drums out of the way. They came back a few minutes later with some long planks to slip under the wheels.

I turned the key, fingers slippery with sweat and nerves. "What did it cost?"

"A favour owed."

"Whose favour?"

"Mine—yours to pay as I demand."

I nodded—not understanding anything but the wild relief of being free to go.

. . .

On the outskirts of Singleton I bumped onto a rural driveway and bounced up to the farm shed. I killed the engine and climbed down, muscles complaining after the hours of jolting.

Marco Dalla Pozza came out to greet me with a serious look and a handshake.

"What's wrong, friend?" I asked.

He shook his head.

"Has Vox been onto you again?"

Marco had followed me when I went into business with Archie.

"You know me too well."

I smiled. "I know Vox too well. What are they promising you this time? Bigger profits?"

"They say they're buying out the franchise on Middlers."

I whistled. Middlers was a franchise of independently owned mini-marts. Supplied by independent farmers, by a loose co-operative of privately owned trucking operations of which Archie and I were part. Hell, truth be told we were the instigators of that loose co-operative and one of the current reasons for Vox's ire.

"If I sign now . . . They'll keep me on as a supplier when the ownership goes across."

"It's a bluff," I said positively. "You know once they've got you signed up they'll want access to your research."

"You don't know that."

I thought frantically. "Can you stall them? Give me a few days—I'll find out what's going on."

Something in his expression told me there was more bad news. "They've said if I send anything else to market with you guys, the deal is off."

I shook my head. Carol was listening in with obvious interest. I took Marco by the arm. "Walk with me."

I led him away from *Remembrance* and the farm sheds. "Marco, it's a bluff. You know the board of Middlers—there's no way they'd agree to this. It's me they're trying to put the frighteners on. Push back—ask them for evidence of the sale. Say that until you see something solid you can't risk changing the way you operate. Tell them you're thinking about the offer seriously. But let me take the load. You know you'll get better prices from us than them."

"What's with the truck? They said you're in debt—lost your truck."

"They're playing silly buggers. Archie's with my truck—it's just the way it worked out." I didn't want to scare him with the truth.

He thought about it for a moment. "And the woman?"

"A hired gun. She'll see us safe to market."

"You've done alright by me to date. I hope to hell you're still on my side."

We shook hands and walked back to the truck. I supervised the loading while Carol lolled by the gate—half an eye on the road.

It took an hour to load *Remembrance*, then I grabbed twenty minutes shut-eye before climbing back into the cab and setting us back on our way. Marco's payment wouldn't land in our account until we'd unloaded at the market—goods safe in Middler hands.

"We'll go the Pacific Highway on the way back. It's daylight—it'll be safe enough." I didn't want to admit how much the roadblock in the Silence had frightened me.

"If you take the old Highway to the Gosford interchange you'll avoid the privately owned bits of the toll."

I nodded my agreement. "What about you? What's your story?" I asked, more to stop her asking me questions I didn't want to answer.

"Not much to say. Dad had a farm the other side of the Dividing Range—on the Bathurst plains. When the Farms Without Fences legislation went through, the dirt chasers started sifting off our topsoil and productivity dropped. Dad couldn't make the repayments." She shrugged. "I was always good with a gun."

It wasn't an unusual story. Plenty of farming families got forced off the land once the dirt chasers started up—movable farms with enormous windblowing trucks that chased windstorms—herding topsoil before them. Farms, financed by the supermarkets, that stopped when the wind did and set down temporary fields covered in netting to protect their precious dirt.

This side of the Dividing Range the Farms Without Fences hadn't gained a foothold. The land was too developed and too hilly to be farmed that way. Dalla Pozza's farm had been in his family for generations.

"What about your sister?"

Carol shrugged. "She married. They ran a local store until a supermarket moved in next door."

"It's unfortunate—but it happens."

"It destroyed them. They lost the business, their home, everything."

"I'm sorry."

She nodded.

"So you're not a fan of the big supermarkets."

She shrugged. "I take work where it comes. No point in fighting what you can't beat." Her eyes remained fixed on the road.

"What time do you reckon we'll hit the markets?" she asked.

I spoke the commands to bring up the latest traffic reports on my phone. "Around half past three this afternoon. Why?"

She shrugged. "I might see if I can catch up with a few friends for dinner. Will you fit in your call to Macy?"

"Always. We should be clear by 4pm." I bit back a surge of disappointment. Once the goods were unloaded and the funds forwarded to release Archie and Daisy, I had hoped to invite her out for a drink—perhaps more.

"Can you pull in at the next service station? I need the bathroom. I feel a bit ordinary."

I pulled in at the next service station for more fuel. Carol disappeared into the bathrooms and re-emerged ten minutes later looking green. "Must be something I ate." She turned and headed back to the bathroom while I moved the truck out of the way and occupied myself with checking tyre pressure. It was another twenty minutes before she climbed back into the cab.

"Are you alright?" For someone who'd just spent half an hour holed up in a toilet she looked surprisingly good. I hoped to God she was. I didn't want us running so late that the markets had stopped trading.

She nodded and gave me a wan smile.

"If you need to be sick try and give me enough warning to pull over." With that I revved the engine and we were off again.

I kept an eye on her over the next half hour.

"Will you stop staring at me like I'm about to fall over?" she snapped eventually.

"Are you?"

"No! Whatever it was is gone now. I'm fine."

We were running behind the schedule I'd mentally allowed myself. Despite the timing, I stuck religiously to the speed limits. The last thing I needed was a speeding fine.

On the approach to the markets I got worried again.

"You can stop watching the rear view mirror," Carol said. "I've got it covered. Besides, they won't risk anything here—there's too many cameras."

I smiled. It was a new feeling having someone to share the worry.

As we rolled onto the weighbridge the stress that had been sending cords of tension from my gut to wrap around my ribs and squeeze my spine and shoulders started to uncoil.

The screen in front of the truck flashed with figures, our weight, registration, current market value on the load. A green light blipped and I leant forward to switch over the ignition one last time for the day.

"Sorry Tal." The barrel of Carol's gun pressed into my side.

I swung to look at her. "What the—"

Her face was white, lips pressed together. "Get out of the truck. Nice and slow now."

"Why?"

She pressed the gun more firmly into my side. "Just do it and no-one gets hurt."

"What has Vox got on you?" I asked, cursing myself for six kinds of stupidity. I opened the door and dropped out of the truck.

"Nice to see you, Tal." A man's voice rang out. I turned and faced the speaker. Six foot and still broad across the shoulders, despite the grey hair.

"Adrian," I greeted him. Three men stood behind him. There would be a fourth outside watching the door, blocking access to the weighbridge until we were done.

"Do you feel like you've been let down by someone you trusted?" asked Adrian Vox, Chairman of Vox Freight, and my former father-in-law.

"What do you want, Adrian? We're a small-time operation. No threat to you and yours."

"Aren't you? You team up with one of our nation's heroes. You manage to unite other small-time operators into a cartel to increase your scale, and then you start stealing my business."

"Hardly. We pick up the scraps from your table. We've no desire to take the table."

Adrian snorted. "I haven't come here to argue. I wanted to talk."

I laughed. "You could have called me anytime in the last two years. My number hasn't changed." I pulled the phone out of my pocket.

Adrian came over to me. "Come back to Vox. I'll reinstate you at the pay you left on with a bonus pending for when you bring Marco Dalla Pozza back into the fold." His voice was pitched low, giving us a level of privacy from the others.

I shook my head.

"Don't worry about Amanda. I'll keep her away from you. I don't need to lose both my son-in-law and my best business manager."

"I'm happier on the road." It was true. I'd tired of the boardroom battles. I'd dreamed of getting home earlier—spending time with Macy. In time with my thought, my phone vibrated quietly in my hand. It was probably Macy. It was that time of day.

"I'm not interested, Adrian. I just want to do my own thing. We're no threat to Vox. You know that."

"Last chance Tal."

"I'm flattered Adrian—but not interested."

"I could make it impossible for you to refuse." Adrian gestured and suddenly those men of his grew guns.

My phone vibrated again. Macy.

"Are you going to shoot me?" I stared at him in disbelief. "Christ—if that was what you wanted, why did you bother get Carol to save me from the road block outside Goulburn—or in the Silence for that matter."

"It's not what I want. I didn't organise anything. Carol was to get you through safely—to deliver you to me."

I closed my eyes. Adrian wasn't one to lie. More likely the ambush had been the directive of my darling ex-wife. "What about Macy?"

"Keep her out of this."

"If you hurt me, you hurt her. A kid needs her dad."

Adrian snorted. "I'll tell her you're a no good bastard who has done a runner."

"Perhaps you should tell her yourself. Face time with Macy on."

"Dad?" Her voice was loud in the silent shed.

I turned the phone so she had a sweeping view of the room. "Grandpa?"

Adrian turned purple. A gesture, and guns disappeared under jackets—but not before Macy saw the movement.

"Grandpa, what's going on? Daddy?"

"Nothing, sweetheart. Your dad and I were just talking business."

"Macy, I'll call you back later this afternoon. I've just got to finish up here at the markets."

"Promise me you will. Grandpa, promise me Daddy will call back." Macy was a smart kid. Always had been. That had been one of Amanda's mistakes—she constantly underestimated Macy's understanding of what happened around her.

Adrian smiled. "Of course Daddy will call you back. Don't forget our date this weekend. Have you picked which restaurant you want to go to?"

Macy allowed herself to be reassured. I said my goodbyes and switched the phone off. I glanced across at Carol. Her face was bland, gun under her jacket still pointed at my side. She hadn't been sick—she'd known what was coming and silently picked a side.

"I'll be on my way then," I said to Adrian and held out a hand. "Thanks for the offer." It was best for Macy for us all to pretend the last ten minutes had never happened.

Adrian stared at my hand before turning and stamping away, calling his lackeys to him.

"Not so quick." Carol's voice carried across the shed.

She produced another gun and swung so one gun was pointing at Adrian, the other covering the guards. "Tell your boys to drop their weapons."

Adrian stared at her for a moment. "Drop them."

There was a blur of movement to my left and two gunshots rang out, one on top of the other. Two of the guards fell. One: a perfect red dot between his eyes. The other: a dark stain blossoming on the front of his grey jacket. Without shifting her attention from Adrian, or her aim, Carol spoke. "Last chance!"

The remaining guard did as she asked. She gestured at a door that past experience told me led to a small storeroom. "Through the door."

The guard shuffled in.

"Shut the door. If you come out you're a dead man."

Once the door closed behind them, Carol fixed her attention on Adrian again. "Tal, do you want to kill him?"

"No!"

"He was going to kill you. If you shoot him you'll be able to claim it as lawful defence of life and property. I'll co-sign the paperwork for you."

I shook my head. "He wouldn't have hurt me. Not in the end."

"You're a fool, Tal. Get my bike down will you?"

"Don't do anything stupid."

"Just get the bike, Tal."

I went around the back of the cab and undid the cables we'd used to attach her bike to the truck. I hauled it down awkwardly—half dropping it onto its tyres. I wheeled it around the front of *Remembrance.*

Carol sighed. A small puff of breath released, and then her finger tightened on the trigger. "Last chance, Tal."

"No." I stepped toward her, intending to take her gun.

She pulled the trigger. The gunshot filled the space. Adrian collapsed, blood slicking the front of his white business shirt. For an instant it didn't seem real. I hesitated, caught between disbelief and denial.

"That's for my sister and her husband." The gun fired again and the illusion wore off.

"No!" I threw myself at Adrian, dragging my jacket off and wadding it up onto the wound above his heart. "Call an ambulance!" I looked around—the door stayed shut.

Carol was on the bike, key in the ignition. "He's dead."

"Why?"

"He spent his life climbing over little people to get to the top of the pile, to make a fortune he can't spend. My brother-in-law shot himself and my sister miscarried after his company destroyed them. I did it for them." She kicked the engine over and drove out of the shed, leaving me with my former mentor and father-in-law's body next to me.

Outside I heard a shout, and then more voices.

I bent over. Adrian's eyes flicked open.

"Hold on, the ambulance is coming."

"Too late." He shut his eyes again. "I'll get my way."

"Don't talk."

He mouthed something halfway between a wince and a smile. "The will. You take the freight company. In trust. For Macy. Amanda takes the rest." He laughed, a breathless rasp. "Amanda never understood business the way you did. You always had something up your sleeve. Do it for Macy."

"For Macy," I repeated, feeling the tendrils of complication chaining me to a place I'd never wanted to be. He smiled then, and his body seemed to relax, the lines on his face faded. "Hang on," I said uselessly.

I shut Adrian's eyes, and sat back to wait. He might have wanted me dead, but he was Macy's grandfather and a man I'd once respected. Christ—what would Macy think? There were no witnesses to tell her how it had really unfolded. I prayed she wouldn't blame me, even as guilt sat in my gut like a canker.

I thought of unloading the truck for Archie, stuck in Coonabarrabran—then pushed that to one side. There would be time. Archie would understand.

I sat vigil with the corpse, trying to work out what to tell the police, Amanda, and Macy.

I still hadn't solved it by the time the police came and the body was borne away. Throughout the wait my thoughts were filled with Carol; her short dark hair and her smile, and the connection we'd almost made.

A Wondrous Necessary Woman

Janeen Webb

"Tomaso's just not our kind, dear!"

"Mother! Must you always be such a horrible snob?"

"Just being realistic, honey. You'll see the truth of the situation when you calm down."

"I don't want to calm down." Josephina-Jocetta stamped her foot in frustration. Her mother could be *so* unreasonable. "I don't want to go through with it anymore. I want Father to cancel my marriage contract with Antonio."

"You know that's out of the question," Francesca de Glorian replied. She fiddled with her pearls, doing her best to hide her alarm at this sudden turn of events. Deliberately, she gathered up her trailing black velvet skirts and crossed the elegant sitting room with its long windows, its coffered ceiling, and its priceless antiques. She faced her petulant daughter beneath a favourite painting, Titian's *Venus d'Urbino*, recently acquired from Earth's Uffizi Collection—the de Glorian mansion was full of such things.

Francesca crossed her arms, crumpling the stiff lace of her tightly fitted velvet jacket. "It's too late for second thoughts now, Jo Jo," she said. "You've already signed the pre-nuptial agreement with Antonio. Your father has already paid for the genetic matching. Both parties have agreed on a boy child."

"It was what Antonio wanted."

"You signed off on it. It's all arranged."

"So un-arrange it!"

"Don't be tedious, Jo Jo. For once in your life, will you listen to your mother? I'm telling you, if you break this contract, Antonio's family will sue. It could bankrupt us." She sighed theatrically. "I didn't want this match for you in the first place. You insisted you were in love with Antonio. Your father had to call in a lot of favours to get the Fertility Control Board to waive the anti-corporate merger provisions."

"We haven't had the ceremony yet."

"It doesn't matter, dear. The legal arrangements are already in effect. The wedding is just a social convention, a grand occasion for you to dress up and spend your father's money. It's too late to renege."

"But I don't want to be with Antonio any more! I want to be with Tomaso!"

Francesca shook her head. "Even if your father *could* find a way to get you out of the contract, Tomaso isn't a suitable husband for you, dear."

"I don't see why not. His family is just as rich as Antonio's."

It was Francesca's turn to feel exasperated. "But Jo Jo, our family are all high index Jobs. Tomaso's clan are all Gates: you are not compatible."

"Nonsense, Mother! We can get a software patch. We'll be just fine."

Francesca sniffed. 'You still can't know that he'll be a suitable sperm donor for my grandchild: we are breeding for much more than a handsome face. Your child will have to be fit to run a corporate empire."

"He will be," said Josephina-Jocetta. 'Tomaso will make a wonderful father."

"I think you mean Antonio," Francesca said drily. "Your marriage contract is watertight—only death will break it. And since you both look pretty healthy to me, you'd better get used to it."

Josephina-Jocetta was suddenly thoughtful. "We'll see about that," she said. "I'm going out."

"I'll catch up with you later then, dear. Do try to see sense." Francesca stroked a small Donatello sculpture as she smiled encouragingly at her daughter. "You know you can still have

Tomaso to warm your bed, if that's what you want," she said. "There's nothing in your contract about fidelity." She sighed. "Your eggs have been harvested, and Antonio's sperm has been collected. The surrogate womb-mother will carry the agreed child to term. That's not really so hard, is it?"

"You just don't understand!"

Josephina-Jocetta stormed out of the sitting room and slammed the carved oak door behind her, leaving her mother to pour herself yet another very, very dry martini.

• • •

Later that afternoon, Josephina-Jocetta took herself downtown to one of the sleazier orbital colony bars she used when she needed a little something extra. She stepped casually through the holograph of a wild-west saloon that hid the entrance, and sidled up to the owner, Brunelli.

Brunelli—dark eyed, dark haired, and dangerously fit—wiped languidly at the counter with a grubby cloth.

"What'll it be, Princess?" she asked. She adjusted the bar's holo-scene and tucked the tiny control into the folded sleeve of her ripped T-shirt, just above her bulging bicep. Brunelli was a woman who liked to work out, and it showed. An ex-Imperial guard, her physical enhancements were more sophisticated than most—her body tech was expensive, state-of-the-art, finely tuned. Even the seediest of her customers thought twice about forgetting to tip— the word on the street was that Brunelli relished a fight.

"Coffee. Real coffee."

"It'll cost."

"You know I can afford it." Josephina-Jocetta swiped her card through the machine on the bar. "Take it out of that, and have one for yourself."

Brunelli shrugged, rippling her muscular shoulders. She scrabbled about the back of a shelf and fished out a small foil package. She tipped a handful of rather elderly-looking beans into the grinder, and the strong aroma of freshly ground coffee filled the air.

The only other patron in the shadowy bar was skinny man huddled in a scuffed leather jacket. He looked around, breathing deeply. "Wonderful," he said. "That's one of the best smells in the universe. You hardly ever get to smell it anymore."

"True," said Brunelli.

"It's not strictly legal, is it?" said the customer. "Coffee's been restricted since the last crops failed on Earth."

"This is a private stash," said Josephina-Jocetta. "Want some?"

"I'd kill for it," the man replied.

"In that case, be my guest." Josephina nodded to Brunelli. "Another coffee, for my friend," she said. 'Mr . . . ?"

"Rodriguez," the man replied.

"Nice to meet you, Mr Rodriguez," she said.

"And you," he said. "You're an angel. I've often prayed for a woman who could afford black market coffee."

Brunelli slid two cups across the counter, slopping froth on the grimy bar. She dabbed absently at the spill with her cloth, affecting not to be listening to the conversation. She switched her lenses to *Record*.

Rodriguez deftly picked up the cups and moved to a table. "Let's sit," he said. "It'll be more private here."

Josephina-Jocetta slipped into the faux-wood chair opposite him. She looked up, and gasped when the bar's flickering neon light chanced to fall across the man's pale, pockmarked, pimpled face. His lank brown hair hung limply to a weak chin where dark stubble glistened with the pus of a broken boil. A few thin hairs sketched a moustache on his crusted upper lip. He smelled bad.

She shuddered.

Rodriguez wiped his watery blue eyes with a paper napkin. "Something wrong?" he asked. He pushed her coffee across to her, deliberately brushing her hand with his fingertips.

Josephina-Jocetta recoiled. The thought of physical contact with this man repelled her. She shifted uneasily in her seat. She wanted to leave, but she still wanted her coffee. She decided she could bear his presence long enough for that. She didn't want to seem rude.

"Sorry," she said. "I'm just not used to seeing natural people."

"Ugly, you mean."

"Un-enhanced—or should I say un-augmented?"

Rodriguez leaned forward, so that the wavering neon lit up the scabby craters of his face. "Don't worry," he said. "I know my face is bad. But there are plenty worse than mine on the outside."

"I didn't mean . . . "

Rodriguez waved her protestation aside. "No need to explain," he said. "How could a girl like you, born up here on the orbital, have any idea what life is like for the rest of us? You live in a bubble—good food, good medical care, good security, good everything. Life's good for the likes of you." He stared hard at her, quivering—his whole lean, disease-ravaged body challenged her to contradict him.

Josephina-Jocetta took refuge in contemplating her coffee. She sipped, keeping her eyes down, pretending interest in her sugar spoon. The coffee was bitter. "I'm . . . " she began.

"I know who you are, Ms Josephina-Jocetta de Glorian. Everyone knows who you are. Your face is all over the social media." He tapped a line into his old-fashioned phone. "See?"

Her image flashed up on the screen: the total celebrity-heiress package. She had the kind of sculpted face and body that only the best genetic engineering could buy. And to go with it she had perfect white teeth, perfect long blonde curls, perfectly manicured pink nails. She was wearing a collage of expensive designer clothes, shoes, and jewellery. She looked perfectly bored.

Rodriguez grinned, revealing discoloured teeth. "How could I not recognise such a beautiful woman?"

Josephina-Jocetta winced. She tried to turn the conversation. "I've never seen one of those," she said, pointing at his phone. "I didn't know people still used them."

"We're not all as rich as you," he said. "This may be an antique, but it still works just fine." He concentrated on the flow of her personal data. "Your friends call you Jo Jo," he went on, scrolling down his screen. "That's nice. I'll call you Jo Jo too. I'm sure the two of us are going to be such good friends." He leered. "Don't you think so, *Jo Jo?*"

Josephina-Jocetta tried not to cringe. "I have to go," she said. She picked up her bag. "It was nice meeting you, Rodriguez. If you'll excuse me . . . "

"Thanks for the coffee, then. I'll see you around." He paused. 'Congratulations on your marriage, by the way."

Josephina-Jocetta hesitated. She pulled a face.

"Don't tell me you don't want to marry the most eligible bachelor in town?"

"No," she said. "As a matter of fact, I don't."

"So why do it?"

She felt needled. Her words came out in a rush. 'It seems I can't get out of it. Neither of us can, short of the other one dying."

Rodriguez leaned further forward and lowered his voice. 'Perhaps I can help you. Obstacles can always be removed," he murmured. "For a price."

Josephina-Jocetta's sculpted face creased into a frown. "Really?" she said.

"You don't believe me?"

"Why should I?"

"Maybe you just can't afford me."

She shrugged. "I can pay," she said. "I can afford whatever I want."

"You are the most beautiful woman I've ever met," Rodriguez said. "It pains me to see you unhappy. I'd like to make you smile." He hesitated, weighing her up, calculating. "This coffee is wonderful, don't you think?"

She hesitated, puzzled. "Oh, I get it," she said at last. She signalled to Brunelli. "Two more coffees, thanks," she said.

Brunelli gave her a long look as she brought the cups to the table. "Careful, Princess," she said. "Mr Rodriguez here is always cadging drinks." She sniffed. "He mostly gets cheap hooch, not real coffee. You'll have him thinking he's struck gold."

"Ignore her," Rodriguez said, an irritated edge in his voice. He glared at the barkeep. "She's just jealous of my skills."

"Why don't you tell the lady what you do for a living?" Brunelli countered.

Rodriguez' narrow face stilled. His expression grew smooth as butter. "I'm a fixer," he said.

"And what do you fix?" Josephina-Jocetta asked.

"Problems. I know people who know people, if you see what I mean."

"Not exactly."

"I'm good with information. I arrange solutions. I broker deals. I remove impediments."

"And you could help me?"

Rodriguez smiled confidentially, his broken teeth gleaming yellowish beneath his thin moustache. "My clients find me a very necessary man." He lowered his voice to the barest whisper.

"For you, angel, nothing is impossible." He paused, leaning even closer. "I like you," he said. "I'm sure we could work something out."

"You could break my contract?"

"Trust me." He reached out, trapping her hand beneath his own. "I'd do anything for you."

Josephina-Jocetta flinched at his touch. His skin felt dry, scaly. "I have to go," she said again. She snatched her hand away. "I can't stay here!' She scooped up her bag and headed for the smoky-glass doors, desperate to be out of his company.

"I'll be in touch, Jo Jo," Rodriguez said loudly.

Josephina-Jocetta did not look back.

• • •

Brunelli laughed. "Nice try," she said.

Rodriguez drained his coffee. "She might not like me," he said, "but she needs me. She just doesn't know yet how much she needs me." He checked Jo Jo's cup, and drained the dregs of that too.

"And I suppose you'll show her?"

"Absolutely. I know exactly how to do it."

"Good luck with that." Brunelli bent to retrieve the coffee cups.

"Some women are strange feeders," Rodriguez said softly. "I can see it in her, the urge to corruption. I can feel it."

"If you say so."

"I do." Rodriguez shrugged. "Did she close her bar tab, by any chance?" he asked.

"No," said Brunelli. "But I will. And before you ask, the answer is no. She's too good a customer to lose for the likes of you."

"You can't blame a man for trying," said Rodriguez.

• • •

Josephina-Jocetta felt better once she was back outside in what passed for broad daylight on the orbital. She walked at a leisurely pace, enjoying the virtual landscape that masked the ugly steel of the city walls, congratulating herself on having found a person who would help her—and help her just for coffee money. She had no idea how any of it might be accomplished, nor did she want to know. She guessed it was probably something complicated to do with computers. She sighed with relief. This was how her world had always worked: she expressed a desire, and people made it happen for her. She was glad things were getting back to normal.

She didn't want to go home, didn't want to face her mother. She pushed open the swinging doors to the next bar, and the rest of her afternoon dissolved into a pleasant blur of drinks and recreational pharmaceuticals. By the time she finally headed back to the family mansion she was feeling much better about the world. She'd forgotten her instinctive horror of Rodriguez.

• • •

Late next morning, when Josephina-Jocetta finally came down to breakfast, she found a package waiting for her on the dining room table.

"Special delivery, Jo Jo," her mother said. "Did you order anything special?"

"No." Josephina-Jocetta tossed the package aside. "It can't be important. I'll get to it later." She busied herself with the business of tea and toast, spooning a generous dollop of expensive blood-plum conserve onto her gold-rimmed breakfast plate.

"Are you feeling better today, dear? About Antonio, I mean."

Josephina-Jocetta waved away the question. "Much better, Mother," she answered.

"I'm glad that's settled, then," Francesca said. "I was worried about you."

"No need for that," Josephina-Jocetta said airily. "I'm sure things will work out for the best."

"Good. I knew you'd come around."

Josephina-Jocetta just nodded. Anxious to avoid further interrogation by her mother, she loaded her plate of toast and her mug of rare Orange Pekoe tea onto a tray. She tucked the little parcel under her arm. "I'll take this upstairs," she said.

"As you like, dear," said Francesca. "We'll talk later."

• • •

Josephina-Jocetta munched her toast as she idly unwrapped the package. Inside was a long metal jewellery box. *Bracelet*, she thought. *Lovely. Tomaso must have sent it.*

She was wrong. She bit her knuckle to stifle a scream when she lifted the hinged lid. The box contained a severed finger, snugly nestled on a bed of red velvet. The nicely manicured finger was still bloody, the flesh frayed where it had been hacked from its hand. The finger was wearing a diamond ring, the ring she had so recently given Antonio as a token of their betrothal.

She grabbed for the gift card.

My darling Jo Jo: Your ex-fiancée did not part easily with your gift, the note read. *Receive it, Princess, as proof that I have fulfilled your wishes. Antonio is dead. The deed is done. Your loving R.*

The ink was fading fast, disappearing even as she stared at it. Rodriguez wasn't taking any chances.

Josephina-Jocetta felt sick. "No!" she said. "That's not right!" She paced about her room, realising that she didn't know how to contact Rodriguez, even if she wanted to, which she didn't. Her mind was blank with terror.

Her private com link chimed.

"Hello?"

"Hello, Jo Jo." Rodriguez' whining voice grated on her senses.

"How did you get this link?"

"I told you: I'm good with information. Did you get my package?"

"It's horrible!"

"What do you mean? You said that only death could break the contract. I have done what you asked. Your contract is broken."

"I never asked you to kill him. I never meant it to be like this! This finger . . . It's too awful."

"Yesterday you commissioned a murder, and today you can't look at a dead man's finger? Get a grip, Jo Jo. It's too late for second thoughts now."

"But . . . "

Rodriguez' voice hardened. "You're mine, Princess," he said. "I'm giving you a heads up before the police arrive at your door. We're in this together, you and I."

Josephina-Jocetta was frantic. "I can get money to you," she said. "Enough for you to go far away before any investigation starts. Enough for you to go back to Earth, first class—or to go anyplace else you like. I can get enough for you to live comfortably. You can keep the ring, too: it's very valuable. You can leave now, today."

"And why would I do that?"

"You said there was a price."

"You thought I meant money?"

"What else?"

"You insult me. Did you think you could buy me for coffee money? I did what I did to prove how much you need me, to show how much I care for you. I know you want me. I can feel it."

This preposterous declaration jolted Josephina-Jocetta from her shock. She considered her position. She deliberately slowed her breathing as she had been taught, trying to think clearly. "There's nothing to link me to you," she said at last.

"You paid for our drinks on your credit chip," he replied. "That proves you were at Brunelli's bar yesterday."

"But it doesn't prove there's anything between the two of us. Brunelli won't say anything."

"Perhaps not: would you like me to make the transaction records go away?"

"You can do that?"

"I told you, I know people."

"How much?"

"Don't insult me."

"What, then?"

"We have to meet."

"Where?"

Rodriguez named a place.

"No," she said. "I won't meet you in private. I'll come to Brunelli's."

"Very well, Jo Jo. I'll be waiting for you." He cut the connection.

Josephina-Jocetta dressed hurriedly, pulling on the nearest pair of jeans and an old sweater. She stuffed the jewellery box into her bag, and ran from the family mansion by the back door. She was in no mood to have to explain herself to her mother.

• • •

"Jo Jo, darling!" Rodriguez emerged for the shadows outside Brunelli's Bar just as Josephina-Jocetta reached the holograph that masked the entry: today the bar masqueraded as a street cafe in the Plaka district of old Athens.

"How lovely to see you again, and so soon." Rodriguez pulled her to him and kissed her on both cheeks.

She flinched from his touch, outraged at the thought she might catch some horrible skin disease from contact with his pus-smeared chin.

"Don't," she said. "Don't touch me!"

Rodriguez was offended. He yanked her roughly into the bare metal alleyway beside the bar, holding her tight.

"Let me go!" She tried to pull away. She could feel her shoulders bruising from his grip.

"Did you think I would put my life in jeopardy for *money*?" he rasped. "You knew I loved you, loved you at first sight." He was shaking with anger now, the spittle flying from his thin lips. "Did you think you could buy my services, buy a man's death—just like you buy everything else?"

Josephina-Jocetta blanched, caught off guard. "So what do you want?"

"You know what I want. I want you. I want your perfect body in my arms. I want to ride you till you're howling in ecstasy, till you beg me to stop. And then some." He slammed her against the cold steel wall, holding her forcefully.

"No!"

"Don't worry, Jo Jo. I'm ugly and skinny and undernourished, but I'm a proper man for all that. I know what a woman wants— you'll be enamoured of my manly charms soon enough, I can promise you that."

"You can't be serious!"

"Perfectly serious!" He pushed his knee between her legs, forcing them apart. He grabbed her thigh, tearing at her jeans.

"But *I* don't want *you*! You knew I didn't want you."

"Did I? You were quick enough to accept my offer. What else was I to think? A lot of society women like a bit of rough trade— why wouldn't you want me? Plenty of others have done."

Josephina-Jocetta was desperate now, clutching at straws. "But you're not enhanced. We're not compatible."

"We're compatible enough for my needs, Princess. I don't care about the mind-body sync stuff. It's overrated, if you ask me."

Josephina-Jocetta tried a different tack. "You'll never pass in my social set," she said. "We can't be seen together. People would guess."

"A woman dipped in blood to talk of social status?" Rodriguez tried to laugh—it came out as a short, bitter bark. "You're no better than me now, *Princess*," he said. "You're as much a murderer as I am. If I go down, I'll take you with me." He grimaced, his foul breath reeking hot against her smooth white cheek. "Buy my silence with your body, Jo Jo." He wiggled his hips suggestively.

She felt his erection, hard against her. She fought to pull his questing hand away from her jeans' zipper.

"No! I said no!"

"Believe me, it's the only currency you have to offer."

"I won't. I can't."

"You can, and you will." Rodriguez relented a little. "You won't have to be seen with me, my darling, if that's what you want. You won't have to own me in public. You can buy me a little apartment somewhere nice—our own little love nest."

Josephina-Jocetta was appalled. "You won't take my money, but I can buy you an apartment? How does that work?"

"I said you couldn't buy me off," Rodriguez countered. "I didn't say I wouldn't take money from you. A man needs to live. You can afford me, my dear. You need to keep me close to you—very, very close." He kissed her again, full on the lips this time, thrusting his coated tongue down her throat.

She squirmed away from him, trying not to retch.

"Soon, very soon, you'll *want* to keep me close."

"Stop it! You're hurting me!"

A rough voice echoed in the alleyway: "Get off her!"

"What?"

Rodriguez felt a heavy hand on his shoulder, pulling him away from Josephina-Jocetta.

"I said, get off her!"

"Stay out of it, Brunelli! The girl likes a bit of rough."

"Princess?"

Josephina-Jocetta shook her head.

"Doesn't look like it to me," Brunelli said. "Give it up, Rodriguez. You know you can't fight me. I run a clean operation. Nobody rapes my customers—not here on my patch! Give it up, before you get hurt."

Rodriguez pulled a knife. "I'll cut her," he said. "Back off."

Brunelli was too quick for him. Her right hand was a blur of motion: there was a crunching sound as Rodriguez' nose broke, and Brunelli carried the stroke through to knock the knife to the ground. She kicked it into the gutter.

"Get out, Rodriguez," Brunelli said. "Go, before I forget my manners and do you some real harm."

Rodriguez caught a glimpse of the razor-sharp blades that now protruded just beyond Brunelli's fingertips. He straightened up, slowly. "You win," he said.

"I always win." Brunelli's blades slid back under her fingernails. "Go!"

Rodriguez used his sleeve to wipe at the blood that was now dripping from his nose and staining the front of his grubby, rumpled shirt. "All right," he said. "I'm going. But this isn't the end of it, not by a long way."

Josephina-Jocetta edged behind Brunelli, too frightened to speak. She straightened her clothes and rubbed the back of her hand across her mouth.

"You don't get out of it this easily, Jo Jo," Rodriguez said. "Remember what I said. You'll do what I want. You know you will—if you know what's good for you."

"Blackmail?" said Brunelli.

"That's an ugly word," said Rodriguez.

Josephina-Jocetta found her voice. "An ugly word for an ugly man," she said.

Rodriguez rallied, spitting blood. "As you will, my love. Call me whatever you like—you made your bargain, and you're stuck with me now. You belong to me. You're mine. You'd better get used to it." He scowled at Brunelli. "Your *friends* won't always be around to save you."

"That's enough!" Brunelli gave Rodriguez a shove. "Get out, before I call the cops."

"The lady won't want the cops," Rodriguez said. "Ask her."

"I will," Brunelli said. She put a brawny arm around Josephina-Jocetta's shoulders and shepherded her towards the door.

Rodriguez tried a parting shot. "Don't forget, Jo Jo—you're my creature now."

Josephina-Jocetta peeped out from the safety of Brunelli's protective embrace. *We'll see about that*, she thought.

• • •

"Come on Princess, out with it," Brunelli said. She led Josephina-Jocetta into the bar, settled her in a chair, draped a blanket around her shoulders, and poured her a very large brandy. "You'd better tell me what this is all about, and quickly."

Josephina-Jocetta was still shaking with shock. She clung to Brunelli. "Antonio is dead," she whispered.

"I know: it was on the vid."

"And Rodriguez says he killed him. He says I asked him to do it."

"Did you?"

"No—at least I don't think I did."

"Give me a moment." Brunelli switched her lenses to *Replay*. "Let's see exactly what was said."

Josephina-Jocetta's eyes widened. "You *recorded* my private conversation?"

"Just a precaution, Princess," Brunelli said. She was concentrating on the replay. "He didn't actually say the word *murder*," she concluded, "but then again, he wouldn't. There was clearly some sort of transaction going down." She shrugged. "He's small time—mostly known around the traps for petty computer fraud—fiddling accounts, that sort of thing. I thought he was just making out he could find a way to break your contract so he could hit you up for more drinks. You can afford it, so there'd be no harm done. I figured he'd sneak a look at the contract, realise your family lawyers are Middleton and Rowley, decide the whole thing was beyond him, and move on." She paused. "I never imagined he'd turn assassin," she said. "Are you sure he killed Antonio? Could he be lying?"

Josephina-Jocetta reached into her bag and pulled out the jewellery box. "He sent me this," she said.

Brunelli eased open the box and examined its contents. The finger had oozed a bit more, staining the velvet a darker red. She snapped the lid shut, and let out a long breath. "You'd better leave this with me," she said. "I'll take care of it."

"What do I do now?"

"Finish your brandy, Princess. I'll close up here, and then I'll take you back to your mother. I'll need her authorisation."

"Mother? No way!"

"She's the brains of your family, child," Brunelli said softly. "Did you not know?"

• • •

An hour later, Josephina-Jocetta sat stiffly in an overstuffed antique armchair in a family living room dominated by a Michelangelo marble, listening while Brunelli discussed the nature of the problem with Francesca de Glorian. The women were calmly sipping tea, sharing tiny iced cupcakes and glistening marzipan sweets as they talked.

"Jo Jo must have looked to him like the chance of a lifetime," Francesca said at last. "Why else would a man like that take such a risk?"

"It's clear enough," said Brunelli. "Rodriguez figured that if he could get his hooks into her once, he could bleed her dry. Blackmail never ends."

Francesca took another sip of her Orange Pekoe. "So you'll end it?" she said.

"Yes. Of course."

Josephina-Jocetta was ready to scream. "Will you two stop this? Please?" she said. "You're talking about me like I'm not here—like Brunelli's my nursemaid or something."

Francesca and Brunelli both laughed.

"What's so funny?"

"That's exactly what I am," Brunelli said. "Your nursemaid, that is."

"You were micro-chipped at birth, darling," Francesca said. "Brunelli here has always been your protector—your security guard, if you like."

"But I found her bar for myself," Josephina-Jocetta said stubbornly. "You couldn't know that, Mother."

"We guided you," Francesca said. "It's easily done: a tweak to your program, a gentle suggestion of the right path through your v-r lenses, and so on and so forth."

Josephina-Jocetta was speechless.

"Your mother always wanted you to have your freedom, Princess," Brunelli said. "But you're a valuable commodity—we have always kept track of you."

"You mean you've always been watching me? Watching *everything*?"

Francesca frowned in distaste. "Not everything, darling," she said. "Don't worry—you've had your privacy. There are things a mother definitely does *not* wish to see."

"Nor does your protector," Brunelli added. "I have better things to do." She turned her attention back to Francesca. "Are we agreed on a solution, then?"

"You'll have to persuade Rodriguez to leave," Francesca said firmly. "Whatever it takes."

"Understood," Brunelli said. "He'll be on the shuttle back to Earth, first thing tomorrow."

"A distraction might also be useful."

"I'll see to it."

"And Tomaso?"

"I've already had a word with him. I contacted him as soon as I heard Antonio was dead. Tomaso's family won't allow a match. Sorry, Princess, if Tomaso married you now he'd always be suspected of involvement in the murder. His family can't risk the taint of scandal."

Josephina-Jocetta began to cry.

"That's the way, darling," Francesca said. "In these circumstances, a good cry always helps."

• • •

Next morning, a tearful Josephina-Jocetta featured on the orbital's media, vowing, through carefully smudged makeup, to honour her contract with her dear, dead Antonio. The surrogate pregnancy would go ahead as planned. Her family would bring up his child—their child—as agreed in her contract, as a living memorial to her fiancée. Antonio's lawyers had already seen to it: this family merger was far too profitable to be hindered by the death of one of the parties—not since the genetic engineering had, fortuitously, already been completed. The little embryo was already on its way to a life of privilege and power.

Francesca de Glorian stood beside her weeping daughter, comforting her and grimly assuring the media that Josephina-Jocetta would honour her obligations—all of them. The family's good name was at stake, and her daughter would not be found wanting.

Josephina-Jocetta's star performance as the bereaved bride was interrupted by a newsflash: the morning shuttle to Earth had exploded, killing all on board. The live emergency feed streaming across her lenses showed the exact instant when the ship was blasted to pieces. She saw a lurid red-gold fireball, dramatic against the inky blackness of surrounding space—and then, nothing. The brightness of the after-image hurt her eyes.

Next moment it seemed that everyone on the orbital colony was messaging at once. The questions were flying, the fears escalating:

Who was on the shuttle? Was it sabotage? What happened to our security? Are we under attack?

The reporters scrambled for the doors, all heading for the spaceport—Antonio's untimely death was old news now.

The space station's controller was already issuing reassurances, trying to calm the panicking population.

Francesca took her daughter's arm. "We need to leave now, Jo Jo," she said quietly. "There's nothing more for us here. Our security people will want to lock down the house as soon as possible." She leaned a little closer to add: "You can always count on Brunelli—she is a most wondrous necessary woman."

Josephina-Jocetta just nodded. As she stepped down from the podium, a very private message flashed across her lenses:

"Attention Princess: Problem solved. Solution status: Permanent. *Brunelli.*"

Broken Glass

Stephanie Gunn

The woman in White is making cakes for the ghosts.

Echo watches from the building known as Blue, her limbs pressed against two crumbling balconies. Below her there is nothing but empty space, all the way down to the greyish smog that breaks across the City twenty storeys below. Above, low clouds mirror the smog, and in the near distance dust thickens the air to the same flat hue.

The City—five buildings known as Blue, Green, Yellow, Black and White, all named for the colour of the glass tiles that ring their roofs—seems to float, a cluster of islands on a sea of grey that never clears, not even in the most violent of the windstorms.

Not that Echo has seen an island, nor the sea, except in the books that she and Darwin have collected. She's not even certain that seas and islands are real things at all. It's hard to believe in anything but the glass and concrete and smog that are all she has ever known.

This is the first time Echo has been here early enough to see the woman in White begin her work. The woman moves slowly around her kitchen, movements oddly stilted, though Echo can see no sign of Twisting in her bones. Sealed behind the glass-and-steel skin of White, she shuffles back and forth, the loose flesh of her arms jiggling as she opens cabinets. A door stands open behind the woman, vague shadows beyond. Echo can just see a faint light in the darkness flickering red then green, red then green. She leans forward, trying to see it more clearly, and the concrete beneath her right hand loosens, cracks and falls away. Moving from long practiced instinct, Echo tenses her other limbs to hold herself in place, finds another handhold. Her heartbeat remains steady, even when she looks down, sees the hunk of concrete swallowed by the smog.

The City keeps her safe, the City will not let her fall.

White stands apart from the other buildings in the City. The others are connected by dozens of ziplines used by couriers like Echo, but White stands too far away for such connections. It is the only building that possesses an intact glass-and-steel skin, and all of its windows are shuttered from within. The woman's window is the only one that Echo has ever seen with the shutters open, and only on one day per year—this day, when Grandmother used to say the ghosts come.

For all of Echo's childhood they left offerings for the ghosts. Grandmother used to fold sheets of paper into clever shapes—tiny houses, miniature dresses and shirts and shoes—and burn them, along with food, in the offering bowls left outside the wind barrier.

The woman in White reaches into a cupboard, withdraws a canister. She opens the vacuum seal, pours a handful of rice into a bowl and begins grinding it into flour.

Now Echo's heart beats fast.

White still has stocks of rice.

The last time Echo tasted rice, she had been six, just learning to mark off the days on the calendar scratched into the wall. Grandmother had commandeered the last of Blue's rice stocks, rolled them into rice balls for the then-children. The air in the kitchen had grown warm and close with so many of them crammed into the small space. Echo's cousin Mei, eldest of the children at ten and already promise-bonded to Masao from Green, had corralled the younger ones, made them line up and wait. Echo remembers the way Darwin had slipped her hand into hers while they waited, how Mother smiled at them both. Echo's brother Tommy, a babe in Mother's arms, had smiled and gummed the fingerful of rice he was offered.

That moment is frozen in time for Echo. Tommy smiling, their mouths full of rice, and the light falling through Mother's skirt from behind. Her legs silhouetted, no longer straight but beginning to curve in almost delicate lines from knee to ankle. Mother was beginning to Twist.

The woman in White pauses, stares out of the window. She doesn't look at Echo. She never seems to notice Echo, or any of the other couriers moving over the other buildings. This year, she doesn't seem to look at anything. She just stares, and the unfocused expression is too much like the way Grandmother stares out at the City now, and Echo cannot watch any more.

Echo climbs across the face of Yellow, hands moving over concrete worn smooth by the passage of many couriers, catches the zipline to Blue. Her carrysack is still half full, and the clouds are beginning to gather fire as day slides into evening. She's spent too long watching White, and she'll have to hurry to finish her deliveries if she wants to earn any barter tokens today. She climbs faster, but her joints have stiffened with inactivity. Both hands cramp hard, and she slips and falls.

She catches glimpses of faces as she falls, all of them staring out, unseeing. She closes her eyes.

The City will keep us safe, the City will not let us thirst, the City will not let us hunger, the City will not let us fall.

Here, in the darkness behind her eyes, she can feel the weight of the City around her. It comforts her, protects, her, anchors her.

She lands heavily on a jagged outcrop of steel. Everything is silent, the air damp and warm as breath against her skin. She lies back against the steel, working the joints of her hands to ease the cramping. Above, waves of fire have begun to roll behind the clouds; nightfall is imminent.

It's only when she sits up and sees stacked stone in the window instead of the wind barriers of the populated storeys that she realises how far she has fallen.

She is less than half a storey from the top of the smog. It is completely still, the dense grey appearing almost soft, as though it is a vast blanket that she could wrap herself up in. If she hooked her knees around the outcrop, lowered herself down, she would be able to touch the smog, feel if it is as soft as it looks.

She is reaching down, moisture beading on her fingers, when the surface of the smog vibrates. And she remembers Father.

It had been after the rice balls, but before Echo had begun working as a courier. Grandfather had Hollowed; unlike most, whose Hollowing set them to silence and staring, his disease had been a thing that sent him wandering, searching for something which he no longer had the capacity to name. Mother had eventually resorted to tying a rope around his waist to tether him to the apartment. One morning, they had woken to find the rope chewed through, Grandfather gone.

Echo pulls herself up, climbs to the lowest wind barrier. The rooms beyond are empty and smell of damp. Flashes of orange light slice through the open wind barrier as Echo crosses the apartment, heads for the centre of the building.

Two shafts run down the centre of Blue. One is filled with rubble and odd chunks of frayed wire thicker than Echo's wrist. The other shaft houses the central staircase. The entrance down here has been blocked up with hunks of concrete.

On the floor near the blockade is an old piece of rope, frayed and brittle. It had been Echo who had found it, who discovered the place where Grandfather, sick and frail as he was, had managed to haul away enough concrete to enter the staircase.

Echo moves close to the barricade. Cool air moves against her face from beyond.

Father had wrapped his face with strips of linen, climbed through the hole Grandfather had made. Mother had begged him not to go, but there was little she could do, her legs already Twisted so much that she was unable to walk.

Half a day had passed before Father returned. The linen wrappings were stained almost black, and his face and arms were striped with angry red burns. When he had tried to speak, Echo had seen that the burns continued down his throat, his voice seared away.

Despite the best of Mother and Grandmother's efforts, Father's burns had suppurated, infection sinking down to his bones. Within days he was dead.

Echo wonders who came down here, replaced the rocks that Grandfather had removed. After Father died, Mother had forbidden them from descending so low, fearing that the smog would burn them as it had burned Father. Echo had always obeyed, even after Mother died. Until today.

She raises a hand to the barricade. It would take the removal of only a few rocks to be able to see through.

She's reaching for the first rock when a low, ululating noise shudders through the building. Echo jumps, her nails scraping concrete, her heart hammering hard. She tastes metal in the back of her throat. It takes her a few moments to recognise the noise as the wind barrier shaking. A windstorm is brewing, and unless she wants to spend the night down here alone, she needs to climb back home now.

Outside, she breathes in deeply, aware as she never has been before of the City's air pressing against her body, filling her lungs. How much it weighs her down.

• • •

The last of the fire is fading from the clouds as Echo climbs into the rooms she shares in Blue with Tommy and Grandmother. The air pulls hard at the wind barrier as she hauls it closed, fixes it in place. She lights the lamp, waits for her eyes to adjust.

Her carrysack is still half-full, her day's deliveries incomplete for the first time. She'll have to start early tomorrow, climb extra hours to make up the loss.

Grandmother is standing just inside the wind barrier, staring out, her arms lax at her sides. She doesn't react to Echo, or to the wind barrier closing. The sour reek of urine tells Echo that Grandmother has not moved from the spot all day. Guilt pulls at Echo as she leads Grandmother away from the barrier, sponges her down and changes the linen pad in her underwear. Grandmother bears it all with a waxen pliability, as she has borne everything since she began to Hollow.

Echo hates leaving Grandmother like this, but she has no other choice. If she doesn't climb, they do not eat.

She mixes some of their rationed soy protein with water to make a gruel that she spoons into Grandmother's mouth. It is a slow process, and by the time she's finished, the wind barrier is rattling hard. Echo is glad to guide the old woman to her pallet, cover her with a blanket. Grandmother blinks twice, and then her eyes close. Within minutes she is asleep.

Tommy's pallet lies next to Echo's at the back of the apartment. Tommy is in it, apparently asleep. He's awake, of course, but he pretends in order to ensure that Echo tends to Grandmother first, no matter how bad his pain is. He feigns sleep still while she changes his pads, sponges him down. Pretence is the only dignity Tommy has left now, with the Twisting in both his arms and legs.

Next to Tommy's bed is a stack of books that Echo has collected for him—all brightly coloured, and all featuring birds. Like the sea and islands, Echo does not know if they are a thing that ever existed, but the presence of them in so many of the books is enough for Tommy. Before his Twisting was so bad to keep him confined to bed, he would sit for hours at the wind barrier, looking up at the clouds, waiting for one to appear. None ever did, but still he kept looking.

Tommy cannot see the clouds from his pallet now. The wall next to his bed adjoins the apartment where Mei and Masao live. When Tommy grew too ill to move from his pallet, Echo knocked a hole in the wall so Tommy could talk to Masao as he worked spinning reclaimed thread. When Tommy still had use of his hands, he had begun scratching a mural onto that wall: trailing vines and flowers surround the hole, and around them, a flock of birds lift into flight. The last bird is incomplete, a thing with half-made wings and no legs.

Through the hole, Echo can see Mei and Masao, both of them sleeping. Mei's stomach is bowed out beneath the weight of the child she carries. She sleeps close to Masao, but she does not touch him. Not six months prior, Masao began to Twist, his illness burning through him, faster than Echo has ever seen.

Tommy opens his eyes, smiles as Echo brings him a bowl of gruel. When she feeds him, he averts his eyes. It is only recently that his hands have Twisted badly enough to render him unable to hold his own spoon, another indignity on top of all that he has already borne.

When Tommy has finished, Echo gives him three drops of breakback infusion. Breakback is a pain-relieving herb grown by Mei in Green's rooftop garden, the only thing they have to ease the pain of Twisting. There is only a little left in the bottle, and Echo curses herself again for wasting time instead of climbing.

Tommy swallows the infusion and lies back, eyes closed. Like Grandmother, he sleeps within minutes.

Exhaustion drags at Echo as she forces herself to chew solid soy protein, sponge down her hands and face and douse the lantern.

She makes her way in the dark to her pallet, lies down already half asleep.

The wind barrier rattles, a thin whine rising as the wind finds its way through the tiny cracks that Echo never seems to be able to find, no matter how hard she looks. She is drifting down into sleep when the sound changes, sharpens. It sounds like a woman screaming.

Echo's eyes fly open. It is the first time that they have forgotten to leave out an offering for the ghosts.

She squeezes her eyes shut, tells herself over and over that it's just the wind. That Mother had always said that the ghosts were only a superstition, that they were never real.

Grandmother always said that the ghosts were hungry, that the offerings were put out to appease them, to stop the ghosts from devouring the living instead.

The screaming of the wind grows louder. Maybe, unappeased, the ghosts were here to devour them now.

Echo opens her eyes again. She can just see the strange lumps that Tommy's Twisted arms and legs make beneath his blankets. Maybe the ghosts *had* devoured them all long ago, and no one had noticed.

. . .

Echo stands on the edge of what remains of Yellow's roof. There's only a single corner remaining of the original structure; the rest of it slopes down into rubble. There are planks and odd pieces of furniture scattered amongst the debris, evidence of the efforts that someone once made to repair the crumbling roof.

If she reached down from here, she would be able to touch what remains of the band of coloured glass that surrounds the edge of the roof. When Echo was younger, she would circle around the buildings, collecting the tiles that fell after each windstorm, fix them back in place. Each time the tiles fell, the glass became more brittle, until eventually all she could reclaim were handfuls of glittering dust.

Echo closes her eyes and raises her arms, palms turned up towards the clouds. If the woman in White opened her shutters now, she would be able to see Echo, a cross suspended against the sky.

She does not open her eyes as she counts: "One, two, three."

She jumps.

If the woman in White had been watching, she would see Echo arc out into the air, twist her body, aiming for an opening in the wind barrier below. From above, the opening is impossible to see, but Echo knows where it is all the same.

She jumps, she falls, and Darwin catches her.

It's the way it has been since they were first learning to climb. Darwin catches her, and she catches Darwin. It is the way it always will be.

The concrete and steel mouth of the building closes over her. A heartbeat later, Darwin is there, pulling her in through the wind barrier. When Echo opens her eyes, Darwin is grinning, teeth bright against her dark skin.

"One day I'm not going to catch you," she says.

Echo punches her lightly on the arm, grins back. She always feels lighter when she's near Darwin. "Right now, you just did. And now is all we have to worry about. For everything else, the City will keep us."

Darwin's smile fades. She moves across the room to the water filter, tops it up from her watersack. While Echo is a general courier, delivering goods like soy protein and vegetables and linen, Darwin is a water courier. All day, every day, she hauls her heavy watersack around the City, dispensing water rations to everyone. It is hard work, and most couriers cannot bear it for more than a year, but Darwin has been doing it since she began to climb.

Echo sets down her own empty carrysack. The windstorm blew out early; she's been out since climbing without a break, trying to make up for the lost hours. She sits down, stretches out her legs, the small joints of her feet popping and cracking.

Other people have lived in this space before Darwin, remnants of their lives layered on the walls. There's an old painting of a girl dressed in red, her hand held out. Scraps of wallpaper hang here and there, flaking away occasionally like old skin to reveal more layers of paper beneath. When Darwin had first claimed this place, she had found a hidden cavity in one wall. Within, she had found a white velvet dress wrapped in layers of clear plastic. Attached to the back of the dress were wings made of lace that fell to threads at a touch.

"White still has stocks of rice," Echo says.

Darwin does not turn from her work, though the muscles of her shoulders tighten. "How do you know?"

Echo looks down at her hands. There is dirt engrained in the lines of her palms and fingers that never comes away. When she had touched that white dress, she had left a smear of black behind. "I saw the woman again. I was there early enough to see her grind rice into flour. I always assumed she was using soy protein, but it's rice."

Darwin scrubs a hand over her short hair, stares down at the dripping water filter for a long time. Finally, she fills a beaker and brings it to Echo. She waits until Echo has finished the water before she kneels down, slips off Echo's shoe and begins massaging, fingers going deep. Echo knows that, even as Darwin is trying to help ease her cramped muscles, she's also measuring the straightness of her bones, just as every time she looks into Darwin's eyes, Echo is looking for any sign of Hollowing.

"I see lights sometimes in White," Darwin says.

"When?" Echo asks.

Darwin looks down. "At night."

Echo stares at her. "You go out at *night*? During the storms?"

"Not the worst of them. You can tie yourself to the building, so if you fall—"

Echo pulls away, a sour taste rising in the back of her throat. "Ropes don't always hold. You shouldn't go out at night. It's not safe, even if there's no storm."

Darwin meets her gaze evenly. "Says who?"

"Says everyone."

"The same *everyone* who tells us the City always keeps us safe? That's keeping Tommy and Masao *safe*?"

Echo moves across the room to the shelf where she and Darwin keep most of the books they've found. They can only read bits and pieces of them—Grandmother began teaching the children to read, but her Hollowing cut the lessons short—and so they try to find books with mostly pictures.

There's a new book on the shelf. Most of the pages are water-damaged, but near the end is one untouched page. A woman stands on the edge of a cliff, the sea churning below, sending up lace-like froth that just touches her bare feet. She is naked, her body thin and pale. From her shoulders stretch vast feathered wings, white edged with silver.

Echo stares at the picture for a long time, a feeling that she cannot name moving within her. When she puts the book back on the shelf, she breathes in deeply, tastes dust and rot. Her stomach clenches hard.

She turns around. "How low did you climb?"

Darwin is sitting in the chair Echo vacated, the beaker of water in her hands. "There's lots of stuff down there still. Some of the apartments are still sealed. There could be stored food. Rice. Real medicine for Tommy and Masao."

"Tommy has breakback," Echo says. "And we have food. The vats produce enough soy protein, and we have the gardens." She crosses her arms. "You can't go down there. The smog burns."

Darwin holds out her arms, the skin unmarked. "It doesn't."

Echo looks away, remembering the cool air that had moved through the barricade in Blue. Remembering wanting to reach down and touch the smog, wanting to feel, wanting to *see*. "White has rice. We'd be better off trying to find a way there."

"Everyone has failed. It's too far away, unless you've found a way to fly?" Darwin shakes her head. "You don't even know that it was the smog that burned your father. It could have been steam from pipes, chemicals, anything."

"I know that I saw him die screaming in pain," Echo says. "Even if there is anything down there, we don't need it."

"There are water pumps down below the smog in Yellow," Darwin says. "I saw them, the pipes rusted through. If there are pumps here, there must be pumps in Blue, too. We might be able to fix them, have water in every building—"

"No," Echo says, her voice flat. "This is the way the City has always been, and it is all that we need."

Darwin takes her hands, twines heavily calloused fingers with Echo's. "What about the books, Echo? There was another world once. There might still be another world out there."

"*This* is our world."

Darwin looks down at their intertwined hands. "Nothing has always been, and nothing will always be, Echo."

Echo looks closer at her, sees the tightness in her jaw, the way Darwin is holding herself as though she is made of glass. "What's happened?"

Darwin slumps, her spine bowing as if beneath a great weight.

"I was delivering water, and I figured I'd check on Masao. He's been trying to hide it from everyone, but his teeth are falling."

Echo closes her eyes, presses her forehead against the curve of Darwin's clavicle. Twisting moves from the ground up: the bones of the legs curve first, then the pelvis, spine and arms. Last of all is the jaw. When it Twists, the teeth are forced from their sockets one by one. After the teeth fall, it's only a matter of time before the throat Twists closed. Mother had lasted only a week after her last tooth fell.

"You can't go down there again." Echo listens to the beating of Darwin's heart, the steady tide of breath in and out of her lungs. "We don't need to go down there. The City watches over us. The City will not let us fall."

"What about Masao and Tommy? Your Grandmother? We're falling, Echo, all of us."

Darwin moves away, cold air filling the space she had occupied in Echo's arms. When Echo finally opens her eyes, Darwin is gone, slipped out so silently she might never have been there at all.

• • •

A week passes. Echo sees Darwin only occasionally, and only then as a distant figure sliding along a zipline or swinging around a corner. Always moving away from Echo. Masao's teeth have fallen one by one, each leaving gaping holes in his gums that do not heal but bleed and bleed, filling the air with the scent of decay. Even the breakback does not touch his pain now, and most nights the windstorms are drowned out by the sound of his screams.

That morning Echo had woken to silence. When she had looked over at Tommy, she had seen that he was awake, staring at the hole in the wall. It had been covered over from the other side.

Echo wanted to stay, but they were running low on breakback, and she had no barter tokens to trade for more. She had to climb.

She had worked solidly all day, the work a welcome distraction. Now she stands halfway up Green, her carrysack empty and barter tokens in her pocket, staring at the side of Blue. She's never noticed before that remnants of old pipes cling here and there to the side of the building. She can trace where she thinks they should meet, weaving in and out of each apartment. Darwin had said that there were pumps in Yellow below the smog, that there were likely pumps in Blue, too.

Echo shakes her head. Whatever has gotten into Darwin, she can't let it infect her, too.

"The smog burns," she tells the broken pipes. "The City will keep us. The City will not let us fall."

She heads up to the rooftop garden. Halfway up, she catches sight of a bundle being attached to the zipline connecting Blue and Black. The bundle is tightly wrapped, so light that it barely bows the line.

Echo looks away, keeps climbing.

Green's roof is fully intact, the space filled with rows of hydroponic trays, gardeners moving between them tending to the crops. At one end, a drying shed and workroom. In storms, everything is tied down or covered. Few plants are ever lost to the wind. The City does not let them hunger.

The beans are flowering, and Echo's fingers itch with the desire to pluck a few of the blooms for Tommy. Before he began to Twist, he spent most of his time up here. The other gardeners said that fruits and vegetables sprang forth at his touch, growing healthy and strong. They had said that one day he would run the gardens and they would prosper like never before.

Mei is in the drying shed, which does not surprise Echo. The shed has always been a place of solace for Mei. Echo is surprised to find her not alone. Darwin is there, both of them bent over a tray of seedlings. Darwin's skin is damp with sweat, and though it is late in the day, her watersack still bulges full, her deliveries unmade.

As Echo approaches, Mei looks up. Her eyes are bloodshot and swollen.

"I'm sorry," Echo says. The words feel useless, but she has nothing else.

Mei holds out her hands. Three small envelopes are cradled in her palms. "Darwin found seeds. Peas, chilli, sunflowers."

Echo looks at Darwin. Darwin does not meet her eyes.

"You can eat the sunflower seeds," Mei says. "And they're pretty. Tommy would love them. So would—" Her voice breaks. She presses her hands to her belly, the seed packets trapped between her palms and the swell of the child within. The paper crackles as the baby moves.

Echo digs in her pocket for her tokens. She wishes she could ask one of the other gardeners, but the breakback has always been Mei's domain. "I don't . . . I need . . . "

The tokens are fewer than she would usually trade for the herb, and she expects Mei to say no, but Mei nods, moves into the work shed.

The air stirs slowly, fire beginning to gather behind the clouds. The moisture is drying on Darwin's skin, leaving a powdery residue behind.

"You went down there again," Echo says.

Darwin pulls a piece of linen from her pocket, the white fabric stained brown. "Your father had the right idea, Echo. It's hard to breathe, but not impossible. It's . . . " She looks up at the sky, her eyes reflecting fire. "There's a whole world, Echo. The way people lived before: it's so different. It wasn't always like this."

"It doesn't matter how things were," Echo says. "None of that matters. Whatever is down there, it doesn't change anything. Not for Masao, or Tommy."

"You don't even want to see what it was like?"

"I . . . " Echo crosses her arms, shakes her head. "It doesn't matter if I want to or not. I *can't*."

Darwin looks at Echo for a moment, then turns and moves back through the garden, vanishes over the edge of the roof.

Echo fists her hands, presses her nails into her palms. Anything to stop her from running after Darwin. Because she wants to, more than anything. She wants to run, wants to dive headlong into the smog, wants to be anywhere but here.

Mei returns with a bundle of breakback far larger than Echo's tokens are worth. The bitter scent of the herb catches in Echo's throat, and she swallows hard, thinking of Mother choking as her throat Twisted closed. Thinking how Tommy will do the same one day.

"I had some stockpiled," Mei says. "It loses strength as it ages, so it may as well be used now. Darwin's seeds, they cover what it's worth. I think I remember hearing that chilli can be used for pain, so maybe . . . " She trails off, her eyes unfocusing. One heartbeat, two, she is staring at nothing, and then her eyes snap back into focus. " . . . we can use them for Tommy." She hands the bundle to Echo.

Echo turns it over, sees that there are three small flowers tucked into the bundle's binding.

"They just fell," Mei says. "It happens sometimes."

Mei returns to work, and Echo climbs down from the roof. Her joints have stiffened, and she has to concentrate hard on keeping her hands and feet steady as she descends.

• • •

The next morning, thick smoke rises from Black. It lingers in the air for a moment only, before it is swallowed by the clouds.

At Tommy's request, Echo leaves the flowers Mei gave him outside the wind barrier that night. Grandmother watches, her eyes as blank as ever.

There is no windstorm that night, but in the morning, the flowers are gone.

• • •

The days pass.

Echo tends Grandmother and Tommy. She climbs.

The seeds that Darwin found all fail, but for a single sunflower. It pushes up a pale shoot that twists and lengthens, trying to find the light. The shoot never develops a single leaf.

• • •

One night, Echo wakes to a sound, sees Grandmother standing at the wind barrier, staring out. The barrier has been opened, and a thin light falls into the room, throws Grandmother's shadow across Echo's pallet.

Echo gets up, starts to close the barrier, and pauses. That light is coming from the clouds and the smog, an eerie bluish glow. She leans out, sees movement lower down on Blue. Darwin, her dark skin drinking in that strange light.

Echo closes the wind barrier, guides Grandmother back into bed. When she lies down, she sees that the covering over the hole in the wall has been removed. Through the hole, Echo can see Mei standing at the closed wind barrier, staring, her hands lax against her swollen stomach. The child within her turns, but Mei does not react.

• • •

Echo stands on the edge of Yellow's roof, counts one, two, three. She jumps, arcs out, then in.

She reaches the opening in the wind barrier, begins to fall past. At the last moment, she grasps the edge of the barrier, hauls herself inside. Darwin is not there.

She sinks down to her knees. Darwin has always been there to catch her before. Darwin has always known when Echo was going to fall.

Darwin's watersack lies empty and abandoned in a corner. Dozens of boxes are stacked around the room, all of them soft with moisture and spotted black with mould at the edges. Papers spill from the split sides of one, and another stands open, hundreds of small white bottles within.

Echo feels something give way within her. She had stayed away from Darwin, hoping that she would give away this idea of climbing beneath the smog, that she would come to her senses.

She curls her fingers over the edge of the last box, pulls. Cardboard tears with a wet, harsh sound, and the bottles tumble free, rattling across the floor. Anger rises as Echo tears again and again at the boxes. She wants to rip them with teeth and nails, wishes she could unmake them entirely.

When there is nothing more to destroy, she climbs out, catches the zipline to Blue. In the distance, White gleams perfect, inviolate. Echo wishes she could throw a rock far enough to shatter the woman's window, to make her look out and see, just once, what the rest of the City has come to.

Below, the smog is moving in slow waves, utterly indifferent to her, to any of them. Echo descends faster than she ever has before, anger propelling her from handhold to handhold. By the time she reaches the outcrop, the smog has stilled.

Echo stares at it, her anger ebbing away, leaving her feeling hollow. She knows that she should climb back up, go back to Tommy and Grandmother and Mei. And then what lies before her? Climbing, caring for them, watching black smoke rise and be swallowed by the clouds again and again?

She climbs up to the first wind barrier.

The barricade in the stairwell is untouched, the frayed rope still there. Next to it is a pile of linen strips and an oil lamp and flint. There's no sign that Darwin has done anything but leave these items there. She's leaving Blue to Echo.

Cool air moves through the gaps in the rocks. It's only when it brushes against Echo's cheeks that she realises she's crying.

She lights the lamp, wraps linen around her mouth and nose. Kneels down next to Grandfather's abandoned rope. She looks at it for a long time before she reaches out and attempts to pick it up. It's glued to the floor, the fibres swollen with water and dried so much that it is impossible to dislodge.

Echo stands, tasting salt in the back of her throat. Pulls concrete from the barricade, climbs through.

Her feet sink through the smog on the other side, find solid ground beneath.

The grey rolls away from the light of the lamp, clearing a small space around her. It's still dusty enough that it's hard to breathe, but clear enough for her to see. She breathes in, tastes rot on the back of her tongue, imagines the smog coating her insides. All of her grey, inside and out.

Darwin was right about one thing: the smog does not burn her.

Echo moves carefully, the smog rolling away with each step down the stairs. She tests each one carefully before resting her full weight on it. The stairs are thickly coated with dust. She comes across clear spaces here and there which may or may not be footprints. Father's, perhaps, or Grandfather's. For want of a better direction, she follows them.

The maybe-footprints end at a door that stands wedged open. Beside it, a small clutch of pipes dangle from the ceiling, all of them corroded, metal fallen away in chunks that have scattered to powdery rust on the floor. Echo skirts the pipes carefully, goes through the door.

The space seems crowded, the walls too close together and too much furniture crammed into the room. When Echo touches a cushion, it falls to threads and dust, the fabric long ago rotted but somehow still holding its shape. She is careful not to touch anything else as she moves around. There are chairs and tables, as well as many other things that she cannot identify: a great black thing pressed up against one wall, an odd shape with numbered buttons on the wall.

In the space before the concreted window hang two small cages. In each is the remains of a bird. They are long dead, their small bodies desiccated and covered with dust, but she can just see the blue of one's feathers, the green of the other.

The first room leads onto a kitchen, then a corridor from which three rooms branch. Two stand with their doors open. The first is a bedroom, the bed higher and vaster than any she has known.

The next is, she thinks, a bathing room, though only the sink looks familiar. She pauses, her heart hammering, before opening the third door.

It is a room made for children, the furniture scaled down to their size. Two beds, two desks, two chairs. The desks hold paper and crayons, both chairs pushed back, as though the children had left, just for a moment.

Only one of the beds is empty.

The man in the bed is curled up, knees pressed to his chest. The small quilt only partially covers him, his bare feet sticking out, the soles scratched and torn. He is as dried as the birds in the main room, his skin shrunk tight to his bones, but there is enough of him left for Echo to recognise Grandfather.

He holds a picture frame to his chest. The picture within shows a family: a mother and father, two children just beginning to stretch towards adulthood. They stand, hands linked, smiling at each other. Apart from the differences of gender, they are almost mirror images of one another.

Echo reaches for the frame. As her fingers brush its edge, she hears a sound. It is something like breaking glass, but not quite. She jumps, adrenaline rushing through her, thinking for a moment that it is Grandfather, that she has woken or broken him. She pauses, listens again. No, it is coming from somewhere else, deeper in the apartment.

When she moves back into the corridor, it is louder, and louder again in the other bedroom. Loudest when she moves into the small wardrobe—clothing falling to dust as she brushes past it—to a door half hidden in the back.

The door has been sealed, its edges smeared with a substance that has hardened into a clear shell. Something is written on the door, but Echo cannot read it. She touches the shell, and it falls away, scatters to dust at her feet. Unsealed, the door swings open.

Beyond, everything is dark but for a series of small lights that blink red then green, red then green. The noise seems to come from somewhere behind them.

Echo steps across the threshold. The breaking glass noise comes once more, then is silent.

Echo blinks. The air is clear in here, the smog stopped at the door as though there is an invisible barrier there. When she breathes out, the smog ripples and dances, but it does not enter the room.

The lights are still blinking. They look like small pieces of coloured glass set into a black box. She cannot see how they are illuminated, their light too steady and bright to be a flame. She touches the top of the box to see if it is warm, and the lights go dark. At the same moment, the flame from the lantern goes out.

Echo stands in the darkness, frozen. Always before when she has closed her eyes she has felt the weight of the City there, a comforting presence. This darkness is deeper than anything she has ever known, and in it she can sense nothing at all.

Something moves against her skin, soft and warm, and then light flares in the room, so bright that it hurts Echo to look at it. Almost immediately it dims, and she blinks hard to clear her vision.

A woman made from light stands before her. She is smaller than Echo, dressed in loose trousers and a sleeveless shirt that shows the way her bones press against the skin of her shoulders. Her eyes are dark, her long hair caught up in a braid.

The light woman's mouth moves silently, and then something clicks in the box. The woman's voice fills the room, coming from everywhere and nowhere. "—had to go. You were all too small, and we worried what the fallout would do to you. Better you stay here in the city, where the radiation levels are low. Samson says that the weather is changing, and that there will be storms, but the buildings are strong. I know how the two of you are afraid of the thunder, but you will be safe." The woman pauses, blinking rapidly, as if to clear away tears. "It's not forever, my darlings. The older children will look after you, and you will want for nothing. The water filtration systems are rated to last for over a century, as are the protein vats. You will not hunger, you will not thirst. It will be hard, but you will both be safe, and that it what matters most. Just thinking about living each day, and don't worry about the next. I love you, my children, my Keiko and my Yuuta. We will find the others, and we will return as soon as we know we can keep you safe on the crossing. We will come back for you."

The woman smiles, then the image fades to motes of light. They hang in the air, spinning, then slowly dissolve.

Echo stares at the place where the woman had been, the ghost image of her burned into her eyes. "Keiko? Yuuta?" The names, horribly familiar, set the smog outside roiling.

Echo sinks down onto the floor, presses her back against the wall. It's utterly smooth, nothing to hook her fingers into to keep herself from falling.

When she looks up again, Darwin is there, standing just outside the invisible barrier. She says nothing, just watches Echo, her expression hidden by the bandages swathing her face.

Echo holds out a hand. After a moment, Darwin steps into the room, takes it. Darwin's fingers are smoother than Echo remembers: her climbing callouses peeling away to reveal new skin beneath.

"It's like a flame, I think, but somehow made of light," Darwin says, gesturing to the black box. "There's one of them in most of the apartments, though only a few of the rooms housing them have been opened. I think that when they left, the smog wasn't this high. They expected the children to come down here, to listen to the messages a long time ago."

"Children," Echo repeats. "She spoke of her children. Keiko, Yuuta. Grandmother's name, Grandfather's. They must have been named for them, the ones the light woman spoke of."

Darwin looks at her. She has not removed her linen wrappings; in the shadows they cast, her eyes are bright.

Echo shakes her head. "It has to have been longer than that. The City has been here for longer than that. Grandmother would have told us."

"I suspect she never knew. The smog rose too fast, and everything was lost."

Echo swallows hard. "But they were brother and sister."

Darwin just nods. "They were left alone, maybe they didn't know. They had no one else."

"There were older children. They would have remembered."

"Maybe they Hollowed. Maybe they Twisted. Maybe they just forgot."

Echo stares at the black box. She wants to smash it beneath her fist, kick it to pieces. "How could they just leave them? They were *children*."

"They thought they were making the right choice," Darwin says. "Maybe it was the only choice they could make."

"But they didn't come back."

"Maybe they couldn't. Maybe they're out there still, waiting for everyone to follow." Darwin pulls the linen away from her face. The dust has masked the skin around her eyes, turned it grey. When she breathes out, it plumes from her lips, a miniature cloud that dissipates into the air. "Don't you see what this means, Echo? This isn't the whole world. They all talk about going to find the others. There are other people out there. And we can go and find them." She smiles, squeezes Echo's hand. "We don't have to stay here waiting to die."

Echo pulls her hand away. "Mei's still Hollowing. Tommy's still Twisting. Nothing's going to change that."

"We're not Hollowing. We're not Twisting." Darwin lays a hand on the box; the lights flicker green. "*We* can go. We can find them."

Echo stares at her. "Are you suggesting that we just leave them? Who's going to look after Grandmother and Tommy? Mei? Mei's baby?"

"I know it sounds heartless, but what else can we do? We're both healthy, Echo. We can survive. Maybe we can find medicine, come back for them."

"She said that she was coming back too." Echo taps her fingers hard against the black box. The lights flash red. "I'm not leaving them. They're my family."

Darwin takes a step back. "I thought we were family. I always catch you, remember?"

"I can catch myself. I did last time." Echo crosses her arms. "I'm not going to stop you, but I can't leave. I won't."

Darwin's eyes search Echo's face, but finally she nods. "It will take me a day or two to get everything ready, so if you change your mind . . . " Her hand comes out, as if to grasp Echo's, but she stops, lets it fall back to her side. "I'll leave markers. Birds, like the ones Tommy drew on the wall. And you can follow me, find me, when . . . " She trails off again, looks away.

Echo says nothing, and finally Darwin rewraps the linen around her face, turns and vanishes into the smog.

Echo stays in the darkness, breathing in the cool, clean air. It tastes of nothing, and she imagines it washing away all of the dust from her insides, clearing away a lifetime of dirt from her skin.

She wraps her face again and makes her way back up through the smog. When she emerges from the barricade she finds that Darwin has left her watersack. On top of it, a piece of glass. It is clear, worn smooth at the edges and fitted perfectly to Echo's palm. On the glass is painted the figure of a bird taking flight, wings stretched out in what looks like pure joy.

• • •

Echo sees Darwin only once more.

She is standing on the edge of Yellow's roof, looking out towards White. Without the usual weight of her watersack on her back, she looks oddly diminished, almost vulnerable.

Darwin stretches out her hands, palms up to the sky. Echo is too far away to see Darwin's face, but she knows that she is smiling.

Then Darwin starts to climb down. Her movements are light and easy, almost as though she is dancing across the face of the building. It's not vulnerability at all, Echo realises, but freedom that she sees.

Darwin pauses, looks back towards Blue. Lifts a hand in a wave, then vanishes around the corner of the building and is gone.

• • •

Smoke rises from Black. It hangs in the sky for a long time before it begins to bleed into the clouds.

Echo stands on the roof of Yellow, watching. She stands in the same place that Darwin had two years ago, the straps of Darwin's watersack wrapped around her body. Echo has never used the sack to carry water, but modified its body to allow her to carry Mei's child on her back while she climbs.

During the last months of pregnancy, Mei had Hollowed quickly. Even in the throes of labour, she had only lain back staring at the roof, not making a sound. She only reacted when Echo put her daughter in her arms, raising her mechanically to her breast.

Mei did not speak after that, not even to name her daughter. Echo had named her Keiko, and she had grown strong, even as her mother had grown weaker. The day after Keiko weaned, Mei curled up on the pallet that had been Masao's, closed her eyes. She had not woken again.

Only weeks later, Echo had woken to find Grandmother kneeling before the wind barrier, cold and still, her hands folded as if in prayer.

This is the third time Echo has watched the smoke rise from Black since Darwin left. First Mei, then Grandmother. This smoke is Tommy's.

Only when the smoke has been completely swallowed by the clouds does she turn. It's then that she notices the shutters drawn away from the window in White. It is the day that the ghosts come. She's been so busy tending to Tommy and Keiko that she hasn't noticed.

The woman's movements are slower than Echo remembers them, and she pauses often, as though thinking of what she needs to do. The door is open behind her, those lights blinking red and green, red and green.

Echo resettles Keiko on her back, the lax weight of the girl telling Echo that she is still asleep. Echo climbs down, moving carefully as she descends.

She stops at the place where she had once wedged herself between balconies and watched the woman bake her cakes. One of the balconies is gone, torn away by a windstorm. Echo stands on the remaining one, watches.

The painted glass that Darwin left her is in her pocket, as always, a comforting weight against her skin. The paint has never worn away, though the back surface of the glass has been polished to a shine from rubbing against the fabric of her trousers. She pulls it out, turns it over in her palm, sees how the polished surface gathers the dim light of the clouds, reflects it back focused to a bright point.

The woman in White pauses, a canister in her hands, stares out of the window.

Echo does not think. She holds up the glass, reflects the light towards the woman. She's not certain at first that it is bright enough for the woman to see, but then the woman starts, drops the canister. The lights in the shadows behind her blink green.

Something rises in Echo, like wings unfolding within her chest. She slides the glass back into her pocket, descends again. Keiko does not wake. She's used to being on Echo's back as she climbs. For a while, she wouldn't sleep at all unless she was strapped into the watersack and Echo was moving.

When Echo reaches the zipline leading to Blue, she looks back up at White. The woman is watching her, and she is not alone.

There is a younger woman standing next to her, a child in her arms. That thing lifts within Echo again; this time she recognises it as hope. Echo lifts a hand in a wave, slides across the zipline.

Maybe once she's found Darwin, they'll go to White. Maybe the people from White will come here first. Either way, it is a beginning.

The things she has gathered wait at the barricade. There's not much, but Darwin left with less. Echo wraps her face and Keiko's, climbs through into the smog. It reaches higher now, almost a half storey higher than it had been the first time Echo climbed through.

Echo takes advantage of Keiko's slumber to move fast, the smog rolling back from the light of her lantern. She's been down here so many times now that she knows her way through corridors and stairways, all the way down to the ground level.

She has been down here many times since Darwin left, each time moving farther down. The first time she ventured from the building itself had been a week ago. That day, she had walked only far enough to find the first of Darwin's birds scratched into a metal sign, lines of blue paint scraped away to form wings lifted into flight.

She finds the bird again now, pauses to run her fingers along the lines of the bird's wings. Sets off in the direction that the bird is flying.

Through the smog, she catches glimpses of curved metal, broken glass scattered here and there. She's not certain, but the smog appears to get thinner with each step, colours bleeding through the grey: blue and yellow, green and red.

She finds the next bird, and the next, all of them flying in the same direction, leading away from the City. She closes her eyes, feels the weight of the buildings in her mind, the City so far behind her already.

Something lifts within her, stretching wings, reaching out for fresh air. She smiles as she walks, following the birds, following Darwin.

A Hedge of Yellow Roses

Kathleen Jennings

Vagabonds leave signs in the road for those who know how to read them. Royalists also have their secret language of warnings and betrayals. This story too, in its fashion, is a sign to mark the way I went.

As with all the lessons of my life, no human voice told it to me. I gathered the threads from spindle-grass and crow-black clouds, from amber autumn roses and the thorns that tore my sleeves.

Once, there was a prince . . .

• • •

Having given myself, body and soul, to the service of my prince, I, Vermeille, found myself fleeing armed rebellion. This, at an age when one of my career and ambitions might have hoped to be settled in a fine house, with a garden and even children at my knee. But that carefully husbanded future had been rent asunder, and now I was homeless, far from the city where I'd dwelt for more years than I cared to admit to those who would scoff at my true age. My lord was said to be exiled, yet I still hoped then, to meet him in a land far beyond the hills.

Certainly I could not stay in the beautiful city, for that cloud-kingdom to which I had struggled so long to ascend had already been torn apart. No matter how humble my birth, I had allied myself with the royal house and in doing so had marked myself out as surely as if I'd worn a traitor's brand. No concession would be made for me by revolutionaries or otherwise.

I rode disguised as a common soldier; not so common that I could not afford a horse, but I took good care to make both the beast (a grey, shabbily caparisoned) and myself appear sufficiently disreputable as to make neither halt nor hindrance worth a vigilante's trouble. I shall let you imagine how that abraded my sensibilities, for I had become accustomed to damask and carriages, satin and featherbeds.

I bore three messages, none conveyed by ink: news of the murder of a King, a sword wrapped in a cape and tied to my saddle, and a secret so close to my own heart that even I did not then suspect it. Beyond these I had only my wits, and few enough of those.

Anxious and fearful, riding hard and sleeping rough, I sickened. My thoughts strayed to happier times past and those I hoped would come—moonspinnings, all. The horse, too, wandered. When at last I roused it was to find that we stood on a hillside gold with clattering spindle-grass, and the lowering clouds too close.

Spindle-grass is no better for horses than storms are for benighted travellers, and there was no more food on that slope than there was hint of shelter. I had resigned myself to pressing on, when the last escaping light of the sun struck fire from what had seemed only a nearer cloud. It was instead, I realised, a stand of trees, with something radiant within.

We crossed the grey stones of a cold hill stream. My horse made a good deal of fuss, and perhaps the water was deeper than I'd thought, for by the far side I was splashed to my thighs.

As we drew closer it became apparent our goal was not a forest, but a low large thicket. A few late birds still settled to its branches, and beyond its highest reach was the unmistakeable haze of moss-grown roofs. The beckoning gleam glanced once more then faded with the sunset. Whoever had built and tended this place had long since abandoned it. To my way of thinking and given my current circumstances, this was all to the good.

"We may spend the night dry, or at least in the lee of a wall," I said to the horse, and urged him onward.

The wind sank, gathered itself again, and tore at the sparse grass and me in equal measure. The air grew grey with dusk. The hillside was poor, stony and ridged, with but a few starved weeds, which my horse snatched at greedily. If ever there'd been fields, they were long worn away, stone walls disassembled by winters and the slow shifting of the earth. We found the faint hollow of a ditch, which became rough with tilted stones and resolved at last into the remnant of a path. This brought us to the entrance of the compound.

Vintners grow roses beside their vines to warn of pestilence; royal gardeners raise them (costly stock!) as a boast and glory. Whether the bushes surrounding this house had been planted for service or beauty I made no guess. They now stood guard for a place that needed none. Thick and unnaturally thorned, spikes as long as stilettos and bright as needles, the woody branches had woven themselves into a thick wattle fence, daubed with leaf-mould. I could hear birds settling in the upper branches, but the net was too dense to see them.

From afar, I'd thought a shattered windowpane had thrown a reflection to draw us here, but now I realised otherwise. The hedge was heavy with roses, blown and blossoming, and all rich as amber, bronze, butter, parchment. At the hedge's crest, twice as high as I sat on horseback, some few still gleamed the dull gold of lanterns.

Their perfume was sickly sweet.

Though the path bade fair to be overgrown, I urged my horse on and soon discerned the deeper shadows of what had once been a gate. I ducked my head and shrank from the barbs, while the grey horse pressed slowly forward. Once, twice and again I felt a tearing on arm or cheek, and bethought myself to back out of the leafy tunnel. But finally stone overarched us, purple light opened ahead, and I sighed in relief as I straightened.

We were in a walled courtyard. Weeds grew through cracked stones, and the several doors that faced us all hung ajar. Grey-green roofs of the towered house, outbuildings and a vacant dovecote angled down to us. Tall cold chimneys were topped with bristles of twigs and the broken wheel of a stork's nest. Dry leaves, like the shadows of birds, rustled past my horse's hooves.

I slid to earth, clinging to the saddle. As I steadied myself I looked back the way we had come. The tunnel must have turned sharply for it now seemed blocked with blossoms and briars. Where the hedge overtopped the wall, the roses were reddening.

"And so they came to the Tower Perilous," I murmured. Ah! So recently surrounded by salons of poets and there I was addressing a horse.

When I faced the courtyard once more, it was to find we were not alone.

The woman appeared terribly young, frail as an ivory fan. Her antique dress was frayed to threads that, like the strands of her hair, lifted in the breeze. I could discern little of her features in the half-light. Yet for all the poverty which clearly beset us both, for a heart's beat I felt as if we were players in a romance on a courtly stage: I no shabby soldier but a knight; she no starveling peasant but a lady waiting to greet a noble guest.

"Good den, my lord," said she, with quaint formality.

I swept as theatrical a bow as I knew, but with the movement, the overgrown courtyard bucked beneath my feet, my empty stomach revolted and my hand lost hold of the shifting saddle. I fell.

She caught at me and for a breath I thought her hands crabbed and clawed. Her fluttering sleeves struck at my face like feathers.

"Hush, hush," said the girl, steadying me. "I cannot carry you, good Sir Knight. Hush, you are come very far to sleep on stone or in hedge." Her cool hand—human, untaloned—touched my face briefly.

I blinked and stared. Her face was near, her eyes wide and luminous as the roses. Her expression was unguarded, and I was disconcerted. It had been very long since I'd seen someone who had not learned to wear a mask either of subservience, civility, or war. The first flecks of rain fell, and they stung like ice.

She stepped away. "You should not bow to me," she said, lowering her gaze. "No wealth or title belongs to this land. I am only Enna."

"You are the mistress of this house?"

She looked up again and smiled. "As much as any can make such claim," she replied. I marvelled at how much beauty could appear, where there was no cold jewelled facade to hide it. I wondered if that was how I had appeared to my lord, when first he took up with me.

"Then I am Miles," I said. "I am but a masterless knight." She seemed to accept this answer though it would never have satisfied anyone from the city I had so recently fled. The girl was not worldly-wise.

"Come. There is still room for guests. Your skin is hot as a flame."

Once within the shadowy ruination of the great house, she produced a shaded taper, then led me up bowed stairs and along a dust-hung hall to a chamber which must have once been a large salon or gallery. There were no furnishings. The candlelight, though dazzling in the dark, was small—I could only tell that the space was airy and broad, filled with what I first thought drifts of gold, then of straw, then as I looked longer, piles of leaves.

"The beds have been long since burned for winter kindling, but you may sleep here. At least you are beneath a roof," said Enna. She gave a quick, hopeful smile and left.

I'd barely wrapped myself in my greatcoat before falling asleep. I did not expect to dream.

• • •

The first time, rain hissed outside, the frail roof groaned, and darkness spread like moss and water stains down the walls. I told my dream-self the house had stood too many years to fall in one night. I told myself the night-fancy merely echoed the sudden decay of our bright kingdom.

I slitted my eyes and peered out, and found the room full of light. It hung like golden tapestries, and painted the sackcloth of my hostess' dress like damask. She stood at the threshold of the gallery, and another figure—something like a woman—stood beside her, in a robe soft with plumes.

"Do you think he will be the one?" asked the girl.

"If he were, he would wake and see you for what you are," answered the other. "Resign yourself to disappointment, goddaughter."

"Perhaps he wakes and merely pretends to sleep."

"Then he is still not the one we require, for he is no gentleman," said the other. "It is only tricksters and common soldiers who feign sleep to gain an end, and such are not for you."

She crossed the room with a rustling swoop of wings as if to shake me—and I woke to the sound of pigeons rummaging in the rafters, the wind like voices in ruined towers.

• • •

I slept again, and thought myself surrounded by many mirrors. They doubled back a crowd of folk in velvet finery, masked with glass-and-ivory visages of birds: I was in a ballroom. Their clothes were wonderful, fantasies for a masquerade and yet with silhouettes long-lost to fashion, sleeves with a queer cut, full skirts falling short of soft-heeled, square-toed shoes. The beaks of their masks were sharp, ground like razors, and the eyes that peered out were very beautiful, and wild.

Yet they were all faintly transparent, as if the mirrors in reflecting them had drawn out their reality, their substance. Through sleeve and epaulet, peplum and bodice, ribbon and lace, I could see at the epicentre a single, solemn figure. It was the girl, Enna, but much younger, in primrose silk, with saffron ribbons in her hair and a crow (glossy blue and stars of candlelight dancing from its back and brows) perched on her shoulder. "Not a true prince among them," rasped the crow, and again with a sound of nails on glass, "Not a one!"

I awoke in the tangle of my coat, breathing in crushed leaves. Lightning leaked briefly through shrunken shutters. The walls were still bare, no mirrors in evidence, no revellers, no crows. Rolling onto my back I stared blindly at the ceiling. (Had it been painted with stars?) In more innocent days I might have counted this a nightmare, but since then I had stood before a palace and been spattered with blood from the throat of a king.

When I wept, I rather fear it was for lost festivals such as that in my dream. All the cruel beauty I had made my own was shattered like porcelain. All the gilt and satin were gone, leaving nothing save dried leaves.

• • •

Yet a third time I dreamt. This time Enna lay a little distance from me. Her dress was all the colours of night and dawn; pearls and feathers were tangled in her hair with a disorder that would have cost time and care to achieve, had it been brought to existence in the waking world.

"You have a gentle face," she said, and reached towards my lips with one finger—but her hand was crabbed and clawed.

I flinched and opened my eyes.

I was cold in my sweat-soaked clothes, half-buried in dead rose leaves. Morning light, the colour of milk-and-water, seeped through the slats of the shutters but brought no warmth. There was a lingering stench of bile and my mouth was as foul as if birds had nested there.

In all my dreams the threshold had been hung with a door carved of interlocking branches, but in the daylight the hinges were rusted and unburdened. In the empty space stood the girl, a basin in her hands.

"I trust you slept well," she said, eyes downcast, and brought me the dish of water. Her fingers were roughened by no more than ordinary work—if there was ordinary work for one who dwelt in such a place. The fine dress of my dreams was replaced by the same drab rag of my arrival.

"I thought I would have slept as the dead," I answered. "But nightmares troubled me."

She looked up. I could see the amber ring about her irises and her wide pupils cast back the reflection of my face hawk-sharp with fever and hunger.

"You will sleep better far from here," she said. "I let you in because of the storm, but it has passed and ordinary decency will not permit that you stay."

"You fear for your safety?" I asked, amused. Even disguised as I was, she was clearly far healthier and stronger than I. And who was there here to be affronted by my presence?

"I am protected," she said coolly. "I fear for yours. You dreamed of flying. Travellers before you have leaped from the tower, or tried to soar across the river. Others . . . "

"I did not dream of flying."

She had no ready words.

"I dreamed of birds," I confessed. "But they were revellers at a masque."

Enna left the dish of water by me, and walked quickly away.

After I had washed as well as I might, I wandered to the courtyard and found her combing the grey horse's tangled mane with fierce intensity. The beast bore it well enough, but in the overhanging branches of the hedge an ill assortment of birds swung and shouted at me, before they beat their way up into the sky.

"This is a fine animal, beneath the mud," she said.

"We have that in common, though both of us suffer from hunger."

She turned, eyes dark with contrition. "Forgive me," she said. "I forgot."

"That men must eat?" It was a jest, but she looked at me in reproach.

I sketched a bow, cautiously, and this time the ground stayed where it should. "It is I who must crave forgiveness, fair Enna. I impose on your hospitality. But if you would have me leave, and not simply become bones whitening in the hedge, then I must beg alms of you."

I do not think she was the sort to long hold a grudge. Though there remained no table in the kitchen, she laid a cloth upon the floor and served what seemed a slurry of chaff and water.

"Can this sustain life?" I asked.

"It has sustained yours these three days past. What you did not cast up again."

I mused on this while I ate. Three days of dreams, while I thought but one had passed. The dish was more substantial than it appeared and the emptiness in my belly and the weakness in my bones eased. Though my stomach was still unsettled, I did not shame myself by vomiting.

"Are you a nobleman?" she asked.

I thought before I answered. "Times are bad for noblemen, child. A wise person will answer they've never held a drop of such blood in their veins. That, if you had, you would have spilled it yourself. Tell anyone who asks that you tore this house to ruins with your own hands for liberty and loyalty."

"That would not be true."

"Yet sometimes lies may be the only thing to save us."

She regarded me solemnly until I spoke again. "Why are you alone, Enna? Where is your family? Have you no . . . " I regarded her, but could not guess her age. "No husband?"

Enna glanced out the doorway. A little whip-bird strutted proudly along the horse's back. "May I tell you a story, Sir Miles?"

"What else do our kind do?" I asked lightly, but she had not the self-deprecating humour of a self-made courtier and looked blankly at me. "Yes," I added, and leaned my head against the wall, much wearier than I felt I had cause to be.

• • •

"Once upon a time, a very long time ago," she began, a child telling a tale using the rules of the stories she has heard, "there was a green valley and in that valley was a wealthy farmholding. The couple who lived there lived well. They were happy and proud, but they had no children.

"'Will you wish for a child?' their friends and relatives asked. 'Will you summon the old powers of the hills? Will you pray?'

"'We may as well call to the birds,' said the farmer and his wife. But in time they had a daughter.

"'Who will stand at her naming?' their friends and relatives asked. 'And who will you choose as her godparents?'

"Now, the parents had no wish to give offence to those who were not chosen. 'As well ask the birds,' they said.

"Their daughter grew, and seasons were rich. The valley flourished, the house was made larger. Dances were held there, minor noblemen journeyed to visit, and rode and hunted in the hills.

"'Who will marry your daughter?' asked the friends and relations.

"'A prince, and no one less,' laughed her parents. There were many princes in those days.

"But before her parents could see her of an age to be wed or betrothed, death came to the valley and took them away.

"Among those friends and relatives who survived, there were many who wanted the rich farmland. They planned to marry the girl to their sons and brothers—but who was to decide which suitor would do?

"Now," said Enna, "you must see it was only in jest that my parents made the birds my godparents. But birds take their responsibilities seriously."

"I did not know that."

"Well, they have so few." Enna shrugged. We sat in silence while, outside, roses wept soft petals, tawny as velvet, into the courtyard.

"I did not even know that crows could speak," I offered.

She made a small noise, as if it were a matter of no great note. As if everyone knew it.

"What happened next?

"The rival suitors came upon an idea. They did not know how, whether it was whispered at their windows as they fell asleep, or murmured in the trees when they went riding. But it was decided a ball should be held so that the girl herself might choose from any suitable admirer who met all appropriate requirements. This was still a rich valley, this farmholding the lock and I the key. There were those who hoped to grasp it—me—not for my own sake, but for the land's. There were, I understand, rather many such men."

"You understand?" I echoed.

"I was young. It was a very long time ago." She pulled her knees to her chest, folded her arms about and rested her chin on them.

"None proved worthy, for although there were noblemen among them, there were no princes—and birds, who listen at windows, knew what my parents had required. When none of their suits were acceptable, the gentlemen grew irate and insulting. The birds said none should have me until I found someone who valued my heart above my land. When the suitors threatened to take what would not be given, the birds turned all their minds to madness, and every man who has reached this place since has gone mad. With the years, the land grew untended and sour, the road was slowly lost and I have waited ever since."

"How long has that been?"

"I don't know. I cannot even remember the name of the Queen who ruled. I was very young, and birds take little notice of such things."

I thought of the unprincely candidates. "Didn't your godparents think the punishment a little extreme?"

She shrugged. "They are birds."

"And the roses?" I asked, considering the only plant that thrived in this desolation.

"I planted them on the graves, and there were so many graves . . . They grew into the hedge you see now. But the suitors didn't all die. Some only thought they had turned into birds. A few really did, and flew away. Some soared and sang in the branches for a long time."

"And you've seen no-one since?"

"Only from afar. But they tell me stories, my godparents. They listen at windows, and bring me word of the world. Only—only I think it is not the same as being in it."

I had no answer to this. Her recounting was no more fantastic than any I could spin. Who would believe that in a rose-hung city— the most civilised in the world!—street-sweepers would drag a king from his palace of white and gold, out into a common square, and cut off his head? Who would believe that peasants would grow to hate the beauty of the realm so much they would set it to burn?

Though I did not believe in nursery tales, anyone would be forgiven for thinking that my own fortunate rise and meteoric fall were no more than the substance of a fable.

I stood, swaying a little, and returned to the courtyard. The birds, on roof and hedge and wall (different feathers flocked together), watched me with unnerving steadiness. Their eyes— orange, black and blue—followed my progress. I reached the arch by which I had entered and found the way matted with roses blooming, here a bloody orange. My little strength could not shift them.

"They will only part for princely blood," said Enna. "But for them to do so, you must take me with you."

"You are welcome to come, though I do not know where I ride. I can take you to a town, find a place where you will be comfortable." As if I knew where I myself could go.

"You must take me with you as your bride," said she.

"I cannot marry you, Enna." I laughed, though I meant it kindly.

"It is the only way we may leave!" she cried. "I do not want your bones to whiten here!"

"I passed through once," I said, and touched the scabbed lines where thorns had scored my arm. "Though I am no prince."

In the outbuilding where my horse had been stabled there was no straw, only the dry golden petals which lay like grass, matted with feathers. Through the unshuttered windows winged shadows drifted.

I saddled the grey, wondering where I might find sanctuary, if indeed there was sanctuary to be had anywhere. I closed my eyes and saw the head of the king as a great golden rose, snipped away and rolling along bloodied cobbles. After so many years of schooling my emotions, it felt as if a dam had burst within me, and I had not the strength to hold it back.

And Enna followed, still talking.

"You were courteous to me. I nursed you and watched over your sleep. You passed through the hedge of thorns. You woke in dreams and saw not madness, but truth. You believed my story! It proves you are a true prince!"

"Your head is filled with fairytales, child!" I said, and bent to pull the sword from its wrappings. How heavy it was, and how weary was I, my tiredness born of something deeper than travel, my illness of more than heartsickness. "I did not seek this valley, nor you. I am only fleeing death."

I carried the blade to the gateway in the wall, swung it with what remained of my might. The branches shook birds into the air, petals fell like sleep and the rents in my flesh stung anew. Yet there was not a mark on the twisted limbs.

"I love you!" said Enna.

"I am not even a false prince," I said. "And I do not love you."

"You were kind!" she almost wailed. "You are here!" She stretched out her hand and—may I be forgiven—I took it and held it in my own.

I felt the weight of flesh and the lightness of her bones, the quick-pulsing blood in her palm. I was not tempted by the land, or the ruined house, or even the dreams of what they had once been and might be again. I was not tempted even by the unkempt beauty of the girl. But her cry for kindness, for companionship, for love—oh, I heard that in the chord of my own being.

"Sir Miles!" she began again.

"That is not my name," I said, returning to the stable. As I rewrapped the blade, I saw a scar in the watered steel, a mark in the shape of a rose-barb.

"You travel in disguise, but you are a prince! What other knight is masterless? What other blood may pass the roses—did you not see how their colour changed?"

I did not answer. There must be a way, another door, a farm gate. Fire—fire would burn a passage through. I would be ready to leave with the grey horse if I could, else over the hedge if I had strength to climb. I could stand on the horse's back. Perhaps from outside I could open the hedge again. I ignored my shaking hands as they made the bridle ring.

"Look at me!"

Enna had pulled her shabby dress over her head and her fine hair blew like silk in the light through the stable door.

Her body was thin and dirty, a maze of gooseflesh, ribbed with scars and welted with scabs. Some had lifted, and from beneath the stubs of young feathers sprouted. She stepped forward, grasped one of my hands and held it to her stomach, where the bones of her ribs began. Her skin, there unbroken, was already raised and rough with the pressure of feathers thrusting from below.

"What is this?" I asked, numb.

"This is what shall become of me, or what I shall become." She released my hands, then pulled me to her and kissed me with uncertain lips. She was still a child, no matter how long she'd lived, and fumbled inexpertly with the collar of my shirt. I caught at her trembling fingers while she begged, "It is the only other way out of this place."

"Then I am sorry for you."

"You do not want me?" she pleaded.

"No, Enna."

"But I am yours for the having! You must! You are a prince, and I have waited so very, very long. I have lost count of the generations of my godparents, of how many have watched for you. Please, you must—have you no heart?"

"It is given to another, child."

"As desperate as I?"

"Desperation is not love, Enna, and don't believe anyone who tells you otherwise!"

"But you're a prince—"

I cried out, though it broke more hearts than hers, though I shouted the words at myself as much as her. "Do you not understand, foolish child? There are no princes left! If your fate hangs upon one then you are truly doomed!"

"No, that is not true! You are here!"

"I loved a prince, Enna. I still do. But I fear he must be dead. He has not turned to a bird, he shall not fly over borders and meet me in some foreign court no matter how much I yearn and pray. He loved me, but he is dead, and he shall never know his son. The blood of the child I now know I carry is the only princely blood left in this land. How else could I have passed the roses?"

"A child?" echoed Enna.

"I am no secret prince, girl, but base-born, a prince's mistress." I tried to speak harshly, but we both wept. I gathered her to me, wrapped her in my long coat and we sank down into the leaves. "Hush," I said, through my own sobs. "Let us think. There must be some escape."

"There is only one," said Enna to my collarbone, where her hands were knotted into fists. Her nails felt sharp against the hollow of my throat. A crow in the window-embrasure clacked its beak impatiently. I believed I felt my own fingers twisting into claws.

"Perhaps my godparents never meant to give me up," said Enna quietly. "Maybe it is not love that will free me, but having my heart broken."

"I have found," I ventured, "that birds and princes break hearts very well. They both live such short lives."

Enna cried herself to sleep. I extracted myself and stood, looked down at her, half-hidden by my wretched soldier's coat. She was—must be—so much older than I. Yet I had lived far more, been made and unmade by the world, bereft and unwidowed, nearly a mother. There had been no godmother, avian or otherwise, to guide me, and perhaps that was as well.

As quietly as I could I went back into the courtyard. The grey horse dozed in the pale sunlight, and the watchful birds had settled again: crows in the branches, whip-birds on my mount's shoulders, pigeons, long-wild housedoves, and little quarrelling sparrows on the cracked pavement. On the roofs, light elegant egrets waited like sentinels, and owls shifted irritably in the shadows.

In the centre of the enclosure, I turned a full circle and cleared my throat.

"Oh, most gracious watchers and guardians," I said, for I had been used to treat with similarly vain and status-conscious creatures. "Most venerable and honourable birds, wise avians, strigidae, corvidae, passeridae ... " I reached the limit of my scholarship and felt my folly; then I rallied. I had weathered the scoffing of the greatest, most glittering of courts—why should I blush for these feather-dusters?

I conjured my best memory of a true courtly bow, swept off my non-existent hat, flung out one arm and bent deeply, until the nettles and the incursions of spindle-grass nearly pricked my face.

The birds strutted and shuffled, swayed on their perches, tilted their heads. I glanced at them from under my brows, drew breath and balance, then straightened.

"Through your wisdom and keen observation, you will by now understand that I am no prince. I do, however, carry within me the blood of the royal line. As such I, Vermeille, am the only and last claimant ever likely to cross the hedge. I beg that you hear my words, and let the girl Enna go free."

"What would you give us?" demanded a crow. Its voice startled me, but I had heard such harsh and avaricious mockery before and steeled myself to wait.

"Gold?" asked a magpie.

"The light of your eyes?" A raven.

A whip-bird piped, "Your first-born child?"

They were knowing ones, and I imagined it was not the breeze but their wild untidy magic which swirled the leaves about my feet. I kept my arms at my sides, palms open.

"No doubt such gold, light, and children as I carry will all fall to your kind in the fullness of time. I owe nothing, I do not seek to buy your charge, and I request no favour beyond this: that you release the child.

"But you have discharged your duty as godparents admirably and in reward I will offer a word of advice. I have travelled from the plainlands where cattle-birds tag at the heels of oxen; over gentle lands where wrens sing; across the crane-stalked river that leads to the sea of gulls and flows about the island city where pigeons and sparrows strut at their ease between the houses of men. And each of their kind could tell you, wise lords and ladies of the air, these two truths:

"The first is that while birds cling to their nature, mankind are changeable, and must be so, else they die. If you hold Enna here any longer you cease to protect her, you will render her unable to change. Even your own kind must fly or fall from the nest, but cannot stay there forever.

"The second is that war and rebellion turn rich pickings up to the light just as a plough's blade does worms. You may stay here in this untilled country and leave the bloody spoils to your gentler rivals. Or you may free yourselves from your own spells, and those of your forefathers, and leave this stagnant land to seek your fortune."

The creatures shifted and conferred among themselves in their own languages. A feathered parliament of nobles who had forgotten why they'd been elevated, who remembered only the power of their position, not its responsibilities. Such revolutionary thoughts made me sink my nails into my palms. *I'm sorry, my love.*

But they were blunt and artless birds for all their self-importance, and wielded no court airs or subtleties. In their thirst for princes they had almost forgotten their charge.

"What—what will become of the child? Without us?" asked a mottled, fan-tailed dove.

"Is she a child?" I asked. "You have held her here so long, waiting, that she is barely able to grow. So long, that there are no princes left in the land. This I swear to you."

"Save one," said the low voice of an owl beneath the eaves.

I rested my hand on my own stomach. "And he shall have neither crown nor country," I said.

I sensed a presence at my elbow, and with my free hand reached for Enna's.

The birds spoke among themselves once more until at last an old crow dropped from the hedge and landed on the hand I'd raised to shield my eyes. There were grey feathers among the black, and its gnarled claws bit into my skin.

"If what you say is true—and we have no reason to disbelieve— then you have done us a favour, servant-of-the-dead-princes. All our lives, and our mothers', for a hundred nestings, have been devoted to raising and protecting this one. We are agreed, now that we think on it, that assuredly, she is more than of age.

"But let her leave with you, that we may not have failed the trust we were given. And we will serve you likewise."

Before I could ask what that meant, they lifted up from hand, roof, courtyard, branch and chimney, a dappled whirlwind, a mottled cloud that cleared the wall and beat away across the fields. I caught myself wondering what manner of power Enna's folk had possessed, to tie that mismatched flock so casually, so tightly, to such an obligation.

"Come," I said to her. "We must seek our own fortunes." She was dressed again. Her eyes had already lost their inhuman light, and she seemed more present, too, than when she'd first met me in the courtyard. As if she had matured in the minute it took the birds to pass.

Before we left, I bade Enna wrap up in strips of wet cloth such cuttings as I could take from the hedge, which yielded at last to the blade of my sword. I filled, too, the secret pockets of my coat, and weighted my saddlebags with heavy yellow petals, their fragrance now rich and rare with the promise of freedom.

I remembered the roses grown by vineyards and in kings' gardens. These must be such as had rarely, if ever, been seen elsewhere in the world. I said, "We may yet turn them to gold. We shall have need of it."

We mounted the grey horse and the hedge gave way before us. Enna's arms wrapped around me and her cheek pressed to my back as we rode out down the ditch of a path and up through the rattling spindle-grass. A whip-bird darted behind us, a solitary escort.

I did not look back at hedge, valley or kingdom and, though I cannot speak with certainty, I suspect Enna's thoughts were fixed on the horizon of the future as firmly as mine.

Dustbowl

Kay Chronister

Looking at her, you would never guess that my dog is a machine. Head laid out flat on the floor and feet resting over mine, her trust is real as trust can be. She flinches when someone comes by but she never wakes, doesn't even lift an ear. The sun is covered in dust and the world is sinking but Sadie knows the soft thud of the wool on the loom means she's safe.

I am Nathalie Winchester, the last Spinner, the woman who has to stop the world from unravelling. I did not have a daughter. I do not have a niece. They never appointed anyone to follow me.

While the dust settled down on our heads, Sheriff Booth sent men on mechanical horses down the ravine to the wasteland. He hoped they might find a ship that was still working. In the meantime, everyone else heaped their scrap metal and said their prayers and left me alone, forgetting that Spinner's wool meant anything at all.

I spin as I always have, humming hymns out of one corner of my mouth and holding a line of dull pins in the other. I am making what the Spinner before me said was a masterpiece. I take her word for it. When the Sheriff stood on my threshold a month ago and pounded on the back of my open door, he asked me what I'd made and I said I didn't know.

Sheriff Booth forgets, sometimes, that I am blind. He once asked if I knew what would come. I yanked the wool up onto the loom until I reached the end, laid unknowing fingers over the perfect stitches that the town's first Spinner made.

"You know what this means?" he said.

"No," I said.

"You can't tell anyone, Nathalie."

I nodded my head and said yes, I could do that. I would not say anything. I shut my eyes so that he would not have to see their murky whites, and climbed onto my stool. My work is never finished. As long as there is wool, as long as there is a future, I go on spinning.

"Is it bad?" I said while he stood on the stoop, a shuffling pile of fringe and leather.

He wouldn't say. "We're the last ones on the surface, and that must be for a reason."

Maybe there is a reason. Or maybe not. This was the last outpost of civilisation, the final frontier. Turns out, it didn't take kindly to being conquered. The air dried up. The livestock died of dehydration and the automatons starved for oil. The government back home stopped sending rations. Every other trading post within fifty miles either headed for the hills or left a pile of corpses half-buried in the dust.

I struck up the loom again and waited for the receding sounds of boots and spurs.

"Can't you spin it into something else?" he said, after a while.

I laughed, hunching down over the wool. Other towns had Spinners, once. Then they had spinning machines. Automatons, like Sadie, that never had to eat or sleep or blink back tears when the dust hit their eyes. At last, the cost of oil climbed too high and they abandoned divination altogether.

"Would be easier for you if I had a lever on my back, wouldn't it? Or maybe a crank."

He coughed. "I brought something for you, Nathalie." When I didn't say anything, he added, "In case you need some help around here, when things get rough. Folks back home shipped us a Spinneret 84x." He sounded embarrassed. He should, I think, have been embarrassed. "We're not replacing you, but I know that this work is tiring."

"I can't spare the oil." Or the pride.

"You don't have to use it. But it's here if you need it. Plenty easy to get set up, I promise. Just take her out of the box, put a fuel cell into her belly, some oil . . . "

"It doesn't have its own fuel cell?"

I could hear him fidgeting. "There are ways to get a fuel cell," he said, and I could hear him eyeing Sadie. Dogs are non-essential, to hear Booth tell it. Not only that, but they waste buckets of fuel. When things got tough, mechanical dogs were the first to be harvested for parts. But I'm old and stubborn and the Spinner, so my Sadie is still sucking down her share of oil.

"I won't use that thing," I told him.

"I know," he said, and didn't go to the trouble of sounding disappointed. I don't think anyone had much faith in Dustbowl's staying power by then.

· · ·

I haven't heard another human voice in days. They must have found a ship, or maybe a ship found them, but I wasn't invited along. Far as I know, I'm the only one left with breath still filling old-fashioned lungs. Sadie woke me with a whimper this morning, hungry for fuel. My gut twisted when I found my oil can empty.

"I don't have anything left," I tell her, and she rests her dry nose on my knee. Saying sorry, I have to reckon. If I don't have any, there's not any left to be found in town limits. And leaving town means not coming back. The end feels like everything that came before it. The wind howls and the world seems to be ending; after sixty eight years I still don't want to be left alone on this broken scrap of dirt.

"Not yet, dog."

I rip the wool from the loom. Then I reach for a leather canteen, drop my feet into riding boots, and wrap the wool around my shoulders.

Outside, the crows have starved, the mechanical horses have stopped screaming, and the scuff of wool on dirt splits apart the silence. Quietly, Sadie shuffles along beside me. The proper road ends a ways down, and she sighs her disapproval as we tread on desert. The sand crumples under my boots and my robe tangles in the weeds but I yank it loose, pulling scraps of cactus along with me, and take to stepping down so hard that the earth shrinks back from my feet.

• • •

Sadie and I go slowly down the ravine, so we don't get thirsty. I fall sometimes, sucking sand into my throat and scraping up my elbows, but I don't stop. If I stop, the sun will soak into me. Nothing lives out here. The air thickens in the folds of the wool and makes it heavy. When I rest a hand on Sadie's back, it's hot as a spark.

I know when we're close to the wasteland on account of the smell: burning rubber and wet rust. When my eyes catch flashes of white—sunlight glinting off steel I figure—I cast the wool from my shoulders and fold it into a pile. No sense in dirtying our history. If Booth was here, he'd laugh that dusty laugh and say a blind old woman has no business doing the work that proved too hard for six able-bodied men on the backs of automatons. That may be true, but my business is survival, sand in my teeth and scrapes on my knee. I don't know who he thought wrote destiny in this godforsaken little town, but it don't tend to be men, or machines.

When the air cools and the steel doesn't shimmer anymore, I pick through piles of scrap hoping to feel the slick unforgiving rubber of an oil can. If there were oil left anywhere, it would be here. Sadie lies beneath an upturned furnace and pants to the rhythm of my work as I scavenge. To be candid, I wouldn't bet any respectable sum on the outcome of this venture. But I've never been much for gambling.

When midday comes and burns the back of my neck, I creep beneath the furnace and let the sun bake me to sleep. The heat makes it almost intolerable to have Sadie at my feet, but I let her stay there because I don't want her to be lonely. She's gotten clumsy, moving like a factory machine and not an automaton, but she's a good dog. Trusts me as much as any scrap of flesh and bone ever could.

• • •

The last Spinner was born before the first automatons came to Dustbowl. Sadie was hers, originally, and before Sadie she had other mechanical dogs. She told me once how the prototypes looked, expatriates running on steam and bedding down in sawdust as if they had any right to rest their iron eyes. "The more you see them," she said, "the more you know that they're not really the same as the animals on your granddaddy's farm. Sadie was the first one to look real. Seeing her, you knew she was real."

"Well," I said, "I can't see anything."

"You could feel her," she said. "Spend enough time with the old ones, and you'll feel the difference. And that's why they haven't replaced us Spinners yet. We live to be ancient, and it's our lives that end up in this ratty length of blanket. But animals die after not too long. You can shut them in the barn and forget about them. When they're gone, no one remembers."

• • •

The wind comes screaming down the ravine into the wasteland, flinging sheets of tin at the sun and covering my hair in sand. My throat burns and my eyes feel too dry to open or shut, and I know that soon I am going to die.

When the dust settles, I find a full can of oil turned on its side.

I hunch over the thing and clutch it to my chest. The scent is thick and awful and I thank God for it. I push my fingers down over the opening so the wind and sand can't touch what's left inside. Behind me, Sadie whimpers and rests her nose on my shoulder.

I could open the hatch at her side and pour the oil inside. She would stop whimpering and maybe for a good while I wouldn't remember that she's getting as close to the end as I am. But then she'd burn the last of the fuel and slow down again.

I cover the oil can with a scrap of cloth and hold it close to my chest. Sadie is smart enough to know what I'm withholding from her, but she can't do a thing about it. She settles down after a while, rests her head in my lap and only whines when her oil gauge sends its hourly reminder that supplies are getting low. When the dust kicks back up later that night, we sit in the wasteland with our backs resting against the furnace and let the wind slash us to ribbons. She's only wood and iron, but I fool myself into thinking that she feels the storm on her face too.

I have never seen her face, but I imagine it like the last Spinner used to say it was: a wooden snout for a nose, eyes, small scrappy ears made of leather and wire. My mother died sixty years ago and I have no daughter, but I have a pile of scrap metal pretending to breathe so that I won't feel lonely.

• • •

Sadie dies at dawn. The air is cool and mild but she's still hot as hellfire, her innards overloaded with the effort of staying alive. I hardly feel the heat; I hold her to my chest and inhale the tinny scent of her skin and wish she could cover me until the dust settles in my throat.

At nightfall, I wrap the wool around my shoulders and get to work on taking her apart. Feels like swallowing my pride, admitting that soon I'll be another pile of bones in this desert, but I love this town much more than I like the notion of outliving it. If the Spinneret 84x has the same uncanniness that I do, that the woman before me did, maybe Dustbowl isn't really doomed.

Climbing the ravine, tasting the salt of the storms, I know that I was right before about leaving Dustbowl and never coming back. The scrap of land waiting for me atop the hill isn't a town anymore. It's property of the dust and wind, and they aren't keen on trespassers. They throw me over one shoulder and carry me halfway to Hell before I find my wits enough to fumble back to living. I keep my head down and cover my mouth with my bonnet, but I can still feel the desert crawling up inside me. I guess I'm due to die soon, so I'd better be efficient about this. I don't intend upon breathing my last until there's another Spinner at Dustbowl's loom.

The walk is long and hard. But Spinners are built to be patient, to mumble hymns out of chapped lips and keep no secrets from themselves so they can think on troubling things when the hours get long. I can't talk to Sadie, so I say to the wind what I want to say to her:

I'm sorry, about tearing your gut out with a crowbar.

It's downright strange how I miss you more than I miss the rest of civilisation.

Don't wander too far, I might need you.

• • •

I can't see her, but I doubt that the Spinneret 84x looks much like an ordinary person. She's a head shorter than me, for one thing, and I'm plenty short of stature. She's got a stove-shaped iron belly, with an opening for Sadie's fuel cell. Long, thin wooden arms and legs hidden beneath a gingham dress that smells factory-fresh. I can't imagine she'll move gracefully, but she'll move. That's good enough. Only the hands have to be perfectly right. A Spinner has strange hands: bristled, rough, and just about bulletproof, but delicate enough to sketch history. You aren't born with hands like that. They're made. In this case, they're made of what feels like wire strung inside old leather workman's gloves. I don't feel too certain that they'll get the job done, but I guess it's her or it's nothing.

When I pour oil into the fuel cell and shut the hatch, she makes a sound like a jackhammer. Then she tells me that she goes by the name Evangeline. The manufacturer must have thought a detail like that would be endearing. Her voice is small and metallic, like she's speaking out of a very long tunnel. Maybe she is. I don't know where they hide her voice box. I wonder how much oil she needs, to talk and move and buzz like that.

"If I remain fully operational," she chirps at me, "I can sustain myself for four days on a full tank of oil."

Four days isn't what I wanted to hear. Sadie lasted for almost a whole week without an oil change. "Well, all right," I say. It's not as if any of this is her fault, exactly. "First thing I want. Find some more oil. Can you do that? Can you see?"

I bunch the wool in my fists and wait for her to say yes. A Spinneret 84x should be able to see what they're doing. They should be competent, since they are also bloodless. To most people, the competence makes up for any other failings. Sheriff Booth said as much at a town hall meeting a while back, when everyone murmured their agreement that Dustbowl could afford the expense of a spinning machine, even if we could scarcely afford our monthly shipments of hardtack and flour.

Someone else might have been hurt, but I was just spitting mad. I stood, holding the elbow of the butcher on my left and the minister's wife on my right, and said, "They might spin all right, but what sort of future will you be looking at? There have been Spinners in Dustbowl since we landed on this piece of dirt, and you're telling me you're aiming to replace them with a hunk of iron?"

Booth assured me that they weren't like that anymore. Like the animals, they wore the faces and made the sounds that told us they were real.

I never minded those lies until I found that there isn't much distance between a stubborn old woman who can't see her handiwork and a competent, oil-hungry machine that doesn't care whether she sees it or not.

"I have excellent vision," the Spinneret says.

My empty stomach hurts. "Good," I say. Really, I reckon it is. At least one of us can see what's coming. "Go. Don't come back until you find oil. You're useless to me if you don't."

I want to imagine that she's hurt by this. Anyone with old-fashioned lungs and a half-decent conscience would be. Useless is the worst thing you can be in a town like Dustbowl, even now that no one lives here. But Sadie learned how to imitate feelings over a stretch of eighty years, and I guess I can't expect the spinning machine to be much quicker.

"Is there anything else I can do for you?" she says, bright as the noonday sun. God damn her. My fists are curled so tight around the wool that they hurt.

"I'll be here," I say, "Spinning."

If she envies me the work, she doesn't say so. Like I thought, bloodless.

• • •

There is nothing the Spinneret 84x can't do. When the wind and dust come down hard over us, she latches the doors and nails blankets to the windows. The water she draws from the well always tastes like tin, but she never forgets about my thirst even though she has no thirst of her own. She makes bread with too little yeast and too much salt. Like a child, I eat it from her hand. At midday, she sits at the loom while I fall asleep in my clothes. When I die, like as not she will bury me.

"Are you not tired?" she says one night. By the sound of her strange little voice, I can tell that she's standing at my shoulder. I'm furiously working the loom, coming up on what must be my sixth or seventh hour here. My dusk-to-dawn shifts are the only point of contention between us, at least the only one that we can talk comfortably about.

I laugh at her and flick my index finger over a frayed bit of wool, tucking it back inside the Dustbowl tapestry. "Been tired for a long time."

"Is this worth it to you?" The question surprises me. It's the rare automaton that doesn't know how to feign polite interest in the goings-on of their old-fashioned neighbours, nowadays, but I never figured the Spinneret 84x for much of a conversationalist.

I wrap a fresh line of wool around the wooden pegs. The twenty-year-old ache in my back has sharpened over the last few days. A pinch of pain ripples down my spine every time I reach down to thread a new line. I can't imagine ten-hour shifts are good for me, but the Spinneret 84x's lines don't feel right. They're eerily even, with the occasional fumble that seems liable to unravel the entire tapestry. She doesn't know Dustbowl like I do, like the last Spinner did. She isn't one of us, even if all the folks back home blessed her a thousand times with whatever uncanniness it is that makes our divinations come true.

"You ought to shut down for a while," I say. "I'll wake you when I'm through here."

"Shutting down will conserve oil," she concedes.

I don't reply. I figured she was obeying, but I figured wrong.

"Have you always been blind?" the Spinneret says, a minute later. From the way she says it, I can tell she's getting at something. This isn't politeness. We passed that a mile back. Automatons collect whatever information their systems think they need. Sadie buried her nose in my hair to know what she could call home; this thing, with its leather-gloved hands, is looking for something else.

I turn on my stool. I want to wince at the snake of pain that bolts up and down my spine, but I've never had much patience for poor health, mine or anyone else's. I clear my dry throat and say, "Always. I was born during a dust storm. Caught the doctor off guard. Things went south, like they do." That was more than I meant to tell her, but it's a story I've told too many times before. "What do you care?"

"You don't know what happened."

If there's one thing I can't stomach right now, it's cryptic prettiness from a spinning machine. "What happened where?"

"Here. Approximately a fortnight ago, by my estimation." Her voice sounds more distant than before. She moves to the door and opens it, I think. Shards of heat fall across my bare toes. "Perhaps you can't smell them because the wind is so strong, but I can."

"What are you saying?" But I know, and am only hanging on to the second before she tells me.

"Everyone in Dustbowl is dead, Mrs Winchester."

"Miss Winchester." I've never had to correct her before, but then she never says my name so formally; never says it at all. Fair enough, I don't say her name, either.

"You're not saying this as some sort of kindness, are you? Because I don't care, that they left me. I'm still their Spinner, till the day the flies eat me."

"There are no flies on the surface of this planet." The Spinneret thinks she's clever.

"Save your oil and shut down," I say, half-knowing that she won't listen, and glad of it. I can't imagine doing this by myself. I leave my post at the loom and hurry out onto the streets of Dustbowl, burning my bare feet on the sand. Dawn is close and the heat has already abandoned the notion of being bearable. I hardly feel it.

I don't know how to go about confirming that an entire town is dead. Truth be told, I don't want to confirm it. I can't think of them all dead. The tailor, with his gable-roofed shop and donkey laugh; the minister's wife with her collection of year-old dresses for redistribution to young and tragically unfashionable Dustbowl girls; Sheriff Booth, his hemming and hawing, the desperation I could just about taste when he came to see me a few months back.

"What happened to them?" I say when I come back into the house, counting on the Spinneret to have disobeyed again.

She didn't. I fumble around for her and find that she shut herself down and is lying sideways across the end of my bed like some ungainly, monstrous excuse for a housecat. I slip my feet into boots and wrap the wool around my shoulders. I didn't want her with me, not really, but I wanted someone. I pretend that Sadie walks beside me while I try to count up the dead. I lose them one by one, and before I go back home I lose her too.

• • •

Before she was much else to me, the last Spinner was my mother. She hoarded cinnamon sent from back home and made decadent breakfasts for us when we were up early, spinning Dustbowl's history in the barn with Sadie at our feet. To me she is still the smell of horsehair and baked sugar, the soft, forgiving sort of warmth that doesn't pool heavily on your eyelids and in your underarms.

Everyone said my blindness was her fault, somehow, and could be they were right. I'd say to her, "Tell me what you see," unsure whether I was trying to rub it in or only showing her that she could undo what she'd done.

"I will teach you to see without eyes," she said once, kissing the tips of my grubby fingers. "With these, the Spinner sees everything."

. . .

Possibly I should have guessed sooner what the Spinneret's tidy stitches meant. She wasn't writing anything on the wool. Nothing left to write, she must have figured. She was spinning empty, perfect cloth, and I didn't know.

"You take me for a fool?" I say. She's kneading a lump of bread, slapping the pile of too-dry dough down on the table with rhythm that only an automaton could keep up. "You thought I wouldn't find out that you're not doing anything at all?"

She doesn't say anything for a minute. The bread slams down onto the table twice before her tinny voice reaches me. "Are you dissatisfied with my work?"

"I gave up the last thing I had thinking that you could help me." If my eyes weren't so dried out, I'd sob and she'd hear it and her mechanical ears would think they'd caught feedback.

"You mean the dog," she says. We've never talked about Sadie before. She knows how I got the fuel cell, but not what it cost me.

"Yes, the dog."

"You would rather have your . . . pet's companionship than my assistance?"

I grit my teeth. How ridiculous it sounds, said like that. Sixty-eight years-old and I am still half a child. "I would rather that you do your job."

She hesitates, the dough slams down on the table again, and then she says, "I am doing my job, Miss Winchester. I am a Spinneret 84x and I am also your caretaker. You told me to see that the town's history did not end, I observed that you were the last remaining occupant of the town—so you are the one who I must keep from ending, as you put it."

"I didn't ask you for that," I say.

"I have failed, at any rate." Across the table, the Spinneret shoves to her feet. I hear her slap the dough down onto a pan and know she'll have it in the oven soon. "Our supplies are dwindling and I have been very thorough in my attempt to find more but have made no progress. You will starve in less than three weeks."

I tell her that it's fine, and it is. Even if I'm gone she can still go on spinning. Dustbowl has a future as long as there is a Spinner at the loom. We might be dead but she won't be, and that's good enough. She'll refine her own oil, if it comes to it; I don't doubt this scrappy little pile of tin. I hate her but I don't doubt her.

When midday comes and she goes to crawl the streets of Dustbowl for something to keep me alive, I think of how easily I could take the fuel cell back. She might put up a fight, but sometime or other she would shut down and I could open her stove-shaped belly, scoop out her guts and give them back to Sadie. But I'm too weak to go back to the wasteland. Even if I could, I would be betraying Dustbowl by leaving the loom without a Spinner.

So she comes back, and I say hello to her, and she apologises for finding nothing. She says, "Won't you ever call me Evangeline?"

I say, "Not on your life."

· · ·

The Spinneret had been quiet for a couple of hours, but I figured that maybe she had shut herself off for once. Precious little housework to do here, and not much left to gather from Dustbowl's dried up reserves. I was at the loom, so she couldn't be.

She comes in the door near dawn, creaking like a prototype, and I hate her more than ever for leaving me without saying so. I choke out something bad-tempered, but she doesn't let me finish.

"Let me tell you what I've seen," the Spinneret says. "The people did not die on the same day or in the same week. Every hospital and hovel in this town is packed with bodies. They died of dehydration, but other things too: polio, influenza, syphilis. They felt pain, I suppose, but they were not alone. I saw it on your wool, and I saw it every time I left this house."

"Enough."

Like always, she doesn't listen. "Your wool was not what I expected. I thought I would see depictions of environmental distress, attempts at emigration, a heroic story—but I saw only the simple truth of those people's bodies. You illustrated them all. Everyone who died in this town had a place on the tapestry. They are not like you and I, Miss Winchester. They leave no mark on anything besides the wool that you spin."

"And we leave more?"

"Less." She almost spits the word. "We are narrators of their story, and leave nothing at all. But you have a beating heart, a hyperactive amygdala, and I think you could have been one of those people. I do not understand why you shut yourself inside here, though I am sure that you have your reasons."

When her strange voice recedes into the almost-human pause between one thought and another, I want to tell her to stop talking and let me alone. I don't.

"I do not see any machines on this tapestry. I suppose it doesn't belong to us. But you wrote one name, over and over again. I was envious, I think. I wished it were mine. But I want you to remember me, just the same. I want to leave a mark. So I will make a choice that you would never make. I will make it for you. I hope you are wise enough not to reverse it."

I don't ask what she's doing, because I already know. Without a fuel cell, her motor holds out just long enough for her to bring Sadie back to life.

· · ·

At midday, Sadie and I bury the Spinneret 84x in the sand. The Dustbowl tapestry hangs from my shoulders, bloodstained and perfect. I shove her body down deeply into the earth and sing hymns and don't understand why we never buried our mechanical dead before this. At my side, Sadie is panting. Enough oil to last a month: that was the Spinneret's promise.

The last Spinner went mad over her work. She was thankful for her daughter's blindness, people said, because she thought that anyone sighted couldn't tolerate that inheritance. It wears you out, spinning. You squint through one eye at the bloodshed. Sometimes, you trace the lines of your own death.

Maybe I should have thanked Evangeline for spinning blank wool; probably, she would want me to follow her lead and try to stop myself from becoming another picture in the Dustbowl tapestry. But I'm an old woman from a short-lived town. Tradition means something to me, and I reckon I will stay at that loom until it turns me and Sadie both away.

Catalysis

Alter S. Reiss

There was the clatter of boots in the hallway as Jehan came in. Anthea smiled, tucked her gold-tipped rod behind her ear, and retrieved the solution from the athanor. She had solved the problem hours earlier, but she had wanted him to be there when she applied it. He had tried so hard to keep her spirits up when nothing seemed to work; it seemed only fair that he should be there when she triumphed.

Their rooms were in a crooked old house on Black Carol Street. They had a little patch of hallway on the ground floor, then a long narrow stair up to their rooms proper—the rest of the ground floor was let to other tenants, as was the middle floor. Jehan liked it because it was cheap, and Anthea liked it because she could use the roof when she needed sunlight, or moonlight, or open air.

As Jehan thumped his way up the stairs in stocking feet, Anthea put her notes in order. Her client wanted pure dovestone, and she had cleared all the impurities in the ore, but the stone was now bound with the alkahest in which she'd dissolved it. If she let it cool, it would be bound more tightly, but the heat of the athanor had kept it ready. Perhaps a greater heat would separate the dovestone, but her client wanted a process that would work for large quantities of the element, without the expense of a blasting furnace. It was an unfortunate marriage between the two components, and at last she knew what would be required to effect their divorce.

"I think I've solved it," she said, as Jehan came through the door. "Watch."

Gold was the noble metal; it did not rust or tarnish. But it was not the only noble metal. From the secret compartment in the side of her desk, Anthea took out her platinum rod, the most expensive of the tools she employed. If she had misjudged the strength of the alkahest, the platinum might dissolve, and she would have another metal to extract.

This was right. She knew it. The rod went into the solution, and as she had hoped, it did not steam, or show pitting, or dissolve. It sat in the liquid, unchanged. And all around it, flakes of the dovestone started to fall.

Alchemy wasn't a mechanical discipline, like sorcery or natural science. It was riddles and metaphors and spiritual meaning. The search for a method of turning base metal to gold was a search to make a perfect spirit from imperfect flesh. That was why it always failed, and why it was always pursued. But it was not the only great metaphor of alchemy; this was another. The catalyst, that which brought about change without being changed or consumed—that was the model of the ideal alchemist.

"Oh, that's wonderful," said Jehan, coming up behind her. "You've been working on that for weeks."

Anthea turned and smiled at him. "Yes," she said. "It's affordable, as well; the platinum is not consumed by the reaction, so it can be reused. I think . . . " Jehan was watching the dovestone fall through the solution like snow, but while he was honestly delighted, there was something else in his expression.

"I think it's what was wanted," said Anthea, and began putting away her tools and setting the solution into a sieving separator. Whatever else was happening, it would not do to leave things half-finished, or improperly stored. Jehan went over to the sink, and started washing the equipment that Anthea had left out. Not many men would do that sort of work, and there weren't many people Anthea would trust with her crucibles and retorts, but Jehan was always careful.

"What's the trouble?" asked Anthea, once the last of her vials was stoppered and put into its place.

Jehan gave a slight shrug. "Really, it is not a problem for me," he said. "It's a problem for their majesties, and for the palace officials."

"You guard the palace," said Anthea. "You guard their majesties."

"No," said Jehan. "No, I am furniture in the palace."

Anthea gave an annoyed tch. "The king and queen will need guards more than furniture," she said. "Bread riots again today, and two newspapers shut down, their presses seized. It won't hold."

"They need guards," said Jehan, "and they have guards; men who do not wear so much gold and crimson, men who have the authority to do more than strut along a walkway for six hours at a stretch, or stand beside a door." He shook his head. "No, we are furniture, and it may be that we will be smashed along with the other furniture. But that is in the hands of God."

"Then what is it?" asked Anthea, coming to stand next to him, to put her tools away after he washed them clean.

Jehan put down the cucurbit he had been cleaning, and took a rose from inside his jacket. "The Palace of St. Donic is a large and ancient building," he said, "with many hidden rooms and chambers. But I know it. And there have been walls where there ought to be corridors, gardens where there ought to be chambers."

"What do the other guards think?" asked Anthea.

Jehan shook his head. "We don't wish to talk of it. The queen is in a frightened rage, and furniture or not, the guard may be dismissed, or dispersed to other units, or court-martialled for failing in our duties."

Anthea picked up the cucurbit and returned it to its place. "And the flower came from one of these gardens," she said. "You want me to see what it will tell me."

Jehan nodded. "If you will," he said. "You've said that in alchemy, the whole is reflected in the part. I couldn't take the whole garden, so I hope that this will serve. I know that this might be the crisis that will end the monarchy, and free your university friends from the prisons. But . . . "

"Of course," she said. "I'll see what I can learn." She took the rose from him and put it beneath a glass dome. After some thought, she vented it with rebased air.

"And now?" asked Jehan.

"We wait," she said. "It's rebased air . . . " She hesitated. Jehan wasn't stupid, but he wasn't familiar with more technical aspects of alchemy. "It's like natural air, but more so. If the flowers aren't natural, aren't suited for the natural world, they will show signs: it might wilt, or show spots. If, for instance, it is a Dhari blind mage tampering with the past and present, prolonged exposure will leave the rose covered in white mould."

He stood closer to the dome, looking intently.

"It will be at least three hours before we'll see anything," she said.

He gave a slow smile. "The theatre?"

Anthea smiled back. "If you wish," she said. "And perhaps a dance, after."

"Nothing less, to celebrate your triumph!" said Jehan, all worry forgotten. Perhaps he over-valued her ability to solve all problems, but that was fine, in its way.

The two of them went down the narrow stair together, and out into the streets of Oain Michel. The bread riots of the morning had been forgotten, and the night lay open, full of promise. The shop windows gleamed with the ever-burning light of fuming air lanterns, and the puddles glimmered with reflected glamours.

Anthea was taller by a head than was fashionable, and she could not dance as well as Jehan, but they were both young, and they made a splendid pair, he in the crimson and gold of the palace guard, and she in the green and grey of the alchemists. They ate, they saw and were seen in the theatre, and then they danced at the Marovia Hall, with spell-woven lights settling in their hair like fireflies. It was a fine night, another pearl on the string of fine nights in Oain Michel.

When they returned, the flower beneath the dome had gone to rot and ruin; it was as though it had aged a month in a few hours. It did not bode well, but since Anthea could think of nothing to do that night, she went up to bed with Jehan. She did not sleep well. She woke later, came out into the sitting room in her night robe, and stared at the ruins of the rose, lit by the moonlight.

When dawn came, Jehan found her still sitting there, still looking at the rose, which was nothing more than a withered twig. "Morning?" he said, not yet entirely awake.

"Yes," said Anthea. "Has there been any change in Prince Erenlan?"

"Change?" Jehan found the coffee urn, empty. Anthea passed him her mug; she had already drunk half, and the rest was cold. Jehan drank it anyway, down to the grounds, and seemed to revive slightly. "I don't see much of the prince," he said. "He is confined to the nursery for most of the day."

"Have the nursemaids complained?" she asked. "Have you heard more cries, or fewer cries, or the sounds of more things being broken?"

"I don't know," he said. He looked down at her mug, set it aside with a disgusted face, and set another pot of water to boil. "One of the nurses was crying," he said. "I had thought it was just the usual sort of thing. What do you think has happened?"

"I had expected spots, or a slight change of colour, to identify the sorcery that had made the rose. But it wasn't just that; it all fell apart. It's entirely made of sorcery, not just a product of sorcery."

"I don't understand."

"It is the midnight court come to St. Donic," she said.

Jehan paled. "I've plucked a rose from the Elf Queen's garden?"

Anthea looked away. She could not cry. What was done was done, and Jehan needed her to be strong. She also could not deny his guess; all the signs pointed in that direction. And it was no trivial thing. Even the gifts of the fae carried a terrible sting, and their punishments and pranks were things of dread legend. It was unwise to take gifts from the fae, but much worse to steal from them.

"They will have called in sorcerers," said Anthea.

"Yes," said Jehan.

"And the sorcerers will have made no progress, because the fae are a wellspring of magic, and what they do cannot be undone by human hands."

Jehan made no response, merely stood there, looking asleep and frightened and trying for brave.

"I will have to come with you to the palace."

That woke him up more than the realisation of what he had done. "What? Anth, maybe you could do something, but they can't bring in alchemists after the sorcerers have failed—not with sorcerers being royalists, not after the university riots. And even if they did, three of your instructors and two of your fellows were arrested! Even if they would be able—"

"You're right," said Anthea. "I can't go as myself. But you've said often enough that they don't look at the guards when they're on duty."

"They'll know!" said Jehan. "The guards at least will know."

"Yes," said Anthea. "But they also know you, and you will have told them of me."

"No," said Jehan. "They might . . . but any questions, and they will do as they are ordered."

"Of course," said Anthea. The water sitting on the open furnace was bubbling, so she tipped it into the coffee urn. "But as you say, you have plucked a rose from the elf queen's garden."

"Yes," said Jehan, decisively, as Anthea poured herself another mug of coffee. "I plucked the rose. And I will face the consequences."

"Fair," said Anthea. "But I do not believe that the queen of the fae sees you in the same way I do, Jehan. I do not think that you are the target of the Midnight Court's visit."

"The heir," said Jehan.

"People have made poor bargains," said Anthea. "So the stories go. And kings and queens make worse bargains, because they never expect that anyone would dare make them pay. I cannot say what her majesty purchased—the hand of his majesty, perhaps? But the price of a bargain with the fae is often a first-born child."

"They wouldn't have . . . a changeling prince? Now?"

"I think so," said Anthea. "A prince with all the capricious cruelty of the fae, but no particular care for the safety of its human body. A prince like that, and smash goes the furniture in the palace, polished shelves and golden braids alike."

Jehan looked at her, and she looked at him. "If you get killed, I'll never forgive myself," he said.

"Well, you've certainly spent a lot of time and effort trying to talk me into going," she said. "It would be only fair to blame you."

"It's not a question of fair," he said. "It is the logic of the heart. But if you are right, this needs to be done. I will get you a jacket that is too small on me; if you wear thick stockings, the boots might not be too awkward."

"Yes," said Anthea. "And I will make my own preparations."

It was a damnably foolish thing that they were about to try, and if she died in attempting it, one of Anthea's great regrets would be knowing that her library would be dispersed. All her three-hundred-year-old folios on rag stock, all the pamphlets printed last week, the ink smeared and poorly applied, all her books and scrolls and tablets, everything gone to other people's shelves.

There was not much in any of it about the Midnight Court, and less that was helpful: some stories of the punishments of the fae, some warnings on how not to approach them. Not much, but enough. The problem was the same as the problem with the dovestone—an unfortunate marriage between the mortal court and the elven court, so perhaps a similar solution might apply.

Anthea knew she was not the ideal alchemist: too much dancing and not enough study; too high a self-regard and too little spiritual perfection. But the platinum was perfect, and one of the principles of alchemy was that perfection could be used to create perfection. It would be dangerous. All short cuts were. In this case, the perfect platinum would not mix easily with the base matter of mortal flesh.

It did not dissolve easily, either, and once it was dissolved, it took more than one change to render the resulting poison into a slow enough acting thing that she might take it and still live. Perhaps. It would be a last resort. She would go, she would see, and she would return with more information.

By the time she was done, Jehan had assembled for her an outfit of his clothing. The jacket was loose and the boots were awkward, but there was no time for any further alterations; they were already running behind. Anthea felt a dozen times a fool as she tripped along the cobbles of the street, sure that every eye was on her, that women were laughing at her behind their fans, and that cold-eyed men had marked her for death.

But nobody stopped her in the street, and nobody stopped her when she walked through the little barred postern gate where the palace met one of the alleys on Sharpside, not even the guards who stood there, looking straight ahead. She was right. They knew that Jehan loved an alchemist, and they knew that they needed an alchemist, for all that the science was out of favour in the royal court.

Anthea had known Jehan for seven years; they had been lovers for three. He had been a guard at the palace for all that time, but she had never been inside.

It was as beautiful as she expected. Even the obscure corridors had marble tile and golden fittings. Beautiful, yet over-ripe. The walls were covered in dark red satin, with figures of men and women, of overflowing cornucopias, of apes and birds and coursing hounds, all given life by glamours, running and playing through the walls. A fortune in spells, for the sake of there having been a fortune to spend—it was ornate but not pretty, and nobody in the palace seemed to see it.

Neither did they see her. As the pair had made their hurried way to the palace, Jehan had told her that a guard who looked uncertain or who walked without confidence would be noticed. Once she was noticed, she was lost. So she walked with purpose, looked as though she knew where she was going, and she was as invisible as the wall satins.

It worked so well that she could no longer dispute Jehan's characterisation as furniture. Guards were there for the same reason as the apes and birds on the walls and the gold in the fittings—because they were expensive, because even the wealthiest of subjects could not afford so many guards, so splendidly uniformed.

Anthea's intent had been to establish the truth of her two major deductions: that the Midnight Court was filling the same places as the palace of St. Donic, and that the prince had been replaced by a changeling. The first was confirmed simply enough. She found a garden whose leaves showed brown spots when exposed to rebased air, and where the powder of Etienne burned with a clear white flame.

The other was not so easy to prove.

It would be a simple matter of pressing a bit of iron to the child's skin. If the skin burned, he was fae; if not, he was human. But this was not a thing that a guard could do, even if that guard was an actual guard, rather than a woman in a guard's uniform. The same applied to anything she might try with rebased air, or the powder of Etienne. A nursemaid might be able to apply the test, if she was foolish, or brave, but not a guard.

There was no way that Anthea could approach a nursemaid. Perhaps Jehan knew one who would try it? Sometimes the guards and maids ate together at the servants' tables. The test had to be done. If her deduction was false, if there was some other reason why the Midnight Court had come, it would change her entire approach.

She went to Jehan's station, but he was not there.

It was a doorway that was supposed to have a guard at either side, but there was only one man there, standing uncomfortably stiffly. Jehan's absence was like a missing tooth.

Anthea stood and stared, forgetting what he had told her about remaining unseen. She willed him to return, to be where he wasn't. It was the sort of thing that the fae would do, but wasn't fair that they'd done it so soon.

An older man, wearing the stiff black coat of a senior servant came through the doorway. "Hey, you," he said. "What are you—"

Anthea turned on her heel, strode in the opposite direction with as much confidence as she could manage.

"But you're not—" she heard, as a door closed behind her. Forgetting all dignity, she ran around a corner, down a flight of stairs. Voices raised behind her. It was a miracle that the deception had lasted as long as it had, but it was done. If she were caught, it would mean the eternal night of the royal jails or the headsman's axe. And Jehan was not there to aid her.

While she could scarcely pretend to have the skills needed for the life of a guardsman, Anthea had an excellent sense of direction. Two more flights of stairs, then down a corridor, and then she would be back at the gate where she had come in. They might pursue her out of the palace, but they might not, and if they did, she would be able to . . . There was a blank wall, where before there had been a corridor.

Anthea swore softly, hearing footsteps behind her. She wasn't ready—the visit was supposed to be a first test, merely to confirm what the reactive agents were. But even if she could leave, now she would never be able to return. She took the vial she had prepared in her room on Black Carol, uncapped it and drank, before she could second-guess herself.

It was acidic, but not enough to burn; her mouth felt raw, like she had been vomiting, but she did not need to cough, and there was no blood. She hadn't killed herself yet, then. The footsteps behind her grew louder.

She opened one of the doors beside the new wall, stepped through, and was in a forest glade beside a stream, lit by moonlight. There were rose petals floating in the stream, and nightingales calling from the starlit trees. No doorway behind her. That wall had not been an accident. The fae must have felt the tests that she had been doing, and they would not like to see her leave with what she had learned.

Very well.

Anthea sat herself down by the bank of the stream. It wasn't a forest, any more than a painting of a forest was a forest, but it was pleasant to look at. She took off the ill-fitting boots and the thick stockings, and stretched her feet out on the grass. There was no way of knowing if what she had done had worked as she wished, but she was feeling distinctly unwell. Anthea sat and waited, and hoped that the poison would not kill her, and would only harm those whom she intended to harm.

She was not suffered to wait long. Two huntsmen came to collect her. They might almost have been mortal, but they were taller and more fair, and their eyes were flower petals: honeysuckle and heliotrope. They said nothing, but they motioned for her to stand, to walk between them, and they led her from the forest out into a palace more grand by far than that of St. Donic.

Its spires were of crystal, and its flagstones were of porphyry veined with gold, lit by firefly lanterns and globes of floating light. It was all so fair and splendid that Anthea felt shabby in her too-large jacket and bare feet. It was a beautiful thing, the Midnight Court, and she felt a distant pity. It was glorious in a way that the mortal palace was not, but it too was over-ripe.

They took her to an audience hall, where the fae queen sat amidst her court. They all had eyes of flowers, and some had wings of gossamer, or feathers instead of hair, or cloaks of butterfly wings. Some were four or five times her height, others small enough that they could have ridden on the backs of sparrows. Few looked anything like the children of man.

The queen might have been able to pass as human, if she chose. She was about the height of a mortal woman, and her eyes were not flowers—the story of the trick she had played to gain those eyes was one that Anthea had heard as a little girl. She was dark as the night, and fair as the dawn, and her dress was iridescent glory.

"You have trespassed on our lands, child," said the queen. "And your stinks and powders have been distressing our servants."

Anthea bowed, stiff and awkward against the sinuous grace of the fae queen. "You have taken things from the palace of St. Donic," she said. "I have come to ask you to give them back."

There was laughter in the court, and the queen's eyes sparkled with mischief. "Give them back?" she said. "We do not give. We take. But what do you think that we have taken?"

"A child," said Anthea. "Erenlan Varin Ardaugi IV, hereditary prince of Oain, baron by blood of Oain Michel. And a man, Jehan Arpine, a guard in the palace."

"Very good!" said the queen. "Bring them out, bring them out, so that this child can see how well she has guessed!"

The prince was in a bassinet of golden thread and clouds, with a spinning, whirling mass of colour hanging by a thread of pearls near his head. He was utterly entranced, cooing and reaching for the colours, which spun just out of his reach. Jehan had his wrists bound with a flowering vine, and he walked like a man asleep, or stupefied with drugs.

"And tell us then, child—why should we release these baubles we have taken? They are fairly ours, after all."

"Because it is not right," said Anthea. "The child . . . changelings are capricious and cruel, and there are revolts and mutinies across the breadth of Oain; even in Oain Michel there are bread riots and marches. A prince like that will embolden the worst, on both sides of the barricades. And the man has done nothing to you; he has—"

"He has stolen from us, child."

"Then he ought to pay you back," said Anthea. Jehan could hear her; he was trying to say something, but was too stupefied, too bound up in spells.

"Of course," said the queen. "The value of the rose is fifty years service, and he will pay what he owes."

"No," said Anthea. "No, that is not right. The value of a rose is a few pence, if it is particularly fine. I do not deny that you have power, but what you do is wrong."

The court laughed at that, the giants and the tiny sparks, and the queen clapped her hands. "Such a delight!" she said. "We think it is your potions and powders that preserve your innocence for so long. 'Though changed, I arise' is your creed, is it not? That nothing is lost, and that all your equations are balanced?"

"That is a principle of alchemy," said Anthea, slowly. She had not expected the fae queen to know anything of alchemy; if she knew well, she might—

"And if I take these two, and leave nothing, are the equations balanced? Will they arise the same, though changed?"

Anthea shook her head. "No," she said.

"And thus the idealist is confounded by experiment," said the fae queen. "The value we set for our roses is right, little potion girl. It is right because we say it is, and it is done because it is right. Let a thousand people die for our bargain to be fulfilled. Let ten thousand, let ten thousand times ten thousand, and it will still be right; we are the queen, and we are the fae, and what we will is what is right."

"Thus says the bear, or the tiger," said Anthea. "Or a winter storm."

"Yes," said the queen.

"There are no more tigers in Oain, and there are bears only in the most isolated and mountainous districts. We have stone houses, heated by coal and candescent air." She had not meant to say that; she had not meant to say most of what she had said. That was why she studied alchemy, rather than law, or religion, or art. One did not have to consider how a solution would react to hearing the truth; one did not have to lie to alloys.

But it was said, and the midnight court grew silent as she said it, the flower petal eyes of the fae turning dark and wild. They could kill her and there was nothing she could do to stop it.

Then the fae queen laughed again. None of the others laughed with her this time, and it was a dangerous, terrible laugh. "You interest us, child. So brave and clever and foolish."

The queen leaned back in her throne of ice, and for a time, there was silence. "Very well," she said, finally. "You wish for these two to be returned to Oain Michel. They are ours, and we do not lightly release that which we have taken. But perhaps you will be more entertaining than they are, for longer. Will we trade, child? Would you have us release them, and keep you?"

Anthea fought back her hope. Perhaps her poison would not do what she had hoped—it was, after all, a first experiment. Perhaps she would say the wrong thing, and the agreement would not be made, or the agreement would not achieve what she hoped.

"No!" said Jehan, his eyes momentarily clear. "No, this is wrong. You've done nothing—they have no hold on you. Anthea, no, I should be far happier within the prison knowing you to be free, than free and knowing you to be—"

Anthea could not look at him, could not take the chance that he would see what she was thinking, and the fae would learn it from him. "I do not acknowledge that either of those two are yours," she said. "They are their own people. But I admit that they are within your power. I will put myself in your power if you release the two who you have taken."

"Anth, no," said Jehan. But it was too late to second-guess, too late to change her mind. He was gone, as was the prince. Anthea was left alone in the audience chamber filled with fae all watching her with hunger in their flower-petal eyes. The queen came down from her throne of ice, and laid a chain of flowers around her neck.

Anthea wanted to argue the point further, but she found she could not speak. The fae queen laughed at her panic. "Perhaps at some point we shall see a need to allow our court alchemist to speak. Or perhaps we shall need another cobble for a path, or another rose for our garden. Perhaps you will be changed, child, and perhaps you will not arise the same."

The queen was not so ungainly tall as Anthea, and she pulled on the flower chain, bringing Anthea's face close to hers. She studied it minutely, a smile growing on her face, the smile of a child with a new toy, the joy of a cat with a new mouse.

"Take it to the stables," she said. A snake-faced crone came up and took the end of the chain and led her out to the stables, where proud-necked horses and unicorns snorted in their stalls. The crone tied her chain to the bar in one of the stalls, and sat a few minutes longer, perched on the stall gate.

"Do not worry, little alchemist," it hissed at her. "It won't be long. You have such lovely eyes, and there are so many changelings who need them."

Then it was gone, and Anthea was left by herself, on the sweet smelling hay. The chain had wrapped itself around her wrists as well, held them tight. Even if she could get loose from the chain, there was nowhere she could run. She had made her choices when she had a chance to make choices. Now she waited, and hoped.

She could not tell how long she was left there. There was always moonlight and cloud, always the sound of a wind in the trees, the songs of nightingales. Anthea drifted in and out of sleep, dizzy, feeling the aches in her joints and back. Perhaps her poison had not worked in the manner she had intended, but it was having some of the effects she had anticipated. No urine or faeces, though, and no hunger or thirst—the rules were different in the lands of the fae, and that was all for the best.

The first sign that what she had done was working was a spatter of rain on her arm. She looked up, and saw that it had eaten through the corner of the roof. The water that rolled off her arm was reddish, and each drop steamed slightly as it touched the hay. In the distance, there were shrieks and howls, as the rain fell on the ordered perfection of the midnight court. Anthea smiled, and slept again.

She was awoken by a series of stinging slaps. The queen was there with her huntsmen clad in green, and she was in a towering rage. "Tell us, creature, why our gardens are turning to iron?" she asked. "Why iron falls from our clouds, and pits and scars our works and our subjects?"

Anthea could not keep herself from smiling.

One of the huntsmen brought down a lash, and Anthea's back lit up with burning, blistering pain. She whimpered, curled up, moved as far away as her chain would let her, all without any thought at all.

"Speak!" said the queen, and Anthea felt her jaw and throat loosening. She could speak now, and as the huntsman raised the lash again, she knew that she would, sooner or later. No reason to delay; the work was already done.

"Catalyst," she said.

The lash came down again. Again she whimpered, again she cowered, though she had told herself she would not.

When the huntsman brought the whip up again, the queen held back his hand. "Speak clearly, and tell the truth," said the queen, bringing Anthea's face up to hers with the tips of her fingers. "Or you will take so long to die, and in such agony, that the stars themselves shall weep to see it."

"The catalyst," said Anthea, "is a thing that causes or speeds a reaction, but is not part of the reaction. I have made myself a catalyst."

The huntsman raised the whip again, and Anthea curled away from it, though he did not bring it down.

"So much has been taken from the mortal realm to here," she said, talking as quickly as she could to keep that lash at bay. "So many children, so many lovers. In every mortal there is iron; that is why our blood is red. So many have come here and left their blood behind. Though they may have left, in the end, each left a residue of blood. If they left weak and broken, they left their iron behind, you see? The iron had to still be here, bound up in a form that did you no harm."

"She's causing it," said the second huntsman. He reached for the bronze-bladed knife at his belt.

"Wait," said the queen, "and be silent. Are you doing this, child?"

"Yes," said Anthea, and turned away, dreading and hoping for the knife.

"No," said the queen.

Again the lash came down, biting through Jehan's coat, and the shirt and vest she wore beneath, leaving a trail of pain and blood.

"You are not lying," said the queen. "But you are not telling the entire truth. What can we do to stop this curse, and return my gardens to what they should be?"

"I don't know," said Anthea. Neither the knife nor the whip came down.

"I will take your heart from your chest," said the queen, "and send you to wander without it, as a snowflake in the springtime. Tell me."

Anthea drew herself up, stood. "What price do you offer?" she asked.

That brought the whip down, but she did not cower this time, or try to escape it. The whip was only pain, the knife only death. There was nothing there to fear.

"You would bargain with us, child?" asked the queen dangerously.

"You would bargain with me?" asked Anthea. She was not strong like Jehan. She could not fell a man with a punch, nor was she expert with rapier and musket. But she would not be talked to like that, not by someone who was asking for her help.

"You are ours!" roared the queen. "By blade and bone, you are ours to do with as we please. Now, speak!"

"I am in your power, as I have said," replied Anthea. "And now you are in mine. Turn me into a snowflake, if you please, and I shall laugh as I melt. What will you do after?"

There was a silence between them. "Here are my terms," said Anthea. "You shall not harm me, or mine, my children or my children's children, until the end of time. You shall not harm us, and those who serve you shall not harm us, by deed or by thought or by word, or by any other means. In return, I will tell you how to end the transformation that is affecting the lands of the fae."

Another silence, longer and deadlier. Anthea could not stand so proud as the queen with her hands and neck still bound to the bar of the stable, but there was no need for that. They were both what they were, and the fae queen had a decision to make.

"Majesty," said one of the huntsmen. "Majesty, you need not suffer this. Let us—"

She raised a hand, and the huntsman fell silent.

"I agree to your terms," she said, every word dropping like a red hot coal from her lips.

"You will have to wait," said Anthea. She shook herself clear of her bonds, the chain no longer having the power to hold her.

"That is all?" asked the queen, her eyes widening, like a cobra's hood spreading before it struck.

"A more precise catalyst, and a larger quantity might have had a permanent effect. Perhaps if you had killed me, it would never have reversed. You did not, and as things stand, you will have to wait. One of the principles of alchemy is that the larger mirrors the smaller. As a body can heal, so a realm can heal; the process that I started is limited and incomplete. If I had—"

The queen screeched. "We could have just waited!" She slapped at Anthea, but her hand passed through her cheek, and out the other side. There was no pain. Anthea was an alchemist, not a sorcerer, but she could recognise magic. The queen of the fae was bound by her words, in a way that mortal princes never were.

"—been able to complete my observations, perhaps I should have come up with something better," she continued. "If the catalyst is removed, the reaction will cease more rapidly, and your waiting will be reduced."

"You think that you will trick us into letting you leave?" asked the queen, drawing back. "Perhaps we cannot harm you, but—"

Anthea hauled back, and punched the queen in the eye. That did not pass through harmlessly; the queen fell back, into the arms of her huntsmen. "If you do not let me leave," said Anthea, "I shall stay, and I do not think that you or yours will much enjoy my company."

The huntsmen moved to keep her from their queen, but they could not grasp hold of her. She walked past them. "In addition, majesty," continued Anthea, "I have made more complete observations."

"Go, then," said the queen. "All doors will take you back to where you wish to go. I am so bound by your trickery that I cannot even send you to a time or place that will harm you."

Anthea swept past her, headed for the door of the stable. It would not do for the queen to see her stumble, to know that by making herself a catalyst, she had also poisoned herself; that to have their revenge, the fairies need only wait.

"We cannot do you harm," said the queen, behind her. "But we can withdraw our gifts, and the gifts of our realm. Unless you wish to make another bargain."

For just a moment, Anthea hesitated. "No more milkmaids earning kingdoms," said the queen. "No more doors in the hedge. Glamours will fade and be forgotten, and all will be left grey and dull. We cannot harm you, child, but we can leave your world a dry and empty husk."

Anthea turned, faced her. "I would not trade a single hair from my head to let a milkmaid earn a kingdom," she said. "How many milkmaids are princesses, and how many men do you keep in your chains? But even if it were one princess for every slave, or ten, or a hundred I still do not want it; the world has had enough of both kings and slaves."

She had more to say, but she felt her gorge rising. She turned and left, as proud as she could manage. The door to the stable opened up into the palace, and she fell out through it, into Jehan's arms.

"Hat," she gasped, and he grabbed it off his head and passed it to her, his face still awakening to who it was he held in his arm. She vomited, twice, three times. Some of the poison. It was a start.

When she was done, he was carrying her through the hallways, out to the postern gate. "How?" he asked.

"Catalysis," said Anthea, sleepily. Her thoughts had been clear enough in the realm of the fae, but now the platinum was catching up with her. There was very little left in her stomach, but she vomited again, making sure to catch it in Jehan's hat.

"You don't need to keep the floors clean," said Jehan. "They'll—"

"No!" said Anthea. "There's at least a hundredth weight of platinum in the vomitus. Can concentrate and reduce it. Recover at least fifty royals worth of . . . " she trailed off.

The apes and birds and coursing hounds in the wall satin were slowing down, freezing into place. It would be a smaller world that she had made, in some ways. Smaller, with less terrifying beauty. But the world was terrifying and beautiful enough without glamour, and there was a sufficiency of human autocrats who imposed their will and called it just.

Anthea settled into Jehan's arms. He had to return to his post as soon as he could, to avoid the court martial, so once they were out of the palace, he transferred her to a hansom cab, which took her back to their rooms on Black Carol. Out in the streets, spells were fading—buildings with glamoured fronts looked shabby and worn, all-winter cherries were turning brown and rotting. But chelating agents still worked their purging effects, and Anthea began recovering from what she had done, as well as the work of recovering the platinum that had been part of her.

People would wonder at the failure of sorcery, why the milk they left out behind their cottages was not drunk, why night breezes no longer carried strange music, but there would be no reason to suspect her of any part in that. They would wonder, and they would forget, and history would become myth. They would not believe her if she told them what had happened and why, and she had no reason to tell. It was not in the nature of the catalyst to become part of the reaction.

When Jehan returned, he at least would believe what she had done. If he had not been threatened, perhaps she would not have faced down the queen on her throne of ice, or half-killed herself to dissolve the bonds between the Midnight Court and the sons of man. He had been, and she did, and it was well. It was an unstable solution, and if it had not been broken at low energy, it would have had to be broken at a higher and deadlier heat.

Chapter Six

Veterans Day

Cat Sparks

"Those ain't no virgins!" screamed red-faced Maria, sweat streaming off her shiny cheeks, words that set the other girls off into shrieking fits of laughter.

Safia looked down to where Maria pointed. Way down below where the parade coiled through city streets like a giant many-coloured serpente. Past the lower balconies—always the first to fill on Veterans Day. Beyond the bridges and walkways spun like webs connecting slender minarets. At the serpente's head walked the city's finest daughters. Veiled, their pale white shifts blending with sandy paving stones. One would be selected and offered to the Veteran in celebration of Veterans Day.

There had always been a Veterans Day as far as anyone remembered. Events requiring sacrifice stood out amongst the many. Veterans Day was better attended than The Day of Blessed Mothers, Annunciation, or even The Culling of All Souls.

Safia adhered herself to Maria's gang of scruffy shanty girls. Safety in numbers, they climbed the walls in packs. Safety in scrabbling beyond the reach of priests and their swinging silver staves. Far from the guardsmen with their wicked blades and ways.

The city's ancient crumbling brickwork was peppered with footholds. Safia had been poked with brooms, swatted at with horsehair brushes, sworn at in a dozen disparate tongues. But the girl was quick and fleet of foot. She did not steal fruit from unguarded window boxes, nor leer at things she wasn't supposed to see.

Safia kept her wits about her, slinking at the fringes of the pack, both on the streets and when climbing high above them. The girls were climbing up to gawk at handsome drummers escorting courtesans in gowns of gold-and-lapis borne on palanquins held high by bare-chested men in pantaloons.

And the acrobats: white faced, coal-eyed, limber, juggling and prancing in their lace and feathered plumage. Flinging themselves from rail to rail, tumbling and screeching like monkeys. Choking confetti, swirling scented smoke.

Drums pounding like the beating of a million human hearts, winding their way up to the citadel—a windowless, glowing cylinder topped with a dome of sheer translucent crystal. Prison of the God-King Ankahmada, a being feared by all, but never seen. Surrounded by the spirits of the dead, the only ones fit to keep him company.

What precisely lay within the citadel? Nobody knew for certain. There was no entranceway or windows, but they'd all glimpsed shadowy figures through the blue. Guardsmen manned its base at compass points. Call to prayer sounded dawn and dusk, when the pale tiles shone with startling luminescence.

Maria and her girls threw stones, the younger ones whining in the heat. Safia craned her neck, but the citadel's blue shimmer remained nothing more than soft, translucent blur.

Ghosts were nothing special. Everybody saw ghosts, just as everyone had lost somebody dear. People vanished in the city of gold-and-lapis. It was the way of things, the price to pay for the protection of the God-King Ankahmada.

Safia learned the hard way that that no place was truly safe—and none less so than the Fancy House from which her beloved Mama had disappeared. Too young to work and without protection, Safia had been cast onto the street, forced to fend for herself amongst the rats and garbage.

Safia climbed with grim determination. The House said her Mama was dead and gone but if that were true, perhaps she was not truly gone completely? Perhaps her Mama walked amongst the citadel phantoms? Stranger things had happened in this city.

Maria spat her warnings as the girls kept climbing higher: *Touch the blue and it will burn your hand. Don't stare too hard or the shimmer-blue will drive you mad-bad-crazy.*

"I can't see anything—we'll have to get in closer!"

"Not too close, you stupid girls. Don't want to wind up caught."

"Those fat old dogs are way too slow for us . . . "

Maria shushed them, harsher this time. "It's not so bad," she assured the younger ones. Maria had been caught and branded twice, plus two more times she'd shrugged off like a joke. Marks she wore like a badge of honour. Jokes you had to be old enough to understand.

The wall's inner balustrade was the girls' favourite haunt. On tiptoe they could just make out the pilgrim camp that dogged the outer walls. Where people walked out of the Dead Red Heart, come to throw themselves upon the mercy of Ankahmada. Beyond their camp, a thousand miles of sand. Further still lay nothing but bones and ruin.

Wedged inside the walls lay the shanty strip, bathed in a sickly glow. Soaked in the relentless hum and random pulses of the outer city wall. Somehow, the barefoot girls and boys learned to sleep with its curdling vibrations, its cold-beyond-cold that burned those fool enough to touch.

The shanty boys and girls slept light, one hand on the three-inch blades they sharpened to points against foundation stones.

"Let's hop it to the Hydroponica," piped up Deean, little sister of Maria, named for a long-forgotten saint like so many other girls.

"No way—guards will climb up if they spot us."

"What of it?" Maria interjected, wielding the authority of her extra years. "They never climb as high as the spiral rail."

She winked at Deean and then across at Safia. A fit of giggling erupted from the rest of them, louder this time until a long blast on a brassy horn drew all attention back to the parade. One by one they hopped down, following little Deean's lead, still peering and craning as the parade choked up the streets.

That a year ago Safia had lived a stone's throw from the citadel was a secret she kept close. When Mama had worn the gold-and-lapis, when they'd lived well in a Fancy House five whole storeys high.

Ahead, Maria, red-faced again, shouted insults. Maria who thought she knew everything, but didn't. Her boastful dreams of living in a Fancy House, dressed in finery, strolling casually down terracotta streets. Abandoning shantytown—and the rest of them—in her wake. She didn't know that gold-and-lapis courtesans were trained from birth, not snatched from slums and spirited away. That the priests who used them did not have human hearts—or human skin. Cold to the touch just like a lizard's belly. Mama had whispered the truth of it. She had wanted something better for her daughter. Safia's own belly soured from an irregular diet of bitter skinks and nettle stems. Scraps from bins when the dogs didn't beat her to it.

Up high beyond the drummers, stilts and acrobats was the one place she felt safe. She did not care to push her luck by jeering at the city's finest daughters, one hand-chosen to be fed to the thing that lived beneath the city streets, the veteran of wars that had long ago been forgotten.

· · ·

The Hydroponica was fashioned from a million ivory tiles, each one smooth and identical to every other. The spiral rail wrapped around its girth connected it with the distillery and the mill.

The closest possible vantage point. The girls leaned over, craning for a glimpse. Those luckless virgins: pretty girls with neat-combed hair, balancing bowls of offerings or hand stitched flowers, eyes downcast beneath diaphanous veils. Nobody knew what happened to the chosen. Deean said the Veteran ate them. Maria reckoned he chained them up and made them bear his demon babies. Nice girls, they were all supposed to be, selected from the city's higher families.

The chattering girls blocked Safia from the blue. She hadn't come to jeer at wealthy daughters or dream of palanquins, lapis-gold or priests. She'd come to see the visions of the dead. To find out if her Mama stood amongst them.

"Look! It's happening. The blue, just like you said!"

Maria smiled triumphantly at the lurid, fading glaze. Safia looked right past her, straight into the shimmering field that moments before had been impenetrable ceramic.

"It glows!"

Safia stared hard, curiosity burning white-hot. Were there ghosts in the citadel or weren't there? A boy called Aeron swore he knew a guard who had put his hand right through one. Ghosts were the reason a bank of spirit houses lined the citadel's west aspect. Ghosts need not be seen to be believed, and Safia did believe: she couldn't help it.

She wanted to show her Mama that she was surviving on her own. That neither hunger nor uncertainty had claimed her. That she could stand her ground against girls and boys twice her size and half again as mean.

"Look—there's Madame Peshari and her poor dead twins!"

The gaggle of girls fell silent, gawking and craning, trying to see what Deean was pointing at. Something that might have been a swirl of parasols and frilly skirts. A blur of colour, difficult to make out at a distance.

"I swear that's Madam Peshari inside—look!"

"Shhh, I can't hear the drumming over the top of you."

"Shove over, I can't see a thing. They're picking the virgin and we're missing it!"

"Gimme the glass. Hasn't someone got a spyglass?"

"Move your arse, you're hogging all the room!"

The shanty girls made too much noise. Safia separated herself from the seething, boiling mass of them, edged her way along a jutting spar that bent beneath her meagre weight. She leapt to a ledge, then across to the spiral walkway. Let them have their cruel parade. Something was happening within the citadel's ceramic glaze. Indistinct shapes coalescing into human forms. If only she was closer. The drumming intensified. Another blast of the long, brassy horn, drowned out beneath loud squeals of uncharitable delight.

The blue light of the citadel, so dazzling and bright. She blinked. Coloured blobs swam before her eyes. For a moment—just a moment—the shimmer thinned and she could see right through. An empty street with whitewashed walls. A woman in a gold-and-lapis dress. A woman who tilted her head and smiled, held out her hand and reached towards . . .

"Mama!"

Safia scurried along the walkway, almost slipping, scurrying faster, reaching out her own hand. Not being careful where she was going, she slammed into a city guardsman heaving and puffing in the opposite direction. The man grabbed hold of Safia's arm and twisted.

"Mama—no!"

The blue-and-lapis woman vanished; the citadel walls became opaque again, glowing faintly like the resonance of sunset.

A second guardsman appeared behind the first, bulky men who blocked the narrow ledge. As one bound her wrists with scratchy rope, she considered flinging herself into the air. Quick as a skink. Fall like a stone. Let them catch some other girl—the streets, walkways and roofs were crawling with them.

But Safia didn't jump or struggle. Where there was life there was hope, as Mama said. Not that words like life and hope had done her Mama any favours in the end.

• • •

There was no sign of Maria's shanty girls as the guardsmen dragged Safia down the spiral walkway. They took her somewhere underground that stank of damp and rot, bundling her into the arms of older women with hard faces and stained aprons.

"Here's your virgin sacrifice," said the fatter of the two, pocketing the coins the woman gave him.

"I ain't no virgin!" Safia screamed.

"I couldn't give two shits, you shanty skank. You look the part—or at least you will when we're done scrubbing the filth off ya."

The women stripped her dirty clothes, dunked her headfirst into a bath. Beefy arms held Safia still while another scrubbed her skin until it stung. Something clattered from her pocket. Her three-inch blade, now kicked against the wall. They washed her hair and combed out all the matted tangles. Hard-faced bitches, every one, avoiding eye contact like it might bring shame on them.

They dressed her in a plain white shift, soft like it had been washed a thousand times, yet the fabric seeming newly off the loom.

"I ain't going in your parade. You won't get me promenading the city street!"

The woman who'd held the scrubbing brush gave her a sour look. Her face was old. Somewhere near forty, were it not for the creases on her forehead and the terrible bags and droops beneath her eyes.

"You don't get to promenade," she said matter-of-factly. "Like anyone's gonna want to look at you."

Safia's feet were jammed into beaded slippers, her hands tied tight in front of her while a thin, pale woman braided her hair too tight. Another threaded paper flowers through it. When Safia squirmed, the sour-faced woman punched her in the gut.

"You really think they'd go wasting the lives of the city's finest daughters? No one's even going to know you're gone."

Safia felt her eyes begin to water. She fought it hard. They didn't deserve the satisfaction. It wasn't true. Deean would miss her. So would Aeron and maybe even lying, two-faced Maria.

When her hair was done they yanked her to her feet.

"There's words to learn," said a scrawny woman standing to one side. "Make sure you don't jumble 'em up, else it'll be the worse for you."

Safia braced herself to kick their shins and make a break for it. She knew all the backstreet nooks and crannies. Even with arms bound, she could outrun them all.

Only she couldn't. One of the women bent and cuffed a chain around her ankle. She yelped as cold iron bit into her flesh.

Sour Face took a vial down from the highest shelf. Pale green glass with something dark inside. When she unstoppered it, a pungent scent leaked out.

"Know what this is?" she said.

Safia nodded. She knew.

"Good. That means I won't have to use it but if you don't stop struggling, Angel help me, that's exactly what I'll do. Don't matter two shits to me what way you want to die. My job's to see you past the temple gate. A swig of this'll burn out your insides, nice and slow. Without it, I cut your bonds, you walk on yer own and take yer chances with the thing that lives beneath our feet."

Safia swallowed the hard lump in her throat. "I can walk," she said.

The sour-faced woman slipped the vial into her apron. "Good then. Looks like we're all done here."

They made her wait in a passageway that stank of piss and rats. With bored-looking guardsman on either side, she listened to the screaming crowd as the procession continued outside. Drumming. Always drumming. She pictured priests with smooth round shaven heads, physiques outlined in clinging silks and satins. Fabric refracting tiny shards of diamond light. Cloaks that flowed and twisted like living things.

Each bearing shiny two-pronged staves, the God-King's symbol emblazoned upon their chests. Chanting prayers, their voices loud enough to wake the dead. Blasting occasional potted palms with lightning; a yapping dog or child not quick enough to move.

Children scattering petals before the sacrifice. They didn't call it that, of course. The word they used was *maiden*. Neither were the petals real. Not much grew around the city walls and what did could not be spared for treading underfoot, not even by the city's finest daughters.

Safia stood tall, ignoring the chill of the chain around her ankle, still hoping an opportunity might present itself. Whatever chance, no matter how small and risky, she would take it.

The drummers ceased their mesmerising rhythms as one by one they entered the passageway. Backlight made them difficult to see. Now and then, a tiny glimmer. The smell of strong tobacco, wafting.

Then the maiden: stark in silhouette. Strong hands pushed her forward until the girls stood face to face.

The maiden held out her bouquet. "Here. Take it."

"I . . . my hands are tied."

The corners of the maiden's lips turned up in a cruel smile. She dropped the flowers. They landed with a dull thud on the passageway's cold stone. The maiden spun on her heel as a stocky woman stepped out of the shadows and wrapped the rich girl protectively in a cloak.

"Untie my hands!" Safia begged.

Nobody spoke. She was pushed for the second time and the flowers were trampled underfoot.

"Watch your feet, you clumsy girl; those took me a week to sew!" The angry woman snatched them up and jammed them between Safia's palms.

Safia couldn't see where they were taking her. She tripped over her ankle chain as the passageway's darkness closed around her, thick and enveloping like fog.

• • •

At the entrance to the temple, a guardsman freed her ankle and her wrists, then pushed her through a gaping, rocky maw. Icy chill bled through her beaded slippers. When she looked before her, all she saw was darkness.

"Walk!"

Safia stumbled forwards. Darkness gradually gave way to a grotto weathered from thick, crumbling stone. And something else. Something unexpected. Lights. Hundreds of them, yellow and winking in the draught, like glowing jewels. Candles placed upon altars: high ones, low ones and plenty in between, each illuminating framed images of a woman's face.

The rough-handed women who'd scrubbed Safia clean had made her memorise a string of words, but the further she moved inside the cool interior, the more those words fragmented and slipped away. Something about creation and destruction. A virgin princess called Diana, the once-living legend. A goddess and a saint. Words didn't matter. Only the offerings mattered: the trampled flowers they'd jammed between her hands. The sacrifice she was supposed to be.

Safia paused before the central altar, breathed in the stink of tallow and expensive wax. Incense too, a mismatched blend of cinnamon, clove and lemongrass.

Diana's face was everywhere. Perhaps she was a goddess? She was beautiful enough. Spaced between the frames and candles stood ceramic figurines, each one a woman in flowing robes. Some showed a heart at the centre of her chest. Others a band of gold around her head. The glow of holiness. The radiance of good.

A noise disturbed the dark behind her. Something moving, much bigger than a man. Her breathing steady, she clutched the trodden flowers against her chest.

"Don't you dare touch anything." A male voice, deep and old, a mix of strong and feeble in one breath.

That noise again, a dragging, rasping shuffling. Louder this time. Closer too. Her pulse began to quicken as a jumble of words spilled out between her lips. "A highborn daughter of Ankahmada stands before your greatness . . . I bring . . . " her voice trailed off to nothingness.

"Liar. You got the stink of shanty on your skin. Do you reckon I can't smell it?"

The sound again, this time even closer. The ground trembled beneath the creature's weight. In fright, she almost turned.

"Don't you look at me," he barked, a sound sharper and more terrifying than the grate of metal scraping metal.

She froze. "I only want . . . "

"I know what you want, the whole damn lot of you. You think I'm stupid? You think I can't see through your games? Desecrating *her* holy temple. Poisoning *her* memory with your lies."

A harsh clunk and clatter nearly startled her out of her skin. The thing behind her wasn't human. It was a warrior demon from the time before the Ruin, risen to slay her for her wickedness. Something cold and hard pressed into her back.

"One inch more and I'll snip your spine in two."

The demon wasn't joking. She sucked in breath, eyes on the sea of flickering lights. Waiting for the beast to make its move.

"So. What have they told you about me?"

"That . . . that you are the Veteran. A holy man."

"More likely that I am a merciless eater of babies. Did they tell you that one? Did they?"

"No, Master . . . " Her voice, weak and insipid, trailed away. She was scared now. Really scared. The Veteran was going to kill her.

"I am master of nothing. Peek into the corners, little girl, and tell me what you see."

The grotto did not have corners. It was wide and squat, its low ceiling choked with jagged mineral spikes like broken teeth. Shadows pooled around the edges. Murky smudges that might have hidden many things.

"Look harder," he growled. "You're not even trying."

Safia looked: first up at the central altar, with its many flickering flames, then at the faces of all the holy Dianas. From there to the ground, hard-packed earth tainted with dark patches that might have been spills or stains. They might have been a lot of things and she didn't want to think about any of them. Finally she saw what he wanted her to see: a neat pile of shiny, polished bones. Arm bones and leg bones. Pelvises and skulls. All human. All the bones of girls.

He laughed when she gasped, a hideous sound not much like laughter, yet she was certain laughter was intended.

"I don't eat babies but I do eat little girls. High-born virgins or shanty gutter trash, you all taste the same when I'm hungry enough not to care."

In that moment, Safia understood. Every tale was true: the demon who lived in the bowels of the citadel—who had lived here since the time before the Ruin. Older even than the wars he fought in. Older than the mighty God-King and his priests. Some even whispered they were brothers. She'd never seen the God-King, but the Veteran was standing close. His dank breath filled the space between them, souring the air she fought to breathe.

She turned her head the smallest fraction, towards strange shadows splayed along the floor and walls. Harsh, jagged spikes. When the Veteran moved, the shadow spikes moved too.

"I told you to be still," he warned. "None have ever left here."

Was she to die by a sharp thrust of his blade? Some said his fingers had long rotted off, replaced with razors. His feet were hammers, his cock a coil of rust.

Atop the altar, the Princess smiled out through a hundred windows, her skin made soft by coercions of dark and flame.

"Is Diana buried here? Does she sleep in this holy place?" Safia closed her eyes—the only way she could squeeze words out at all. Her voice was dry as an abandoned well.

"What do you know of the People's Princess? You and your kind, you have no concept of blessings. Your minds are blasted hollow with false gods."

The blade pressed sharply through her shift. The stink of his breath enveloping.

"Why won't you let me see your face?" she blurted. When she opened her eyes, the Dianas seemed to smile. She would be brave and speak her mind as her Mama had spoken hers. Like Mama, she was dead already, so what could be the harm?

"Hers is the only face you want to see," he growled, and then, a heavy sigh like wind rattling through broken eaves. "So beautiful. Men died for that beauty. Women for the want of it. What makes you think she'd have time for the likes of you? Your petty causes. Your simpering demands. All you people ever do is *take*."

He spat that last word out like sour wine. She turned her head just a little more, winced at the knife dug harder into her back.

"Shut your eyes and I'll make it quick."

And she almost did exactly what he said, only in that last crucial second she did something else instead. Something stupid and crazy. Why not? Stupid and crazy had carried her through hunger and spirited her away from ill-intentioned guardsmen more times than she was capable of remembering.

Safia took a deep breath, then three brave leaps ahead. Right up to the altar, then spun around to face him.

The grotto echoed with a frantic clattering and clanging. Nobody stood behind her. Nothing but a sea of winking flames refracting off the walls and ceiling teeth. How could he possibly have moved so fast? *Demons travel faster than the winds.* She knew that. Everybody knew that.

"Why won't you let me see you?" The flowers were gone. She must have dropped them. The flowers didn't matter.

"They killed Diana, you know," said his voice from one of the darkened edges. "Hunted her down like a slavering pack of dogs. All across the land, the faithful had visions at the precise moment of her passing."

Silence again.

"I'm so sorry."

"Such a long time ago . . . "

"But you keep her memory alive."

"She's all that's left of beauty in this world." He sighed heavily, a sound like wind stirring through fallen leaves.

Silence upon silence. A sudden gust set a row of flames to flickering. She cast her gaze across the images of Diana, drawing strength from them, and courage. Young Diana, child Diana, Mother, Wife and Lady. "You're not a monster. You're a lonely old man. So old, you've forgotten how to die so you hide down here where no one else can see. They forced me in here. All I wanted was to see inside the citadel. To find my Mama or the ghost she has become."

"You don't want to see in there," he said. A quiet voice, every trace of the demon gone from it.

"Yes I do. More than anything."

"They'll hunt you and they'll kill you."

"They? Who are *they?* The ghosts?"

"The priests." He paused, considering his words carefully. "I can't let you pass. Princess Diana is my liege. I guard the entrance to the reliquary built for sainted bones: Saints Madonna, Theresa, Maria, Fatima, Diana. All the blessed holy, but Diana is my liege. She came to me in a dream and never left me."

Silence filled the grotto. Even the flame tips lay completely still.

"Tell me, Veteran. In that dream, did she ask you to kill for her?"

A long, silent pause and then the Veteran roared and charged.

She screamed, then clambered up the central altar, the safest place—the only place—candles tipping and spilling in all directions.

"How dare you desecrate *her* shrine," he bellowed.

There was nowhere to hide. Safia scrabbled on all fours, scattering figurines and offerings, dropping down behind the altar in a crouch, frozen in fear, not knowing where to go.

He came for her, a blur of meshed flesh and metal. She tried to leap to her feet, only suddenly he seemed to be coming at her from both sides at once, pinning her down with metal appendages that shot forth from some part of him she couldn't even see. The Veteran wasn't human. He wasn't even close.

Safia screamed.

"Be quiet!"

Fallen candles burned upon their sides, hot wax pooling and spilling across stone. Her trembling hand—the only part of her that she could move—reached out and righted the nearest.

"If you have cracked a single glass frame, I will kill you."

"You're going to kill me anyway," she whispered. "I saw Mama standing with her parasol. Inside the citadel when the walls went thin—I saw her!"

He snorted hot, foetid breath. "No you didn't. Your mother is dead. The priests took her. They take whatever they want. Everyone's dead and soon you will be too."

"You're not dead—you're talking to me!"

"I died in the wars."

"No you didn't!"

At this, he laughed. A sound like the rattling and scraping of tin cans mixed with the rusting squeal of ancient hinges.

"I'm a ghost, my stupid child. As dead as dead can be." He raised a blade above her head. Cold steel glinted in soft yellow light.

She fumbled for her own stone-sharpened blade. Not there—the washerwomen had taken it. "You won't hurt me," she sobbed. "Not in Diana's holy temple. Not in front of *her*."

His blade came down, stopped a hair's breadth from her neck. Safia screwed her eyes up tight.

And waited.

Nothing happened.

She waited for the longest time, then opened them a crack.

Up close now, yellow light revealing all. She found the part of him that most approximated a face, stared into what she hoped might be his eyes.

"What you saw was an illusion," he said softly. "No people dwell within the citadel. Nor ghosts. Just bones and dust. The blue is a weapon, same kind as protects us from the Dead Red's pilgrim hordes. But the citadel roots sink deep down into sand. Roots that suck up mineral replenishment."

The man he had once been still lived within his eyes.

"Get me inside the citadel," Safia pleaded. "I've nowhere else to go."

The Veteran didn't answer, but the metal tools that pinned her retracted one by one with a wheezing like the bellows on a pump.

Free at last, she didn't move. Diana watched them both in silence with her many, varied faces. Different ages, different skins. Not judging, just watching. Safia was beginning to like this ancient goddess.

"How long have you lived down here?" she asked.

"Long enough."

Moving slowly, so as not to startle him, she pushed herself gently to her feet, then waited until the grotto fell completely silent. She watched without staring as each of his extra appendages folded in upon itself, repacking and nestling beneath his leathered hide.

He turned away, blushing. "You can climb up through the roots, but it won't be easy. Most who chanced it died a nasty death."

"But some have tried it?"

"Aye. Straight up and in. A vein spiked into the living heart. It'll try to flush you out again, make no mistake. You might get in but you won't last long up top."

"I'll take my chances."

The Veteran coughed, a sound like scraping rust. "Touch only the dead roots. Be very quiet, moving like a skink below the sand. Hollow, flaccid things, those roots. They wither and drop off over time. The citadel tears them when it shifts and realigns. Some are choked with slime and ichor. Avoid the blue ones—that stuff will burn your flesh right to the bone."

"But how do I—"

"I didn't say it would be easy, shanty girl. You young want everything handed on a platter. In my day we'd have blasted holes clean through the fresh ones, drained them dry and hauled ourselves up through."

She smiled and nodded. "In your day. Come with me! Show me how."

"You're talking to a long-dead soldier. Not much sense in dying twice."

Safia smiled. She touched the nearest of Diana's faces. Gently. "Come with me. What if there's not just bones up there? What if—"

"Don't try and mess with my head, shanty girl. I'm giving you your life back, so now *get!*"

With that came an aggravated clanking, as though someone was hammering pots and pans. He pointed at a deep fissure set into the far wall, a crack she had thought nothing more than shadow.

"Thank you, Veteran. I'll prove you wrong, and I'll come back for you."

He laughed, a mean, dispirited sound. "You'll wind up dead as your long-dead Mama. I'll light a candle to your new-dead memory."

Too late. She was already on her way. When the sound of her had faded like mouse scratchings in the wall, he stepped out into the open, retracting the last of his spider-splayed appendages. Diana stared smugly from her scattered frames as he bent to pick them up.

"What are you gawking at?" he grumbled, shaking shattered glass shards down like rain.

Diana's soft voice echoed in his head. "Get on after her. You know it's time to—"

"Shut up. I'm not talking to you."

Diana laughed. "Of course you are. I'm the only one you ever talk to, day in, day out and all the brooding night-time in between."

He mumbled something incoherent, slammed the broken frames upon the altar top.

"You know I'm right," she continued. "You've outgrown this lair of polished bones. Get on after that shanty girl. Be a soldier once again—be a man. Give those priests what they've had coming since they killed their king and allowed his corrupted program to run rogue."

"Shut up shut up shut up," he said as he clamped his leathery palms across his ears. But he knew she was right—she was always right. It was time to move on, time to make a stand.

He brushed the sheen of crumbled glass from a faded photograph, tucked it into the pocket above his heart. "You'll wait for me?"

"Of course I'll wait." Diana smiled, benign and strong from a hundred picture frames as the Veteran strode boldly towards the fissure.

Cursebreaker: The Mutalibeen and the Memphite Mummies

Kyla Lee Ward

"Ah! Allah have mercy!"

"Hello to you too."

"Ouchioch! Osoronophris! Ouserrannouphthi! Do not touch me, foul *ghul!*"

"Now that's just rude . . . by the Fates, is this a *tomb*?"

Zakiyah bint Hayan had never believed in *ghuls*. But the flame of the lamp she carried revealed to her a woman pale as death and corpse-naked, and nearly as tall as the roof. This apparition had appeared as suddenly as if sprung from the walls around. Idolatrous images covered every inch of these walls: terrifying processions where men carried coffers and collars, and naked children, and live animals, towards monstrous, standing giants. The gazelles and ducks seemed yet to struggle against their fate, as the flame trembled in her hand.

"It *is* a tomb," said the *ghul*. A woman found this deep in the desert, so tall, strong and *naked*, could only be an eater of the dead. "Egyptian. Looking a little old and, despite what you just said, you are not a priest." Her eyes narrowed, which made her face no less a skull that had somehow retained its long, dark hair. "So what are you doing here?"

"Allah, have compassion on the line of Hayan!" Zakiyah cried. In that moment, she regretted the expedition, her disguise: everything she had done. "Though I sin, let me not be eaten!"

"Guess that answers my question. Salaam, friend treasure-hunter: I'm the Cursebreaker and you summoned me."

Zakiyah stared like an imbecile at the *ghul*'s white and rounded flesh.

The *ghul* sighed. "Look, an Egyptian curse generally isn't that serious a problem. We'll be done in no time. May I please borrow your coat?"

As Zakiyah felt the old, grey *binish* slipping from around her shoulders, she reacted instinctively. No one, not even a cannibalistic monster could touch her, or get close enough to discover her real sex. With another burst of what was probably gibberish (although the surrounding Greek had been clear enough), she drove the lamp into the obvious target and flung herself aside. As the *ghul* yelped and utter dark descended, she hit first the wall, then open space, and ran.

"Hey! I'm not here to eat you, I'm here to help you!"

When Zakiyah had descended into the tomb with her father's servants, they had discovered a huge chamber, empty except for the sand that had preceded them down the hole. But a succession of smaller rooms had led them to the stone door, its face unbroken, its seals intact. Rafq and Mubar had started work with the picks, while she had prepared the spell, which was titled (again, in Greek) "A rite that turns away the anger of the dead". Every *mutalib* knew the ancient treasures were protected by demons wielding knives, and this spell, the Greek gloss said, was in the ancients' own tongue. She had already prayed and performed her ablutions. The incense had been of the specified kind. Under the gaze of those stony giants, she had poured the libation and whispered the words. But the only effect had been disaster.

The sound of picks had ceased. She had glanced upwards to see old Mubar standing there with his big shoulders shaking, and face nearly as white as his hair. The eyes of the Hayan retainer had seemed to rove beyond the walls, and when Rafq questioned him, he had fled back towards the first chamber, and the rope. Rafq had drawn his scimitar and followed, telling her to tend the lamp and keep chanting. She had, switching to the prayer of deliverance for the first-born god. "*You who are lord above all; shield me against all evil magicks, the maleficence of daimons and fate . . .* "

Now, as the *ghul* raged behind her, Zakiyah stumbled through the utter darkness. When her outstretched fingers discovered another wall, she crept along it until she found another gap. By her reckoning, she should now be back in the first chamber. So she stepped out blindly, swinging her hands from side to side in search of the rope. Then behind her, still distant, a light blossomed.

"Whoa!" the *ghul* crowed, in her strangely-accented voice. "I just lit a lamp with a flint! I've never done that before. I suppose it was a flint. Look, hunter, boy: what should I call you? It's obviously some time after the Arab conquest, but have the British have arrived yet? Do you even know who they are? Say something!"

The light was growing stronger, coming closer. Then Zakiyah realised that she was now treading sand rather than ancient stone. The sand had been under the hole! She plunged forward, and immediately stumbled over something the shadows yet concealed. She fell headlong, arms out—

At the touch of cool flesh, Zakiyah jumped back up, stifling a scream. The back of her head hit something else, something that swung, just as the edge of the light caught up with her and the horror below wavered into sight. Rafq, O Allah, *Rafq*—

"There you are!" cried the *ghul*.

One mighty leap, and Zakiyah was swinging above the floor. The rope burned her bare feet as she grappled for purchase. Backwards, forwards she rocked; above the floor, but scarcely out of reach. Advancing any higher seemed to involve letting go with one hand, and that seemed completely and utterly impossible. She cried out as the light drew yet closer, illuminating pavings, carvings, a row of squared pillars, and at last the *ghul* herself.

And suddenly, it all fell away. Without any effort beyond clinging, she was being hauled upwards towards the roof. As she was dragged through the hole, she heard voices above. Had Mubar escaped the calamity?

"Wait!" Below her, the *ghul* pawed the air. "You summoned me! I have to help you, break the curse, or else I'm stuck here—by the Fates, *listen*!"

Zakiyah lay panting on sand, gazing up at the desert stars. They were the most beautiful thing in all creation and among the most meaningful. For the moment, the identity of the men gathered around her was irrelevant: why they spoke to each other only in low voices, with but a single lantern to illuminate the scene. For just this moment, it seemed possible that they too only desired to gaze on the stars.

All around them spread the great stone field of Saqqara. The Greek writers transmitted the name of Memphis, and what those buried here had called it, only Allah knew now. The mighty pyramid raised black steps into the sky, surrounded by a maze of half-ruined walls, standing columns and statues both shadowed and silvered. It was a landscape at once familiar to any of the house of Hayan (Rafq, eyes staring from a face sheeted in blood . . .) yet now utterly remade. The sandstorm had shuttered the city of Fustat for two days, and its passing still stained the horizon, where the dust in the air made the stars blur and shimmer as if through glass. The storm that had uncovered this accursed tomb.

The men around her were wearing *trousers.*

Zakiyah curled up like a cat protecting its belly. Some of the men laughed. There was no sign of Mubar, only a mass of strangers wearing the low-slung trousers of the *futuwwa.* But what were they doing here? The Young Men had their halls in Fustat. There was nothing to steal out here, nothing to drink, nothing to . . .

"A boy," a voice rasped from the shadows. "Some might say, but I call this a talisman. A charm fashioned for the protection of man. What is your name, boy?"

"Al—Al Jawbari!" It was the name she always gave, when she went out on the streets. The rasping man stepped into view, a monster with a gleaming eye and grotesquely hunched back.

"A Syrian? Well, I prefer Charm. Because you have emerged from a maw that has swallowed three of our number since the storm broke." Another gleam: the hunchback had drawn a blade. "So you see, Charm, I must know what you saw down there. What is that voice that wails even now, like a woman fucked by her brother?"

Swallow fear, Zakiyah told herself, along with grief. Above all else, let no one come near. For Al-Jawbari was indeed in dire trouble, but Zakiyah bint Hayan would know far worse.

. . .

"Well now, this is great." The Cursebreaker spoke loudly to the carven walls, but even though her Arabic was presumably as perfect as her Pharaonic Egyptian, no one answered.

In the totally incalculable time since she had become the Cursebreaker (cursed herself by threefold Fate and flung into eternity, with only immortality and her universal knowledge of languages for succour), since that distant day (which had been just before the mid-year exams), she had materialised in many places under many different circumstances. What they all had in common was a man or woman (or in one memorable case, an entire city), who had incurred a curse. They were usually quite distraught, and the young treasure-hunter wasn't the first to panic when the summoning actually worked. But he was the first to climb up a rope, leaving her stuck in a tomb while he went off and did the Fates knew what. Hopefully not die, but the curse would be following him. They always did. And at first glance, she had thought this might actually be simple!

As she'd tried to tell the little fellow (he'd been cute, too, with smooth skin and a mop of curly black hair), the curses on Egyptian tombs were professional jobs, which was always preferable to somebody operating with a grudge and raw talent. That mess she'd had to sort out in Wales, for instance, that didn't bear remembering: at least sober. But Egyptian curses were always written down. The entire curse with its conditions and qualifications was here on one of these walls, where a less magically-orientated culture might have placed a warning about the security system and fine imposed on trespassers. But the Egyptians were magical; they harnessed magic like other cultures harnessed wind and water. The . . . *royal chamberlain, overseer of the great mansion, Ankhm'ahor,* had been buried with food and clothing, furniture, jewellery and weapons in kind and effigy, because inclusion in the tomb meant possession in the spirit realm. The entire place was an ongoing magical ritual, which would have originally been overseen by attendant priests.

Obviously, he didn't appreciate his ritual being interrupted.

The corpse she had found lying beneath the hole in the ceiling had provided her with an attractively-striped galabeya, bearing only the slightest of bloodstains. It wasn't the first time she had stolen from the dead, or dressed as a man for that matter. It was amazing what men had worn throughout history: in another time or place, she would have been wearing a nightgown. If I could go back, she thought, and alter just one term of my curse, it would be that I appear in appropriate clothes.

But *this* man had been killed by a blade, something much smaller than the scimitar he had carried himself. And he wasn't alone. After a more thorough search of the entrance chamber (during which there wasn't so much as a peep from up above) and the rooms between it and the door where she had first appeared, she had a total of five dead, a skin of oil for the lamp and another of tarry-tasting water. In her reconstruction of events, the man with the scimitar had struck down a big, elderly fellow, whose only weapon had been a pick. He had, in turn, been stabbed in the back, as had one of the unfortunate pair of men in baggy trousers, who she had found behind the row of columns at the far end of chamber, well beyond the spill of sand. The hands of the one still gripped the other's throat.

She found the dagger itself in a small niche or closet off the second room. The defunct wielder was likewise small and wiry, clad in trousers and a yellow headclout. Here, the carvings depicted a procession of priests male and female, bringing the daily offerings of water and incense to sustain the blessed spirit and his patron deity, depicted here as his Pharaoh. The workmanship was exquisite: the translucency of the fabric expressed in delicate lines and the remnants of white pigment. From the equally fine glyphs, she learned that Ankhm'ahor was furthermore due bread and beer on the festival of Sokar, and the burning festival, but nothing about the curse.

"All right," she spoke to the carvings, and the dead man. "Let's try and reason this out. If we take the Trousers for a separate party to that of my young summoner, then I guess they entered first and promptly killed each other, all except this one. Then, the second party entered. The fellow with the scimitar did for the old guy with the pick, only to be stabbed by Yellow Headclout here, who I guess must have stabbed himself somewhere, I can't quite—"

"Aargh! He wakes, he wakes!"

"Steady now." Jumping back through the doorway, the Cursebreaker eyed the bare-chested man, taking note of his dark-flushed face, bulging eyes and the drool trickling down his chin.

The dagger, once loosely clasped in hand, now hovered in the air between them. "All right, so you're *not* dead. And before you jump to any rash conclusions, I'm not a *ghul*."

"Die, says Yousef! All who trespass must die, that he remain sleeping!"

"Damn."

. . .

"Speak to me, brother, of the proper remedy for *ghuls*," said the hunchback, who called himself Al-Uqab.

"Dismemberment," replied his second, a tall and lanky fellow whose face was so scarred he could only manage one moustache. "And yet a *ghul* is a fearsome opponent. The tales often say it is best to approach them with a suitable offering. Their hunger sated, they may be reasoned with."

"This suggests that there is more than one." Al-Uqab stroked his own luxuriant facial hair. "For one *ghul* alone could not consume such plenitude as our three brothers. Added to the former possessors of this charm. Speak, Charm."

"I saw but one *ghul*, and none of your beneficent brethren, O legend among thieves," said Zakiyah, thinking, the real Eagle died in Babylon a hundred years ago, you crooked-pissing fool. And he was a thief!

Thieves could be relied upon for a degree of professionalism. The Young Men were thugs, drunkards and eaters of *bhang* who took money from shopkeepers in return for not disrupting their trade. Members of their fraternity were often guests in Fustat's prison, a circumstance of which the entire city became aware as the trouser-wearing hoard descended on the Zuweyla Gate, roaring like desert beasts and smashing stands and shutters. Even on the Street of Scholars, you could hear them.

Their purpose here was obvious enough: despite the repeated deaths in the stone fields and constant official warnings, they fancied themselves *mutalibeen*, capable of extracting treasure from the grip of the ancients. As Zakiyah had fancied herself.

" . . . come from, Charm?"

"Fustat, O great one."

"Well of course, Fustat! You're no Berber. Those soft cheeks—" A harsh hand came groping, and she flinched away. "—and curls didn't spring from the desert!" The hunchback bent close now, studying her more carefully. "What's your family, Charm? Who's going to miss you, eh?"

"I am of the house of Hayan the Mutalib."

"A servant, eh?"

"I tend upon Hayan, who is great of years. This morning, very early, I accompanied his men into the desert. Now . . . now they are all dead."

"And so are our brothers," said Scarface. "Let us take what we have already collected back to the apothecary and sell this boy to the Berbers on the way."

"I know the spells that bind the ancient demons," she spoke steadily, despite the sudden thudding of her heart. "Hayan trained me himself."

"Spells, you say?" rasped Al-Uqab.

"They would appear to have been of limited utility," spoke Scarface. "Given the rest of his party is dead."

"The spells protected me," she said. "Because I am . . . pure."

Some of the shadows laughed at this, but not Al-Uqab.

"That should net a higher price," said Scarface.

"We had just broken through the door of the burial chamber when the *ghuls* attacked. I saw gold," she said, shifting ever so slightly towards the hunchback. "Glinting in the light from our lamps."

"Gold and jewels, I'm sure," spoke Scarface, "and the cure for leprosy as well. Come, brother, the longer we delay, the more likely the Naqeeb will catch—"

"Hayan was a great *mutalib*!" Her voice sounded too high, she lowered it quickly. "He retrieved exactly such things!"

"This is but a tale of the evening!" Scarface raised his hands.

"And yet, the boy lives," Al-Uqab stroked his beard. "There may indeed be gold in that tomb. Or there may be more of such items as we have already collected."

"Yousef would have preferred gold," said one of the shadows. "*I* would prefer that my brother died for gold, rather than a load of black-faces."

"O thou deficient in mind," cried Al-Uqab. "You are deaf as well, and must now run with the beggars. I have repeatedly told you how the apothecaries in Fustat and Damascus will pay the weight in gold—or good value, at any rate—for such corpses.

"Bodies such as are safe from *ghuls*." The hunchback bent towards Zakiyah, loosening the neck of a large sack. "Bodies such as these." She repressed another squeak as she saw a human hand. It was gnarled and blacker than any southerner, but for all that perfect in every detail, down to the glassy nails. Had a craftsman among the Unfaithful contrived it, he would have been a master. But it had not been contrived; the ancients had practised such techniques upon their dead to preserve them, as they had protected them with bound demons and terrible curses.

Al-Uqab made an expansive gesture. "We shall return this charm to the tomb. What's the matter?" For she had flinched again. "You won't be in any danger, if you spoke true."

"If—if I bring you treasure, will you set me free?"

"Retrieve us such a body and any gold that might happen to accompany it. Then we shall discuss drawing you back out, and perhaps granting your master the option of ransom."

"Douse the lamp!" Scarface hissed like a startled cobra. "See, see the torches! I told you, it is the Naqeeb Al-Mutalibeen!"

Zakiyah achieved one glimpse of the flickering stream of light entering the stone field, painting the near walls bright and plunging the far into darkness, before rough hessian smothered her. The stench of pitch was overwhelming and the ghastly hand seemed to paw at her as the Young Men secured their charm. *O, you who are lord above all; shield me . . .*

. . .

"So, Yousef is you, right? "

"Yousef says that all must die!" With one hand, the lunatic kept unravelling his head clout. The other held the dagger ready. The Cursebreaker held the lamp and kept stepping backwards, slowly.

"Who told you that, Yousef?" she asked. "When you broke into the tomb, did someone tell you that? What did you see?"

Yousef drooled. The veins stood out on his forehead and in his thick, red neck. *His blood pressure's through the roof*, the Cursebreaker thought, *and his adrenaline levels must be toxic. He can't last much longer.*

When did she become so cold?

She smiled, as kindly as she could manage. "Please Yousef," she said. "I know that you're frightened, but you don't need to be frightened of me. I'll not wake old Ankhm'ahor, and if you just calm down, we can sort all this out." She reached out towards his shaking hand.

The blade flashed, and pain shot up her arm. For a moment she saw red welling from her pale skin, marking the dagger's passage. Then the red retreated, closing the cut behind it. By the time the dagger had cleared her arm, the wound was gone. So that was how immortality worked. By the Fates, it still hurt.

She turned and sprinted. *Just* two *terms, two little refinements of my curse . . .*

Once she was back in the first chamber, she dropped the lamp. The flame flickered, but didn't expire. She kicked sand, but she was already halfway across the floor. Exposed in the light, she glanced around at the mound, the columns: up at the hole. "Hey, treasure-hunter! If you can hear me, this might be your only chance!"

"Yousef says what's cut should *stay* cut!"

She angled for the pile of sand and bodies, and leapt nimbly to the other side. But despite his flailing, Yousef proved sure-footed and landed right behind her. He'd probably been just the man to send down a rope into an unexplored tomb: the last man standing when this act incurred a curse of homicidal mania. Nice choice, Ankhm'ahor.

It wasn't affecting her, she noted, dodging through the columns where the strangler and his victim lay. But then, the ordinary run of curses never did. So far as she could tell, the almighty curse of her nature subsumed all others. But—as Yousef skidded through the gap, she dodged behind a column bearing a life-sized portrait of a remarkably fat man—her summoner had not been mad either. Terrified, yes: but not mad.

Was *she* terrified? Was not even that much humanity left to her?

As the lamp flickered, the carvings on the wall behind the columns seemed almost to dance with tiny shadows. Yousef stopped dead, watching them. Pictures of dancers, a row of sandblasted women, each raising one leg above her own head. Sand, lots of sand in this corner as well. Stealthily as she could, she began to move. Yousef turned towards her.

"Double damn."

"*He must sleep!*" Yousef plunged forward, blade raised. The Cursebreaker ducked through the colonnade and headed back across the hall towards the lamp. And halted, when she realised her pursuer was viciously attacking the column. The portrait rather, she decided. That must be of Ankhm'ahor himself.

If that was enough to keep Yousef occupied, she might just return to the first chamber. None of the men had died in there, but they had definitely been working on breaking down that door . . .

Suddenly, bright light broke over her from above.

"You down there, don't think you can hide!" It wasn't the boy speaking. This voice was at once deeper and snappier, suggesting a full-grown man with an equally well-developed sense of his own importance. "We heard you screaming," he called. "So give yourselves up!"

Blinking frantically, she replied, "Who so addresses the cursed?"

"Why, no more than the Naqeeb Al-Mutalibeen!"

The Caliph's Officer, in charge of all Treasure Hunters? "Then Allah is merciful! O great one, please extract me from this place before I am devoured by *ghuls*!"

"Who are you?" demanded the vague silhouette.

"Ah . . . but a humble servant of the house of Hayan!"

"Hayan? And is the old man now so deficient in mind, as to think himself beyond the law? He has not applied for a license in twelve years! Tax evading miscreant: say I leave you down there, as a lesson to all?"

She sighed. She was going to regret this, only not as much as she would staying here. "Oh please Sir," she cried. "Despite this garb I am no *mutalib*! I am but a woman used most cruelly!" And heaved her chest a little.

"By my death!" swore the Naqeeb.

"I was abducted this morning by—by the most foul ruffians, and brought here as an offering for the demons within!"

At that moment, Yousef let out an obliging shriek. She shrieked herself and in response to this bit of drama, something slithered above her. She looked up, only to get an eyeful of sand, and was slapped in the face by an uncoiling rope.

"Ouch!"

"Yousef says—*wait*!"

She grabbed hold and was hauled rapidly upwards. Below her, Yousef staggered into view. She lifted her feet out of his reach, which set her to spinning as the men above heaved. The madman swiped at her with a mangled stub of steel. His eyes bulged and blood ran slick from his lower lip as he wailed. But it seemed to her the swipes were at least partially attempts to grasp hold, and in the wails was a plea he not be left alone.

• • •

"They have extracted one from out the tomb," reported Scarface. "And are interrogating him."

"Yousef?" Al-Uqab enquired, but Scarface shook his head. "Slippery Ahmed? You think it one of the Charm's party, then."

Despite the weight on her back, Zakiyah's heart leapt. Mubar had escaped after all! Instead of the gulf of death, all that separated them now was a mere fifty cubits or so, of mostly flat desert. She knew this because she had been dragged across it, and then slung over a low wall, or something. But the bag was still over her head and Al-Uqab was pushing her down into the sand. "One shout," he had rasped, "one cry, one overloud fart will be your death."

She could hardly breathe. The black hand was hard and cold as wood, and those nails jabbing into her cheek felt like broken glass. Her own hands were twisted beneath her, and the weight and stench of the hunchback's sweat was like every nightmare she had ever had.

But the Naqeeb was there. When laying their own, hasty plans during the storm, Mubar had judged that the Caliph's officer would take at least another day to reach the stone field, having to sort through the license applications and assemble a proper complement of guards. Perhaps he was even hunting the Young Men. A noise, a signal, somehow she must contrive . . .

"I counted eight soldiers," continued Scarface, "armed with scimitar and bow."

"And we are now but eight ourselves," said Al-Uqab. "Whatever lies within the tomb, lies beyond us now." This caused a general rustle of agreement.

With a tremendous effort, she managed to turn her head. "Gold," she whispered. "I swear by—"

Pain drove phantom lights into her skull, as her face was ground into the sand. The motion shifted her—for an instant she could move her hands. Instinctively she clawed at the sack and as Al-Uqab resettled himself, she was clutching the dead hand like a saviour.

" . . . slit his throat." Scarface, again. "Only way to be sure."

"O, thou deficient in mind!" The weight shifted. "One by one we shall depart. Once all others are safe, I shall bring the boy."

"You are certain, brother?"

"If he does not behave, I shall kill him myself. Go now, and wait for me by that giant pair of feet which fronts the avenue of rams!"

She lay absolutely still, her face throbbing. Tried not to breathe. Let him think her stunned, perhaps already dying. Give him no reason to suspect that once they were alone, that she, that Al-Jawbari . . . what could she possibly *do* that wouldn't result in a sharp sting across her throat, her blood gushing into the sand like a goat at the butcher's . . .

How could she pray? By her sorceries and impious masquerade, she had placed herself beyond the concern of the Compassionate. What more proof need she, than the way the *ghul* had appeared, as if in answer to her supplication?

Of course she was a *ghul*. A woman discovered this deep in the desert: what else could she be?

Zakiyah's grip tightened on the ancient hand.

As the sixth shuffling sound receded into the night, the hunchback's hand returned to her, rough and hot, and this time merciless. She did not move, as he groped and squeezed as if seeking to judge the quality of fruit in the market. It was bad, and terror sent pangs into her stomach. Any moment now, he would realise. But inch by inch, his motions permitted her to draw the dead hand into position. She would only get one chance.

"To think that my brother would prefer you a corpse. Lop-sided degenerate, what a treasure is here! You understand how this goes, don't you my Charm? What a little favour gets you? What a clever boy, what a sweet—what in Allah's name is *this*?"

"O thou deficient in mind!" she hissed. "To believe you drew a boy from out a tomb. But you're so *plump and juicy*!"

• • •

"And so at long last, I gaze upon the countenance of the daughter of Hayan." The Naqeeb pursed his lips as a slight frown puckered his forehead. "I would that it had been some years sooner."

When she'd first cleared the roof of the tomb, there had been gasps and murmurs of unease, but the Naqeeb had barked orders and draped a sweaty horse blanket over her head. He was still the only one who would come anywhere near her, or the hole that gaped at the edge of the firelight. Even though it was some time now, since Yousef's screams had died away.

She fingered the edge of the blanket, and dropped her eyes to his gold-embossed boots. "Do I disappoint you, O great one?"

"It is no matter. There is in truth only one reason for father to leave daughter unwed so far past her prime."

Oh thank you, thought the Cursebreaker. The Naqeeb himself was okay, if you liked oiled beards and a bit of a belly, but nowhere near as pretty as her summoner. Her curly-haired, smooth-cheeked summoner with the big, long-lashed eyes, who panicked when she started to remove his coat . . .

The Naqeeb took a few restless steps. "Do you know how many times I petitioned your father? The stubborn old goat; and this for a concubine's child! A northern concubine, by your skin."

He'd never even seen the poor girl. At least, that he knew. The Cursebreaker took a quick glance around, and wondered how best to raise the subject of a missing boy. She could not see him anywhere in the impromptu campsite. Soldiers in quilted jackets cut thorn bushes and watered horses: the nearest cover was a ruined wall, protruding from the sand at the other extreme of the light.

"He knew I had fathomed his secret." Suddenly, the Naqeeb was there, squatting right in front of her. "The secret of the house of Hayan." And the smile spreading across his face had indeed nothing to do with lust. Nonetheless, his voice took on a wheedling quality. "How cruel, not merely to deny you a husband, but to force you to accompany him on his expeditions." He leaned closer. "Was that your father wailing below?"

"No, O great one."

"This is a unlicensed expedition. I am well within my rights to leave him."

"O great one, I was in truth abducted—myself and a boy, who is my servant. A most lovely and innocent child—"

"But you know the spells, don't you?" He nodded encouragingly, which made his beard drip. "Only one of the sorcerer's bloodline may incant the spells to bind the ancient dead." And now the frown was back. "And you are yet pure?"

"I—great one, I beg you. Help me find the child."

"Is this child the secret, then?" He rocked back. "Did Hayan sire a *son* and disguise him as a servant?"

"Find him," she said, "and you may see the truth for yourself."

It was then that a rasping scream broke across the peaceful crackling of the fire, the whickering of the horses. It came from a section of the wall, and soldiers were already running towards it, scimitars in hand. Before they could reach it, a monstrous figure appeared over the top, like a huge bird with the face of a bearded man. Another glance: it was a man with a grotesquely deformed back, which turned every motion of his arms into flapping. Dark droplets sprayed across the sand from his bleeding throat.

"*Ghul*!" He screamed, "She's a *ghul*!" He lost his balance and fell.

As one, every bearded face turned towards the Cursebreaker.

"I believe he meant whatever's griefing him behind the wall," she said. The vanished hunchback moaned, and at least some of the faces turned back towards the sound. But no one was now advancing. Taking a good grip on the blanket, she stood up.

"Nock your bows," ordered the Naqeeb. His face was several degrees paler than it had been. "And keep the fire high."

The Cursebreaker raised her eyes to the desert stars. "This is my task," she said. As the Naqeeb opened his mouth, she raised one hand. "I am the daughter of Hayan and vessel of his magic. I assure you, O great one, I know more about curses than anyone else here."

With all the dignity she could muster, she strode forward. The Naqeeb didn't stop her. None of the soldiers stepped in her way, or even whispered as she passed.

Behind the wall, once her eyes had adjusted to the shadow, she found the moaning, trembling hunchback. The fall seemed to have hurt him more than the *ghul*, who had only managed a series of shallow claw marks. "You'll live," she told him. "That is, if you stay down."

In the sand, she found the scuff of feet. Most of the tracks ran straight, away from the wall and towards whatever cover had seemed best. But one pair followed the wall. Once the wall ended, they ducked across to the plinth of a ruined statue, and continued in this way, slowly arcing around the edge of the fire. She was creeping herself now, only hoping that the hunchback's moans would keep the arrows pointing the other way.

She found the slim figure in the *binish* hunkered in a ditch not far from the hole. Those big eyes watched silently, as she knelt down beside her. "You're not a *ghul*," she whispered to them. "Or a boy."

"And you aren't Mubar." Her summoner turned her attention back to the camp. "I'm guessing you aren't a *ghul* either."

"As I said before, I'm the Cursebreaker."

"We can try to steal one of their horses." The girl's voice didn't hold much hope. "The young men fled into the ruins, but in the dark we might get through."

The Cursebreaker shook her head. "There's only one way out for either of us." She pointed towards the hole. The rope still lay beside it, secured to a spread of pitons. "After you," she said.

• • •

Zakiyah bint Hayan decided she had been too hasty in revising her judgement of the stranger. The so-called Cursebreaker was wearing Rafq's galabeya, and had clearly taken what she wanted from all the bodies. And before descending, she had loosened the pitons and pulled the rope down behind them, trapping them both in the tomb. If that didn't make her a *ghul*, then what did?

Right now, the pallid monster was using the lamp to peruse the carvings around the stone door. Zakiyah sat with Rafq's scimitar across her knees, staring at the stain of Mubar's blood. The old servant had abetted her every effort to maintain the household and her father's reputation after his wits had fled. Once Hayan's guard on his desert expeditions, Rafq, too, had been loyal. But not sufficiently, it seemed, to prevent him from severing Mubar's neck.

" . . . and that's why an Egyptian curse can generally be reversed. They just want everything to stay the way it was. All we have to do—" Interrupting herself with a great sigh, the Cursebreaker straightened back up. "Is find the curse itself."

"This is the curse." Zakiyah slumped forward, gaze still glued to the blood. "What more do you need to see?"

"I need to know the precise conditions that triggered it. I mean, obviously sinking that pick into the door did the trick, but was it 'whosoever shall work harm upon my house of eternity?' I don't think so, because there's no sign that Yousef did any defacing before he went mad. But it can't be 'whosoever shall enter my tomb', because you didn't go mad."

"I cast the spell," she said dully. "It was supposed to bind the demons from harming any of us. But it only worked for me. I am pure."

"Hmm, yes, well. From what I remember, the Ancient Egyptians weren't so fussy about that. Not the last time I was there, certainly. They were more concerned with *ritual* purity. A binding spell, you say?"

"A rite that turns away the anger of the dead," she recited drearily.

"Is that why the first thing I heard you say was the name Ousir?"

"It was just gibberish," she said. "Magical words."

"Ah, no, it isn't. You really don't know? You were speaking Greek earlier, weren't you? The Greeks called him Osiris, the Egyptian Hades. Not that that's really accurate: the Egyptians had a rather different idea of death."

"I don't understand anything you've just said!" Although part of her speech *had* sounded familiar, just those two syllables.

"Ousir is the Egyptian god of the dead. He's that figure there with the crown." The *ghul* pointed towards the wall, quite close to Zakiyah's head.

"Stay back!" She grabbed the scimitar, by hilt and blade. "Stay away from me! O, *you who are lord above all; shield me . . .* "

She kept it up until realising that the *ghul* was reciting it with her.

"Yes, that was the summoning. A very poetic one. I must say, you are the best-educated person I've met in—oh, I don't know. A very long time. Look, Zakiyah, or whatever you want to call yourself." The *ghul* had something approaching compassion in her dark eyes. "It's not the first time I've been summoned by someone who well, wasn't expecting me."

What was I expecting? Zakiyah wondered. For all my troubles to just *stop*?

Suddenly, she felt unbearably weary.

"And I'm sorry about your friends. They succumbed before I got here. The thing is, though, the first thing I heard you say wasn't the summoning: it was, 'the beautiful being, Ousir of the good name.'"

"I don't understand."

"No, you don't. To you it was just some magic words, taught to you by your father who learned them from his father and so on . . . yes; your father, the secret: I got all that up top from the Naqeeb."

"He . . . he knows?" She glanced back at the blackness of the vestibule. "About me?"

"Apparently, he's been trying to marry you for years. To get the words, I might add."

No wonder he had insisted her father apply for his license in person. And her father, why hadn't he told her? Had he thought she would want it? Or had all his care, his teachings, their secret come down to *keeping* her! "Those are the secrets of the house of Hayan!" It came out a sob. "They are my birthright!"

"Ssh! Keep it down! If Yousef is still alive, then he's likely to be very close by."

Zakiyah fell silent. The Cursebreaker had warned her that one of the Young Men survived, though with his mind devoured by demons. Just as age had devoured her father's mind. He would be better off dead, and now, so would she.

All the time she had been struggling for her life against the Young Men, she hadn't realised. Even if she somehow escaped from the tomb and got past the Naqeeb, she was still a full day's journey from Fustat, with no supplies and above all, no escort. Making it through the desert would be a miracle exceeded only by that of getting through the Zuweyla Gate and back to the Street of Scholars.

Even that would be no use. Because without her confidants, there was no way she could continue her masquerade: answering her father's letters, paying his taxes and the household bills, protecting her mother, repelling a suitor who was the Caliph's own officer . . .

She gripped the hilt of the scimitar in her hand, feeling its cold striations. She had gambled everything on this expedition, and the *ghul*—woman—*thing* she had supposedly summoned was prattling on about the incense she had burned and the water poured before the door. As if that was important! As if the spell had done anything more than condemn her to a death as slow and agonising as anything the Imans would have ordered, had her flouting of Allah's law, above the mere laws of the *mutalibeen*, been discovered.

She could reveal herself to the Naqeeb and beg his protection.

She stood up. The *ghul* was bending over the remains of her little ritual. "That's it, then," the creature said. "That's how we break the curse. Though I don't know how we're going to get—"

"Hey *futuwwa*, you diseased prick!" Zakiyah yelled louder than she ever had in her life. "Over here! Come here and see what kind of charm I am! Understand that a *charm* got the better of you!"

"No Zakiyah, wait—" But as the Cursebreaker turned, a hideous wail rang from out of the darkness.

Zakiyah readied the scimitar. She knew it was too heavy for her to wield, but if she could strike just one blow in her own vengeance . . . . But then, as a red-faced maniac burst into the room, blood and froth spilling down his chest, eyes veined with crimson, the *ghul* threw the water skin at his head.

The impact stopped him as surely as the scimitar could have. As the liquid ran through his hair, down his chest, he was teetering, chest heaving in shock. He stopped waving around the stub of a dagger, and started beating at his own face.

"Steady on, Yousef." The *ghul* was approaching him now, very cautiously.

"What are you doing?" Zakiyah snarled. "Stand aside and let me finish him!"

"No. Because I can't leave until we break the curse and as *you* aren't cursed, it has to be him . . . that's right, Yousef, just calm down." Slipping behind him, she slipped an arm around the man's chest.

"This dog killed Rafq!" Zakiyah felt her wrist beginning to tremble, under the weight of the scimitar.

"I think you'll find that Ankhm'ahor doesn't care about that either. Ah! Easy—"

The man thrashed, and a lean-muscled arm broke free. "Yousef says that all must die!"

"Yousef says he must lie down," said the Cursebreaker through gritted teeth, as she held on.

"Yousef says . . . lie down." The man dropped with a whoosh of air. He slumped so bonelessly at the *ghul*'s feet that Zakiyah thought he must have died.

But the *ghul* bent closer. "Yousef says, 'Ouserrannouphthi'."

The bleeding lips moved. "Yousef says—"

"Those words are mine!" She hefted the scimitar.

"They are an invocation of the Egyptian god of the dead, that somehow survived in a Greek manuscript for a *mutalib*'s daughter to recite phonetically while making the prescribed offerings. If you ever wanted to witness a miracle—not to mention get back to Fustat with your disguise intact—then stop waving that thing about and help me teach him. There should still be enough water left for the libation."

"But . . . " Finger by finger, the scimitar sank towards the floor. "You think *he's* pure?"

"Zakiyah, you didn't survive because you were a virgin, or because you bound the spirit of Ankhm'ahor. You survived because *he thought you were a priest.*"

• • •

Once the rite of offering had been completed, and Yousef had recovered somewhat, the three of them stole back into the entrance chamber. With Zakiyah's consent, the Cursebreaker had given the fellow Rafq's galabeya, and herself taken the *binish*.

In the chamber, all was as silent as stone. The only thing that fell through the crack was a pale, greyish light.

Dawn? The Cursebreaker stared; was it dawn already? Now that the curse had been broken, she might have only moments remaining here, and there were still things that she needed to do. That she wanted to do. She turned to her companions. Yousef still looked pretty wild, although he was breathing easily now. Zakiyah was sunk deep in thought.

"You understand that this tomb was not originally buried," she said. "When the Pharaoh who lies in the Stepped Pyramid lived, they formed a city around it. A city of the dead."

"Attended by priests both male and female, who came with prayers and offerings," said Zakiyah, then her lips twisted. "So priests are like Imans? It would have been a fine thing, to live in the days when women could hold such rank."

"The ancient gods are all still there." Her own lips twisted. "Not realising that was *my* mistake. But if there's one thing that being the Cursebreaker has taught me, it's that every different era has its own problems." She paused, thinking, this one would have made a wonderful student. Become a linguist perhaps, or archaeologist. Here, the best she can hope for is to pass completely unnoticed.

"But there are always opportunities, too. For instance, if you were to look over there."

The pale light painted the faces of the columns and sections of the wall behind them. It revealed quite clearly, that the damaged carvings broke completely around an eroded rectangle. It looked a lot like the door they had left behind, but again the light made it clear that the rectangle was not stone, but layers of packed sand. The pick would make short work of it. "That's your way out. I fancy you'll come out in that ditch we were hiding in."

"Our way out?" Zakiyah frowned. In that moment, she could have passed very nearly for the Naqeeb. "What are you going to—"

"Yousef!" the Cursebreaker cried, and the man jumped. "You who were formerly of the brethren of the Young Men—do not protest the oath you swore! That life is behind you. Know you that I am not mortal?"

"Y—yes . . . "

"This good sorceress summoned me and bound me to her protection while in the desert. I now bind you to her service and protection as you journey back to the city, and for all the years thereafter. You are to obey her absolutely: in return, she will have you in her household and make of you a respectable servant. Fail her in any way and the madness from which she saved you will return. Do you understand?" The man nodded frantically, as Zakiyah looked from him to her, and back again. "Good. Now, Zakiyah, I appreciate you're a bit hard up, but I'm sure you now appreciate that no good can come of robbing tombs."

"Indeed," Zakiyah said fervently, still glancing sidelong at her new servant. He was still nodding.

"But they can still help you. Your knowledge of them, what you have observed here and what you learned from your father . . . may I suggest that you write a book?"

"A book?" As though the words were a flint, Zakiyah's face lit up. "I *could* do that! I could say it was by Al-Jawbari . . . and if Yousef handles all the copying, then none need ever see me. Zakiyah . . . Zakiyah could die in the desert."

"Promising to reveal the secrets of Hayan should attract plenty of readers." Zakiyah's frown deepened. "Oh, you don't have to reveal the real ones. But, teach people to respect these old places.

Emphasise their dangers. And of course, make yourself sound so manly and courageous that no one will ever question—"

And here it came. The first spark of true daylight, lipping the crack like molten metal about to pour down and gild the floor below, preserving Mubar and Rafq, and Yousef's dead brothers for all eternity. She, it would dissolve. She drew a breath and spread her hands. *To break a curse I never even saw, now that's a first.*

But already she could hear another voice intoning the words, the meaning the same whether recited as poetry or gasped in agony, whether in Greek, in Arabic, Egyptian, English, Sioux, Korean, Maori, Chinese, Scythian, Peruvian . . . *You who are lord of all the angels, shield me from fate . . .*

Lift you His judgement . . .

Lighten my dharma . . .

Please, please, won't somebody help?

Al-Jawbari is the author of The Unveiling of Secrets (Kashf al-Asrar), which describes his experiences as a treasure hunter and con artist in 13th century Cairo. The tomb curse of Ankhm'ahor is inscribed on the exterior of his mastaba, just beside the front door. "As to anything you might do against this my tomb of the necropolis, it will be done the same against your property for I am an excellent lector priest, knowing the book, never was any efficient magic hidden from me. As to all people who will enter into this tomb in a state of impurity . . . I will seize him forcefully as a bird, the fear of me is cast in him, so that spirits and those upon earth see and fear."

The Fruits of Revolution

Eleanor R. Wood

The guy in the alley wasn't my typical client. My regulars were antioxidant junkies or buyers procuring goods for ill family members. This guy was new, and the new ones were usually nervous, edgy, terrified of being caught. They weren't sure what they wanted or they were clueless of the cost. But he was confident and discreet from the outset, handing over a loaded credit chip before we'd even discussed business. I noted the flicker of his gaze as he sized me up. Young, slender, female . . . everything he wasn't. *Yeah, keep looking, mate. Snap judgements only make my job easier.*

I plugged the chip into my tablet and the relevant app pinged to life, confirming a hefty sum. I whistled. "I take it we're not talking dried goods. You after seeds? Fresh stuff?"

"Fresh," he said, eyes shadowed under his wide-brimmed hat. "And I'm not just talking greens. I need fruit too."

"Ah." The six-digit amount made sense. "You know I can't guarantee that, right?"

He wasn't put off. "My client was very specific. Apples, oranges, lemons—whatever you can get, and plenty of it."

Right. He was a go-between. The kind of sub-dealer really anxious clients would use. Really *rich*, really anxious clients. Guys like this didn't come cheap, any more than the goods did.

"I'll see what I can do. I take it the chip's not activated till handover?"

He snorted. "My client may need a go-between, but he's no fool."

"I'm sure he isn't. But I'll need something up front to cover my costs. I don't grow the stuff myself, you know."

He nodded. "How much?"

"Fifty percent."

"Yeah, right. I'd never see you again."

"I have to pay my suppliers. Fruit doesn't come cheap to me either."

"Thirty percent, then. I doubt your fellas are awash with buyers."

I narrowed my eyes. He was right. They risked everything importing the goods, with no guarantee they'd offload the stuff. I figured they deserved an even cut. Their risk was greater than mine, and they provided a lucrative line of business.

"Fine," I sighed. "Give me access to thirty percent and I'll contact you when I've got it."

He nodded and stalked off. Experienced clients had their plusses and minuses. This guy struck a hard deal, but at least he knew his business. And he hadn't tried to shake my hand on it. The rookies did that almost every time.

. . .

I managed to avoid two night patrol units en route to my next stop. I heard the nearby megaphone orders of a third as I trotted down the steps to Hal's basement flat. I'd been caught out past curfew twice in the past three weeks, and I knew I'd be tagged if they caught me again this month.

I rapped on Hal's door and double-blinked to deactivate the recording chip in my temple. It was rare black market tech, a prototype. I'd got it cheap for beta testing, though it worked like a charm. It was smart to record client transactions, but I wouldn't put my best suppliers at risk. The chip would reactivate itself in an hour's time unless I overrode it again. I only stored what I needed, deleting most of my dull daily-goings-on. Hal opened the door a crack before unbolting the chain to let me in.

"Hey, Ro," he said, stepping aside. "I didn't expect you again this week."

"I've got a repeat order for you, along with a new one you could partially supply."

"Come through," he said, leading the way through his low-ceilinged apartment. "The faster I harvest, the quicker this bunch seem to grow."

Hal had been in the business long before the ban. He and his wife April had grown vegetables in an allotment, and he swore he'd seen no evidence of the blight the Agricultural Ministry said was in the soil. When they'd come with their supposed anti-blight crop sprays, April had opposed them. They had forcibly injected her with a powerful sedative, and she died along with all their plants. Her death was one of many as people defended their orchards, garden plots, and patio tubs. I knew Hal defied the law as much to honour April as to keep doing what he loved. And his goods were among the best quality I could get.

He unlocked the door to a back room, the warmth from within hitting me as I stepped through. The small windowless room was full of tall racks of plants arranged in a grid. Banks of bright lights gave the room a stark appearance, but the plants loved it. They stretched up towards the light, jostling each other for position.

Most of Hal's current crop were tomatoes. Their distinctive peppery scent filled the air and many of the plants were laden with heavy red fruit. I spotted lettuces as well, and what looked like bean seedlings in one corner.

"Was it the same again?" Hal asked, the twinkle in his eye suggesting he was as proud to show off his babies as he was glad of an outlet for them.

I nodded.

"What was the new order?" he asked as he tenderly plucked fat tomatoes and placed them in a burlap bag.

"I've got a buyer who wants as much fresh as I can get. I figured you might be able to help out with some of it."

"Sure. You can see what I've got right now."

"Yeah. All looks great. This guy's after fruit too, though."

"Tree fruits?"

"Yup. He has expensive tastes."

"Wish I could help. I thought about trying some dwarf apples, but even if I could get hold of dwarf seeds, I doubt they'd thrive indoors."

"You'd know better than me; I just deal the stuff. I'll be back once I've sourced the rest of the order."

He handed me the bag of tomatoes. "Look out for those patrols, now," he said as I paid him and left.

I grinned. I'd never be careless enough to be caught carrying goods. That'd earn me far worse than a tag. I rounded his building, climbed the fire escape, and took my well-practised route over the rooftops to my drop point. My client was waiting on her own roof as arranged, and we exchanged goods and payment in silence.

Once she'd gone, I descended the nearest fire escape to pavement level and made my way home, sticking to the shadows.

• • •

I changed and shook out my dreadlocks, still undecided on their new purple look. I grabbed a vitamin bar and sat down to read the Government-Accepted news pages. VitaCorp had just patented a new immune-boosting drug. Their marketing slogan, 'An Immuno a day keeps the doctor away', made me slightly nauseous. People were less resilient now than a decade ago, but it wasn't VitaCorp's sleazy junk they needed. I tossed away my half-eaten vitamin bar. The VitaCorp logo on the wrapper was subtle, but just knowing it was there killed my appetite. I took a swig of water to dilute the cloying taste of fake banana.

I scanned the remaining headlines. "Smuggling Ring Busted" was further up country, so thankfully not one of my supply links. "Minister's Daughter Taken Ill" concerned the daughter of Phil Maythorpe, the Health Secretary, ironically enough. "Terrorist Ringleader Sent Down " . . . I fumed as I scanned the inaccurate article. Damned Accepted bias.

I activated my illegal unblocking app and headed to a Blacked-Out news page. "Revolution Leader Loses Final Appeal" was more accurate. Jimmy Vance was outspoken, passionate, maybe even a touch fanatical, but he was no terrorist. He hadn't intended to spark the Health Revolution—his ideas and down-to-earth approach simply appealed to the masses and took on a life of their own. Yes, he'd vehemently opposed the Government's backlash and placed a wealth of accusations at VitaCorp's door, but he was innocent of the plots he'd been accused of. He was such an obvious hindrance to their joint propaganda that his public vilification was inevitable.

But money and power had again won over Parliamentary common sense and reasoning, and Vance was locked up, unable to interfere further with their lies and extreme policies.

I threw my tablet down in disgust. I'd been too young to remember the height of the Revolution, but my parents were Healthers and I recalled their delight when the big food and drinks corporations started reporting heavy losses and going into administration, one by one. I didn't think much of it; all I'd really known was fresh, raw, unprocessed food, so it made no difference to me.

The difference came when they took away our food and replaced it with synthetic alternatives. I sure as hell noticed that.

I fished the credit chip out of my pocket to see if the promised thirty percent had been activated. I plugged it in and a melodic *bleep* told me money was available. I scanned the details:

You have immediate access to £36,000 of a total £120,000, transferred to this chip from an encrypted account.

"Hmm." I liked to know who I was doing business with, and really, all security precautions begged to be hacked. I pulled up the encryption code. It only hid the client's identity. There'd be a fortress of firewalls around the account itself, but I had no interest in that. This code was basic at best. It might have kept a casual observer out, but anyone with a little know-how could hack it in no time. I had more than a little know-how.

Five minutes later, I knew who my client was.

A chill ran over my body. "You've got to be kidding me." I stared at the screen. The account belonged to a Mr P. G. Maythorpe. The ID photo showed me the Health Secretary. Phil Maythorpe himself.

It was a mistake . . . wasn't it?

Phil Maythorpe certainly made enough dough to afford a hundred and twenty grand's worth of illegal goods, plus the extra for an anonymous go-between. And . . . he had an illness in the family. Why else would he need a shedload of organics?

I re-opened the Accepted news pages. There it was: "Minister's Daughter Taken Ill". Maythorpe's 12-year-old daughter Jenna had been diagnosed with some unnamed disease. Whoever had leaked the story wasn't privy to the details. The child was believed to be at home, family deeply concerned . . . The rest was speculation, but any doubts were erased.

The guy in the alley was a go-between for the bloody Health Secretary.

My blood boiled at the man's hypocrisy even as vindication crept over me. He was acknowledging Nature's food was best for his daughter, not the chemically-derived dead nutrients promoted by his Department. This was huge. If word got out that Maythorpe was sourcing fruit and veg for his kid, the Government would never recover from the blow to their fascist policies. Other people's ill children had to suffer the side effects of ever-more complex drugs and synthetic supplements. Most of us had to watch ourselves slowly deteriorate as our bodies succumbed to a processed diet. All in the name of protecting society and infrastructure. All because the pharmaceutical giants felt their livelihoods threatened.

I'd never much cared who my clients were; we were all citizens damaged by the system. But Maythorpe had influence. He supported the draconian measures that kept us dependent on VitaCorp and its partner companies.

No doubt VitaCorp supplemented his income in exchange for further promotion. I was about to use VitaCorp's own money to pay smugglers for the fruit that VitaCorp had helped ban. Talk about twisted justice.

I mulled it over. I could meet my client's needs. I could get his family hooked on the beautiful stuff. When he was a regular and his money was lining my pockets, I could use his status to my advantage. To everyone's advantage.

I sensed potential here. I never wasted potential.

• • •

I arranged to meet the go-between a few days later. I'd procured the order, but only brought part of it. He parked his black van across the end of the alley, blocking us both in. The subtle threat wasn't lost on me. If I was here to deliver the goods, it wouldn't have worried me, but I doubted the guy would like what I had to say.

"Where's the stuff?" he said as soon as he got out of the van. It was obvious I didn't have it all with me.

I handed him a small brown sack and tried to sound casual. "Part of it's right here."

"Part of it?" His fists clenched.

"I've got the rest. But I need to deliver it to our client in person."

The go-between's lips twisted in a snarl. He wasn't the type to be messed with, and I'd be out of my depth if I let him get angry.

"I know who he is," I added.

That gave him pause. For all his posturing, he cocked his head at me like a dog trying to understand. "I doubt that," he said at last. "I've been in this game a long time. I know how to cover my tracks."

"I'm sure you do. But the client's a newbie. Maybe you should have given Mr Maythorpe a few pro tips before offering your services."

He inched back a step. To his credit, it was the most minor flinch. This was a man who wore his armour well, but I knew I'd got to him.

"I want to see him," I repeated.

The go-between laughed. "Why would he agree to that? He didn't hire me for fun."

"If he wants the rest of the goods, he'll agree to it. If you tell him I have no qualms about revealing our little transaction to the media, I'm sure he'll leap at the opportunity."

"It'd be your word against his. A prominent Cabinet minister against a shady criminal? You're hardly going to incriminate yourself, now, are you?" He wore a superior smile, as if he'd called some sort of bluff.

"I have proof of Maythorpe's involvement, and I can reveal it without incriminating myself." That *was* a slight bluff. The proof was on the hacked credit chip, but it was unlikely I'd be able to sell it to the media without a personal testimony. Recorded evidence would come later, if Maythorpe agreed to meet.

The go-between glowered. He was bigger and stronger than me, and we both knew it. I'd be faster, but he'd still follow me up the fire escape ladder if I took my preferred getaway route. I waited, tense and ready in case he decided he could solve his client's little problem himself. He sighed, and I relaxed. Obviously his fee wasn't worth the messy business of taking me out.

"I'll meet him here, alone, this time tomorrow. Otherwise the deal's off and his name's all over the news pages in far more than a sympathy-swinger about family illness."

The guy tossed the sack of tomatoes and lettuces over his shoulder and left me with a final glare.

I knew I was getting myself into deep shit. I hadn't revealed the nature of my proof to the go-between, but I still needed insurance if Maythorpe decided it'd be easier to eliminate me. I copied the data from the credit chip and sent it to a trusted associate with instructions to reveal its contents should anything untoward happen to me.

• • •

Next evening, I was back in the alley with my nerves on red alert. I had another sack with me, this time containing some fruit, to show I had the goods. I'd arrange a complete delivery once I knew Maythorpe was on side.

I arrived early to be sure Maythorpe didn't get there first. If he ignored my requirement to come alone, I'd leg it up the fire escape ladder and be gone before they ever knew I was there. I bundled my dreads up in a scarf; distinguishing features seemed risky when meeting with an official.

Ten minutes dragged by. I forced myself to stop checking the time. He'd either show or he wouldn't.

At the sound of a car door, I peered down the alley, ready to flee if he wasn't alone. I exhaled when I saw a single figure silhouetted against the far end.

He looked pale and nervous when he reached me, and shorter than he seemed on the news. He held out his hand in the typical rookie fashion. This time, I took it.

"You're the dealer?" he asked. Whose hand did he think he was shaking? Presumably politicians greeted everyone with that fake openness.

I nodded. "I'm Rowan."

"Phil Maythorpe."

"Yeah. I know who you are, Phil. That's why I asked you to come here."

"What do you want?" he asked, trying and failing to appear confident.

"I thought we could work out a deal. I can provide the goods you need; you've got the money. We can sort out a regular order if you like what I'm flogging." I handed him the sack.

His eyes widened as he looked inside. "Oranges." His voice was hoarse. "I can't remember the last time I saw an orange."

"They're good, too. Sweet, juicy, and fresh. That's top-notch fruit. Even the apples are as fresh as I can get 'em. Most of them are still crunchy."

"Is this all of it?" he asked, seeming to recall how much he was paying.

"Nope. The rest is elsewhere. I'll arrange delivery if you agree to my terms."

He looked up at me, wary-eyed. "What terms?"

"In short, I won't reveal our little business arrangement as long as you keep buying. I've got solid contacts. I can get the stuff. And your family will love you for it."

"I can't afford to do this regularly. Your fees are extortionate."

"Extortionate? I'll tell you what's extortionate, Phil. Your twisted government taking away our basic right to have fresh food in our diets. Your corrupt laws that destroyed an entire farming industry overnight, making thousands of people penniless as well as desperate for their greens. You expect me to believe you can't afford to pay the price you created by banning natural produce? I'm sure your pals at VitaCorp will provide a nice fat bonus for publicly feeding your sick kid more of their drugs. That should cover it and then some."

He turned spiked-blood-pressure red and prepared to utter an outraged retort, but I wasn't going to let him insult my intelligence with more bullshit propaganda. "I've got proof you and I have done business together, Maythorpe. Revealing your hypocrisy to the media won't upset me one bit. It'll be revealed if anything should happen to me, so don't even think about spending my fee on hired thugs."

"What proof?" It wasn't quite a whisper, but I knew I'd startled him from defensiveness to capitulation.

I smiled. "You used substandard encryption on the credit chip. Something you might want to remember for next time." He didn't need to know I'd have additional proof of this very meeting on the chip embedded in my skull.

He paled. I could almost hear his brain registering my hacking abilities. His shoulders sagged and I knew I had him.

"Tell you what . . . " I injected my voice with a touch of sympathy. "I'll deliver the goods personally. Save you having to sneak around in dirty alleys."

"You expect me to give you my address? Don't be ridiculous."

He attempted a dismissive laugh which sounded more like a cough.

"Oh, I already know where you live. Your account ID was most informative. This'll make our transactions easier on you. If you set up a regular order, we won't have to keep meeting like this. I've got a mate with an unmarked van and I'll hide the fruit in cardboard boxes. It'll look like an ordinary delivery."

"I'm not allowing you access to my home!"

"I think you are, Phil. Regular bulk orders aren't easy to hand over. It's better for both of us. You're hardly in a position to refuse my terms, are you?"

His eyes radiated resentment, but he agreed. I promised his first order would be delivered the following day. As long as he made funds available to the credit chip, I'd keep him and his family in the freshest fruit and veg I could get and his secret would stay safe. For now.

The mate with the van was an occasional flame I hadn't seen in a while. I knew he'd let me borrow his wheels as long as he wasn't running jobs of his own. I couldn't get to his place over rooftops, so I called first to make sure he was in. I didn't want to risk running into a night patrol for no reason.

"Ro! Long time no see. How's things?"

"Hi, Troy. You at home?"

"Planning to break curfew for me again? That's enough to send a guy's heart aflutter."

"There's a new drug for that, I hear."

"Ha ha. Very funny."

"I need a favour, actually. Okay if I stop by?"

"I'm not going anywhere. Got tagged last week. Can't have it removed for a month."

"Idiot. I told you to be more careful." I sighed. "I'll see you in twenty minutes."

Troy's place was spacious, with a great view across town. We'd sat drinking and talking in front of his big picture window countless times. We'd done other things in front of it too . . . his apartment was high enough not to be overlooked.

"You hungry?" he said after letting me in. "Fancy a shake?"

"I probably should have something."

He pulled out two sachets of VitaMinerals drinks. "I've got mint flavour—your fave." He whisked the powder with water, which thickened into a frothy drink. We sat on his couch in front of the view.

"You said you had a favour to ask?"

"Can I borrow your van tomorrow?"

He shrugged. "Yeah. Not a problem. I need it in the morning, but you can have it later on."

"Great. Thanks."

"Dare I ask what for?"

"Probably best if you don't."

He gave me his disapproving look. "Still raging against the machine, then."

"Still trying to make a living, actually. It's good money."

"Dodgy money. Don't try and kid me you don't love undermining the system."

I rolled my eyes. "It's a hideous system! You know it, I know it, everybody knows it. I'm just not willing to be a mindless, drug-fuelled sheep like the rest of society."

Troy held his hands up in surrender. "Okay, okay . . . I don't need another lecture on the evils of VitaCorp." He was laughing. "So, you staying the night, or what?"

I stayed the night. Troy left in the morning to run his errands and I lounged around his place until he returned with the van.

"All yours, babe," he said, planting a kiss on my forehead as he handed me the keys. "Bring her back safe."

I drove back to my place, disguised the crate of apples and oranges in a cardboard box, labelled it with Maythorpe's address to look like any courier delivery, and loaded it into the van. It was bulky and awkward, but I managed.

Maythorpe's house was on the outskirts of town, in one of the expensive leafy districts with pristine streets and manicured hedges. I pulled up outside his place and spoke into the intercom on his gate.

"Delivery for Mr Maythorpe," I said, like it was just another stop on my rounds.

"Drive up," said the voice from the speaker as the gates swung inward.

I drove along the gravel driveway and stopped outside the main door. Maythorpe's wife came out as I hopped down from the driver's seat. I recognised her from the news articles and wondered if she knew about her husband's illicit deal.

I slid the box onto a two-wheeled handcart and followed Mrs Maythorpe into a wide hallway. I left the illegal goods on the tiled floor, produced a legitimate-looking form for her to sign, and bid her good afternoon.

A doctor's car was waiting to turn into the driveway as I pulled out. The VitaCorp logo stared impotently at me from its rear windscreen as I drove away.

. . .

I dropped the van back at Troy's, lingered for a quick fumble, and headed home. Troy would have had us spend another night together, but I missed my own bed and he wasn't allowed out after dark. None of us were really, but his tag forced him to behave.

The Blacked-Out news pages had nothing interesting to report. One was protesting Jimmy Vance's incarceration by continuously looping his famous speech decrying government spin.

"If all our essential nutrients are in these pills, bars, and drinks, why are people getting sicker? Why aren't we just as healthy as before? The Government would have you believe they're simply making food production more efficient, but the fact is, the health and longevity of our population frightens them. How dare we aspire to live longer?"

I turned off my tablet, having heard the speech so often I could recite it by heart. I grimaced at the thought of what Vance would say about the Health Minister's indiscretions.

I didn't sleep well. I awoke once thinking I was still in Troy's bed. I reached a hand over to his side before remembering I was home. Missing him surprised me. I usually preferred sleeping alone, and my relationship with Troy had always been casual.

I'd never put much faith in intuition until that night.

My phone's chime woke me early. I ignored it, pulling my pillow over my head and willing it to shut up. It was the number I only gave to friends. When it chimed again, curiosity got the better of sleep. No one called me before dawn.

I shoved the pillow aside and grabbed the phone, blinking bleariness away to see the screen.

Troy. That was weird. He was no more an early riser than I was.

"Hey. You're up early," I croaked, still half asleep.

"Ro . . . " He sounded odd. I sat up. "I'm sorry. I don't know what they want, but—" He was interrupted by a new voice, harsh and angry.

"We've got your friend. Hand over the chip and he gets to keep these pretty blue eyes."

I hadn't realised I could wake fully in four seconds flat. My heart went from a sleepy beat to full pounding.

"Wh-what?" I managed. "Who are you?"

"Be at your friend's place in half an hour with everything you have on Maythorpe. Half an hour. Not a minute longer."

The line went dead.

I sat catching my breath. They had Troy. How did they know about Troy? Had they followed me? That made no sense. They could just as easily have followed me home and ambushed me directly.

The van. How could I be so fucking stupid? Nausea rose in my throat at my moronic mistake. Maythorpe's gate was bound to have surveillance. He'd have images of Troy's van and I'd done nothing to disguise the registration plates. *Stupid, stupid, stupid!*

Maythorpe knew I'd copied the chip's details. With that and my recorded evidence, passing over the chip wouldn't deprive me of proof. Still, I didn't see that I had much choice. Troy had sounded scared, which scared *me* even more. I'd never seen him anxious, let alone afraid. These guys obviously weren't messing around. They said they'd take his *eyes*, for God's sake.

I dressed in a rush and shoved the chip in my back pocket. It was still early, but curfew was over. As I hurried along the bare streets, rising anger muted my fear. Maythorpe was welshing on our deal in spectacular fashion while threatening someone I cared about. Did he really think he was going to get away with that? He was a fool not to take me seriously. My fury spurred my pace, and I reached Troy's with ten minutes to spare.

I took the lift up and knocked on Troy's door. Troy opened it himself, pale-faced, his dark hair a disarrayed mop. They'd obviously dragged him out of bed. He said nothing, just pulled the door open to let me through, and I saw the heavyset brute behind him holding a weapon to his spine.

"This her?" he asked.

Troy nodded, regarding me with a haunting look of apology and accusation. I felt guilty enough for getting him into this. None of it was his fault. The brute gestured me through, ushering Troy along behind me. There was another thug, tall but slimmer, admiring the view from the picture window. I had an urge to rush forward and shove him through the glass, but my acute awareness of the weapon at Troy's back held me in place.

The thug turned around, a shark-like grin on his face as he looked me over. "You made good time," he said, and I recognised his voice from the phone. "That's your first smart move."

"Hardly my first," I said with contempt.

He ignored that. "Where's the chip?"

I tossed it to him. He pulled out a pocket tablet and slotted it in. Satisfied, he tucked it inside his jacket. "Our favourite minister will be delighted to have this back," he said. "But of course, you have copies." He paused. If he was waiting for me to deny it, we'd be here a while.

"Something tells me your assurance to destroy them would be meaningless. We're under strict instructions not to harm you thanks to your guarantee of Maythorpe's exposure should anything happen to you. I expect you're bright enough to have actually set up that sort of insurance, so you're free to go about your business."

Somehow, that didn't assure me at all. He continued. "But Maythorpe needs a little insurance of his own. We'll be taking your friend with us. If any hint of this is leaked to the media, he dies. If we have *any* suspicion that you're sharing information elsewhere, we'll send him to you one piece at a time."

I seethed, my fists clenched at my sides, unable to pound that smirk off his face. "Troy has nothing to do with this. It's between me and Maythorpe. I'll talk to him, give him whatever he wants. Just leave Troy the hell out of it."

He had the gall to chuckle. "If you'd wanted him left 'the hell out of it', you'd have used alternative transport. He's coming with us."

"That's crazy. What are you gonna do, keep him forever, just in case?"

He nodded thoughtfully, as if the question hadn't occurred to him. "If need be."

He pushed past me towards Troy and the brute and pulled out a pair of handcuffs. Troy's brow was beaded with sweat. The look he gave me was painful, for both of us.

"You can't be serious," he said. "What did you do, Ro? What the fuck did you do!" He struggled as they wrangled him into cuffs.

"I'm sorry . . . " My voice sounded pathetic in my own ears, never mind Troy's. Maythorpe's spokesman backhanded him and the brute pressed the knife—I could see it was a knife now—harder against his back.

"You'll be quite comfortable unless she does anything stupid," the mouthy one said as they hauled Troy away. He called back to me as they left the apartment.

"Oh, and in case you're still wondering, Maythorpe says the deal's off."

• • •

However callous it might seem, my immediate instinct was to expose the hell out of Maythorpe. If he thought he'd pulled the rug out from under me, he could think again. But as I stood in Troy's abandoned apartment, I realised I couldn't betray him further. I'd got him into this. I couldn't let them kill him any more than I could let Maythorpe continue enabling VitaCorp's stranglehold while breaking the laws he swore were crucial to our society.

I knew I'd be followed if I went home. I couldn't have them knowing where I lived; my flat was my sanctuary. I'd stay at Troy's, since his place was already compromised. I'd have to buy clothes, but it was as good a spot as any to weather the storm.

I sat on the floor in front of his window that evening, watching the city lights brighten as darkness encroached. My desire to expose Maythorpe ate at me. He thought abducting Troy would shut me up, but it only forged my determination to bring him down. I had all the proof I needed of his illegal transactions, but how could I protect Troy?

The solution hit me like a taser. *Of course!* I slapped my forehead—the turn of events must have fried my brain. I didn't just have proof of Maythorpe's dealings with me. I had proof he'd abducted Troy.

I'd left my tablet at home. My heart raced as I searched for Troy's. I downloaded the app I needed and activated the tablet's wireless connector. My embedded chip's recordings appeared. I opened the most recent file. A video popped up and began playing my day, from the moment my phone had woken me. I scanned ahead and sat in the darkened flat re-watching Maythorpe's thugs kidnap my friend.

It was all there. Alone, it wasn't enough. Maythorpe's name was mentioned, but not his initial crime. If I released this alone, he'd kill Troy, dump his body, and somehow spin his way out of the whole thing. But if I released it along with my alley recording and the chip details . . .

I had proof Maythorpe had arranged Troy's abduction, and proof of why he wanted to keep me quiet. If I exposed both crimes at once, Troy might be protected by the public's awareness of his predicament. If Troy disappeared, people would know Maythorpe was behind it. But Maythorpe might be able to salvage a shred of his reputation by releasing Troy.

It was risky, but it was a chance. I didn't see another option that offered Troy any hope. Even capitulating condemned him to a lifetime of unjust imprisonment. He'd simply be another missing person who never resurfaced.

It was just as risky for me. My face didn't appear on the recording, but my voice did. I sighed. It would be worth it for Troy. It would be worth it to prove Maythorpe wasn't so bloody untouchable after all.

I collated my evidence and approached a Blacked-Out news page who offered me a huge sum for the recordings and the chip copy. I can honestly say I hadn't even considered the money, but it made up for what I'd lost through Maythorpe's failed deal and then some. They broke the story the same day. They even disguised my voice and agreed to protect me as an anonymous source. Troy had to be named and shown fully—that was vital so Maythorpe would release him instead of some stooge.

"SCANDAL: Health Minister Procures Fruit, Takes Hostage As Protection" read the first headline. It was under an hour before every other Blacked-Out page picked up the story and raced with it. By the time the Accepted pages began addressing it, their bias looked pretty foolish. The picketers calling for Jimmy Vance's release soon had placards demanding Troy Bingham's safe return.

I sat in Troy's flat watching the spectacle unfold with increasing anxiety. What if I'd got it wrong? What if I received pieces of Troy as they'd promised, despite the media's call for his freedom? I paced the flat, feeling caged and helpless. I ate some dried blackberries I found stashed at the back of Troy's sock drawer, which had been supplied by yours truly after an illegal countryside forage. They helped calm my jittery stomach. I ignored the half dozen or so of Troy's friends and neighbours who came bashing on his door, presumably to assure themselves the abductee on the news was a doppelganger who also happened to share Troy's name. They left with no such reassurance.

By the end of the day, the headlines read variations of "Maythorpe Arrested" and the Government was releasing statements trying to distance itself from his activity. I watched as alliances such as CaFNaF (the Campaign For Natural Food) arranged demonstrations outside the Houses of Parliament. Police in riot gear met them, and sadly they all went home at curfew like good little citizens. I cheered them for protesting and cursed them for being too cowardly to break a few draconian laws while they were at it.

I left the flat the next morning after a sleepless night. A crowd of reporters besieged the building—God knew how they'd discovered Troy's address—but I pushed past them with my head down. A few shouted after me, but they obviously figured I had little insight to offer. I laughed under my breath as I walked away. Anonymity had uses besides staving off arrest.

The CaFNaF demo was in full flow again by the time I got across town. Thousands of people were there, demanding fresh vegetables, Troy's release, Government accountability, and countless variations on those themes. I mingled with the crowd, one eye on my borrowed tablet, desperate for news of Troy.

My phone vibrated in my pocket. I couldn't hear its chime over the chanting crowd, and the screen showed a number I didn't know. I answered it, sticking a finger in my other ear to hear better.

"Ro?" came a muffled voice.

"Yeah . . . sorry, you'll have to speak up. I'm in the middle of a crowd."

"It's me. It's Troy."

I gasped and clutched the phone tighter to my ear. "Troy?"

"They let me go." He sounded as though he didn't quite believe it.

"Where are you?"

"They threw me out the back of a van on the outskirts of some village. I'm at a police station."

I grabbed the arm of the nearest person to stay upright. Troy was okay. My crazy plan hadn't killed him. "Are you all right?"

"A little bruised. They broke my nose and knocked some teeth out. But I'm okay. The police . . . they said Maythorpe's been arrested, not just for abducting me, but for purchasing fruit. Is that what this is about?"

"I'll tell you everything, but not over a police phone." I'd have to get a new number as it was now he'd shared mine with the fuzz. "Right now, I'm just relieved as hell that you're okay."

"And you?" he asked. "You're okay?"

I swallowed a lump in my throat. "Yeah, Troy. I'm okay."

I wasn't sure the same could be said of our revered lawmakers. I looked around at the growing crowd and realised I hadn't seen a protest this big since my childhood. People shouted, waved banners, stomped, chanted. They had spent too long repressed and drugged into submission.

Now they were angry again.

Star Bright

Cherith Baldry

Iristain Antoqana stood on the balcony outside her apartments and looked out to the glimmering line of the horizon. The sun had disappeared behind the low hills that cradled the western side of the bay; the sea was a soft, dusky green, reflecting the greenish sky where the first stars began to awaken. The harsh heat of the day was fading and a breeze sprang up, fluttering the edges of Iristain's white mourning robes.

The marble balustrade was cool under her palms. She looked down, past the sandstone terraces of the palace, past the tops of eucalyptus trees in the palace gardens, to where she could just catch a glimpse of the broad stairway that led up from the town. At this hour it was deserted. Somewhere out of sight a priest was shaking a branch of silver bells to call the faithful to evening prayer; the sound shivered upwards, half lost in the serious babbling of Iristain's small son Amal as he squatted on the marble flagstones of the balcony and played with his carved wooden horse.

A voice behind Iristain's eyes said, "Go home."

She froze. Her husband Malik, Lord of Gaith-Rabi, had died ten days ago. Three days since they had laid him on his pyre; his bones were calcined, dissipated as flecks of ash upon the wind. She had thought never to hear that voice again: velvet with a glittering edge that could turn to anger or amusement. She could visualise him now, leaning indolently in the doorway behind her, in the plain linen robe he wore when the duties of the day were over, a smile lurking on his mouth. She did not dare to turn in case he was not there.

To go home . . . The word conjured up the wind of the north, carrying the resinous scent of pines as it swept down from the mountains; the river that foamed down towards the city in a long series of cataracts; the gleam of rain on grey stone. Homesickness stabbed her to the heart, but how could she go, when the child playing at her feet was now the ruler of Gaith-Rabi?

Somewhere inside the apartments, a door was flung open; Iristain heard footsteps and the high, hectoring tones of her husband's brother Umar, though she could not make out the words. The door banged shut again, and the voice was cut off, but the moment was past.

Iristain's sense of awe, of something transcending the actual, died abruptly. She stood immobile for a second longer, vainly willing the fugitive presence to return. Sighing, she held out a hand to Amal and turned to see no familiar figure in the doorway, only her maidservant Merope slipping into the room beyond, a lamp held high in one hand, turning the gathering twilight to true dark.

"Mistress!" Iristain felt a prickle of unease at the urgency in her maidservant's voice. Merope was beckoning to her, then raised a finger to her lips for silence.

"What is it?" Iristain whispered; though she had no idea what was going on, she kept her voice low as she led Amal inside.

"Mistress, I overheard them talking—Lord Umar and the Patriarch Fath."

Umar. Her husband's younger brother, a man whom Iristain had tried in vain to like. She had always thought him a pale copy of Malik: not so tall, his features sharper, his eyes without the depths where wisdom or delight could lurk. Uneasiness stirred inside her, especially as she could see it was not idle gossip that Merope had come to repeat.

"What did they say?"

Merope's dark eyes widened, the flame of the lamp glinting in their depths. "They mean to kill your son, and set up Umar as Lord of Gaith-Rabi. The Patriarch says that God has ordained it."

After the first shock, cold as a shower of ice water, Iristain discovered that she was not surprised. Instead she was furious with herself because she had never expected this. Fool! she berated herself. Fool to think that they would ever let Amal succeed. Umar had always envied his brother's position, and he was a weak man who would allow the Church, and through it the Patriarch, to wield the real power in Gaith-Rabi.

In the five years she had lived here, Iristain had found it hard to believe that the people of Gaith-Rabi worshipped the same God that she had known in her home land. Her faith was gentle, with openhearted charity for the poor, and tolerance for the weak and wavering. The God of Gaith-Rabi ruled through implacable decrees. As Malik's lady, Iristain had attended the public prostrations out of a sense of duty, and only realised now how much Malik had shielded her.

Fear prickled her skin and dried her throat. The God of Gaith-Rabi would endorse the murder of a child if it would reinforce the power of the Church.

"We can't stay here," she said, sweeping her son up into her arms. Echoing Malik, she added, "We must go home—home to Herria."

Merope nodded. Passing through the outer room into the nursery, she flung open the door of the clothes-press and began tossing out garments. Her cat, Acantha, dislodged from her favourite sleeping place, leapt to the floor with an outraged yowl.

Iristain stood frozen for a moment, then picked up one of her son's striped woollen caftans as Merope extracted it, and tried to stop her hands from shaking as she pulled it over his head and fitted the small wriggling arms down the sleeves.

Meanwhile Merope spread out a gauzy silk scarf on Amal's bed, and fetching Iristain's jewel casket from the storage chamber, upended it and poured out all its glittering wealth onto the scarf.

Iristain stared blankly at the ropes of cool sea-pearls, opal and lapis from the mountains above her home in the city of Zubizarra, finely worked gold from the smiths of Limairac, flashing emeralds brought by camel-train from the deserts to the south of Gaith-Rabi. Merope knotted the scarf into a tidy bundle and fetched an indigo cloak, servant's garb, which she held out to Iristain.

"Put this on, lady. Then we can go."

Iristain almost said, *Now?* only to realise how stupid that would make her sound. What was there to stay for, except for the knife and the fire?

She wrapped the cloak around herself and took Amal in her arms. Merope picked up the bundle of jewels and crept cautiously through the outer room as far as the door. The cat Acantha padded silently at her heels, slipping out into the passage when Merope cracked open the door. A moment later, an inviting trill came from the darkness beyond.

"Safe . . . " Merope breathed out.

On the word of a cat? Iristain thought, bewildered. But she followed Merope out without protesting, along the whisper-silent corridors of the palace, down the marble staircase to the garden atrium where she and Malik once used to sit, stretching fingers into the silver spray of the fountain and watching the scarlet flash of carp in the pool.

Everyone was at evening prayer, everyone except for the two motionless guards out on the terrace, whose spiritual health was presumably less important than the palace security.

Merope and Iristain paused in the shadow of a palm tree, its serrated leaves arching between the pillars that separated the atrium from the terrace. The guards had their backs to them, their feet apart and their hands on their spears as they gazed out over the city. Moonlight spilt over the terrace paving, which stretched as far as the balustrade and the stairway that led to the town. No great distance, yet Iristain had no idea of how they were to cross it.

She turned to Merope, looking a question, but her maidservant was silent, biting her underlip in perplexity. Acantha sat beside her, tail wrapped around her paws. After a moment she raised one paw, licked it, and drew it luxuriously over one ear.

Small help you turned out to be, Iristain thought.

She looked back across the terrace to where the guards still stood, keeping their implacable watch. Has Umar given them orders? she wondered. Or is it still too soon? Dare we risk it?

She leaned towards Merope, ready to whisper the question in her ear, but before she could speak, Amal dropped his little wooden horse that he had clutched to him all the way from their apartments. The tiny sound as it hit the marble paving rang out like the clang of spear on shield.

Amal opened his mouth to yell; before he could utter a sound Iristain clamped a hand over his mouth. As his face grew red with indignation she murmured in his ear, "Quiet, little one. It's a game."

Unconvinced, Amal started to wriggle in her arms, wanting to be set down.

At the sound of the horse falling, the two guards on the terrace spun round, their spears levelled. "Who's there?" one of them called.

For reply, Acantha sprang to her paws and dabbed at the horse, sending it skidding out into the open. She leapt after it and pounced on it, as if it were a mouse.

"Godforsaken cat!" one of the guards exclaimed, relaxing.

Merope thrust the bundle of jewels into Iristain's hand and darted out into the open, her arms outstretched. "Acantha! Here! Come here! Bad cat!"

Iristain watched, desperately trying to manage the bundle and restrain her struggling son, while the guards strolled over towards Merope. The taller of them raked her with his eyes, as if his look alone could strip off her gown.

"Hey, pretty one," he said. "Come to keep us company?"

"Maybe." Merope tossed her long dark curls. "But you've got to help me catch the cat. That's the little lord's toy she's got."

The other guard, an older man with a thin beard, reached out to caress Merope's shoulder. "Forget that, sweeting. The little lord won't—" He fell silent as his colleague nudged him roughly.

So they know, Iristain thought.

The two guards stood close to Merope, crowding her, their attention distracted from the balustrade and the stairway. Iristain realised that this might be her one chance.

God be with us, she prayed to the kindly deity of her girlhood, the God who cared for the fall of a sparrow, and would surely never decree that a child should fall into the hands of his enemies.

Clinging to the shadows of the pillars and encroaching foliage, she slipped along the front of the atrium until she was as close as she could get to the stairway without revealing herself. Then she launched herself across the void of the terrace, braced for the shouts of the guards, the flung spear in her back.

But all she heard was muffled laughter, and Merope's voice. "Quiet, fool! What if your sergeant hears you?"

Iristain fled down to the first turn of the stairway and halted, panting, in the shadow of a bougainvillaea where it poured in a white cascade over the banister. Her arms ached so that she had to set Amal down, a finger over his lips to beg for silence.

His voice came out in a plaintive whimper. "Want horse . . . "

A screech from above set Iristain's heart thumping, and a moment later Acantha fled down the stairs, the horse clamped in her jaws. She brushed past Iristain, a tortoiseshell streak, and vanished into the darkness below.

Merope's voice followed her. "Demon-possessed cat! Come back!" Her footsteps pattered on the stairs, almost drowned by the guffawing of the guards.

When she reached Iristain, she scooped up Amal and hurried on down the stairway. Iristain stumbled after her. The cat waited at the bottom, her eyes small moons. Beyond her lay the wide roadway that encircled the palace, and beyond that the dark streets of the town, the distant tang of the sea, and freedom.

But as Iristain set out across the roadway, with Merope and Amal at her shoulder, torches flared in the night. She heard the silken sound of swords drawn from their sheaths. Blinking, briefly dazzled, she realised that they were surrounded. Men had crept up on them, silent-footed, and stood around them now, their eyes gleaming dark from leopard masks: the Temple Guard. And thrusting his way through the cordon to stand in front of her, the Patriarch Fath, with Umar close on his heels.

"Foolish woman," the Patriarch said, his voice cold. "Did you think that we would not be watching?"

Fear stabbed deep into Iristain's heart, though she refused to let these men see it. Instead she raised her head, fixing them with an icy stare, hoping that she managed to convey the utter contempt she felt for the pair of them.

"What do you want of me?" she asked.

"Of you, nothing." Umar pressed forward to stand beside the Patriarch. "We want the child."

"And we know why, you heap of sheep-droppings," Merope snarled. At her feet, Acantha let out a threatening yowl.

Umar raised a hand to strike Merope, but the Patriarch stopped him with a gesture. "Pay no heed to the vain babblings of women," he said, then added to Iristain, "While I was at prayer I heard the voice of God speaking clearly to me. I cannot doubt that it is His will that we should set aside Amal and anoint Lord Umar as the divinely ordained ruler of Gaith-Rabi."

For a moment Iristain allowed herself to hope. If that was what they wanted, then why should she and her son not go free?

"You will see the wisdom of this," the Patriarch went on smoothly. "Amal is a small child, and bears the blood of an alien nation. The people of Gaith-Rabi would never accept him."

Iristain doubted that. Malik had been well-loved, so why would the people not welcome his son? At least they were not accusing her of adultery, she reflected, even though Amal shared her pale, northern complexion, not the honey-gold skin of his father.

And what was she to fight for, she asked herself. The right of her son to rule this arid, thankless kingdom, to see him grow up twisted in the service of its harsh God? Malik had been strong and clever enough to win a space of freedom where he, and she, and their child, could live at peace. Iristain did not know if Amal could grow into such a man. Once again she tasted the snowy tang of the winds of Herria, almost felt their breath lift her hair.

And it was Malik who had told her to go home.

She bowed her head submissively. "If it is the will of God, then I must obey."

A bubble of laughter, instantly suppressed, rose inside her as she caught the suspicious glance the two men exchanged. If she had meant to temporise, to deceive, she might have spoken so. But could they not recognise sincerity when they heard it? Could they not even imagine she might not want what they were snatching from her, for herself or her son? Smiling, she pictured Amal running across the moors above Zubizarra. *He shall learn to ride a hill pony, and climb the hills to see the sun rise . . .*

"We will leave immediately," she said decisively, "and you will not be troubled by us again."

Umar stared at her, a sneer on his thin face. "You are more foolish than I thought, woman," he said. "Do you think that we will let you go, to raise an army in Herria and return to put your half-breed son on the throne of Gaith-Rabi?"

Once more fear froze Iristain. *They cannot believe that anyone would choose freedom over power.* But with the fear came the realisation of what she must do.

Iristain drew herself up. "Then you are more foolish still, my lord," she said. "And so is the Patriarch, and so also was my late lord Malik." It tore at her heart to speak his name so coldly, so dismissively. "Amal is not Malik's son."

"What?" The Patriarch's single word was full of outrage.

"See, my lord," Iristain said, with a gesture towards her son, still clasped in Merope's arms. Does he *look* at all like Malik?"

Oh, but he does, she thought. The bright intelligence in his eyes, his quick movement . . . But these men would see none of that, only the colour of his skin and his hair glinting chestnut in the torchlight.

"This may be so . . . " Now the Patriarch sounded uncertain.

Umar grabbed him by the shoulder. "Don't listen to her," he urged. "Would not a woman confess even to adultery, to save her child? Kill him anyway, and be safe."

The Patriarch gave him a displeased look, a rebuke without words for his insubordination. Turning to Iristain, he asked, "Then if not Malik, who is the father of this child?"

"A . . . a sea captain," Iristain replied, improvising desperately. "He was my lover in Herria, before ever Malik and I looked on each other. But as the Duke's niece I knew we could never marry. And when I was tossed into Malik's bed for the sake of an alliance, why should I give up the man I truly loved?"

Oh, forgive me, love, she said silently, wondering if Malik's shade was able to hear her. She would never forget the moment she had first seen him, when he arrived as Ambassador to her uncle's court. The moment her heart stopped, the sudden fall down unimaginable steeps; between one breath and the next her life changed for ever. The wonder when she realised that the same lightning had struck him too. It hurt to deny him now.

"That's right," Merope put in. "He would send word when he was in port, and I would bring him to the women's quarters by night. A fine man, handsome and generous . . . "

"She lies!" Umar hissed. "They both lie. Kill the child!" He gestured violently towards the nearest of the swordsmen, but the man stood fast, awaiting an order from the Patriarch.

"A child's life is not so small a thing," Fath told Umar. "We must try this further." To the guards he added, "Bring them."

The Patriarch led the way. Two men flanked Iristain as they climbed the steps again and followed the terrace wall until they reached an archway which led to the Temple courtyard. The others crowded around Merope and Amal, with Umar bringing up the rear. Iristain could not see whether Acantha was still with them.

Fath climbed the long flight of steps towards the looming columns of the Temple and passed through the gold-ornamented doors into the echoing space beyond. Two rows of marble columns marched down the centre, leading to the altar, a vast block of obsidian.

By now the evening service was over. A priest was quenching the last of the tapers; the only light came from the charcoal in a wide copper bowl, burning perpetually before the altar. The light flickered over the paintings on walls and ceiling: warriors and horses, fantastic creatures and the twisting stems of vines. To Iristain, walking in a fog of apprehension, they seemed to writhe and reach towards her, claws and tendrils ready to strangle and tear.

The Patriarch beckoned to the priest and spoke briefly in a voice too low for Iristain to catch the words. The priest scurried off, passing behind the altar and through the silken curtains that led to the sanctuary where only priests were permitted to enter. Meanwhile Fath halted beside the copper bowl and gestured to Iristain to join him.

"You will undergo the trial by fire," he said. "If you speak the truth, it will not harm you. But if you lie, it will consume you."

Iristain stood silent for a moment, her stomach churning as she fought for self-control. Her own God and the God of Gaith-Rabi were united in this: the trial by fire would reveal the truth. But she had no choice now; she had to continue.

Briefly she formed a silent prayer: *Dear God, protect me. Protect my child.*

She handed her bundle to Merope and stepped forward to stand beside the copper bowl, but before she could do more the priest returned from the sanctuary. He carried a branding iron, a heavy rod with a sharp-pointed star at one end. Thrusting it deep into the coals, he stepped back with a bow to the Patriarch.

"Proceed," the Patriarch said to Iristain.

Iristain raised her hands, palms outward, and let her voice ring out through the Temple. "I swear before God and these witnesses that Amal is not Lord Malik's child." Then she took a deep breath and plunged her hands into the coals.

The heat was gentle, pleasant, like the water in the pools where she and Malik had swum together. Iristain bathed in it, letting the flames lick up her arms and into the hollows of her neck. She cupped her hands and held flame in them like roses. Though her mind was spinning, though it took all the strength she had to stand erect and play out the ordeal, she made herself smile.

At last she let fall the burning coals and faced the Patriarch. "Are you satisfied now, Father?" she asked.

The Patriarch bowed his head. "I am." Looking up again, he added, "And that means, lady, that you are a self-confessed adulteress. For that there is only one punishment."

Two of his guards stepped forward and gripped Iristain by the arms. Merope let out a cry of protest, but no one listened to her. The Patriarch himself took the branding iron and pressed the star-shaped end against Iristain's brow.

This time the pain was instant, intense. Blackness enfolded Iristain, shot through with jagged lightning. A cry was wrenched out of her. But for the guards holding her up she would have fallen.

Gradually the white-hot agony ebbed to a burning pain that Iristain could bear. Light seeped back until she could make out the stern face of the Patriarch, Merope watching her with horror while she kept Amal's face pressed into her shoulder so that he should not see. The little boy was wriggling, his muffled protests rising to a wail. Shuddering, her legs scarcely able to support her, Iristain went to him, murmured words of comfort and stroked his hair.

"The trial is over," the Patriarch pronounced. "The punishment is meted out. You may go."

"No!" Iristain had lost sight of Umar until now, when he barged forward through the guards and stood in front of the Patriarch. "The bitch is lying. The child must die."

Fath turned a flint-hard face on him. "You question the judgement of God?"

"She tricked us somehow!"

"How?" the Patriarch asked. "You saw the trial for yourself."

For answer, Umar seized a sword from the nearest guard and swung it at Amal. Iristain flung herself into the path of the blade, but before the blow could land, the cat Acantha shot out from behind a pillar. Letting out a screech she hurled herself at Umar; her claws scored down his face, blood spattering over his robes. Cursing, Umar staggered and dropped the sword.

"Go!" ordered the Patriarch. "My lord Umar, how dare you commit this blasphemy in the Temple?"

Iristain did not want to listen any more. Side by side, she and Merope stumbled from the Temple and down the steps towards the harbour and the ship that would take them north. Merope held Amal's hand as he trotted along beside her, while she gave her other arm for Iristain to lean on. Acantha brought up the rear, letting out furious hisses as her neck fur bristled and her eyes gleamed green-gold in the moonlight.

"Cover your head, lady," Merope said as they headed into the town. "If folk see the brand, they might stone you."

Iristain nodded. She had seen wretches like that before, condemned for the mark of shame they bore. Malik had tried to put a stop to the cruelty, but even he had not been able to root it out completely.

But as Iristain raised the hood of her mantle, she became aware that the pain of her branding had disappeared. She felt stronger, refreshed as if she had just risen from a good night's sleep. And all around her diffused a silver light that did not come from the moon.

Merope was staring at her in awe. "Lady," she whispered, "the star is shining on your brow."

Iristain raised a hand to see the light stream over her fingers. Even as she did so, the light began to die, until it was the merest glimmer. Iristain drew her hood down over it, to hide it from prying eyes.

But the star still blazed out within her, showing the way to freedom.

Generation Zero

Kathryn Hore

Henriette picked up a chunk of scarred metal. It was cool in her hands, lying in shadow and unheated by the too-near sun. There was no shade here except that offered by the hulk above, the wreck of the ship left abandoned once they'd clawed all they could out of it. Nobody came here now. Nobody except her.

She kept to its shadow. This was not a planet favourable for blonde-haired pale-skinned types and she could feel her shoulders burning in even the short walk out of the camp—or was it a town, now?—to the wreck. Sunblocker. They needed to do something about sunblocker. There must have been stores of it, surely, along with food, construction and medical supplies. Maybe it had been in the section of the ship destroyed in the crash. Maybe it was just lost down the back of the hastily constructed storage sheds where everything they could salvage had been dragged and was still waiting to be inventoried. There had been more important things for Marcus and the rest to think about in the immediate aftermath of the crash. Such as building shelter and feeding almost two thousand starving, grieving colonists.

That was all who had survived. Barely a couple of thousand. Out of tens of thousands, almost a hundred thousand.

She tried not to think about it. There were too many dead to comprehend properly.

Above her, metal groaned. There was no wind, but the sands shifted below her feet. The hulking remnants of the ship shifted with them. She ignored it, clambering inside the mostly intact front section. The trail of debris stretched for kilometres beyond, a burnt scar on an already heated planet. Most of the back of the ship hadn't even made it down, still floating in bits somewhere beyond the atmosphere above. Metallic moons. Forgotten pieces of scrap doomed to float in deep space for the rest of eternity.

While those who had made it down were doomed to spend eternity, or at least the rest of their lives, here.

She wasn't sure which fate was worse.

Inside, at least it was cool. She felt at home here in the confines of the slowly sinking ship. The sands would take it eventually, cover it. Wipe out its memory. There wouldn't be anybody who cared enough to preserve it, even as some kind of relic or memorial to the dead. They were all too busy focussing on the future to care that the past would be left to rot.

The metal ticked, expanded, contracted. It was a mess inside the cockpit. Any reusable circuitry had been ripped out already; the engines, the guts of the ship cannibalised. Behind the pilot's station, maintenance galleys, which had once led directly to engine rooms, were twisted, impossible to traverse. Ripped metal where the hull of the ship had hit against rock, dragged along the ground at crash speed. Sealed interiors suddenly opened up to the elements.

She knelt to look under the crooked, over-turned chairs, scrabbled about down the back of the pilot's station. She pushed hard against a panel down low, a small storage space, trying to release the warped metal. A grunt of effort, pulling with fingers, a quick shove with the heel of her palm.

It opened.

She sat back to catch her breath, wiping sweat away from her forehead with a dirty hand. It was going to take time to get used to the thinner atmosphere here. This planet was almost like Earth. Close enough for the ship's computers to find during the emergency, somewhere possible to sustain life, and send them hurtling towards it in a burning downward spiral. But it wasn't Earth. And she found the differences stark.

Behind the panel was a large, hard case. Black, moulded polymer. She dragged it out, clicked it open. Exhaled in sudden relief.

The cartridges were safe. Thin multi-discs: the combined memory of a millennium of human history. Maybe nobody else here cared about the past, but if they were the only survivors from all the colony ships a dying Earth had sent out—and there was no way to know that they weren't—then she didn't want the final archives of all Earth's history to be forgotten.

"Thought you'd be here."

She jolted and whacked the back of her head on the chair, resenting momentarily the interruption to her solitude. She glanced over her shoulder as she rubbed the back of her head. He was standing in the angled doorway to the cockpit, looking tall, authoritative, not in the least puffed or sweaty from the walk over. Typical. Never a hair out of place, never out of his depth. He had seemed in control even when scrambling out of the immediate bloody aftermath of the crash.

"Marcus."

She turned back to the case of multi-discs, flipping through carefully, checking to ensure none were physically damaged. She did not look back at him again.

"So you're overjoyed to see me, then."

"What do you expect?" she muttered, reluctant to buy into this. It was done, it was decided. What point was there talking over it all yet again? "So what are you doing here? Aren't you busy? Don't you have a society to organise? A future to plan?"

She heard him step forward, the dull thud of rubber boot on twisted metal. Was aware of him pausing, looking around. Seeing what was left. Had he even been out here since the crash? Probably not. He'd organised a memorial, of course, but it had been held in the new settlement. Not out here where the reality of their situation was stark and looming, etched in chunks of burning debris across a barren landscape.

There had been a night, before the memorial, where the two of them had sat with one of the last remaining bottles of gin between them, getting slowly drunk. It had been the first chance they'd had to stop, to consider, to breathe. To wonder *what next?* They'd pulled people out of the wreckage. They'd found every survivor. They'd located a water source, a desert spring enough to support everyone, giving thanks to the final intervention from the ship's computers sending them down as near to water as possible. They'd set up an emergency hospital, then emergency accommodation.

Organised what remained of the food supplies. All the things you had to do immediately after crash landing a colony ship on an unknown, inhospitable, but technically habitable planet.

Let the sands take the wreck, he had said over the gin. They had to concentrate on what was important for tomorrow, not yesterday. Forward-looking strategies. That was all Marcus could see. It was his job, she supposed, to concentrate on the future. To be prepared to do anything to secure it.

He had the survival of the human race to worry about now.

She dragged up the case, pushing herself up from her knees and finding some bench space tilting to the left as the ship shifted in the sands. But it was straight enough for her to rest the case on so she could stand among the wreckage. It was heavier than she remembered, or maybe it was just the effort of lifting it in this atmosphere. It did contain possibly the only remaining archives of all humanity, after all.

She felt him come to stand beside her. Close. She didn't glance across, kept her eyes on the multi-discs in their slim cases before her. On her hip was a manual reader. She pulled out a disc, no bigger than her thumbnail, and slipped it into the reader. Held her breath while she waited to see if it would work.

The screen flickered, came to life. Too dark. She tapped the screen, pulled up the contrast manually. The colours began to gel, the images shifted. A rugged figure, handsome if you liked that kind of thing, dressed in clothing outdated by at least a couple of centuries, appeared etched across the screen. A flashing smile caught forever, dark skin, darker hair; every school child knew this image, this man a long time dead, but forever a hero.

"Terryian. The first of the great explorers," said Marcus, by her ear. Trying to get her to look at him. She resisted.

"If it weren't for him, we wouldn't be here."

"We'd be trapped on a dying planet."

"We may be now, for all we know of this place."

With jerking movements, she pulled the disc out, slipped it back into the case. Shut, snap locked. Hauled it off the slanted bench and pushed past him to scramble out of the cockpit.

"Henri!" he called after her. She heard the exasperation in his voice, knew she was being childish, but didn't care. If anybody had reason to be childish right now, it was her.

No children had survived the crash. Not a one.

The thought made her stop, a physical impact. The memory, trying to pilot a disintegrating ark to the ground, realising half of it was already gone. The understanding, rancid in her belly, of knowing even as she fought to save what was left, that the sections containing the pods of the children were already lost. The recall halted her in the shade of the torn ship, out on the edge of the shadow, as if afraid to step back out into the burning sunlight.

When she heard him scramble out of the crooked doorway, safe too out of the twisted wreck, she glanced back. He had worn long sleeves, long pants, despite the heat. Protecting his skin: always practical. She should have thought to do the same.

"You know, I came looking for you to apologise." He said it like it was some kind of accusation.

"For what? You're doing your job. And I'm just a pilot; what do I know about securing the future of the human race?"

"You saved our lives, all our lives, just getting us down here."

"That was the ship's computers. And if you want to look at it that way, I killed over ninety-seven percent of those on the ark."

He pulled a face. "Henri, quit the bullshit. I know you're pissed with me. But you said yourself, I'm just doing my job."

"Yeah, okay. Survival. But survival doesn't need those measures."

"Not just survival. Continuation." He stepped forward, reaching out a hand to her arm. "We don't know how many other ships made it. We have to assume none, that we're it. The last of the human race."

She closed her eyes and tried to imagine it. Worst case scenario: life gone on Earth, all the big colony ships sent out in opposite directions to the deepest of space, destroyed, crashed, no survivors. Only them, the handful who had made it down here. There was no way to know, of course. No way to even know if all that panic way back when the decision had been made to push forward the colony program, too quickly, too many, was deserved. Maybe the Earth had survived. Maybe all the other colony ships had made it to their destinations safely.

No way to know.

"We have a duty to ensure the continuation of the human race," he said.

Her eyes opened. His face was close to hers. In a moment, he would kiss her.

She looked up into his black eyes. "Am I to be part of your official breeding program, Marcus?"

His momentum stopped. "You're being unreasonable."

"Tell me. Am I to be one of your brood mares?"

He pulled back, stepped away with agitated movements, running his hands over his black hair as if it somehow needed smoothing down further. She waited, wanting an answer he did not want to give.

"No," he muttered at last, a reluctant sound. "You know I wouldn't. Not you."

"So I'm the exception. That's nice. Everybody else is bullied into their so-called duty, but I don't have to worry because our leader gets jealous."

He glared at her. "You know, before we left Earth I was going to ask you to marry me."

"Yeah? Well before we left Earth, I might have said yes."

She turned and began the short, if difficult, hike back through the sun to the rocky valley in which the last remnants of the human race across all the galaxies and all the universe—at least as far as they knew—were trying to build a future.

• • •

She thumped the case down on the long bench so hard the thin, temporary wall behind it shook. She thumped herself down on the high chair in front of it and ignored the obvious glance from Astrid down the far end, where she stood at her usual station.

It was a restricted area. Only the scientists and the engineers, the expedition leaders, were allowed in here. And one wayward pilot, now self-appointed historian, with a developing habit of scowling at them all so they would know just how unhappy with the lot of them she was.

Astrid was obviously smart enough to keep her mouth shut and her eyes on her work.

The place was ghost-empty, except for her and the scientist. They'd all be trying to ward off the intense middle-day heat in the tiny, form-fit, click-together buildings that could be easily shipped and quickly erected and had become a hasty camp. Town. Settlement. Whatever. This one was more solid than most, which wasn't saying a lot considering how badly it shook and shifted with the sands. At least it was cooler than out in the sun. The materials it was made from were designed to be self-insulating, or something. The engineers would know. The scientists would know. Astrid would know. Henriette didn't ask her.

Instead, she clicked open the case of archival multi-discs and flicked on one of the few computational stations they had so far set up. It was meant to be for the scientists, but nobody questioned her. She wasn't sure if it was because Marcus had told them not to or if they really did feel she had somehow saved them, got them down to the ground alive. Whatever it was, everybody else seemed to have jobs and tasks and a purpose for the future. Growing food, building more permanent shelters. Everybody was strictly necessary. Except her, whose job was done. It wasn't like they'd ever be flying out of here, after all.

She slid a disc into the computer station built into the bench, ran her fingers across the screen, flicking through to check its contents hadn't been corrupted in the crash. Maybe that was why they let her play at preserving their history. Because it kept her busy and quiet and out of the way. And maybe she was just being cynical and bitter and looking for things to be peeved about, too.

She made a conscious effort to focus on the screen, on the tasks she had found for herself. They had no idea what planet they were on, some unknown ball of rock in some uncharted part of deep space, but it wasn't like the big colony arks were the first ever sent out from Earth. They'd ramped up the existing program, sending out large-scale ships in the panic, filling them with carefully screened, selected, useful people who could all contribute to building new futures on other planets. No riff-raff, no poor, no rebels. No artists, no musicians. No historians. But the colony program had been around for over a century and there'd been others before them to venture into space. Small ships of early volunteers, whose routes the big arks had followed when disaster had struck the Earth.

So maybe there was some record, some reference, sent back by the early explorers, the first settlers. Maybe she could even find out something Marcus and his newly set up leadership team would find of use.

"We missed you at the Council meeting."

She looked up with a jolt. Outside, the sun must have been heading further toward the horizon, for the shade of light through the translucent walls had darkened. She hadn't realised, had been too engrossed in the archives to notice the progression. Stories of travellers did that to her. Explorers, pioneers, discovering new places and new things.

Astrid was standing next to her, waiting for a response.

"Uh, yeah, didn't think I'd have much to contribute," she said, trying not to sound too bitter.

The other woman shifted forward. She was young, had been some kind of child genius, or something, back on Earth. Was all of twenty-five now, acknowledged the foremost expert in some complex bio-physical field of science, if not in life experience. Brown hair pulled back tightly off her face, small, angular. It gave her a severe look. Reminded Henriette of a child pouting.

"All contributions are welcome," Astrid said. Henriette tried not to give sound to the cynical laugh in her throat.

"Yeah? Well, mine haven't been too well received in the last few days."

"Though the Council has not agreed with you, it does not mean you are disallowed your opinion."

"Huh. So long as I keep my opinion to myself." She glanced darkly at the younger woman. "Don't worry, Astrid. It was very clear: don't stir up trouble with the survivors. Don't undermine the Council. Keep my mouth shut. I got it."

Astrid stepped away, no doubt deciding it was not worth a fight. Henriette wasn't sorry. The formality of conversation with Astrid was tiring: the stilted manner of her speaking; the complete lack of irony with which she stuck to the company line. The woman may have been a child genius way back when, with all the driving ambition that entailed, but socially she was as awkward as . . . well, as a teenager who had worked through their youth instead of learning how to socialise.

"Astrid?"

The young woman glanced back. "Yes?"

"Are you really okay with it?"

"With what?"

"With being reduced to nothing more than an incubator for future generations of the human race?"

Astrid turned, a soft glide on the spot. There was rarely anything sudden with that woman. Everything from her public behaviour to her casual conversation was studied, considered well in advance.

"There is no greater goal or purpose to put one's life to, than ensuring the future of our species. The future of humanity itself."

Henriette pulled a face, waving a hand to stop the sermon before it began. "No, stop, wait. Forget the public statements for a minute, the blah-blah-blah greater good shit. I want to know about you. You personally. Aren't you even just a little bit . . . angry? Frightened? Unsure?"

Astrid opened her mouth to provide immediate response, but Henriette jerked her hand to stop her: no formal words, she was after a personal reaction. If the girl was capable of one, which Henriette was beginning to doubt.

The young woman hesitated. "I . . . I am glad to do my part," she hazarded, as if unsure what Henriette was looking for.

"Yes, sure, but look at you. You're practically a certified genius. Back on Earth, world leaders the planet over were taking your advice and you weren't even fucking twenty-two yet." She sat forward, aware the girl was listening, maybe for the first time. "You're ambitious; I know you are. Are you really ready to give all that up?"

"I do not plan on giving anything up."

"You won't have a choice. You have seen the scale of the proposed breeding program, haven't you? More men than women survived. Far more men; it's like three to one out there." She stood up, needing to move. The solo-female pods had been on the side of the ship sustaining the most damage. Did this girl really not see what that meant? "It's not the men who will be taken off other tasks to focus on only the one."

She was standing close, towering above the smaller woman, who might be a genius but still didn't seem to understand human nature. She put her hands on Astrid's shoulders, tried in touch to convey the sense of urgency, even of terror, that churned in her own gut.

"They're talking about keeping the women continually pregnant," Henriette said. "Year after year, birth after birth. To build the population. To . . . to replace the dead kids who didn't make it down."

Astrid stared up at her. That same pursed face, the same considered expression. Henriette had never seen a wayward emotion mar those composed features. The girl focussed on her science, on her research, on the facts and figures, the logical and the straightforward. When presented by something as illogical as a human emotional reaction, she didn't seem to know how to approach it.

Or maybe she did. The girl raised her fine eyebrows. "Of course I am aware of the scale of the breeding program, Henriette. I designed it."

A moment. Just one moment of still, of her fingers tightening around the arms of the small, bony child-woman before her. Then she took her hands off the girl, jerking away. She stepped back. Stared with all her own messy emotions, which she could not help but show.

She didn't know what to say. The breeding program wasn't just some committee-generated mistake from a group of mostly men who hadn't thought through all the implications. It was the deliberate design of a single, obsessive, increasingly ambitious woman. She opened her mouth, but couldn't find the words. So she turned, back to her computer station, back to the explorers, early settlers, pioneers. History.

"Henriette?"

She did not glance back. She could not. "What?"

"You are a hero here. The survivors look up to you. So you tell me: are you okay with the consequences of not supporting the most efficient, scientifically sensible method of ensuring continuity of the human race?"

She swallowed, hard, against a suddenly dry mouth. "People will breed. They'll do that anyway."

"So you would leave the future of our species to the ad-hoc whims of a surviving few?"

"Astrid, they're people. Not components of an experiment, not cogs in a bigger wheel. Just people. And you cannot use them like lab rats because you're afraid of not being in control of the process."

Astrid's stare was intense. "I work to ensure the future of the human race. The last hope for our species. Henriette, are you really okay with opposing that?"

Henriette closed her eyes. Wanted to scream that they didn't know that, they had no way of knowing that. There was not even any real surety as to the fate of Earth. The planet left behind may well still be there, might have found a way to ward off the menace, might have survived. The other colony ships, nine arks in all, each carrying near a hundred thousand, sent out along known colony routes to planets already explored, in some cases already settled, early outposts. Deep space travel was dangerous. She knew that better than any. She had piloted a burning, tearing ship down through a searing atmosphere to the surface of this planet. But that was why they'd sent so many, in so many different directions. At least one or two could get through. Start again. Keep humanity going.

It didn't have to be them, the handful of survivors from their crash.

It didn't have to be her.

No way to know. She opened her eyes, gulped a breath. What if they were the last? What if no other humanity survived anywhere? Her eyes stung with the comprehension of such an enormity.

"Yes," she said. "Yes, I am perfectly okay with it."

She didn't need to say she was talking about the extinction of the human race.

• • •

Dusk took a long time to fall here. Time was different. If time was measured by the progress of the sun across the sky, daylight lasted maybe sixteen hours and darkness maybe four.

It would be different elsewhere on this planet, wouldn't it? Like it had been on Earth? There would be places of different climes, maybe even colder places. Maybe there were oceans. Forests, ice-caps. Something other than sand and desert and the occasional, if plentiful, fresh water spring amid the dunes, fed by some unknown underground water source. It couldn't all be heat and sand and nothing else planet-wide, surely.

She walked down the centre road; well, she supposed it was a road, even if there were few vehicles to move along it. A wide space along which they had constructed the main habitation blocks in neat rows. Small squares erected in a grid-like pattern, the one primary street right through the middle like a spine, the settlement expanding out from it. Budding, early farms beyond that. At the one end was a kind of community hall where large meetings were held. At the other were the restricted buildings. The science lab. The Council meeting spaces. Where the decisions were made.

She wondered if all those survivors who huddled now in their grief and trauma in the little squares of pre-fabricated construction material understood what was to happen now.

Some had ventured outside now the sun was beginning to fall. Sharp-edged shadows, long against the sand, movement around the camp. They looked busy, most of them. All had tasks to do. As she passed, some smiled, others raised hands. Some just stood and watched. None ignored her. She wanted to tell them they should. That she was hardly the hero they thought her to be. So many had died; how could she claim she had done something heroic when she had saved a bare couple of thousand?

What would they say if she told them what their leadership Council's plans for them were? The Council she was meant to be a part of, though only because Marcus insisted. How would these people react?

How would they react if they knew she, the supposed hero, fought against those plans?

On her hip was her portable reader. In her pocket was a small, hard case containing selected archive multi-discs, those she had identified as key. She moved steadily, slowly, looking around but trying not to catch anybody's eye. Wanting to see, not wanting to interact. Her throat was dry; the air was still so hot, though it would fall freezing once dark really set in. She would need to get into her shelter soon enough. It might be hard being outdoors here in the sunlight; it was worse in the darkness.

Her shelter was at the far edge of one of the outer grids. Marcus' was on the opposite side. Without thinking about it, she found herself turning right, towards his place.

He let her in with barely a word.

"Hey."

"Hey."

He had to shift sideways to let her in. She shuffled past him, bodies pressed together by necessity. Not even the Council leader, the head of the whole expedition, was afforded much private space; his quarters were as cramped as hers. Or maybe that was deliberate. Maybe he wanted to be seen as just the same as everyone else, with no more advantage than anyone. A political decision.

He found her a chair. There was only one, in the kitchenette, which she sat on in the internal doorway while he sat on the cramped bed. They looked at each other. She bit her lip, trying to hide a sigh.

"Sorry," she said, after a bit.

"What for?"

"Everything?"

He sighed too. "Yes. Well. Sorry back."

Not that it resolved anything. Not that it changed anything. But she was sorry. Sorry they'd found themselves at this impasse. Sorry she couldn't agree with him. Sorry for the position he was in.

She wanted to kiss him. She leant over and he let her. It was the first time she was glad for the cramped confines of living spaces since they'd set the township up. His lips were warm. Salty. Lingered on hers. She knew it changed even less than the exchanges of apology did.

"Henri, you know I'd never . . . Well, I'd never place following a principle as more important than you."

"Shut up. Nothing you can say will make it better. So just shut up."

She kissed him again. Pushed him backwards. Moved to lie on the bed beside him, unclipping the portable reader, putting it and the case of discs on the shelf beside his bed. Told herself seducing him wouldn't help, that she was deliberately letting herself be distracted and she shouldn't. That she was deliberately distracting him, which was worse. Pulled her shirt off anyway. Dragged off his. Needing to feel physical connection, skin on skin, no matter all the things that could not be fixed, not by anything, even this.

They lay there in the dying heat, in his humid, sweaty cubicle of a living space, cramped and wrapped together. She looked up, forehead against his, meeting his eyes at close range. There was barely any room on the bed.

"If we were back on Earth would you still want to marry me?"

He blinked, rapidly. His eyes watered. "I want to marry you now."

She stopped him from saying more by putting her lips against his. She didn't want him to make excuses or offer apologies. She didn't want to hear why he couldn't, even though he was brought to tears when he said he wanted to.

Sweat, heat, arms about each other. His skin against hers.

Banging on the door and cries from the outside to open up.

She froze, arms tightening about him. A kick-in-the-guts sensation. *No, not now.* There was a crash, the door flung open—*how? Someone with an all-access pass?*—and stomping boots. The small sleeping cubicle was suddenly crowded with bodies and yelling, and there were hands on her arms and shoulders, yanking her back. She cried out, struggling, glimpsing confusion on Marcus' face as their grip on each other was forcibly severed. Heard anger in his shouted demands this be explained. But they hauled her away, all too fast, and she lost sight of him. There were only limbs and fists and indistinguishable faces, and Henriette fought a losing battle against them.

They dragged her outside, men and women in a kind of uniform. Guards. Newly designated guards—she'd heard the Council discuss the possibility; she really should've paid more attention to it. Hard-edged frowns glared down and someone flung her own shirt at her, a flicking movement of disdain. She caught it, put it on. Where was Marcus? Was he okay? Somewhere beyond the wall of uniforms she could hear him, all futile anger, but she couldn't reach him. They must have been ordered to keep him away. That made sense.

She wished this surprised her.

Her heart hammered into her throat, but she swallowed it back and turned to look for the one she knew must be here. There. Over by the door, watching, impassive and calm, an all-access pass still held between pale fingers.

"Ah, Astrid," Henriette said, and stopped trying to fight.

• • •

She sat on an uncomfortable, hard moulded plastic chair and stared at the ground. Debate raged around her. She decided not to listen, instead concentrated on the uneven seam in the floor beneath its synthetic fabric covering. Large sections of thin, pre-fabricated flooring slotted together too quickly, too rushed, in the first days when they were still trying to set up shelter to protect from the freezing dark, from the sun. Survival the only necessity. Fineries, details, they could all be dealt with later.

She wondered if later would ever come.

Marcus was furious. She didn't think she'd ever seen him try to pull rank like he was doing now, reminding all in a thundering voice just *who* was expedition leader and final authority. It wasn't doing much good. Power was already too diffused, with too many competing interests. He had set up the Council and created it as a leadership team, wanting to share power, disseminate it amongst the many. Encouraged engagement in how their society was run. Dictatorship was not his style.

He would have to be careful. She raised her eyes to where Astrid stood, impassive in the face of Marcus' emotion. There were others on his Council whom dictatorship suited very well indeed.

The younger woman had called the Council together. A smart move, putting her opponent on the back foot; Marcus had wanted to keep this just between the three of them. But by the time he had ordered the guards down, had understood it was Astrid who stood as her accuser and who had organised the guards to find her, wherever she was, even if that be in the leader's own bed, there was little he could do. Astrid had dragged her before the whole Council. It had become suddenly political.

"You cannot do this. She saved our lives. All our lives, yours included!' Marcus cried, playing the hero card for her.

Astrid, the only other standing, faced him. "Nobody wants to do this, Marcus. But we have to ensure the Council's authority is not undermined. We have to protect the future of the human race."

The two of them circled each other, watched by just over a dozen scientists and engineers, most blinking in surprise at finding themselves in what was quickly resembling a mock court with Henriette, hero of the crash, positioned defensively in the middle. She could feel their eyes upon her. Wondering, questioning. Probably only four or five had any real enmity. Ambitious types, political types. Power-hungry types. Those eyes were calculating, shrewd. How would this help them? How would this further their own agendas?

This was not just about her; she understood that. It was about the future. About how their society would be structured and power divided up within it. Humanity in its finest glory.

"I have convened the Council to bring my concerns before it, as is our agreed procedure," Astrid said. "Such is the purpose for which you set up the Council to begin with, Marcus."

"You do not drag people here under guard simply because they disagree with you!"

"This is not a matter of simple disagreement. I believe Henriette seeks to actively undermine the Council's position." Astrid's voice projected to the entire room. "She is searching the archival discs for something she can use to convince the survivors to reject the Breeding Program. To stir up rebellion, if you will."

She accompanied that last with a fleeting expression of distaste, the closest Henriette had ever seen the studied young woman come to a grimace. She had to swallow back the cynical mutter in her throat. Instead, she just closed her eyes and let Marcus try.

"Voicing unpopular opinion is no crime. And you have no evidence for any of it," he snapped back.

"Archival discs are missing. Henriette is the only one to have accessed those archives."

"She's the one who retrieved them. She's the only one who's been interested!"

"What does she mean to use them for? What evidence is she so desperate to find, and why?"

"Maybe something to help us with!' Marcus roared, so that even the closest of the watching Councillors instinctively leant back. Astrid herself didn't flinch.

Marcus was unusually emotional. Well, his living quarters had been invaded, his girlfriend dragged out and accused of undermining the future of the human race. He had a right to be emotional. But it still wasn't a good look. By comparison, Astrid was small and certain, a tiny figure of calm logic before which Marcus was losing ground. He needed to appear as the leader, prepared to make hard decisions and necessary sacrifices. Right now he only looked like a desperate man trying to save the woman he loved.

Henriette wanted to pull him aside, tell him his arguments wouldn't matter; they would do this regardless. This was a frontier society, a difficult outpost, like so many before it in history. Frontier justice had never been compassionate, or necessarily just. Not in all the centuries of exploration and colonisation on Earth, not in the exploration and colonisation of space, either.

She said nothing. She was already undermining his position as it was.

"Nobody wants to do this, Marcus. We have no choice. Our survival is at stake and hard decisions must be made to ensure it,"

Astrid said, looking up at the towering, angry man. 'This is what you have told us since the beginning."

"You are talking about her effective imprisonment," Marcus said. 'Worse. About forcing her participation in the program."

"I'm talking about ensuring Henriette cannot threaten the Council's authority or the Breeding Program amongst the survivors."

Henriette sighed. "I'm not threatening anybody," she muttered to the floor, and wasn't surprised when nobody paid her any attention.

She glanced up through her fringe, trying to determine who among them was driven by fear for humanity's future and who was just afraid of losing power. It was a fractious group, given to infighting. But they all agreed on the Breeding Program. The need to ensure the human race continued. It was the priority given to all the arks when leaving Earth—settle somewhere and breed—an established wisdom not one of them had ever stopped to question.

Except her. No wonder they felt so threatened.

"We all have a duty," Astrid said, loudly. "And we must all do it. Regardless of personal feelings."

Surely Marcus had seen that coming? Or maybe in his anger and upset he had not. It was the same rhetoric he had long used with the Council and it resonated now against him, a murmuring agreement from the gathered experts and leaders. They appreciated Astrid's cool logic, while his untrammelled emotion made them uncomfortable, frightened even.

He shook his head. "Don't do this, Astrid," he said suddenly, a very personal plea.

Astrid turned her back on him.

"Henriette, do you understand what will be required of you now?"

She let herself take a moment. Pushing herself straight, lifting her head to look out at each of the Councillors. Of course she knew what was required of her. Just as she knew she was being used to undermine Marcus' leadership by those who wanted more power for themselves. She wasn't sure if it were just Astrid or if there were others. The fact that guards had been used suggested the girl had backing, but impossible to know how many. Or who.

"Yes," she said and her voice was clear. "Yes, I do understand. But it won't work."

"We have some of the greatest thinkers the Earth ever produced in this room, Henriette. There is no doubting the science."

Henriette felt the frown cross her own face. "I'm not questioning your science. But this is about people, not science."

"Excuse me?" Astrid even managed to sound offended.

"It's a reaction. The program, I mean," she said. "It's an irrational, emotional reaction to being cut off and lost out here. Why else would you prioritise this before we even know the farms are going to last more than one crop? You're all just desperate and clutching at anything that lets you feel in control of your fate."

Somewhere off to the side, she saw Marcus' shoulders drop. She did not dare look at him, but from the corner of her eye she could see the tension flood out of him, the resignation kick in. The other Councillors rose up in angry disagreement, but Marcus stood still. He had fought so hard for her. Now she had all but sealed her own doom. She felt sorry for him, wished she could tell him how grateful she was that he had tried.

It took Astrid a moment to regain silence, clawing back control of the room. When she had, she turned back to Henriette, two faint creased lines across her otherwise perfectly composed brow.

"Henriette, your disapproval of the Breeding Program is already well documented. And discredited. The program will ensure the future of the human race. Such is the mission given to all the arks."

She felt her lip turn up in a kind of sneer. "Which geneticist gave you those guarantees?"

"We have no geneticists. Or biologists. As you well know. All such expertise died in the crash," Astrid said, probably to make the point that though they called her hero, many more had died than had been saved when she had brought them down.

"But we do have archives," Henriette said. "History. Did you know most recorded evidence suggests we need little more than a couple of hundred people to start a new world?"

"Of course we know. And the fewer there are, the higher the risks of lasting only one or two generations. This isn't just one colony's survival, Henriette. This is starting the human race over again."

"You don't need an enforced Breeding Program. You just need to let people do their own thing!"

Astrid remained impassive. Behind the small woman, the collective might of the Council looked down just as hard, a wall too solid for Henriette to crack. All those faces staring at her. She was neither a scientist nor an engineer, not anyone useful to their new world, their plans to secure the future of their entire species. If they had their way, her only worth would be in breeding.

She stood up. She did not look at Astrid, instead her eyes met those of each Councillor. Trying to find the chink in their collective armour. Trying to find the one who would listen.

"I looked up the history," she said. "There was a program, a colony on a planet called Terryian Six, and they were trying to populate it, but there was trouble. I'm not sure of the science of it. Maybe somebody could look at the data that's left—"

"The Terryian Colony Program closed over a century ago," Astrid cut her off.

"Dammit Astrid, just look at the reports. They're in the archive. I think they're relevant. It's the same—"

"Reports? The archives contain letters home, Henriette. They contain passenger lists, inventories. Diaries, logs. They do not contain scientific data of any use to us now." Astrid stepped forward toward her, even for a moment, looked understanding. "Leave the science to the scientists, Henriette."

Nods, agreement. Not a single dissenting expression, not a voice of doubt. There was nothing she could say. A pilot with nothing left to be piloted. An amateur historian who shrugged off their expert evaluations of the future. She didn't have enough hard evidence to prove anything; she only had guesses. And that wouldn't be enough. Not from her, not when they were so desperate for certainty.

She took a hard breath, filling her lungs. She would miss a world without musicians, she decided then. Without painters and artists. Without love. She would miss a world without children.

"Fuck it," she muttered, and looked up at the wall of Councillors. "Astrid was right. I took the archival discs to show the survivors. To give them an alternative view, one contrary to what you're telling them. Because none of this will work, and if you keep insisting on it the human race will end here."

By the time Astrid had calmed down their angry clamouring, debate that was not debate, Henriette was sitting again and looking for Marcus. He was the only one who remained quiet. Standing back and not trying to stop her. There was sadness in his face as she found his eyes, but he tried to offer her a smile, wan and faltering. She tried to offer one back. He didn't agree with her, she knew that. But he understood, and that was enough.

Astrid stepped forward. When she looked at Henriette, it was with undisguised contempt. Until that moment, Henriette had begun to wonder if Astrid was capable of feeling anything at all.

"Your confinement will be arranged. You will communicate with none beyond representatives of this Council," the young woman declared as if it were already decided, and Henriette supposed it was. "In your last trimester you will appear publicly, under supervision, to promote the program. To declare your support of it. You will be its figurehead. The hero doing her part to save the future."

Henriette just sighed and looked away. "Won't work, Astrid."

"You must adhere to the will of the Council."

"It's nothing to do with the will of the Council," she said. "It's far more simple. I can't have children. I'm infertile."

• • •

Marcus must have suspected. All those years they'd tried, back on Earth. The discussions about when to seek medical intervention. Only then came the panic, the Earth threatened, and everything else got lost in the push for survival, the future, sacrifice, urgency. Life interrupted.

She hadn't told him she'd been tested anyway, before leaving Earth. Hadn't told him she was one of the 0.9 percent of women even the most advanced of medical science could not help conceive.

If she hadn't been a pilot and already assigned to the job, they wouldn't have let her on the arks. An imperfect human specimen. Or if she hadn't been the girlfriend of the expedition leader and the pilot he specifically requested for his ark, perhaps. In the end, they didn't ask and she didn't tell. Not even Marcus.

He watched her as she packed. Hurt eyes, stiff limbs. There was tension in him, as if he were holding himself back, as if he wanted to hit someone, or hug someone, but knew he could do neither. There were guards, a couple of thugs, which seemed excessive but she guessed it was as much to make a show for Marcus and the Council as for her. She wondered who had decided their new world needed such a policing force. Astrid? Or one of the other power brokers on the Council? Marcus would have to be careful. Somebody else was already in control of the muscle.

His face told her he was well aware of that: the repressed fury every time his eyes flicked across one of the mismatched, cobbled-together uniforms. The guards would not leave them alone together. They were not even allowed a moment. He didn't say much as she packed and neither did she. It was hard to converse with such watching eyes. Even without them, it would have been hard to find the right words to say.

They had given her a choice, the Council. The threat she presented was too much for them. Her own admissions, her declaration she would never just shut up. In the end, she was damned by her own words, by her need to speak. By her influence with the survivors, which was what the Council really feared.

She could stay and be imprisoned.

Or she could go. A kind of exile.

She hadn't been able to look at Marcus when she had chosen the latter.

They gave her an old scooter salvaged off the ship, a tent which would protect from the sun, though it would do little to help with the nightly freeze, and enough food rations to last a week, if she was careful. She thought she would be able to find water. There had seemed to be more than one big spring in the desert when they had been flying over it. Of course, they'd been crashing down at speed, burning up as they did so, and she'd been trying to bring the massive ark, or what was left of it by then, under control. There hadn't been a lot of time to really check those kinds of facts out.

She would get to find out now, she guessed. Either it would work, or . . . well, so be it.

They wouldn't let her take any archives. Not even copies.

By the time she had got together the last of the few things she was allowed to take and strapped them to the back of the scooter, the sun was rising. She raised her head and squinted in the early sunlight. Pulled on a long sleeved shirt over her tank-top, despite the gathering heat, to protect her skin.

Marcus held out something to her. She glanced quickly at him as she took what he offered, still finding it hard to keep his gaze.

Sunglasses. His sunglasses. She put them on to hide the threat of tears.

"You know, Astrid will try to make out that you opposed her because of your own infertility," he said as they stood on the edge of dawn, out on the edge of the settlement.

"Laying my personal hangups over her precious Breeding Program." She almost laughed, but could not quite manage it. "It's not true. I'd oppose it regardless."

"I know."

"You still support the program, don't you?"

"Yes. But a voluntary program. Not enforced. Not like that."

A sigh. To her there was little difference. Worth determined by breeding. Attempts to control the future. But they had argued that one out long before and would never agree. Instead she turned to face him. Looked up into his hurting face and wanting to explain, but too conscious of the guards to try. Anything she said would be noted, would be used against him. She needed to make sure he had the greatest possible chance of success, not hampered by association with her.

"Why?" he asked, a hoarse kind of whisper.

She bit a dry lip. "I might not seem to care much for generations not yet born," she said. "But I do care for those alive now. Today. The survivors. They need a leader, Marcus. One who isn't Astrid."

When the guards came to lead her away from the camp, he took her hand, walked by her side. She was to leave from a pre-arranged set-off point enough distance from the settlement that there would be no chance of any survivor seeing what was happening. The Council wanted no awkward questions, no rumours, no doubt. Nothing left of her to undermine their authority with.

The set-off point was isolated, beyond the rocky valley. Astrid was there waiting for them. A small figure against the dunes, hands clasped neatly in front of her. Henriette felt her mouth settle into a grim line and felt Marcus' fingers tighten around her own. The young woman watched them with those impassive eyes, always so impossible to read. It was impossible to know what really drove her. Was it a desire for power? Some kind of political ambition? Or did she truly see the world only in terms of calculations and logistics?

"Come to see me off, Astrid?" Henriette called out as they approached, not bothering to hide how she felt.

"I take no pleasure in this, Henriette. It was your choice," Astrid said, then paused awkwardly. "The Council wanted me here. As a witness."

Henriette came to a halt in front of the other woman. A girl, tiny against the landscape. In that moment she felt her anger leave her. It just flooded out of her limbs. Astrid, who knew so much about her science, but so little about human social interaction. Who thought she could get the Council to follow her will, but who was here now at the Council's bidding. The girl was being used. One faction or another, it didn't really matter which. She was not going to last against those with less naive understandings of human nature. The politics would end up devouring her.

"Well, good luck, Astrid," she said.

"It is not I who go to face an unknown planet, Henriette. I wish to offer you good luck. I did not want you to think I meant you personal harm."

Her lip twisted, a kind of smile. "Yeah, I know. Nothing personal. You did what you saw you must to protect your program." She shrugged. "Anyway, I always wanted to be an explorer. Now I'm getting the chance. And it won't be me dragged in, locked down and forcibly impregnated."

That hung in the air a moment. Astrid's eyes slid, momentarily, to Marcus, whose anger remained very real. He crossed his arms and glared at her, saying not a word. Astrid would find no ally in Marcus, not now. Was she starting to realise she might need allies? The young woman's eyes moved back to Henriette.

"We all must do our part," the girl said. "My part is in the program's design. In its leadership and monitoring and scientific operation."

"Anyone can lead a program once established. Not everyone can carry a child," Henriette said. "Watch your back, Astrid. They'll come for you too, eventually."

She turned to push past the girl. Could no longer bear to look in her face. Ahead lay dunes, sands. Desert. She would be an explorer, a discoverer of new places. Just like in the archives, the stories. She took a deep breath as she looked out across the washed-out landscape.

Marcus was at her side. She felt his hand around hers and gripped his fingers tight. How to say goodbye? Her mouth wouldn't work, no words came out. But he reached for her, his hands around her arms, her shoulders, turning her to him. Slipping his arms all the way around. She held onto him, clutched him with all she had.

He buried his face in her hair. His mouth right by her ear. "I could come with you." Such a whisper.

"No," she murmured back, almost no sound. "No. You are needed here. You are essential."

"Don't go far. I'll fix this. The wreck: stay near. Be close."

She swallowed. Tasted salt, dry air. Pulled back so she could see his face, his eyes. "Water," she said, as if it explained everything. "Not the wreck. I'll be near water."

And nobody, not him, not Astrid, not even herself, knew exactly how far she would need to go to find another water source.

He kissed her. Clung on until the guards came to pull them apart, haul her away. He tried to hold on even then, but there was no fixing this, not now. She was shoved on by a guard, pushed towards the unknown. She got on the scooter. Looked back to see Astrid standing with an uncharacteristic frown. She was glad for the sunglasses Marcus had given her. She did not want Astrid to see her cry.

Kicking the bike into life. Allowing herself one last look. Marcus stepped forward, one arm stretched out toward her, as if he could somehow hold her back.

"Henri!" he called. "Will you? If I ask, will you?"

It almost made her smile. So foolish. So impulsive and messy and emotional: so human.

"Yes," she cried back, unable to help that lost smile. "Here or on Earth, it was always yes."

She heard him laugh, low and sad, and she laughed too. Astrid stood and frowned, the briefest of creases etched across the girl's forehead. She looked confused, maybe for the first time ever. It was irrational, an emotional impulse, and it would make no sense to Astrid. That human need to love. To breed. To leave something for the future.

To laugh, even in the face of the end.

Henriette turned the scooter and pushed it out into the unknown landscape.

• • •

She survived the day. Found a hollowed-out rock face, harder ground around which she set up the tent. Set a fire with what little synthetic fuel she'd been able to take with her, to try and survive the night. She tried not to think about what she'd do the next night, when her fuel was exhausted and there was nothing in landscape consisting only of sand and rock that she could burn. She'd figure something out. If nothing else, she knew herself to be a survivor.

She sat, watching the low blue and orange flames. Marcus must have found the multi-discs by now, the selected archives she had left by his bed.

She poked at the fire. What would he make of them? Would he understand? He was one of the cleverest men she had ever known; yes, he would understand. He would see what she had seen, those records from Earth's early space exploration. He would have to. The early settlers, the very first attempts at colonisation, so many of which had failed.

Terryian Six.

She wasn't sure, of course. But what could they be sure of in this place?

The archives recorded it as a planet of shifting sands and freezing nights, named for the father of all space exploration, like so many early attempts at colonisation had been. A desert planet with inexplicable fresh water springs among all-consuming sands where nothing else grew. A planet on which the first pioneers had attempted to create a new world and had lasted but a single generation.

There were a lot of desert planets, of course. There was nothing defining in that. No real evidence of anything.

Maybe.

She decided she had better eat. Her food rations were tasteless and she was not hungry, but she would need the energy. Had to keep her strength up. It was hard to tell from the hundred-year-old coordinates copied from the archives into her small box compass just how far she might have to go. If this was Terryian Six, and it was impossible to know, then there would be the remnants of the first colony somewhere. Buried under the sands perhaps, sinking into the desert. Maybe she would be a better archaeologist than she had been a historian.

Closing her eyes, thoughts of Marcus. *Not the wreck. Water.* If she found the first colony, if it existed, there would be water there. She thought of what she had read in those archives. The science of it was beyond her, complex calculations in detailed bio-genetics reports a century old. But she had understood the urgency of their correspondence back to Earth. And she thought she had understood their conclusions.

Not sure. Never sure on anything. Except the one thing: there had been no children. Nobody in the colony had been able to conceive a child.

They thought it had been something in the water.

After a while of sitting and watching the darkness grow beyond her tent, she shifted, found the silvered synthetic of her thermal blanket: thin, strongly insulated, designed to retain her body heat. Hopefully between the blanket, the fire and the hard rock-face around her, she would be able to keep out the freeze. She needed to sleep. She had to conserve energy and survive, because whatever planet this was, Marcus and the survivors would need to know what was out there, and whether it was good, bad or worse. That was her mission now; that was what explorers did: discover.

Maybe this was Terryian Six. And maybe it wasn't. Maybe the colonists had been made sterile from the water, those inexplicable desert springs, or maybe she had misunderstood the science.

Maybe the Earth had not been lost, or the other arks had got through. Maybe they weren't the only humans left.

The future was like that. Impossible to know for sure.

The Silica Key

T. R. Napper

Lynn hated the light. She blinked rapidly as she ascended the stairs from the basement, the bone-white sun searing its afterimage onto her retinas. She slipped on a pair of sunglasses with slim, mirrored lenses and hurried down the footpath, uncomfortable under the oppressive heat. Hard currency from the poker game in her backpack, large manila envelope carrying the instructions in physical copy under her arm. The road was nose-to-tail with traffic, the whine of hydrogen engines filling the street. But the footpath was deserted. Only the foolish ventured out this time of day.

Lynn was up six million and would have been happy to keep playing, turn a twenty-hour session into thirty or forty. But she needed the money for the Dragon, who'd decided the final payment had to be made today, up front. The Dragon wasn't the sort of person you failed to pay on time, not if you wanted to avoid a hole in the back of the head, anyway. So she quit early.

A headache was beginning to form behind her eyes now she was away from the game, the lack of sleep catching up with her. She stepped through automatic doors into a dim arcade, sighing in relief as the chilled air enveloped her. Inside, feed-zombies shuffled over the black-and-white tiles with vacant stares. She weaved past them and pushed through the red-curtained door into Tom Pham's. Shaded lamps cast the inside of the restaurant in a quiet dusk. The familiar, welcoming smells of tea and anchovy sauce hit her as she walked in. The tension eased in her chest.

The old man behind the back counter hurried over to her, his whole face smiling. "Good to see you child. Have you eaten?"

Lynn inclined her head in a small bow. Tom Pham spoke only Vietnamese; she replied fluently. "Uncle, it is good to see you. I apologise, I'm in a hurry. Just tea and some bean *banh bao* to take away."

Disappointment touched his face for a moment. "Always in a rush, child." He indicated a small table near the counter with a weathered hand. "Please, please, sit while you wait."

Lynn sighed as she sat. "The world comes at us faster every day, uncle. I rush just to keep up."

"We make you work too hard, I think." He nodded at her. "I'll make your lunch myself."

Tom Pham disappeared through a beaded curtain to the kitchen out back. Lynn put the manila envelope to one side on the scratched tabletop and was about to pull up her news feed when someone approached. On instinct her hand moved to the pistol hidden in her belt.

"Lynn?"

The man had curly light brown hair, the affectation of horn-rimmed glasses, and an uncertain smile on his face. He was wearing wrinkled pants and a red tie that had been mangled in the tying. His high forehead shone with sweat in the low, red light. A slender, expensive-looking e-reader with a faux leather cover was wedged under his arm.

"Professor Finley." She eased her hand away from her belt.

"It *is* you Lynn. Hard to tell underneath . . . " He gestured at her hair, no doubt lost for a polite descriptor. Fair enough. There probably wasn't a polite way to describe the look she'd cultivated. Her hair was coloured the hue of a freshly-minted gold coin, moulded into a spiked Mohawk. She wore a nose ring, a small black real leather jacket, and was styling a deep green eye shadow and lipstick combination today. She could be mistaken for rebellious teenage neo-punk. Even though she wasn't a punk. Or a teenager. Or particularly neo.

"What are you doing here?" She kept the surprise from her voice.

"Ah." He looked around the dim room. Half the tables were occupied, none of the faces at them white. "I find the atmosphere and the food here *authentic*, insofar as such a term can only ever be applied subjectively. There's a certain . . . " He rubbed thumbs against fingers, though trying to feel the correct word, "timelessness about this place. I can come here, unplug from the world, and let my mind breathe."

"Authentic." Lynn repeated. "Well, they haven't changed the menu or the decor in about twenty years, if that's what you're getting at."

He smiled as though that were delightfully witty. "May I join you?" He pulled out the chair opposite and seated himself before she had a chance to answer.

She looked around the room. Many of the clientele were looking back at her. Wealthy white men in the restaurant were one thing, another thing entirely to be talking to Lynn Thi Vu.

"I'm in a bit of a rush, Professor." She spoke loud enough for the tables nearby to overhear.

"Lynn." He favoured her with a conspiratorial smile. "You were my number one student. And it has been years. Just give me a few minutes until your food arrives."

She glanced around once more, then shrugged with her eyebrows. "Sure."

He indicated her hair. "A dramatic transformation from the buttoned-down woman I knew at university. I wouldn't have even thought it could be you, but ah, that," he nodded at her arm, "jogged my memory."

She glanced down. The immigration markings on the inside of her wrist were showing. A neat, black tattoo detailing her full name, birthdate, arrival date and Medicare number. The imprint was lasered deep, so it could never be removed.

She pulled her sleeve down.

The professor straightened in his seat. "A barbaric practice."

Lynn shrugged. "If people didn't destroy their identification while trying to get here, there'd be no need for it." She pointed at the e-reader he'd placed on the table. "Working over lunch?"

"Ah—it's my new book, *Throwing Away the Key*." His eyes shone in excitement. "I'm reviewing the final draft before publication. Not many read it in a format like this anymore of course—mostly they'll just pull up the c-notes on the back of their eyelids while the car is driving them to work. But some traditionalists still like to read books cover to cover. It is ironic really." he smiled at himself, being one of those people who think any use of the word *irony* is awfully clever, "my thesis argues that constant interconnection with a freewave feed has fundamentally altered human consciousness. And yet, because of these changes, most people won't have the capacity to grasp what the book is saying." He glanced down at Lynn's manila folder. "But here I am talking to someone carrying paper around, of all things. What have we here?"

Lynn's headache was getting worse. She needed tea and something to eat, and soon. She kept the irritation out of her voice. "It's nothing. Please, tell me more about your research."

The professor's favourite subject, like most academics, was himself. Lynn didn't hold it against him, not particularly anyway— the article of faith that is the *glory of me* infected pretty much all of the over-educated and the artists, the privileged in general. Her only concern was that the professor focused on self-congratulation rather than what Lynn's life had held since university.

"Well." He gave a self-deprecating shrug of his shoulders. "I don't want to give you one of my lectures over lunch."

She pushed the corners of her mouth into a smile. "Please."

He didn't need a third request. "Well, the premise extends from my first book—*The Cages of Our Minds*. You'll remember that from class?"

"It was the compulsory text for your course, coincidentally."

He gave her another *my—you're witty* smile. "Well." He inhaled deeply. "We know from the research that as the appetite for the freewave has increased, our attention spans have diminished. As memory pins are used by nearly the entire population, providing all with what used to be called photographic recall, our natural capacity to remember has declined precipitously. So, we have a *paradox*." He smiled the same smile he had used for *irony*. "On the one hand, a desire for news, entertainment and facile social interaction twenty-four hours a day, yet on the other, a need to break down this continual stream of information into smaller and smaller chunks. Slivers of information tailored by complex algorithms to one's political views, aesthetic preferences, sexual orientation, points of prejudice, secret desires, and professional goals.

"This desire for more and more of this input is primordial. As a hangover from our Neanderthal brains, we are hard-wired to hunt for new information as a basic survival instinct: looking out for predators, for food, shelter. Our brain rewards us when we acquire new information with a shot of dopamine. The freewave, therefore, is a powerful drug, a rich source of data dopamine we can mainline every waking minute of the day. The downside of this perennial overdosing is that it crowds out other forms of thinking—in particular, our ability to form and consolidate memories.

"Now, none of this is new." The professor steepled his fingers. "For more than fifty years this has been the case. What *is* new are the technological advances that will allow us to remove ourselves completely from the physical world. In the past five years, people have started using proximity technology developed for automated cars on their own bodies. So they can shuffle around their homes or the shopping districts while they remain plugged into the freewave. It's crude; not particularly effective, but wildly popular nonetheless."

He raised a finger in the perfect imitation of an academic making an important point. "But this development is just the tip of the iceberg. The absolute top-of-the line, next-generation technology can assume complete control of the body's basic mechanical functions. The elementary requirements for human movement have long been understood through cybernetic work on amputees, which has progressed rapidly over the past couple of decades in response to the conflicts in Taipei and Vietnam. The technology is now so advanced that it can be applied to our *physical body*, not just prosthetic limbs." He touched a finger to the smooth metal circle behind his ear. "Through our cochlear-glyph implants, we can place our bodies on auto-pilot, if you will, while our minds are elsewhere."

Professor Finley stopped as Tom placed tea in front of Lynn. The old man didn't give the professor a glass, just a fleeting dour look from out of an otherwise blank face before disappearing back into the kitchen.

Lynn smiled inwardly and sipped her tea, eyes closed, savouring the aroma and feeling her exhaustion abate fractionally while the professor droned on in the background. When she refocused, he was still deep in the groove of his treatise:

" . . . the duality of body and mind. More precisely, this technology separates completely the mind from the body. Yes, only the wealthiest can afford it at the moment—perhaps two or three per cent of the population. But nearly fifty per cent of the population use collision software and most of those will be eager to switch to a more advanced, reliable system; one that will enable them to be fully absorbed into the freewave. It may even be legislated. Think about it: traffic accidents were, for a long time, a serious public health issue. The introduction of strict laws regulating driver-operated vehicles means that today, road deaths have nearly been eradicated. How long before we require human beings to be operated autonomously, for our own safety? No more falling down stairs, into bodies of water, walking through windows.

"Once this technology becomes affordable we'll never have to leave the cage. Our memories and attention spans will continue to shorten; redundant pathways in our brain will atrophy. But that's okay—" He touched a finger to his c-glyph again, "-we have our memory pins. They will remind us of our birthdays and the birthday of our loved ones, when to eat, when to sleep, where we left our keys, what day it is. The advantages it will provide in terms of individual competitiveness will make it compulsory for the powerful. Think about it—CEOs, for example, can instruct the body to play with the children, or make love to their partners while the mind engages in meetings or reads through key documents." The professor smiled, "Or, you know, watches the game."

"All of our day-to-day experiences will be mediated by technology. Physically we will be zombies; mentally we will be machines. Don't you see, Lynn? This threatens the very nature of our existence. Where is *cogito ergo sum* when we can no longer remember the nature of our consciousness? We'll simply be flesh robots for the video game playing inside our heads."

Lynn turned her tea glass slowly in her hand. Her stomach gnawed at her, as did her headache. "Fascinating thesis, Professor. But as you say, there's at least fifty percent who don't use it this way. I'm one. You're another. Technological addictions aren't new."

Irritation touched the corners of his mouth. "Lynn. The early adapters and primary users of this new technology will be the wealthy, the powerful, those at the apex of the information industries—"

"University professors."

He smiled a thin smile. "Yes, but Lynn—"

Tom appeared next to the table, placing a white container in front of Lynn. The aroma of bean and chilli set her stomach rumbling in anticipation.

Tom handed the professor a menu. "All that talking must have made you hungry."

Finley looked up, an uncertain smile on his face. "Sorry, I don't have my translator on. Just a minute." He put a finger on his c-glyph, whispered some instructions.

Lynn stood, picking up her takeaway box. "Professor, it's been edifying. But I really must rush."

"Oh." His hand hovered near his ear. "We should do this properly some time. Dinner perhaps?"

She raised an eyebrow. "Dinner?"

He reddened. "Well, we don't have a professor-student relationship anymore."

"Did you imagine that was the only thing standing in our way?"

He gave her an optimistic shrug, face still red.

"Professor, you don't need me for social interaction. The sound of your own voice is all the company you require."

His mouth popped open in an 'o' of surprise as Lynn turned and walked towards the exit with Tom. She leaned in close, whispering. "Sorry Uncle, he was my university professor. He loves hearing himself talk."

Tom frowned. "A teacher? You shouldn't disrespect him, my child. This society already has little enough respect for learning."

Lynn winced inwardly. "You're right."

He winked at her. "Even if he looks like a balding poodle."

She smiled. "And yaps like one."

He put his hand on the door handle. "I want you to meet Hien. He and his family have not had a chance to thank you since they arrived."

"I'm very busy at the moment."

"They've been here four months."

"That long?" She raised an eyebrow. "You're right. I will contact him soon."

He nodded, opening the door. "Stay safe, child."

Lynn put her lunch in the compartment under the seat of her glimmer bike and rode home. A straight shot between the steady lines of cars bringing feed-zombies from city to suburb. The solar particles coating the bike scintillating white under the stark sun. For a precious half-hour, the rush of the ride cleared the mist of exhaustion from her mind.

Lynn pushed the glimmer bike through the front door into the darkness of her narrow apartment, leaning it against the wall in the entryway. She set the plasteel bar on the door and collapsed with a satisfied grunt into a chair at the kitchen table.

She pulled food and chopsticks from the bag, rubbing the chopsticks over and under each other to smooth off any splinters. The *banh bao* were delicious, and promptly demolished. She sat back, rested her head against the wall, and placed the chopsticks across the lip of the empty food container. Lynn closed her eyes.

Quiet here in her small apartment. Just the whine of the block's hydrogen generator in the distance and a blowfly buzzing against the kitchen window. She breathed in and out slowly, trying to quell the noise in her mind, wound up in the aftermath of the poker game and in anticipation of the meeting later today.

That, and something else. Something else she couldn't quite put her finger on—fretting at her, nagging at the edges of her memory.

Her on-retina timestamp told her:

12:53pm

41° Celsius outside—25° Celsius inside

13/97 Bowden Street Cabramatta

A little over three hours until she had to meet the Dragon.

She put a finger against her c-glyph. "I'm going to sleep. Wake me up at two pm."

A flat, uninflected voice whispered into her ear: "Two pm. Yes Miz Vu."

She shouldered her way through her bedroom door and allowed herself to fall onto the bed, twisting her legs up into the cool, soft sheets. She groaned in contentment. A daytime sleep after an all-night poker session: one of life's great pleasures.

Her mind had started to fade, to drift, to her glimmer bike, flashing down empty roads. Wind in her hair, walkways full with people with empty eyes, watching her as—

"*Du ma,*" she swore.

She sat bolt upright in bed.

Her on-retina display read: 1:31pm

Lynn leapt from the bed, pulled the door open, and went to the kitchen table. She grabbed her backpack, yanking out handfuls of hard currency and throwing them onto the floor. Nothing else was inside.

"*Du ma.*"

She looked around her living room, the tables, the floors, inside cupboards she knew damn well she hadn't opened since she arrived home. Tossed the spare room, where she hadn't been either.

"*Du ma!*"

Then to the bike, shimmering even in the low light of entry hallway. She popped the seat, checking the compartment underneath. Empty.

Lynn slammed the seat closed and hit it with her fist. "*Du ma!*"

Finger to her c-glyph. "Get me Tom Pham's restaurant in Surry Hills."

"Right away," the empty voice replied.

Tom's face appeared to Lynn's eyes a few seconds later, hanging in the air three feet away and to the right.

"Uncle, it's me."

"Huh?" He stared blankly, brows furrowed. Clearly he had no visual function in his c-glyph. "Lynn? Is that you?"

"Yes. It's urgent. I think I left a manila folder on the table today. Did you pick it up?"

Brows still furrowed. "No, no child. Was it important?"

"Tell me, the professor—did he take it?"

"I don't know. It was strange. Half way through his meal he got up and left."

"Uncle. I need you to check your memory feed and see if he took it."

"Child." His eyebrows changed from confused to irritated. "I'm never going to let them put one of those pins in my head."

Lynn gritted her teeth, closed her eyes. A couple of seconds later she opened them again. "You've got that young waiter working today, right? Tell him to check his feed from about forty minutes ago. See if the professor or anyone else took that folder. This is very important; get back to me as soon as you can."

He nodded.

She cut the call, leaned on the tabletop with clenched fists. "Stupid, Lynn. Stupid."

She dragged the small kitchen table away from the wall and pulled the rug underneath aside, exposing the bare polycrete. She placed her palm on the blank floor. After ten seconds, the polycrete glowed in a soft green halo around her hand. A series of satisfying clicks echoed from somewhere in the floor and a section, two feet by two feet, slid back noiselessly. Lynn reached down, grabbed a neat bundle of hard currency, and placed it nearby on the floor. She continued stacking, running over the dimensions of the pile with a practiced eye until it reached the desired size. She stowed the cash, plus her poker winnings, in the compartment under the seat of the glimmer bike. What didn't fit went into her backpack.

Then she paced, from bike to kitchen table, back to bike, slipping the sleek, electric blue nerve pistol from her belt from time to time to check the settings and the clip.

After what seemed like hours, a soft chime sounded in her ear. Her timestamp told her it'd been thirty-three minutes.

"Yes, Tom?"

"He took it. The professor. He looked at what was inside, just sitting there for a few minutes not eating. Then he left."

"*Du ma.*"

He winced at her language. "Is this serious?"

"Yes."

"Do you need me to send a couple of my boys?"

"No. I'll handle this myself. Thank you, Uncle." She cut the feed.

There was no listed number for the professor, and the old one she had was no longer connected. She took her bike to the only place left to go.

. . .

She parked up on some gravel near the entrance of the sandstone Humanities building. The heat was still oppressive, not a breath of wind in the air. Students hurried across the campus, all with eyes glazed or covered with reflective glasses. They ignored the neo-punk and the glittering motorbike she was standing next to.

Her timestamp read: 2:27pm.

She had to have the money and instructions to the Dragon in a little over thirty. Lacking the latter would blow the mission; the former would blow the chances of Lynn seeing her next birthday.

Lynn walked into the dim foyer of the building. The fresh, cool air inside brushed against her face, bringing with it the scent of old wood and pure young bodies. The halls echoed with footsteps and conversation and the petty dynasties of the moderately privileged. She straightened her Mohawk, fixing the ends with open palms while she swallowed her contempt. She made her way up the wide stairs to the floors above.

Lynn knocked on the door.

A pause, then a familiar voice. "Yes?"

She entered.

Professor Finley sat at a large, real wood desk, attempting to hide the concern on his face. Then he attempted a smile, which he failed at as well. Then he pointed at the seat opposite and asked her to sit. He got the pointing right, at least.

The manila folder sat in front of him. The contents—photos and documentation—spread out in front of him.

Lynn remained standing. "Find anything interesting?"

Red rose on his cheeks, his forehead shone with sweat. "I . . . paper is just so expensive and uncommon. I couldn't understand . . . " He straightened in his chair, tried on the voice he used for lectures. "But this really is not the point, Lynn."

She stood watching him, her pupils contracting to harsh pinpoints.

He shifted in his seat, pulled his eyes away from hers. He looked down at the pictures on the table. "Is this what I think it is?" he asked.

"What do you think it is?" Her voice was as hard as her eyes.

"It looks like you're planning to . . . " He cleared his throat, glanced back up at her. "It looks like a detailed travel itinerary for the Tianxian deputy foreign minister's visit to Australia. How did you get this?"

She waited in the silence for a few seconds. "Put it back in the envelope, Professor Finley."

He looked down at the papers. "I don't know if I can do that. I can't just let this—"

"I accept you're good at talking, Professor, and less good at packing envelopes. But you're going to find it difficult to do either after your heart explodes in your chest." She drew the nerve pistol from her belt.

His eyes widened. "Who are you?"

"The one holding the gun. Which means I'm not the one answering questions."

"Lynn—"

"You can call me Miz Vu. Now I haven't slept in a day, bathed in two, or had one off in sixty. That puts me in an ill humour. You rub me the wrong way on a day like this and I'm liable to do something you'll regret. Now give me the fucking envelope."

"Look—" He stopped when Lynn pointed the gun at his face, arm straight out.

He gathered the papers, hands shaking. She waited in silence.

When he was done he pushed the envelope towards her. He stuttered. "This . . . this looks like an assassination."

She raised an eyebrow.

"I mean, I understand your anger towards the Tianxian, and I sympathise, but—"

"You understand nothing. And I need your sympathy about as much as I want your dick in my arse."

His cheeks reddened. "Lynn—"

"Miz Vu."

"Yes, sorry, yes. Miz Vu—if you do this you'll be killing the symbol of a state. It isn't about just one person; it will be seen as an attack on an entire people."

She raised her eyebrow again. "And?"

"It's a declaration of war."

She laughed without humour. "Declaration of war." She stepped over to the table, picked up the envelope. "You're twenty years and twelve million bodies behind the times."

He made a placatory gesture with open hands. "Look, I know the Tianxian Confederation has done terrible things in Vietnam—"

"Most people I deal with in a situation like this try to talk themselves out of a body bag, Professor. You seem intent on doing precisely the opposite. Open your mouth one more time and I'm going to put a nerve splinter in it. Understand?"

She interrupted when he tried to speak. "Don't say anything. That 'o' you make with your mouth is too tempting a target. Just nod."

He nodded.

She watched him in silence, finger tight on the trigger. Footsteps echoed down the hall outside, passed the door, continued on. Lynn took a deep breath, then another. She was too tired, too on-edge. She was going to make a mistake today; she could feel it coming, bearing down on her. But that mistake wasn't going to be shooting the professor in his office. Lynn eased the pressure on the trigger and smiled. As imitation smiles go, it was a very convincing one.

Lynn put the gun in her belt and sat opposite him. "I apologise, Professor. I lost it there for a moment."

"Oh," he said.

She held up the folder. "This isn't going to happen. I called the operation off. After lunch at Tom's I was going to destroy this envelope, never think on it again." She tapped the gun in her belt. "This was just a little sabre rattling. I would never harm my favourite uni professor. I'm just-I'm just under a lot of pressure right now. You understand."

He tried to keep his face blank, but Lynn could see the disbelief in it. The professor wouldn't make a very good poker player.

Lynn weighed her options, watching the curly-haired man as he wiped the sweat from his brow.

She sighed.

"I'm a people smuggler, Professor. That's what I've been doing since university. I pay for residency visas for Vietnamese families trying to escape the Tianxian occupation. I get them clean identification, so they don't show up on any of the Tianxian watch lists held by the Australian government, and help them settle here." She rested the envelope in her lap and leaned back in the chair. "The Tianxian deputy foreign minister is visiting to sign a new treaty with Australia. It will result in Tianxia becoming the biggest importer of Australian basic commodities again. In return for this economic dividend, they have insisted Australia maintain complete neutrality regarding the war in Vietnam. This includes a halt to the refugee re-settlement program. The Tianxian strongly suspect that most of those re-settled are former *Viet Minh*. The program brings out five thousand Vietnamese annually. That's five thousand human beings saved, each year. For a time, I considered exchanging all those lives for that of one Tianxian official."

"But how would killing the minister stop the treaty?"

"The Tianxian would have received evidence, from an anonymous source, that the Australians knew full well *Viet Minh* were being resettled here; that the government turned a blind eye because it was desperate for revenue. Which is true. It's also true that some of these same *Viet Minh* would be behind the assassination." She shrugged. "Anyway, all this is academic. The treaty will be signed, and the lifeline to Vietnam cut."

Finally, Professor Finley was silent. He leaned back in his chair, steepling his fingers. The disbelief was gone from his face, replaced by something new. He breathed a sigh of relief. "I knew it."

"You did?"

"I knew that what I saw in the envelope must have an explanation. I remember that girl from class—quiet, inconspicuous, yet brilliant and passionate in her essays. I knew that whatever I was seeing had to be for the right reasons. You became a people smuggler because you were driven by a sense of social justice."

Lynn watched the professor in silence for several long seconds. She nodded, though not in agreement. "What's the difference?"

"What do you mean?"

"I mean, what difference are my motivations? It's all inside my head. Whether I'm following a moral code, or doing this out of hatred against the Tianxian, or just a mercenary concerned about maintaining a reputation for reliability. From the outside it could be any one of these things. They all look the same. Even if I told you it was one thing, you could just as easily think another, as it suited your interests."

He shook his head. "I know you Lynn. I know this is about a code. I know you believe you are doing what you believe to be right."

"Like I said, you'll only accept one answer to your question, as it suits your interests. You're trapped in the cage of your mind, Professor. We all are. Technology isn't changing our nature; it is bringing perfect clarity to our natural state. It is enabling a pure, unabridged individual uncorrupted by base physical needs." Her tone was as flat and smooth as an ice rink. "We're atomised beings floating in nothing but the sea of our own consciousness. Lamenting this is about as useful as lamenting evolution."

He shook his head again. "You don't believe that."

She smiled. Like the first one, it was a very good imitation. "Maybe. Maybe I'm just making a philosophical counter-point to keep your arguments rigorous. Something I learned from the best."

He smiled back. His was real.

She reached out to hold his hand, fingers brushing his shirtsleeve. "I need to ask you a favour, Professor."

The professor's cheeks reddened. "What favour?"

She held up the envelope. "Never speak of this. To anyone."

He gave her a regretful grimace. "If I'm ever asked about this by the authorities—"

"Professor," she gripped his hand tightly. "Do this one thing. Not just for me, but for the thousands I've brought over here. "

He paused, glancing down at her hand. He nodded slowly. "Okay Lynn, okay. I will." He squeezed her hand back, face sombre. "This is . . . bigger than either of us."

She nodded in reply, mirroring his gravitas. "Yes. It is."

Lynn straddled the glimmer bike and put on her helmet, flipped down the mirrored visor.

"Activate trace. Keep on-retina."

To the right of her vision, an overhead map of the inner city appeared. It was currently centred over the University of Sydney. A soft green pinpoint of light pulsating over one of the campus buildings.

• • •

Lynn sat at the stained faux wood table in the dank café, the ache behind her eyes unrelenting. Her hand shook slightly as she picked up her glass of tea. Exhaustion had won the battle hours ago, pulling her into a sensory demimonde—aware of the world outside, even interacting with it as required, but from a distance. It felt like she was watching the c-cast of her life, but one badly tuned and on a several-second delay. The meeting with the Dragon had gone well though, the last of her adrenalin getting her through the meeting. The deal was done.

Now she had just one more loose end.

"Older sister?"

A young man with short black hair stood nearby, fidgeting with his hands.

"Hien?" she asked, placing her tea carefully on the table.

He nodded rapidly. "Yes, Tom Pham sent me. He—"

Lynn interrupted with a shake of the head and indicated the seat opposite. He took it. She poured him a glass of tea.

"Sorry, I—"

"It's nothing, little brother." She pulled an unopened pack of Double Happiness brand cigarettes from the top pocket of her jacket. "Smoke?"

"Not since I arrived," he said, eyeing the pack.

"Australians like to make laws on everything. Please." She slid them over to him.

He hesitated, then pulled one from the pack. "Thanks."

She lit it for him with her silver lighter, snapping it shut. "Your family has settled in well?"

He nodded, closing his eyes as he took a drag of the smoke. "Our apartment is perfect, the boys in primary school: it's great Miz Vu. Really great. We owe you."

"You're right. You do. That's what I wanted to discuss with you."

He set his jaw. "I'll work hard. We'll pay back every single dollar."

"Yes you will." She pulled a small brown envelope from her backpack, and a flat box wrapped like a present. She set them in front of him.

Hien looked around, his movements sharp. The café was dim, empty except the proprietor sitting behind the counter. He was reading a flexiscreen, studiously ignoring Miz Vu and her companion.

"Relax, we can do business here. Open the envelope."

He did so, removing a colour photograph of a white man sitting at an outside table at a café, a glass of red wine in one hand, looking at an e-reader in the other.

Lynn's eyes flicked to the edge of her vision where the on-retina map had the trace. "That man is at his house right now. I've got a car waiting to drive you. When you get there you tell him you have a message from Lynn. When he asks you what it is, tell him I think his books are heading in the right direction. It's just a shame no one reads anymore."

Hien fingered the photograph. "And then what do I do?"

Lynn indicated the box with her eyes. "Then you shoot him in the face. Take his memory pin."

He put the picture down on the table, silent. His hands started shaking.

"Problem?"

"I . . ."

"You've fought in the war. You were a sergeant."

"Yes."

"So you've killed before."

"Yes . . ."

"But?"

"But they were soldiers."

Lynn put a finger on the photograph. "This man is far worse than a foot soldier. He is a *collaborator*, little brother. Tomorrow morning he will go to the police and give them vital information about my operation. That will put thousands of families in peril. They will be sent back to Vietnam and end up in Tianxian prisoner-of-war camps. That includes you and yours. How long will your wife survive in one of those? How long will your two sons?"

He looked up at her sharply. Then, seeing what was in her eyes, looked back down at the table. He took a deep drag on his cigarette, the shaking in his hands abating slowly.

"Most take years to pay off their debts to me. You can do it in a single night. Your slate will be clean."

He nodded again, face blank.

"Did you think the war ended just because you came to Australia?"

He didn't answer. Just shrugged, eyes distant.

"It never ends, little brother." She took back the envelope and picture. "Now, give me your memory pin. We'll implant an alibi memory for this evening."

Hien popped the pin from his cochlear implant and handed it over in silence, staring at a spot on the table in front of him.

Lynn took the pin and leaned back in her chair, drained. She watched the thin line of white smoke from Hien's cigarette trail upwards to the ceiling. Her voice sounded distant in her ears. "But we're going to win this war. One day the ruling class will disappear down the rabbit hole of their own subconscious. And all that will be left are those with their eyes open."

Hien looked up at her, confused.

Lynn shook her head, refocussing on the man opposite. She cleared her throat. "All you have to do is say a dozen words and pull one trigger. Can I trust you to do this?"

The distance in his eyes was gone. "Yes Miz Vu. You can rely on me."

. . .

Two hours later Lynn sat alone in her apartment, trying to concentrate on a slim paperback volume of poetry under a lamp at the kitchen table. A bowl of noodles and tempeh, barely touched and now cold, pushed to one side.

A soft chime in her ear sounded and a news alert flashed at the bottom of her vision. She touched her c-glyph and whispered. "Bring up the story."

The image of a woman resolved into view. The newsreader looked the same as every other: white, blonde, and square-jawed.

"—come to hand. We repeat: tragic developments tonight as reports emerge of the death of the Tianxian deputy foreign minister. The minister died of a suspected heart attack after a state banquet hosted by the Australian Prime Minister. Sources have informed us that the Tianxian Confederacy has reacted swiftly, mobilising their own physicians to undertake the autopsy—"

"Cut the feed."

She breathed in and out slowly, a small smile at the corners of her mouth. The buzzing in her mind was gone. Lynn rose from her chair, pushing her way through the door to her bedroom.

She was going to sleep well tonight.

Function A:save(target.Dawn)

Rivqa Rafael

That evening was the last time I ever stepped foot in the White House. Not that I was a regular visitor or anything. Still, my best efforts—being super polite, dressed in my nicest clothes, piercings out or covered, hair braided neatly—weren't enough, after what happened. The fact that Dawn instigated it didn't make any difference.

Dinner hadn't started yet, so we were sprawled on Dawn's bed. Sneaking looks at each other. Carefully not touching. Accidentally touching. She was nervous because she was going to give a speech, and I was doing my best to keep her distracted.

We'd lapsed into silence and she was fidgeting, so I pulled my ace from my pocket. "Dawn, this is for you."

That girl had everything, but her grey-blue eyes still lit up when she saw the game box. "You programmed this yourself, Desi?" She flipped the cube, searching for the button, hair falling in a golden curtain.

I ducked my head. "Yeah. It's just a little sim, and . . . " My hand closed over hers as I switched on the game box for her, my skin dark against her pale, which never saw the Sun. My train of thought evaporated.

Dawn glanced up. Her lips curved into the smallest of smiles and our eyes met. She opened her mouth.

The soft metallic tapping of a housebot at the door. "Miss Dawn, Miss Desiree. The other guests are arriving."

"We'll be right there," Dawn said. She pressed her mouth against mine for too-brief a moment, stood and held out a hand.

I took it, grinning stupidly, pushing myself up with my other hand. It was habit to be cautious around Dawn, with her condition and all. She lifted her chin and opened her door, still holding my hand. The housebot trailed behind us, its stainless steel tuxedo gleaming bright.

The Family Dining Room of the White House was dazzling, LED chandeliers blazing, carpet springy enough to be a trampoline. The First Lady was the first to notice us. She frowned, and after a second's hesitation Dawn let go of my hand.

"It's OK," I said. "You don't have to . . . "

"Thank you," Dawn said. She bit her lip, then turned to wave at a woman across the room. "Come on, let me introduce you."

We wandered over. Dawn said, "Lavender, I thought you weren't coming tonight."

The woman was tall, even by gen-modded standards. Her mods were of the delicate, ethereal variety, and her dark, wavy hair was pulled up carelessly into a loose bun. "I shuffled things at the last minute to be here for your speech. Who's your friend?"

Dawn smiled. "Desiree, Doctor Lavender Peters. She heads the research program at FAIRY, well, you know, the research into me." The Foundation for Augmentation and Improvement Research for the Young mainly did gen mods on embryos for the super-rich, but after the attack, they had a whole army of scientists trying to find a cure for Dawn. Fifteen years on, they hadn't had much luck.

I held out my hand. "Nice to meet you."

"Desiree is amazing with tech," Dawn said. "She can code anything, fix anything, and build anything."

"Impressive," Lavender said. She shook my hand with a firm grip. No doubt she noticed my lack of mods—it was obvious close up, from the flaws and all. But she wasn't the sort to surreptitiously look for a neural port, at least.

"Dawn!" I said. My face grew hot.

"Dawn doesn't exaggerate." Lavender pulled out her datapad.

"I'll beam you my details. Maybe you can do a summer project with our biomedical engineering department."

I pulled out my pad to take the beam. "I'd . . . I'd love to."

The housebots began serving food. Dawn was quiet, probably nervous about her speech. She picked at her food with her datapad on her lap. When she eventually stopped swiping through her speech, I reached under the table and squeezed her hand.

After the appetisers, the President welcomed his guests. He was immaculate, as always, in a perfectly tailored suit. His white teeth and glossy hair—a full head of it, of course—shone under the lights. Apart from Lavender, there were some other FAIRY bigwigs and other cronies he mentioned individually by name.

Politicians and businesspeople always made me feel icky, although I never mentioned it to Dawn. Her dad was the most popular U.S. President in centuries, but the way he stiffened up around me and forgot to be President Charming made me wary. My guess was he didn't like that I was a scholarship kid. A reminder of the genetically unenhanced masses who had to resort to neural implants—if they could afford them—to try to keep up with the richer, genetically modified Joneses. Not that we could ever succeed. With so many people around, he just ignored me, his gaze sliding straight past mine.

Suppressing a snort, I turned away and shifted my attention to the First Lady, whose eyes were the same shade as her daughter's, but always held a sad expression. Not everything can be modded or operated out, especially not life experience, and Dawn's condition seemed to affect her more than it did Dawn.

At last the President introduced Dawn. She left her datapad on her chair; speaking without notes was one of her dad's hallmarks.

"People often feel sorry for me," she said, glancing around the room. Her nervousness was no longer evident. "But they shouldn't. Yes, there are limitations on my life because of what a terrorist did to me. Yes, I have regular medical appointments and can't go out in the sun because it would damage my DNA and give me cancer. But I never forget how lucky I am to have received this level of care. With the standard of medicine today, it's easy to forget that some people with conditions similar to mine aren't fortunate enough to have them modded out. And that's why I'd like to remind people that the research FAIRY does on my behalf is not for my benefit alone." She nodded at Lavender and caught my eye for a split second.

"Their work is crucial, not just to increase my chances of ever being able to experience sunshine, but also to improve the lives of hundreds of thousands worldwide. It's incredible that the concept of altering DNA after birth is still revolutionary. FAIRY are at the forefront of this research. Their annual donation drive begins this week, and I urge you all to give generously. You'll be funding the most innovative research on the planet, and you'll be saving lives."

Including hers, but she didn't need to say so. Or that it might mean gen mods for more people. People like me. She slipped into her seat and smiled as everyone applauded. The President beamed at her. If FAIRY's donations jumped that year, I wouldn't be surprised.

Lavender was seated close enough for me to ask about FAIRY between bites. Dawn had questions too, but they were about molecular biology instead of engineering like mine, so we kept her pretty busy. Soon they were talking a mile a minute while I struggled to keep up. Dawn studied this stuff in her spare time and was already at college level, despite her own lack of fully functional gen mods. "It's just code, really, Desi, same as the stuff you do," she'd say to me, but molecular biology didn't obey the rules like programming languages did. Epigenetics confused me as much as F++ confused Dawn.

So while she and Lavender discussed junk DNA and metabolic cycles, I let myself dream of one day working at FAIRY. Joining Lavender's team, impressing everyone and helping them find a cure for Dawn. Or maybe I would be the one to catch the terrorist Lachlan Cara. Plenty of people thought that finding him would be the key to uncovering data that would lead to Dawn's recovery.

Dawn put her hand on my knee and I jumped back into reality with a fizz of electricity.

"You're not listening, are you?" she accused.

"I, um . . . "

"You'll need to learn all about this stuff if you want to work at FAIRY."

I glanced at Lavender.

"It's true, DNA is kind of our thing," she said. "But I'm sure you'll get up to speed."

"I'll try," I said.

Dessert was served and before I knew it, Mom had arrived to pick me up. Dawn walked me out and held me close. She didn't kiss me, but I was floating anyway. She'd fast-tracked my career with just a few words to the right person, and everything was settled between us with no words at all.

· · ·

The next day at school, Dawn wouldn't talk to me at all. I was crushed for a minute, before realising that keeping her distance couldn't have been her own idea. After some manoeuvring I cornered her in the bathroom.

"Did your dad tell you to stop talking to me?"

She stared at her feet. "He says I'm too young to date."

"How did he find out? Your mom wouldn't . . . the housebot."

"Yeah, I think so. Didn't know they were programmed to snoop."

"So, what? We can't even speak? Or be friends?"

Dawn's eyes met mine. "Can we really be just friends?" Her voice was bitter. "He said, if we sneak around, he'll find out, and he'll be really angry."

I swallowed. "We can be friends. It's better than nothing. Much better."

She swiped a hand past one eye and gave me a quick hug. "Thank you," she said.

The President accepted us being just-friends, probably hoping we'd move on from our 'schoolgirl crushes'. It was unfair, but Dawn had demands on her I'd never have. I wasn't invited back to the White House and she was never allowed to visit me at my apartment, in a part of DC considered 'too dangerous' by most. We only had school, which was covered with enough CCTV to make sure I kept to my word. During lunch breaks, she taught me molecular biology in the library. She could explain it so well. Sure, I could infodump through my implant, but there was no substitute for real learning.

"OK, I get DNA," I said, a few sessions in. "Can you explain what's wrong with yours, now? If you don't mind me asking."

She shook her head. "I don't mind. You know Cara injected me with nanobots at my baby naming, when I was just a few days old. You've watched the vid, right?"

Everyone had seen it. The terrorist used holos to disguise a robot first as a sculpture, then as a person mingling in the crowd. The robot slipped past security and injected baby Dawn with nanobots, right in her mother's arms. Everything happened so fast, it was hard to follow the vid without annotations explaining what was what. And in slow-mo.

"Have you seen it? That would be so weird, watching yourself be attacked."

"Watched it first when I was ten. My parents thought I should have waited, but ... " Dawn shrugged. "Anyway, FAIRY still hasn't been able to extract a nanobot from my blood. If they could, they'd know a whole lot more. Their best guess is that the bots do continuous damage to my DNA. That's why I have Sun sensitivity and I'm way shorter than my parents. Tumours grow all the time, but they cut them out straight away."

"And Cara could only do that because you had the gen mods from FAIRY in the first place, right?" I fidgeted, tapping at my implant.

"That's right. The bots attack the vectors that FAIRY used to put in the gen mods. He had all the DNA sequences because he used to work there."

"So if your parents hadn't ... "

"That's what Cara said. But if he hadn't injected me with nanobots, I'd have been fine too. Just taller and brilliant and gorgeous."

"You *are* brilliant and gorgeous," I said.

Dawn shook her head: in denial or warning I wasn't sure.

• • •

We continued like that for the rest of the year, then parted ways on the sidewalk outside school. Any contact between us over summer would be via heavily monitored mails or vid calls.

"It's only a couple of months," Dawn said. "Just keep busy. We'll be back at school before you know it."

My throat caught; I had to swallow before I could speak. "I'm going to study hard. Next year I'll be old enough for the FAIRY summer program."

"You'll get it for sure." She paused. "I still use your game box every night. The whole thing is so pretty, and I keep finding new things in the world you made. You must have spent ages on it."

I ducked my head. "Glad you like it."

Her car dove down to the curb. If we hugged a little longer than just-friends do, if our kisses on the cheek drifted towards the lips, no one noticed in the crush of the last day of school. One last squeeze of my hand, and she was gone.

• • •

Molecular biology was my world that summer. Dawn had taught me enough that I could infodump and make sense of most of the material, and questions were always a good excuse to mail her. My own coding study was never as much of a struggle. Not for me. When my head felt like it was exploding, I played video games until my brain could function again. Nothing wiped my worries like putting on a sim helmet and smashing monsters.

First day back at school, I was ready early. I'd never been happier to sit on those concrete steps, surrounded by red brick and prestige. Eyes glued in the direction of the White House, watching the cars stream by.

Hers never came. I called her over and over, not moving when the crowds poured in. There was no answer.

According to my log, I called thirty-seven times before someone answered. The First Lady's face showed on my datapad, her perfectly sculpted nose red from crying. "Oh, Desiree, honey, I'm sorry. We should have let you know."

My stomach clenched, hard as rock. "What's wrong with Dawn?"

"She's really sick, Desi. She had a brain tumour and they just operated. She's in an induced coma now, recovering."

"Is she going to be OK? Can I see her?"

The First Lady shook her head. "We're not sure just yet. No visitors at this point. I'll beam your details from Dawn's pad and call you when there's news, promise."

I thanked her and disconnected, anxious to get away from those sad eyes.

Dragging myself off the steps, I headed to the computer lab. Class was not going to happen; I mailed my homeroom teacher with my excuses. If she was in a good mood, she'd let it slide.

I switched on a terminal and stared at it, thumbing my implant. The President's second term was almost up. Funny how I'd let myself fantasise about curing Dawn, but I'd never thought about what might change next year. The First Family had planned to stay in DC until Dawn finished school, but we'd never discussed what that would mean for us.

Cara must have devised a way to make Dawn sicker, right before the President's retirement. It was too much of a coincidence otherwise; he was surely trying to distract from that and raise the Luddites' profile. They'd adopted him as part of their cause because he opposed gen mods. Never mind that his brand of terrorism messed with nature just as much, if not more, than FAIRY ever did.

Dawn's illness was already all over the news. Socmed was going wild, posts and updates streaming past with conspiracy theories (I *almost* smiled at the one that Dawn was being turned into a mutant superhero), some concern about Dawn, and lots of support for the President, rather than Dawn herself.

My brain was buzzing; I wanted to do something. Contact Lavender? No—she wasn't expecting to hear from me until internship applications opened. And as much as I'd learned about molecular biology, it wasn't my true strength. Instead, I dug around through the junk in my bag, searching for the right cable. I opened a new window, jacked into the terminal with my implant, and started coding.

It took a while to get it right, of course. It always does. My homeroom teacher mailed back, granting me another day of leave; classes were still settling in so I wasn't missing much. I took her up on that and finished my program the next day.

Testing it was the next step. The program worked, with some revisions, but it needed more processing power. So I set up a little website, asking people to donate their spare CPU to my Cara-finding project. I called it 'Save Dawn' and put a plea on socmed on a separate account and behind a proxy, for some anonymity. It would slow down anyone looking for me, rather than stop them, but that was better than nothing.

To my surprise, a journalist from a major news company picked it up and publicised it, so after a few days, I had enough power to try the program out for real. Jacked into my home terminal, my heart thundered as I pushed the script through the orange and grey corridors of the web. This was what I did best, this was where I belonged; riding waves of data, certain I could succeed and —

Something pushed me, or *flicked* me, it felt like, out of the corridor and back into meatspace. Bile rose in my throat. I jacked out and sipped some water. My spam watcher started beeping and I cycled through my browser tabs. The Save Dawn website had been hacked, defaced with graffiti, as if someone had written it by hand on a datapad. All it said was: *Think a child can stop me?* Over the request for help at the end, Cara had pasted a picture of me, one from my personal socmed.

My chair toppled as I stood. "Mom?" I called. "We have to get out of here. Now."

She must have caught my tone, because she ran in. "What happened?"

"I made a really big mistake. We need to go."

She took out her datapad.

I snatched it from her hands. "Better leave it here. I'll explain on the way."

The early evening sky was still streaked with light. We footed it to the police station rather than risk the car's computer being hijacked. Our implants were a risk too, but we could hardly leave them at home, and they were supposed to be immune to hacking. We ran past the crumbling apartment blocks of our decaying neighbourhood. The acrid smell of leaking sewage flooded the narrow streets. People stared as we raced past. I gripped Mom's hand tighter and pulled her along.

Whatever checks the officer ran on us, they made him take us seriously. Despite my best efforts, I started crying as I explained what I'd done. "I made things worse, didn't I?"

He shook his head, expression blank. "Can't say, miss. I'm going to get one of our lieutenants. This is more his line. And . . . We'll need to search your apartment, with your permission, ma'am."

Mom nodded. She gave me a tissue from her purse and tried to hug me.

I pushed her away, sniffing. "I don't deserve any sympathy."

"Oh, honey . . . "

The officer returned with the lieutenant, who made us go over the whole story again.

"It's true that you were foolish, Desiree," he said. "But you've done the right thing in coming straight to us."

"Please don't tell Dawn's parents," I said.

He patted my shoulder. "This isn't exactly something we can hide from the President. In any case, as a precaution, I'd like to place you in temporary protection. I've taken the liberty . . . " His voice trailed off as he opened up a comm link.

"Doctor Peters!" I sat up, then put my face in my hands. "I . . . kind of messed up."

Lavender pressed her lips together. "Desiree, your mistake hasn't done as much damage as you think. Not to Dawn, anyway. And as far as mistakes go, it's pretty impressive."

Startled, I looked up again.

"The fact that you got as far as you did, working from a home terminal, speaks volumes about your potential as a programmer. There's a place for you with our biomedical engineering team, if you would like it. We can keep you as safe as the police can, and get your career moving while we're at it."

"I . . . what?"

. . .

Mom's work gave her leave and FAIRY organised an apartment for us, right near the main research building. A private entrance shielded us from the street, and burly guards seemed to be everywhere. The police quarantined all our data, but they brought our clothes and other stuff to our new place, so it felt almost like home.

Still, I wanted a fresh start. After some coaxing, Mom chopped my hair down into a short 'fro and helped me dye it bright pink. Short enough to show off all the earrings that I sometimes wondered why I'd bothered getting. Tilting my head revealed my neural implant. I felt a million times cooler. Lots of people hid their implants, but not me.

Lavender did a double take when she met me at the gates the next day. "I like it," she said. "The colour is awesome against your skin. You look like a real hacker now . . . the good kind, of course."

"Thanks." I glanced up at the building. Domed and rounded, it was built to suggest the shape of a curled-up foetus. The current paint job was stark white, but bricklayers and gardeners were working together to scoop away some of the facade and embed vertical gardens. The sterile walls and dirt and greenery were a mess, but it would be pretty when it was done. "FAIRY's getting a makeover too."

She rolled her eyes. "It's taking ages, and there's dirt *everywhere*. Come on, let's get you inside."

Security took a while to go through my bag. "Girl, you need to clean this crap out," one of the guards said to me with a grin. Laughing, I promised to do my best.

Past the automatic doors, Lavender presented me with a swipe card. "This will take you where you're allowed to go. Keep it with you at all times."

She showed me through the labs—some dedicated to Dawn's treatments, some general. They all seemed pretty much alike: bright lights, white benches and lots of complicated machines that scientists used with the confidence I felt when jacking into my terminal.

Then there were training modules to pass. Lab protocols and procedures, OH&S, lots of boring hoops to jump through. They tested me, question after question about anything they could think of. At the end of each day all I wanted was sleep, but I had homework, too; my study was nowhere near enough to keep up with the PhDs, most of whom had gen mods and years of research under their belts. I'd never infodumped so much in one go, and it was a losing battle trying to make sense of it all.

At first I worried about Mom, cooped up in the apartment. But she was determined to treat it as a vacation. She hadn't had a proper one since before I was born, working as hard as she did to pay off our implants. Mom said she was sure she'd get bored of watching vids all day eventually, but it was going to take a while.

While Dawn was under, they filtered her blood to search again for nanobots. They managed to extract a couple this time, a success in terms of research, if not treatment.

"The others must be more deeply embedded in her organs," Lavender said. "But we'll get some good data from these."

I wasn't allowed near them. Frustrated, I offered to help in other ways. Endless, boring data entry and analysis, but at least I knew what was going on—or wasn't. The test results were disappointing.

Nanobots were notoriously difficult to study, being so tiny and all, but I'd never expected everyone to be so stumped.

In a lab meeting full of despondent scientists, I raised my hand tentatively. "What if there's more encryption on the bots than we think? It might explain why we're not finding much."

"Can't be," Jerry, one of the biomed engineers, said. "That much data just can't fit in a bot this size."

My shoulders slumped down.

"No, it's worth checking out," Lavender said.

"Just because she's your wunderkid, doesn't mean you need to coddle her," Jerry said.

Lavender raised an eyebrow. "You started here after Cara was fired, didn't you?"

"Yeah, what—"

"So don't assume anything is impossible. He's much smarter than you, and sneakier."

Jerry ducked his head. "Wait, you knew him? What was he like?"

I leaned forward in my chair. A personal opinion on Cara was worth a million infodumps on his shady activities.

"Not much to tell. In retrospect, it's obvious that he was a sociopath. You know he was fired for building nanobots that could be programmed to stop working if the client fell behind on their payments, right? He was always a bit off, but brilliant. Cramming more data into bots than they're meant to fit wouldn't surprise me in the least."

"Is he modded or planted?" Jerry asked.

"Modded, definitely. Implanted, possibly also," Lavender replied.

"Isn't that—?"

"Illegal? Yeah, and so's hijacking an infant's gen mods." Lavender pressed her lips together in a thin line.

There was a brief silence. How often had she tortured herself thinking about what FAIRY might have done differently to prevent Cara's bizarre vendetta?

"Right," Lavender said, her expression clearing. "I'd like Desiree to have access to the bot we've been working on. See what she comes up with. If she breaks it, we've still got the spare."

"I'm not going to break it," I said, trying not to scowl. Then I noticed the twinkle in her eyes.

Jerry got over being grumpy and taught me how to use the electron microscope. The nanobot was creepy and interesting to see at extreme magnification, but it didn't help me much. What I needed was a way into its data, a way to connect to it somehow. I thumbed my implant as I thought.

"You can't jack into this baby," Jerry said.

"Yeah, I know. But I might be able to interface." I rummaged around in my bag and pulled out a game box, a prototype of the one I'd given Dawn. Its simple wireless capabilities might just do the trick.

Jerry grinned. "With a few over-rides . . . "

We programmed it quickly, arguing good-naturedly about how best to code it. The first time any of them treated me like a colleague, instead of just a kid. When we were done, I started jacking into the game box.

Jerry shook his head. "Stay in meatspace. Let's test it wirelessly first. We might need a better firewall."

It was true that things hadn't gone so well last time I tried to jack into Cara's domain.

"While we're at it, let's back up before we connect, like good little tech heads," he said. He uploaded the code into the lab's cloud, then severed the link. The game box would connect to the nanobot only, projecting any data it found as a holo, which we would then transcribe. Annoying, but it would keep us, and the data, safe.

Neither of us breathed as we opened the connection. As data began to flow through to the holo display, I read the code aloud into my datapad's recorder.

Jerry spoke softly, so my mic wouldn't pick up his voice. "This is the most sophisticated encryption I've ever seen. Lavender wasn't kidding when—what's that smell?"

The game box was blazing. Jerry ran for the electrical fire extinguisher while I shouted the rest of the data at high speed before it vanished.

"All done?" Jerry asked, waving the extinguisher around.

"Yes, that's everything—that was projected, anyway." When my datapad was safe in my pocket, he put out the fire, so tiny it hadn't even triggered the smoke alarms yet. We opened the windows for good measure.

"Bet you're glad that's not your brain," he said.

I coughed as I inhaled some smoke. "Little bit."

Lavender gripped the edge of her fancy glass desk as we brought her up to speed.

"This section here?" Jerry pointed to the last code fragment we'd recorded. "We're pretty sure it's a transmitter."

"So Cara is still communicating with his bots." Lavender nodded. "We'd thought so."

"He also knows we're onto him," Jerry continued.

"Don't forget the good news," I interrupted.

Jerry frowned at me. "Desiree thinks she can trace his signal back to him in meatspace, find where he's hiding," he said. "But I really don't think she should . . . " He turned to me. "Remember what that game box looked like."

"But with better firewalls . . . "

"Jerry, could you step out for a minute, please?" Lavender said.

He left, looking as puzzled as I felt.

"In our line of work," Lavender said, "It's important not to let our emotions cloud our judgement. It often leads to poor decisions that don't hold up in front of ethics committees."

"But Dawn—"

"It's obvious how much you care about her. More than just as a friend, right?"

I nodded, blushing at my transparency.

"So, ethics aside, imagine if something happened to you, and I had to tell Dawn that I'd let you do it."

"Lavender, I can do this, I swear. I'll encrypt to my eyeballs, literally. I'll be careful. Just give me the chance."

She shook her head. "We'll find another way. Thanks to the data you've extracted, the biotech team is closer to a cure, or at least a treatment. You've already done enough. Even if you did actually break the nanobot." She smiled, eyes twinkling with what seemed like a mixture of amusement and pity.

I resisted the urge to kick something on my way out.

• • •

The biotech team worked around the clock, while my team worked on what they called the delivery system, which was basically a nanobot with as many defences as we could code in. I did my best to make myself useful, even if it meant getting coffee instead of doing real work. No one knew how long Dawn could stay in the induced coma, so everyone was tense. After what seemed like endless testing, Lavender decreed Dawn's treatment ready.

"You should be there when we give it to her," she said to me.

"Her father won't let me."

Lavender put her hand on my shoulder. "They know what you've done for Dawn. Anyway, we need a team there to search for rogue tech. You may as well be on it."

We spent ages scouring the private FAIRY facility where Dawn was being treated. Despite its high security, we found and disabled a few small bots. When we were done, Lavender brought me into Dawn's room.

Dawn's parents sat on either side of her; I returned the President's curt nod and stared at Dawn. Paler and thinner than I remembered, she had wires sticking out everywhere. They connected to a central monitor that displayed all kinds of numbers I didn't understand. Lavender put her arm around my shoulder.

"We'll get her healthy again," the doctor said confidently to the President. He checked Dawn's monitor and, apparently satisfied with the numbers, began preparing a syringe with the treatment.

The monitor's display flickered. Before I had a conscious thought, I was elbowing the doctor out of the way to reach it. With trembling hands I plugged a cable into my implant, hoping the monitor had a standard connector. It did.

A voice emanated from the monitors. "Nothing can stop—"

I ramped up my firewalls and jacked in.

In my daydreams, this moment was carefully planned, with protocols and filters and an arsenal of awesome trojans. Imaginary me would match Cara's stealth, slipping in and out of the dark web until I caught him.

There was no time for anything like that. The data streamed by without any anomalies to guide me. Closer. A small empty space that should have been full. I nudged it and jumped back when it tingled like an electric fence. Firewall. I lobbed a giant, overly obvious trojan at it. While the wall consumed it, I used a tiny one to cut through. I jumped through just in time; the hole was reabsorbed in microseconds. The buzzing reverberated through me, then faded. No way back now.

Cara's corner of the web was dark, darker than the shadiest hackers' corner. A slender strip of grey light directed me to where he was likely to be jacked in. I pressed on as fast as I dared, doing my best to hide behind data as it moved through.

The centre of his domain suggested a shadowy castle. Someone had delusions of grandeur. Back in meatspace, my guts clenched. I reminded myself that none of this was real, that all that mattered was Cara's avatar. The entrance was unguarded apart from some easily dodged turrets; his defences would be inside.

Further in, a second firewall presented itself. I threw another trojan. The time for subtlety was over. The wall crumbled easily—more warning system than real defence.

The terrorist stood facing away from me, his flickering, shadowy avatar camouflaging him and making it hard to see particular features. He turned quickly. "Ah, the baby hacker . . . the young lover. Come to save your princess again?"

I reached for another trojan, but my stash was empty. Knocking together another would take time. I angled my avatar away from him. "I've already done better this time." I hoped I sounded braver than I felt. "Haven't I?" Grabbing a fistful of data, I began twisting it to my needs.

"Undeniably," he said, "but you will still fail, and the Luddites will rise!"

My hand stilled for a second. "Luddites? Everyone knows you're just out for revenge against FAIRY for firing you. In the stupidest way possible. All you've done is given them more research opportunities." I resumed working as fast as I could. Almost done.

He bared his teeth, too pointy to be human. "Their cure will never work. I'll always be one step ahead. Always!" His form began to shift.

I jumped back as his avatar changed into a giant dragon. A convincing illusion, even though part of me couldn't believe he was this cheesy. The smell of burning plastic enveloped me as I dodged flames. Yellow eyes glowed in purple-black scales. A lashing tail was another hazard to avoid.

He's still just a man, I told myself, and twisted one more strand of data. Long hours of gaming had trained me to stay away from extremities and find the weak spot, usually the belly. One hand on my implant—I'd only have one shot—I threw the trojan and jacked free as everything exploded.

"Desiree!" Lavender and Dawn's mother called in unison.

"Is Dawn OK?" I leaned on the monitor for support.

"Stable," the doctor said. "After you jacked in, I thought I'd better not proceed with the injection just yet."

"I put a trace in my trojan, Lavender. You should be able to track it in meatspace." My breathing was almost normal now as I beamed the details to her.

She nodded and made the call, stepping outside to speak to the police.

"Sit down, Desi." The First Lady gestured to the bed. Dawn didn't take up much space in it. She was propped up into an almost-sitting position.

It was awkward, but my knees were shaking and there were no free chairs. I sat at the First Lady's side. Opposite, the President smiled at me for the first time ever, and the doctor injected the treatment into Dawn's arm.

We waited. Dawn flinched. Without thinking, I took her hand. She was holding something. "What . . . ?"

The First Lady smiled. "Dawn brought that game box into surgery with her and she's had it ever since. We thought it was best to let her keep it."

Dawn opened her eyes. Her parents hugged her gently but I was in her line of sight. "Desi?" Her voice was croaky, and the doctor held out water for her to sip. She kissed her parents' cheeks in turn.

My hand tightened around hers. "Dawn."

The door clicked as Lavender came back in. "The helicopters are out. They should have him any minute—hey, did I miss everything?"

"Hi Lavender," Dawn said. She let the game box drop and clutched my hand. "So, am I better now?"

"Thanks to Lavender and Desiree and the rest at FAIRY, we hope so," the President said.

"You really did it. I knew you would." Dawn said. I thought she was talking to Lavender, but she was looking at me. She leaned forward and pressed her lips against mine.

Barista

Jane Routley

The cafe had been closed for a couple of hours but Shanna was still there, pottering around in her favourite space, running a cleansing steam through the bright red Lavazza, enjoying the warmth of the fire, the sound of her feet on the wooden floors and the lingering smells of coffee grounds and toasted focaccias.

Outside, the Melbourne winter evening was chill. Drizzle fell in a cloud of bright particles through the beam of the street light. Now the rushhour commuters had gone, it was very quiet. So when something thudded on the dumpster in the alley behind the cafe, Shanna heard it clearly. Assuming some homeless person was outside looking for a dry place to sleep, she opened the back door to see if they wanted some leftover pasta salad or a cup of cheer.

Instead a familiar stocky figure lurched out of the soggy darkness.

"Oh, great. Redback!" she groaned theatrically. "Should've known you'd be out here with the other garbage. What's the matter? Run out of windows to break in Geelong."

"Cheers Barista. How's it hangin'?"

He pushed past her into the cafe.

"Nothin' hanging, cos I'm a girl," muttered Shanna for the thousandth time. It was like a call and response between them.

"Like the new place. Nice pale wood look. Steam Junkies! Hip name!"

"A lot you'd know about hip," said Shanna.

Redback was wearing his hero clothes: a black lycra top with a spider on the chest and a red back. And football shorts. At least he had the legs for them—lean muscular footballer's legs, very nice legs if truth be told—not that Shanna would ever tell him that. He'd once told her that tights made him feel like a poof. Redback was an old-school superhero. As far as he was concerned, political correctness was some kind of bottled white fluid that typists used to correct mistakes.

He gave her his best good-natured Aussie grin.

"Nah darlin', hip's your gig and damn good you are at it, too! Looking good by the way."

The signs were very bad. The clothes and now the charm. Clearly this was a business call. And Shanna had been hoping for a quiet evening, listening to jazz and leafing through tattoo magazines.

She groaned, for real this time. "What do you want?"

"Ah! Nice of you to ask! Got a little fella out there. I need him to spill some beans. Thought you might make him a friendly little cuppa coffee."

"No!" said Shanna, her automatic response when someone asked for the Cup of Truth.

"Now Barista, don't be like that. Sydney Road's in danger. I promise you. That's why I knew you'd help."

One of the reasons Shanna worked with Redback was she that could tell when he was lying. This time he was telling the truth.

The back of her neck prickled. Brunswick was her heartland—sacred ground—and Sydney Road, just around the corner from the cafe, was its main artery—home of coffee shops, recycled clothes stores and Arabic wedding boutiques. No harm would come to Sydney Road while she drew breath.

"What's it about?"

"Got one of Bridgy's accountants out there. Complete with USB stick. Just need the password, and he won't tell."

"Who the hell's Bridgy?"

"Bridget Rostenkowski. That big American property developer. The Pixie, I call her. Teeny, tiny and cute as a button. But poison. More ruthless than a ruckman before the siren in a tied game.

She's got some plan to develop Sydney Road and I'm pretty sure this holds the key."

He waved a USB stick on a BMW key chain. "I'm hoping it's got a list of the city councillors and state planners she's paid off. If I can get that, I might be able to get the newspapers to pay them a little visit. Make a big stink. Put stop to it all. Maybe drive the Pixie out."

Shanna's mind began to list possible journalists she could leak this stuff to. If you made coffee, you knew a lot of journalists. That was a given. But Sydney Rd!

"What's she planning for the Road?" she asked anxiously.

"Details'll be on the stick," said Redback. He knew, but he wasn't going to tell her till she helped him, she could see that. "Come on, kiddo. I've had no luck the guy so far. Threats and promises aren't working. You be the good cop to my bad cop. Make him a nice cuppa coffee and work your magic."

"All right," she said. "But this better be about Sydney Rd. And try not to break anything this time. I always have a hell of a time explaining it to the owner."

"Goodonya kiddo." He smacked her shoulder with a big paw. "I knew you'd come through for me. I'll just get him out of the dumpster."

"What? That thing stinks!"

"Had to stop him running away somehow."

He went out the back door.

Shanna went to the machine and started the coffee.

Nobody made coffee like Shanna. Coffee was her super power. Even though broken windows seemed to follow her wherever she went, and she refused to make little pictures in the milk froth, cafe owners all over Brunswick wanted her working for them. Her fans followed her no matter which cafe she worked at.

Coffee could do a lot of things: it could soothe, it could comfort, it could invigorate, it could make friendships. It could bring forth confidences. Shanna was mistress of all these powers. The trick was in the way she ground the beans, packed the grounds in the group, the way she tamped them down, the heat of the water and the speed she ran it through the grounds.

As she waited for the coffee, she took out the piercing on her eyebrow and pulled the scrunchie out of her hair so that it covered her neck tattoos. Normally she refused to compromise the way she looked, but she had a feeling an accountant would find her less intimidating that way.

She had the Cup of Truth ready by the time Redback brought in the poor shivering little Suit. Perhaps once upon a time the well-cut grey Armani jacket on the accountant's scrawny pot-bellied frame would have made him an impressive figure. Now he looked like a drowned rat, a little weed of a man with only one shoe and thinning grey hair plastered wetly on his forehead.

She didn't need to put on her cry of pity.

"Poor guy! What did you do to him?"

"Just dipped him in the bay a bit as we were flying over to see how easy he'd talk."

"That's water boarding! That's torture! No! No! No!" She gave Redback a hard thump on his beefy arm. He winced, not entirely for show. Shanna worked out. A lot.

"Geez Barista, hold your horses. I'm an Aussie. We don't torture people."

"You poor man!" Shanna took the Suit's arm. He smelt of rotting orange peel and coffee grounds. Crooning soothingly, she led him to a table by the fire and tenderly tucked one of the cafe's soft grey blankets round his legs. Not much different from what she did most days. She could tell just by looking at him that he was a latte-with-two-sugars man. She poured in the steamed milk and the sugar, brought it over and took a seat opposite him.

"I'm really sorry about my friend," she said patting his hand. "He gets over-enthusiastic. But we really need to know what's on that USB stick. Couldn't you see your way to letting us take a little peek?"

The Suit shook his head. His teeth chattered on the edge of the cup as he lifted it to his mouth and took a sip.

"Tell her!" shouted Redback, taking to his role as bad cop with a bit too much gusto.

"Redback, just let the man drink his coffee," said Shanna.

"I'll never betray her," said the suit. "It's more than my life's worth. You don't know what's she's like."

"She doesn't need to know," said Shanna. "We can be discreet."

"No!" said the man and took another sip of coffee.

But by the time he'd had three sips he was smiling at them, and by the time he reached the bottom of the cup, he'd confided the password for the USB stick, as well as his kids' birthdays, his wife's maiden name and the lingerie size of his girlfriend in Williamstown.

Armani suits and girlfriends! Shanna could write a book. The Cup of Truth often made the weaker mind babble like that.

Shanna smiled, patted his hand and brought him another cup of coffee, this time soothing coffee which made him fall asleep on the table after three sips.

"Good job Barista. You're a star. Where's your tablet? Let's take a look at—"

The door smashed open.

"Stop right there!" said a harsh squeaky little voice. The cutest, teeniest, tiniest blonde-haired woman stalked in through the door. She wore a grey business suit with a short skirt, very red, very high heels and a big silver-grey fur coat. She looked like a pixie, but the shotgun toting henchman in black behind her was no fairy tale. Nor was her handgun.

Since neither Shanna nor Redback had been made bullet proof, it was time to stand still and maybe put up their hands.

"Pixie! Whatcha doing here? How's it hangin'?"

"Don't play innocent bogan with me. And don't call me that stupid name. Where is he? Where's my accountant?"

"He's back here, boss," grunted the henchman.

The Pixie stalked over on her spiky heels and poked her gun at the accountant asleep on the table. For a moment, Shanna thought she was going to shoot him.

The she turned on her heel.

"Goddamn useless heapashit. He'd better not have talked." With a quick lunge, the woman snatched the USB stick out of Redback's hand and waved him back with her gun.

Something dawned on Shanna.

"Is that baby sealskin you're wearing? You bitch! How could—"

"Hey!" yelled the little woman. Her voice was like a crystal wolf's, a light, scary growl. She shoved the gun into Shanna's face. "I might be a bitch, but I'm the bitch who's got the gun on you." She smirked. "And I'm the bitch who's gonna own your self-righteous little ass one of these days." She turned to Redback. "Who's this chick? Your squeeze? Black and piercings doesn't seem your type somehow."

"Just the coffee seller," said Redback. "Just friends. Barista, this is Bridget Rostenkowski. The property developer behind the plan to put an elevated freeway above Sydney Rd."

"What?" gasped Shanna. "Why haven't I heard . . . ? That's insane. It'll kill the Road."

"So what?" said the Pixie. "Get with the program, girl. No one wants scruffy little suburbs full of lazy slobs sitting round drinking coffee. They want a fast road to Sydney so they can go places, do business. Make more minimum wage jobs." She tossed her head back and laughed.

A red mist filled Shanna's vision. Her fingers started to boil. Thousands of trucks and cars thundering on a freeway above Sydney Road, cutting out the light and filling the air with fumes?

"Never!" she screamed. She lunged at the woman, but Redback held her back.

"Not yet," he hissed in her ear.

"Goddamn it! May I remind you dumb hicks I'm holding a gun? Are you too stupid to realise you're supposed to be scared of me?"

"No," said Redback. "Look, take your guy and go. I don't want any innocent bystanders caught up in this."

"Sure," sneered The Pixie. "Sure I'm gonna leave you behind. Now you just pick him up for me, nice and slow, and the pair of you can go in the car boot, all nice'n'cosy together. Hey, hold on a minute!" Her eyes narrowed at Shanna. "Hang on just one goddamn minute. How come you brought this guy here?"

"Just wanted to get dry," said Redback too quickly, making to pick up the sleeping accountant.

"Now wait just a cottonpickin' minute. I heard tell of some woman up here. Some kind of hippie witch who makes potions that make people tell the truth. That's you, isn't it?"

"What are you on, lady?" sneered Shanna, sensing danger. "I just make the coffees here."

"Well, well, well! That's why he came here. What a tasty find. I could see you being very useful to me, honey." She seized Shanna by the wrist. "I think you're going to come with me. I'm gonna teach you all about success in business."

"No, I'm—"

"Oh yes you are."

A suffocating cloud of expensive perfume enveloped Shanna as the Pixie shoved the gun against her temple. She was remarkably strong, even though she only came up to Shanna's shoulder.

"Enough chatting. Time is money and the money is mine. I've got the gun. So I get the say. Goddamn it, who would have thought it? A useful hippie. Sykes, cover the Spiderman here. You, Spiderman, pick up that piece of shit on the table and put him in the car boot."

Shanna locked eyes with Redback. He twitched his eye at her, their sign.

She let loose—releasing the angry jet of high pressure steam that had been building up in her fingertips. The Pixie screamed as the scalding water vapour hit the hand holding the gun, flinging it upwards and away from Shanna's temple. Shanna ducked and spun around, gripping the Pixie's wrist in her other hand, forcing it up hard.

A deafening explosion—the shotgun had gone off—Redback and the henchman were fighting too.

As ceiling plaster sprinkled over them, Shanna hit Bridget on the chin and pushed her away with a kick in the chest. The Pixie screamed and staggered back. The gun was in Shanna's hand now.

As she turned the gun on the Pixie, there was a crash and the window behind Bridget exploded. The Pixie's henchman landed in the alley outside.

"Damn you Redback! The boss is gonna scream!" cried Shanna.

Redback shrugged his shoulders. The henchman jumped up and took off at a run down the alley.

"Crap! Don't expect to have a job tomorrow!" screamed the Pixie at the fleeing henchman. She glared at Shanna, still shaking her scalded hand.

"So hippy girl! You got some fangs after all. I'm impressed. With powers like those you should be working for me, not jerking coffees in some lame-ass dive like this. We could make some big cash together."

"But I like pulling coffees," said Shanna. "And I could never work for a creep like you. Anyway, you're outta date. I'm a hipster, not a hippy. And now I've got the gun. So hand over that USB stick, you toxic little pixie. Redback, call the cops."

"Hey now! You don't wanna do that. Why involve the cops when we can come to some arrangement of our own?"

"The only arrangement we're gonna come to is that you leave Sydney Rd alone, Pixie."

"Now don't be so inflexible. Surely . . . " The Pixie caught sight of herself in the mirror above the fireplace. "Goddamn it. I look a wreck."

"Watch it" said Shanna as the Pixie put a hand in her pocket.

"Oh come on!" said the Pixie, bringing out her hand to show a compact. "Can't a girl look her best when meeting the Boys in Blue?"

"Barista, look out!" shouted Redback, as the Pixie opened the compact and with a sudden move, flung it towards Shanna.

An explosion. The world went powderpuff pink, filled with the acrid tang of tear gas.

Holding her hand in front of her face and shooting out steam for all she was worth to clear the air, Shanna flung herself forward into the cloud and managed to get hold of the Pixie's arm as she fled towards the door. Pressing her face into the sealskin to keep out the stinging pink gas, she struggled to get a grip on another limb, or on anything while the Pixie dragged her across the floor, raking her with vicious claws.

With the crash of an opening door and the chill of night on her skin, they were out in the street. The Pixie twisted round and drove a fist into Shanna's gut. The strength of it after all the ineffectual struggling and clawing took Shanna by surprise. She lost her breath and her grip on the woman's arm as she slammed back against the doorjamb.

Something hissed and rushed like steam. A bitter chemical scent filled the street and the Pixie shot up into the air, laughing, her sealskin coat spread out behind her like a stabilising sail and jets of flame coming out of the spikes of those red high heels.

As Redback staggered out of the cafe door coughing, eyes streaming—he hadn't had steam to protect him—the Pixie flew over the roofs of Brunswick, grey sealskin coat spread out behind her like Superman's cloak, screeching with wild laughter. Shanna shook her head and marvelled.

"Jet powered Manolo Blahniks! Never thought I'd see that!"

"Shit," said Redback, leaning back against the door beside her, coughing and thumping his chest. "Pardon my French, but . . . A broken window, and all for nothing."

"Not so," said Shanna. She held up the USB stick that she'd managed to get out of the Pixie's coat pocket as they'd struggled. Superheroing, like coffee making, was all about focusing on the goal. "We've got the stick, we've got the code. We've even— God help us—still got the accountant. I'd say it was mission accomplished."

"Barista, you're a pip," said Redback. He held up his open hand and Shanna clapped hers onto it in a victory salute.

"That woman's never gonna destroy Sydney Road. Not on my watch," she said.

With thanks to Jason Frank and the other members of the "How to Build a Super Workshop" at Continuum 10 2014.

Clara's

Marlee Jane Ward

The diner's just two clicks off the edge of the contamination zone. You want coffee? We've got coffee. It's not good coffee, but it'll do in a pinch, and I guess you could call this a pinch all right.

Clara owns the place and runs the grill. She's a gnarled old bitch, scarred with radiation burns and she don't speak no more, not since her tongue came off. It fell right outta her mouth and onto the grill! She just scooped it off into the trash and kept right on cookin'. I mean, bits are fallin' off Clara all the time. These days she just grunts and points, but she does a mean breakfast with spam and a side of beans. Calls it the 'Big Fry'.

Clara swats me on the shoulder 'cause I'm dreaming again, staring at the scrubbed Formica counter top. Sometimes I'll start on a staring jag and it's like the solid surface just opens up and I can see through it to forever. A part of me knows that I should be filling the salt shakers but I'm lookin' right into the face of infinity . . .

Anyway, Clara snaps me out of it, puts a rag in my hands, points to the dish-pile and grunts. The bell above the door jangles and two scrubbers come in. We've got motion sensors and a three-stage monitored cleanroom system, but Clara still put that bell atop the front door, and it sets my teeth on edge every time it sounds.

"Evenin' Eloise!" Shep booms across the diner as he takes a seat in a booth by the window. There's nothing much to look at but swirling dirt outside, but Clara makes me polish the inside with vinegar every morning 'til my arm aches. She's a real stickler for tidy.

"Hey Shep, evenin' Jimmy," I say.

I pour coffee into both of their cups, full for Shep cause he likes it black, three-quarters for Jimmy so he can stir in milk and sugar.

"What'll it be today?"

"I'll take a double Big Fry, thanks darlin'." Shep grins, a gummy smile punctuated with a few crooked choppers.

"And I'll take a Half Fry with a side of pancakes if you got 'em," Jimmy says.

"You bet we do. I made the sugar syrup myself last night."

I hear the order ping through to the kitchen. Clara grunts and shuffles around, throwing things on the grill. The buzzer goes off again and before I know it, a bunch of girls from the whorehouse out by the dorms flood in. Them girls always have spare coin for Clara's pies. You want pumpkin pie? Clara makes them twice a week.

· · ·

We close up around ten, Clara and I. She counts out the register and I do everything else 'cause she don't trust no one with the money. After I've scraped off the grill she hands me a plate she's kept special for my dinner. I always make a big deal of how good it is, and it seems to please her. She don't exactly smile, but she kinda frowns less, if you know what I mean.

I've got a room to myself out back, just a bed and a sink and a space to keep my things. I guess I just work for room and board. I don't got no family to send coin to back home, so it don't really matter. 'Sides, what else would I do? The scrubber corp wouldn't have me and they'll hire almost anyone. Truth be told, I was on my way to that whorehouse lookin' for work when I washed up at Clara's. That's okay—I like bussin' plates of eggs better than I like bussin' my ass. No disrespect intended, them girls do honest work.

After dinner Clara shuffles out the door, huffing into her respirator. She disappears in a whirl of dirt, the puff of her breather fading off into the night. There's nothing round for miles, so who knows where she gets off to.

Without Clara grunting or any of the Scrubbers bellowing from the booths for more coffee, things get pretty lonely. In the deep quiet night, in this little diner perched on the plain, the only thing for miles that ain't blowing topsoil or roaches—sometimes I don't think that whorehouse woulda been so bad. It woulda been a family, you know?

. . .

In the morning, Clara doesn't come.

I raise myself before the sun turns the dirt swirls to a lighter shade of brown, slice up a brand new pie (careful now, Clara likes it done just so) and set to folding the napkins. I like folding before Clara comes because I can get some quality time with the counter top and infinity without having a spatula aimed at my head.

But Clara doesn't come.

I fold a whole box of napkins and get a good deep glimpse into forever and it's only when my fingers brush the bottom of the box that I realise something ain't right. Usually before this point the buzzer would snap me back to the diner and Clara'd come limping in, drop her clinking bags on the floor, point at the shelves and grunt.

But Clara doesn't come.

I put on a pot of coffee because we still have grounds left, but there are only three cans of beans and a sack of eggs on the shelf. Clara don't bring extra and when I asked her why she wrote on a napkin that no one would bother breakin' in for a few measly cans of beans and a pie or two.

Well, I asked, wouldn't the robbers just get mad at going to all the trouble to bust in for no reason? Maybe take it out on the poor waitress napping out back? She threw the napkin at me and limped off, grunting. She didn't seem to think that part was important.

When the third shift quits and starts trickling in, looking for hotcakes and greasy eggs with ham, I don't know what to tell them.

"I don't know what to tell you, fellas. We don't have no food. Clara didn't show up this morning."

Bernie, Gus, Javier and Dumb John look up at me from the booth like I'm not talking real words.

"We've got coffee or pumpkin pie."

"You don't got any beans?" Javier asks, his face strained as if he's trying real hard to work it out.

"No beans, Jav."

"No eggs?" Bernie chimes in, looking just as befuddled.

"No eggs, I'm sorry."

They grumble, but settle for coffee and the four split a whole pie. On their way out they complain 'bout how they're still hungry. I stand by the door and apologise again.

"Let me know if you see Clara," I plead.

I put a note up on the door to say we are only serving coffee. Folks still come in for a cup, but mostly just to find out what's going on.

"Round lunchtime we see a Scrubber approach, puzzle over the sign for a bit, sounding out the words. As the message gets through, he flies into a rage, screaming and kickin' up dirt, though we can't hear the show he's putting on. Finally, he pulls a shotgun out of his Jeep and methodically pumps shells into the diner's front window until he runs out and shuffles off. The window holds: it don't even chip.

Blonde Sarah and Cupcake from the cathouse look around, wide-eyed, and no one speaks for a few minutes. Dax and Sammy suit up and take off after him. They come back half an hour later and let me know he won't be a problem no more. I give them a free cup and the girls all gush and fawn over them. They won't be payin' next time they stroll into the whorehouse, that's for sure. And they say chivalry's dead.

• • •

On the third morning I put up a sign that says, 'Closed. No food, no coffee. Gone looking for Clara." I zip into a coverall and strap on Clara's ancient shotgun and a respirator before I crack the door. I mean, the Scrubbers do a good job cleanin' the zone, but the dust still blows, don't it? Better safe than dyin' a long slow death is what I always say. My breath echoes through the breather, too loud in my ears. There ain't nothing else to hear out here.

The working girls let me borrow one of their Hovers. It jerks a fair bit when I take off, but it don't stall and soon I'm peering down at the lonely little square of Clara's diner. The open plain feels too much, too big. Like I might just keep expanding outwards until I'm so stretched out that I just stop being. Don't you hate that feeling?

The Hover holds a day's charge. Twenty-four hours to find one grumpy old griller in one big old desert. I don't know why I'm doing it. Maybe because it's this or nothing.

I incline up. If I blink against the sun off in the distance I can just make out the row of Scrubbing machines, giant and inching across the desert like enormous bugs. Closer still, the Scrubbers' dorms, rows of long, low buildings. The whorehouse rises up, a gaudy box panelled in yellow and pink. That's it: that's all there is to see. I bring the Hover around, setting it on the first line of the grid on the nav. The auto does the steering while I peer down, looking for anything that might hide a little old fry cook.

In the late afternoon shadow I spot a cluster of shapes crowding in an old river bed. Tents and Hovers, old Jeeps in pieces and flapping sheets of plastic. As I ease down and land, a man walks out of the closest tent, squinting out from under a cupped hand and I'm horrified to see that he's barefaced. In a minute he's joined by two more fellas, not a respirator among 'em. Not even a particulate filter! One of them has a rag tied round his mouth, though there's not much point to it. These are bandits; no one else would be out here living like this. I put a hand to the shotter in its long holster, fastened round my waist and my thigh.

"Hey fellas," I say, my voice muffled by the breather. "I'm not looking for trouble, I'm just trying to find a friend of mine."

No one says anything. My heart beats quick.

I've made a terrible mistake.

"She's about, uh, this tall?" I hold my hand up to my chin. "Old, wrinkly, goes by Clara?" I don't know why I'm still talking.

"We like your Hover," the first man says, the healthiest-lookin' of 'em. He hacks and spits a great pink wad into the sand. Maybe not so healthy.

"Well, see—it's not technically mine . . . " I say, but they ain't listening.

"We like your breather," says the man with the rag under his nose. I take a step back, and they all take one forward. I whip my shotgun out and they all lift their shooters. There's three barrels aimed my way and inside I'm sinking 'cause I ain't ever even shot a gun before. I don't notice that someone's creepin' up on me 'til they pull my mask down and clamp a stinking rag on my mouth. After that I don't notice nothin' for a good long while.

. . .

"Hey lady, hey, hey," the voice is close, hot breath tickling my ear and it's only when I go to swat it away that I realise my hands are tied behind my back. I jump right awake and wrench my arm 'til my shoulder near pops right out, bellowing around the cottony mass they've shoved in my gob. I shift on the little cot I'm trussed to and a cloud of dust flies up. I panic. I'm not wearing a breather. I hold my breath for a good minute before I realise I been breathing this muck in for who knows how long. I exhale, picturin' the cells mutating in my lungs.

"Hey lady, what's your name?"

There, by the edge of the cot—a pair of wide brown eyes. And another. And another.

"Eloise," I say around the gag, but it comes out all garbled.

"If we take that sock outta your mouth, you promise not to scream?"

I nod and a little brown hand reaches up and plucks the wadded clump from between my teeth.

"Eloise," I say, spitting out the taste of dirty feet. I turn over to get a better look at who's talkin', and my head swirls. I feel like someone took out my brains and replaced 'em with a double serve of scrambled eggs. Out of the corner of my eye, in the dim, I can just make out those eyes, the tops of three curly heads. "What's you guys' names?"

"JimandJebandJoey," they sing. I blink past them. I'm in a vast tent, lit by a solar lantern hanging from the roof on the other side of the room.

"We sure are glad you came to visit," the one in the middle says.

"Our Hover's on the fritz, so our Daddy borrowed yours," says the one on the right.

"Borrowed it, did he?" I say, trying to wriggle one of my wrists free. The binding's tight though, and I just mince my hands a little before I give up.

"Yep, he's gone to get s'plies. I hope he brings us back some Ramen noodles," the one on the left pipes in.

"Or a candy bar!"

They laugh and their little heads bob in unison.

"Are you someone's Mama?"

"I almost was," I say. I'm writhin' on the cot, trying to get into a good position to maybe loosen the ropes on the metal frame. I want to keep 'em talking.

"What happened?"

"I lost my baby. Before he got born."

The boys nod, solemn. "That happens a lot, don't it?"

"It does."

"Our mama passed, when she was havin' us. We nearly didn't get born. We've had lots of mamas, but they always pass or run away. Our Daddy says you can be our new one."

I squeeze my eyes shut, pulling my arms to their stopping point with a new sense of urgency and dread, trying to hook the binds onto a sharp little jut on the frame. Just as I get it there, the tent flap flies open and orange light floods the canvas space for a second. I blink, tryin' to clear the blindness from my eyes.

"JimandJebandJoe, you get away from her!" There's a scrabbling noise. The boys wriggle their way out from next to my cot.

Sometimes babies get scrambled up a little while they are cookin'. Happens more and more these days. The boys, triplets—they're all joined up. Through their wide, skinny, shared chest I can see their little ribcages. One innie bellybutton, two outies, all in a row. They got two hands and six legs between 'em and they jostle and skitter like they wanna tear apart and scatter in three different directions, but they can't. Little boys, you know? It's hard to contain 'em.

The girl is young but tall, with a big mop of curly brown hair and black eyes. She tries not to look at me and she hefts the triplets up under their arms and plonks them on their feet.

"Go play. Go see if Daddy's back." She shoos them away.

"I'm Eloise. What's your name?" I say, all soft.

She shakes her head, picks up the sock and stuffs it back in my mouth. Then she drapes an old, stinking towel over my head. Before the light fades I look into her eyes, beggin' with mine. She looks sad. In the dark I hear her walking away. I swear I hear her say something.

It sounds like, "Sorry."

• • •

The rope on my wrists goes with a whisper of partin' fibres and a flood of blood back into my hands. I been working on it for what feels like half my life, but is prob'ly nearer to half a day or so. The towel on my face has slipped a little and I can see fading light spill around the edges of the tent flap. Right away I sit up, throw the face-towel off to one side and make short work of the cords at my ankles. There ain't no time for caution, but when I spring up and see her by the door, a surge of fear still zings in me. I hold my hands up, a sorry-lookin' pair of rope-burnt wrists topped with measly fists.

"I'll do whatever it takes," I tell the girl.

She blinks at me. She's got a baby in one arm, a little snot-nosed kid with big old eyes. With the other hand she pulls out a flarelaunch and points it at me. I drop my hands. It ain't a real shooter but it'll make a pretty coloured mess of me anyways. I wonder how long I'll last wiping asses, pumping out sick babies and feedin' this bandit brood of kids before I cough myself to death. The baby sniffles, starts to whimper. It lifts one fat brown hand to its face and rubs a dusty eye. The girl drops the launch.

"I can help you," she says. She puts the baby down and it crawls over, clings onto my pants. It looks up at me and a giant bubble of snot grows and shrinks, grows and shrinks over its plugged nostril as it breathes. "But if I help you, can you help us?"

. . .

We wait 'til dark. The Hover comes back in just as the sun burns out for the night and the fellas are too busy whoopin' over their spoils to bother checking in on me. Sylvie tells me to bunker down on the bed anyways, just in case. She's rounded up all the kids and they peer at me from cots and cribs, eyes glimmerin' in the dim lamplight. It's creepy. There's five of 'em plus the triplets. Virginia's twelve but she don't say much. Percy's nine, Amy is eight. The triplets (James and Jebediah and Joseph) are six. Xavier is blind but still rambunctious as all heck and he's three. The little snot-nose, Sophie, isn't even one and she's still snifflin' as Sylvie manhandles her into a sling on her chest.

"Sylvie! Come get some supper for the littluns!" The bellow comes from outside. Sylvie beckons. She's found me a shotter, not the one I brought with me: this one is better. I creep round the edge of the camp with it raised. I sure hope I don't have to use it. It's so big that the recoil will prob'ly take my shoulder clean off and

I'm so blasted inept with firearms that I'll no doubt just end up shootin' myself in the foot.

The Big Daddy of this little clan stands by the fire. Noodle packs drift around his feet on the breeze. He stirs the pot of Mi Goreng, rippin' open flavour packets, cursing at the little foil pouches as he fumbles.

"Sylvie!" He bellows as he drops one into the pot, cursing and kicking at the plastic scattered round his feet. "Come help me with these noodles!" She hurries out the tent flap, wipin' the bub's green nasal flow with a rag. When she reaches her pappy he goes to hand her the spoon but instead'a taking it, she pulls a shooter, a real gnarly hand-cannon, out of the sling with one hand and points it right at his face. With the other hand she draws the flarelaunch and aims it to a point on her left. The baby gurgles in the harness, waves its chubby feet back and forth.

"Where'd you get my shooter, Sylvie? I tole you a hundred times not to go poking round in Daddy's things."

It's then I see what she's pointin' the flarelaunch at—the Jeeps, the fuel cans. She don't say nothing, just pulls the trigger. Bright red light erupts from the launch, and the whole thing goes up with a roar. The kid at her chest starts to cry.

Her brothers are here now, and I come outta my hiding spot, training the shotter right at 'em.

"You're dead meat, Sylvie," the dumbest-lookin' one says, spitting out her name. He looks like the meanest as well. He points at me. "Her too. We're gonna rip you to bits if you don't put that shooter down. Look what you done to the Jeeps."

"Oh, piss off, Harrison," she says. "Who do you think scrubs the stains outta your shorts after a raid? I'm surprised you ain't sobbing into your hanky with that shotter aimed at your face."

I pump the action for emphasis. I don't even know if I'm doing it right, feel like I've probably switched it off or something, but he flinches, so I just try and look menacing and such. I catch Sylvie trying not to smirk. She looks beautiful in the firelight with the fuel-smoke billowing behind her, like a girl I saw in an old comic book one time.

She motions to the kids and they file out in a line. The triplets gallop ahead, bellowing 'bout how they want to sit in the front. I side-step over, gun still trained on Sylvie's daddy and brothers, and help the little ones climb in, try and shoo the triplets into the back.

"You ain't taking my kids, Sylvie!" her daddy wails. He starts towards her, raising a hand, but Sylvie don't hesitate. She fires a bullet right at his feet. He glares at her, wounded, but only in the feelings.

"The kids need to live somewhere clean. They're sick. We're all sick! What's gonna happen to 'em when we die, huh? How long you been coughing blood, Daddy? How long you think you got?"

He pulls himself up tall, his boys clustered behind him. "This is my fam'ly, Sylvie, and you'll do as I say. I've made a decent life out here for you. We got food, don't we? A buncha nice tents? I even found you a new Mama to help with the kids."

"Some life. You and the boys rob and kill good folks for—" She looks around. "For fuckin' noodles," she says, kicking away an empty packet that's come to rest on the top of her bare foot. "Meantimes, we starve and bake under the sun and I try and keep these kids from dying on me."

"Babies die, Sylvie, it's always been like that. And these are hard times. We do what we gotta, we stick together like a fam'ly!" Her daddy's face is flush with rage. A vein throbs in his neck. One of the boys launches into a coughin' fit behind him. There's a wet slap as he hacks a bloody chunk onto the ground.

"This ain't no family," she says, real bitter. "This is just you tryin' to build a kingdom out here. That's why we left the commune back when Mama was still alive. It was clean there, safe, but they wouldn't let you be in charge, would they?"

He steps right up to the barrel of the shotter. She's so mad that it shakes, but she keeps it pointed true. She's so tall that they are eye to eye. "You'll leave your mama outta this if you know what's good for you, girl. I brung you into this world and I'll take you right on out of it."

"You can try, Daddy, but I'm the one with a shooter aimed at your face." For a long second I think she's gonna do it. The tension stretches right out.

"Shoot him!" squeal the triplets together, and I damn near bolt outta my seat. Everyone jumps. I swat at the boys and they wriggle out of my reach. It breaks the moment. Sylvie don't lower the barrel, but she starts to back away. Her arms are like steel, the launch and shooter still poised to fire. She climbs backward into the Hover.

"Go. Now. Before I change my mind and blow his fool head off." I don't need to get told twice. The Hover struggles a little as we top out. Six wriggly kids, plus us and the bub on Sylvie's chest, is a whole lot more cargo than this boat is used to.

"Swing round, Eloise. I wanna take one last look." I bring the Hover round and start a big circle over the camp. Thick black smoke billows from the centre and in the orange light I see the boys runnin' behind the tent, going for the ammo boxes, the weapons. They don't know it yet, but every shooter and shotter and even one pretty slick laser are wrapped up tight and stored under the Hover's seats. Sylvie lifts the flarelaunch and fires off a brilliant purple sparkler right into the middle of the big tent. By the time we turn around, it's already catching.

Her daddy kicks over the pot of noodles, then drops onto his knees in the wet dust. I think he's crying, but with all the smoke and his filthy face, it's hard to tell. He could just as easily be laughing.

"Wave goodbye to Daddy," Sylvie says, and the kids all dutifully flap their hands as we pass. She has to grab hold of the triplets who lean so far out of the Hover to wave that they almost topple right off. Even the baby starts wavin'. She don't really know what she's doing, but she wants to join in.

We skirt the twin plumes of smoke and peel off just as something else inside the camp catches and goes off. I set the auto to Clara's, then turn about to watch the thick dark clouds rise and shrink in our wake.

Lil' Sophie keeps on waving, chanting, "Bye bye bye bye . . . " under her breath. Sylvie ducks her head to kiss her, thick black curls spilling over the both of them. Her shoulders start to shake. I think she's crying, but behind all that hair, it's hard to tell. She could just as easily be laughing.

. . .

"Hey Eloise?" Joey asks, 'cause he's the closest to my ear. "What's your place like?"

"It ain't really my place," I tell him. I gotta yell to be heard over the wind. The air's pretty clean up here, and even though there was two spare filter masks on board, I don't have one on. Sylvie and me strapped 'em on the two youngest, though they both fuss with the straps. It probably don't make much difference, but it feels like the right thing to do. I barely know 'em but I got this urge to protect the littluns that's coming up deep from somewhere in my guts.

I let the auto do the steering. I haven't forgot that I came out here to find Clara, if she's out here to be found, and I scan the ground out the corner of my eye.

I'm not paying much attention to the drivin', so I almost spill right over the edge when the impact comes sudden. Sylvie and the kids cry out. The glowing nav screen shows us almost back to the point I plotted as Clara's.

It comes again right away, crunching up against the right side. Another Hover, edges glowing in the thin silvery moonlight. The slap-up rig is barely flying. It trails long streams of smoke and bobs like a drownin' rat in a sink. I expect to see their daddy behind the controls, but it's them brothers instead. They got looks of all fury and no control. Oh, I've seen that look before, more times than I'd like to tell you 'bout. I'm no swift flyer but I grab the stick and switch off the auto, 'cause by their twisted, set mouths I can tell that me and Sylvie gonna be in a world of hurt if they catch us. I gotta try.

"Hold on, everyone!" I scream just before I peel off to the left. The kids all shriek, but I can hear the delight in the way the triplets bellow.

"Faster, Eloise!" Jeb squeals, and the three of 'em shake the back of my seat as I angle the Hover upwards. I sneak a look behind, real quick. The fellas don't got much by way of manoeuvring, but they ain't wanting for speed. They're gaining.

I try to speed up. It's too late though, they're on us again and this time when they hit, the whole boat tips. I see the dirt racing up to meet us, ghost-lit by the moonglow.

I don't know how we make it, but we must'a hit the dirt only a little off kilter. Whenever I've heard the Scrubbers tell stories of wrecking bikes or trucks or the occasional Hover, they always say *one minute I was 'bout to crash, the next I was waking up in the med bay,* so I expect it to be like that, but it's not. I remember every second. It feels like it happens so slow. We thump down hard and wrong and the Hover tips on its side. I wait for it to go over, but it doesn't, I don't know how. Dirt flies up in a huge spray before us. Beside me, Sylvie holds tight to the baby, her eyes squeezed shut and I reach out without thinking to grab at Virginia, who's tryin' to keep hold of the triplets as they slide across the cargo floor. I see the other boat come down, missing us by just a hair, and it starts to roll. It comes apart piece by piece; sheets of orange flame spring out of the growing spaces between the parts. I see one of the brothers' faces twist in fear, and then the fire eats 'em both whole.

We clang into something and the boat shudders, stops with a lurch. Sylvie tumbles out, awkward, tryin' not to squish the baby, then she starts to pull all the kids off the back. They are too shook up to do much but flop like little dirty ragdolls off into the sand. I'm afraid the Hover's gonna blow too, but I can't move. I'm not hurt, I'm just starin'. In the middle distance stands Clara's, the little box lit against the deep-blue deep-night sky. But right here, so close to where I've whiled away all them years folding napkins and bussing plates, is something I ain't ever seen before. The thing we hit—it's a door.

Not a door like the door to the kitchen, but a door sunk in the ground. It's been covered all over with dirt, but the hover edge pried it up when we hit. It's only the size of a big man's shoulders around. Sylvie don't see it yet, she's looking over at Clara's.

"That your place?" she asks. I don't answer. I unbuckle, drop to the dirt and push the sods away in big handfuls. They are loose, like they've been brushed off and brushed over again and again.

"What is that?" Sylvie asks, coming to stand right by me. The kids all follow in a wobbly line, stunned to silence. I think it's the first time I heard quiet from the triplets, who are usually muttering, squealing or plotting something.

"I don't know."

She drops to her knees and helps me brush the dust away. The handle is a lever in the middle of the round door. I pull it up and the thing starts to hiss.

"It's okay," I say as Sylvie leaps away. White light pours from the inside. There's a ladder and I don't even think before I drop right in and find the rungs with my feet. The climb ain't long and just a few steps down I realise I'm standing in a decontamination room. It's an airlock.

. . .

We find Clara in the sleeping quarter off the main room. She's layin' on a cot, just a little hump underneath a blanket. She's long dead of course, but I feel like I always knew it, you know? She looks peaceful. I bet she didn't even know she died, and that woulda pissed her off! Clara don't like surprises.

The room's cosy and all fit-out like a little house sunk under the ground. In the refrigerator I find a pie, unsliced and covered over with plastic wrap. I hand it to Sylvie and she digs into it, hands clumps to the kids with her clean hands. They look different now they've been through decon, like the camp and desert are far away. Sylvie's cracked brown hands are scrubbed and her big mop of hair frizzes and gleams. Little Sophie smears pumpkin filling over her face and squeals with delight when some of the sweet stuff ends up in her mouth.

I walk around, peering in drawers and behind cupboard doors. When I put my hands to the walls I can feel a thrumming behind. Air filtration, generators. Right on the other side of the room is another door. It's heavy, with a big wheel for a handle. Sylvie helps me turn it, gets sticky pie smears all over the steel. It takes a good minute or two to find the light and while I fumble I feel something strange. The dark space feels too much—like I might just keep expanding outwards until I'm so stretched out that I just stop being.

"Does it feel big in here?" Sylvie asks, coming up beside me. "I hate that feelin'. Like I could get lost forever, you know?"

I smile in the dark. I like her.

There's a mighty click-crunch as the lights go on. The pie plate clatters to the ground, sweet pumpkin splatterin' all over our legs.

I ain't never seen a room so big. I can't even see where it ends. And every part of it is filled with huge shelves in long rows, and every shelf is filled with cans and sacks and bags and boxes. Oh, Clara had a stash all right. It went and outlived her. Hell, it'll outlive little Sophie's kids, if she makes it that far.

"Nice place you got here," says Sylvie.

We both take off running down the rows. She don't even make it halfway before she stops, laughing and coughing and clutching her belly. The kids follow slower, lookin' round with big eyes. The triplets drag Xav along, whispering in his ear about all the treats he can't see.

There's a ladder right at the end and if I'm judging my distances right, I bet it comes up right inside Clara's. All this, right under my feet. All that time. The sneaky bitch. Guess keeping secrets is easy when you got no tongue.

"So, Eloise. What you gonna do with all this?" Sylvie says, catching up to me.

"Well, I got one idea. Do you know how to cook?"

• • •

Next morning we turn the 'open' sign back round. I fold the napkins, Sylvie fires up the grill. Virginia and Percy wipe down the booths and we try to keep the triplets busy with fillin' up the salt shakers, but they just make an awful mess. The smell of hot coffee fills the diner and my heart leaps a bit when the buzzer sounds for the decon room. I straighten my apron, go and polish the windows even though there's not much to see out there. Clara was a real stickler for tidy.

The bell sounds. It don't jangle my nerves this time.

"Morning fellas! Coffee's on. You want eggs? We got eggs. They ain't great eggs, but they sure are better than no eggs."

About the Contributors

CHERITH BALDRY was born in Lancaster, UK, and studied at the University of Manchester and St Anne's College, Oxford. After some years as a teacher, including a spell at the University of Sierra Leone, Freetown, she became a full-time writer. She has a special interest in Arthurian romance and medieval literature, and has published novels and short fiction for adults, young adults and children. She is currently part of the Erin Hunter team writing the Warriors and Seekers series. Cherith has two grown-up sons and a grand-daughter, and lives in Surrey in a household ruled by a cat. She enjoys music, especially early music, reading and travel.

• • •

JENNY BLACKFORD is a prize-winning Australian poet and author, with stories and poems published in places as diverse as *The Pedestal Magazine*, *Westerly*, *Cosmos* and *Penumbra*. Kate Forsyth described her historical novella set in Athens and Delphi, *The Priestess and the Slave* (Hadley Rille Books, 2009), as "Completely fascinating—a vivid and evocative glimpse into the life of the past", and legendary feminist Pamela Sargent called it "elegant". In 2013, Pitt Street Poetry published her first book of poetry, *The Duties of a Cat*. She was one of the World Fantasy Award judges in 2009.

• • •

KAY CHRONISTER's fiction won the 2015 Dell Magazine Award and is forthcoming in *Beneath Ceaseless Skies*. Originally from Seattle, she currently lives in Phnom Penh, Cambodia, in a household of twenty-one children and six dogs.

STEPHANIE GUNN is a Ditmar-nominated writer of speculative fiction, with short stories published in anthologies such as *Bloodstones, Epilogue* and *Kisses by Clockwork*. In another life she was a scientist, but now spends her time writing, reading and reviewing. She has judged the Australian Shadows Awards and is a frequent judge and convener of the Aurealis Awards. She lives in Perth with her husband, son and requisite cat and is currently at work on a contemporary fantasy novel, amongst too many other projects. She can be found online at stephaniegunn.com.

• • •

KATHLEEN JENNINGS is an author and illustrator based in Brisbane, Queensland. Her short stories and comics have appeared in such publications as *Lady Churchill's Rosebud Wristlet* and the Candlewick anthologies *Steampunk!* and *Monstrous Affections*. Kathleen thanks Angela Slatter for her comments on this story, and for pointing out (for example) when characters had neglected to put their clothes on again. If you enjoyed the world of Kathleen's story, she also recommends you read Delia Sherman's *The Porcelain Dove*. Some of Kathleen's thoughts (but mostly her art) can be found at tanaudel.wordpress.com.

• • •

KATHRYN HORE is a writer of dark and speculative fiction, as well as a business writer, researcher and sometime librarian. She has fiction appearing in anthologies and magazines and showing up in the occasional competition, plus a novel in the works. When not writing or dusting library shelves, she can be found taking photos of weddings and spiders (though not usually at the same time), or reading to her kids in their home among the gum-trees on the outskirts of Melbourne.

• • •

FAITH MUDGE is a Queensland writer with a passion for fantasy, folk tales and mythology from all over the world—in fact, almost anything with a glimmer of the fantastical. Her stories have appeared in various anthologies, the most recent of which include *Kaleidoscope, Phantazein* and *Cranky Ladies of History*. She also posts regular reviews and articles at beyondthedreamline. wordpress.com. Somewhere in the overcrowded menagerie of her mind, there are novels. She is even writing some of them.

T. R. NAPPER is an aid worker, stay-at-home parent, former refugee advocate, and writer. He has spent the last decade living and working throughout South East Asia. T. R. Napper has been published in *Interzone*, *Grimdark Magazine*, and several other markets. He is a *Writers of the Future* winner. He currently lives in Hanoi, Vietnam. His twitter is @DarklingEarth, website is nappertime.com, and Facebook is facebook.com/trnapper

• • •

RIVQA RAFAEL is a writer and editor based in Sydney. She started writing speculative fiction well before earning degrees in science and writing, although they have probably helped. Her previous gig as subeditor and reviews editor for *Cosmos Magazine* likewise fueled her imagination. She can be found at rivqa.net.

• • •

ALTER S. REISS is an archaeologist and writer who lives in Jerusalem with his wife Naomi and their son Uriel. His stories have appeared in *F&SF*, *Strange Horizons*, *Nature*, and elsewhere, and his first novel is due out from tor.com's imprint in September. He likes good books, bad movies, and old time radio shows.

• • •

JANE ROUTLEY has had a variety of careers, including fruit picker and Occult librarian, and lived in Germany and Denmark for a decade. Now she's back in her beloved Melbourne and working for the railways. (All the live long day) She's published 4 books and won two Aurealis awards. Her short stories have been widely anthologised and read on the ABC. She's written a blog about Flinders Street Station and another called Station Stories about her life staffing a railway station. Her current life ambition is to see an erupting volcano.

• • •

CAT SPARKS is an award-winning author, editor and artist whose former jobs have included media monitor, political and archaeological photographer, graphic designer and manager of Agog! Press. She's currently fiction editor of *Cosmos Magazine* and partway through a PhD in YA climate change fiction. Her short story collection *The Bride Price* was published in 2013.

KYLA LEE WARD is a writer based in Sydney but ranging freely through time and space. Her novel *Prismatic* (co-authored as Edwina Grey) won an Aurealis and *The Land of Bad Dreams*, a collection of dark poetry, received Rhysling nominations. Her short fiction has appeared on Gothic.net and in the *Macabre* and *Schemers* anthologies, amongst others. For more historical trivia and some creative cursing, try kylawward.com

• • •

MARLEE JANE WARD is a writer, reader and weirdo from Melbourne, Australia. She attended the Clarion West Writers Workshop in 2014. Her debut novella, *Welcome To Orphancorp,* is shortlisted for Seizure Online's Viva La Novella. She digs cats, good coffee and making an utter spectacle of herself.

• • •

SUSAN WARDLE is a graduate of Clarion South 2005. She has had numerous short story publications including in *Overland, Antipodean SF, Fables and Reflections, Shadowed Realms, Ticonderoga Online* and *Lady Churchill's Rosebud Wristlet.* Susan lives in Wollongong and spends her daylight hours (and some of her night time hours) working for local government as well as raising two small boys.

• • •

JANEEN WEBB is a multiple award-winning author, editor and critic who has written or edited ten books and over a hundred essays and stories. Her most recent book is the short story collection, *Death at the Blue Elephant*, released by Ticonderoga Publications in 2014. Janeen is a recipient of the World Fantasy Award, the Peter MacNamara SF Achievement Award, the Aurealis Award, and the Ditmar Award. She holds a PhD in Literature from the University of Newcastle, and divides her time between Melbourne and a small farm overlooking the sea near Wilson's Promontory.

• • •

ELEANOR R. WOOD loves fruit and veg, especially juiced. Her stories have appeared in *Plasma Frequency Magazine, Bastion, Pseudopod, Stupefying Stories,* and *Crossed Genres,* among others. She writes and eats liquorice from the south coast of England, where she lives with her husband, two marvellous dogs, and enough tropical fish tanks to charge an entry fee. She blogs at creativepanoply.wordpress.com.

Acknowledgements

"The Sorrow" copyright © 2015 Jenny Blackford.
"Blueblood" copyright © 2015 Faith Mudge.
"A Truck Called Remembrance" copyright © 2015 Susan Wardle.
"A Wondrous Necessary Woman" copyright © 2015 Janeen Webb.
"Broken Glass" copyright © 2015 Stephanie Gunn.
"A Hedge of Yellow Roses" copyright © 2015 Kathleen Jennings.
"Dustbowl" copyright © 2015 Kay Chronister.
"Catalysis" copyright © 2015 Alter S. Reiss.
"Veteran's Day" copyright © 2015 Cat Sparks.
"Cursebreaker: The Mutalibeen and the Memphite Mummies"
    copyright © 2015 Kyla Lee Ward.
"The Fruits of Revolution" copyright © 2015 Eleanor R. Wood.
"Star Bright" copyright © 2015 Cherith Baldry.
"Generation Zero" copyright © 2015 Kathryn Hore.
"The Silica Key" copyright © 2015 T. R. Napper.
"Function A:save(target.Dawn) " copyright © 2015 Rivqa
    Raphael.
"Barista" copyright © 2015 Jane Routley.
"Clara's" copyright © 2015 Marlee Jane Ward.

LIMITED HARDCOVER EDITIONS

EBOOKS

THE YEAR'S BEST AUSTRALIAN FANTASY & HORROR SERIES
EDITED BY LIZ GRZYB & TALIE HELENE

thank you

The publisher would sincerely like to thank

Elizabeth Grzyb, Jenny Blackford, Faith Mudge, Susan Wardle, Janeen
Webb, Stephanie Gunn, Kathleen Jennings, Kay Chronister, Alter
S. Reiss, Cat Sparks, Kyla Ward, Eleanor R. Wood, Cherith Baldry,
Kathryn Hore, T.R. Napper, Rivqa Raphael, Jane Routley, Marlee
Jane Ward, Lucy Sussex, Lisa L. Hannett, Donna Maree Hanson,
Robert Hood, Pete Kempshall, Penelope Love, Nicole Murphy, Angela
Slatter, Karen Brooks, Jeremy G. Byrne, Felicity Dowker, Kim
Wilkins, Marianne de Pierres, Jonathan Strahan, Peter McNamara,
Ellen Datlow, Grant Stone, Sean Williams, Simon Brown, Garth Nix,
David Cake, Simon Oxwell, Grant Watson, Sue Manning, Steven
Utley, Lewis Shiner, Bill Congreve, Jack Dann, Janeen Webb, Brian
Clarke, Stephen Dedman, the Mt Lawley Mafia, the Nedlands Yakuza,
Shane Jiraiya Cummings, Angela Challis, Kate Williams, Kathryn
Linge, Andrew Williams, Al Chan, Alisa and Tehani, Mel & Phil,
Hayley Lane, Georgina Walpole, Rushelle Lister, everyone we've
missed . . .

. . . and you.

IN MEMORY OF
Eve Johnson (1945–2011)
Sara Douglass (1957–2011)
Steven Utley (1948–2013)